PLAY ON

A PLAY ON NOVEL

SAMANTHA YOUNG

play on

on

SAMANTHA YOUNG

Content and line edit by Jennifer Sommersby Young

Copy edit by Amy Donnelly

Cover Design By Hang Le

E-Book & Print Formatting by Indie Formatting Services

also by

SAMANTHA YOUNG

ADULT CONTEMPORARY

Into the Deep

Out of the Shallows

Hero

One Day: A Valentine Novella

On Dublin Street Series:

On Dublin Street

Down London Road

Before Jamaica Lane

Fall From India Place

Echoes of Scotland Street

Moonlight on Nightingale Way

Until Fountain Bridge (a novella)

Castle Hill (a novella)

Valentine (a novella)

One King's Way (a novella)

Hart's Boardwalk Series:

The One Real Thing

Every Little Thing

YOUNG ADULT CONTEMPORARY

The Impossible Vastness of Us

YOUNG ADULT URBAN FANTASY

The Tale of Lunarmorte Trilogy:

Moon Spell

River Cast

Blood Solstice

Warriors of Ankh Trilogy:

Blood Will Tell

Blood Past

Shades of Blood

Fire Spirits Series:

Smokeless Fire

Scorched Skies

Borrowed Ember

Darkness, Kindled

OTHER TITLES

Slumber (The Fade #1)

Drip Drop Teardrop, a novella

about the author

Samantha Young is a *New York Times, USA Today* and *Wall Street Journal* bestselling author from Stirlingshire, Scotland. She's been nominated for the Goodreads Choice Award for Best Author and Best Romance for her international bestseller *On Dublin Street*. *On Dublin Street* is Samantha's first adult contemporary romance series and has sold in thirty countries.

Visit Samantha Young online at
www.authorsamanthayoung.com
Twitter @AuthorSamYoung
Instagram @AuthorSamanthaYoung
Facebook @AuthorSamanthaYoung

This is for my family and friends, for forgiving my absence and absentmindedness while I lived and breathed Aidan and Nora's story, and also for encouraging me to pursue my dreams. Like Nora, I realize how powerful that support is, and I'm grateful every day.

part 1

prologue

EDINBURGH, SCOTLAND
OCTOBER 2015

MY BEST FRIEND'S MOTHER ONCE TOLD ME, "YOU WOULD THINK AFTER numerous attacks of grief the human body would be unable to process any more sadness. But our hearts have an annoying amount of endurance."

Since she was one of the bravest people I knew, her words stuck with me as I grew older. And I found out she was right. Most people's hearts are built to withstand loss and grief.

No one, however, said anything about guilt and regret and how those two things can haunt you long after loss.

I didn't want to be haunted. No one does. So I was pretending I wasn't and throwing all of my focus at my job. Not my job as a sales assistant in a cute boutique clothing store in Old Town. It just paid the bills. Barely. Which was why I was currently running late after doing overtime at the boutique. I took all the overtime I could get ... unless it cut into my other job.

Not really a job, actually. It was so much more than that.

"Nora, can you help a customer?" Leah's head appeared around the doorframe, looking into the closet we called a staff room. "Where are you going?"

I pulled on my backpack and strode past her. "Remember, I finish at twelve today. It's five after."

"But Amy isn't here yet."

"I'm sorry. I have to get to the hospital."

Her eyes widened. "Oh? What happened?"

Life happened.

"Uh, excuse me ..." A girl stood at the counter looking annoyed. "Can someone help me, please?"

Leah turned to help the customer and I took the opportunity to dash out of the store without having to explain myself. I knew my boss probably regretted hiring me. She hired two Americans: Amy and me. Only one of us lives up to our national reputation of being a friendly extrovert.

Take a guess which one of us.

It's not that I'm not good at my job, or even that I'm not friendly. I just don't share personal shit with people I don't really know, and Amy and Leah seemed okay with telling each other everything from their favorite color to their partners' ability to give them an orgasm on a Friday night.

As I climbed the hill from the shop and hurried up the old cobbled road of the Royal Mile, my anxiety increased. It was stupid because the kids would be there when I arrived, but I hated the idea of being late. In the weeks that I'd been visiting, I hadn't been late once. And I still needed to change my clothes. I'd have to do it when I got there but before any of them saw me.

They called Edinburgh the windy city, and today—behaving like its forces were against me—it lived up to its name. I strode into the wind feeling its icy resistance. A whimsical part of me wondered if the city was trying to tell me something. Would I look on this day in the future and wish I'd listened to it and turned back? Weird crap like that crossed my mind a lot lately. I lived in my head.

But not one day out of the week.

Not today.

Today was for them.

Hurrying, I cut a twenty-minute walk down to fifteen. It would've been less if not for the damn wind. I almost skidded to a stop once I reached the ward, the nurses looking up in surprise when I appeared at their station sweaty and out of breath.

"Hey," I puffed out.

Jan and Trish grinned at me. "We didn't know if you were coming today," Jan said.

I grinned back at Jan. "Only illness or death."

Catching my meaning, she chuckled and came around the nurses' station. "They're all in the common room."

"Where can I change before they see me?"

She shook her head in amusement. "They won't mind."

"I know." I shrugged.

"Alison is in the common room, so her private bathroom will be free." She gestured down the hall in the opposite direction of the common room.

"Thanks. Two minutes," I promised.

"They're already here. Both of them," Jan said.

Relieved, I nodded and darted through Aly's empty private room to her bathroom, the door banging shut behind me.

Yanking off my sweater and jeans, I began to feel a little hum of excitement in my belly, as I always did when I was about to spend time with them. And it *was* about them.

Really.

"It is," I snapped at myself.

I pulled on my green leggings and shirt and was about to button the shirt closed when the bathroom door suddenly jerked open.

The breath left my body as I froze, looking up at his familiar eyes staring down at me.

He was so tall, his shoulders so broad, he almost filled the entire doorway.

I tried to open my mouth, to ask him what he thought he was doing, but the words got stuck as his gaze drifted from my eyes to my lips, and down. His perusal was long and thorough, from head to toe and back up again. He lingered on the sight of my bra beneath the open shirt, and when his eyes finally returned to meet mine, they were brimming with heat.

His expression was determined.

A mixture of fear and thrill and nervousness burst through me, finally melting my freeze as he stepped into the bathroom, locking the door.

"What are you doing?" I stumbled into the wall behind me.

Amusement danced in his eyes as he moved slowly, predatorily toward me. "I'm thinking that Peter Pan has never looked so sexy."

Unfortunately, I was a sucker for a Scottish accent.

Clearly, or I wouldn't have ended up here, so far from home.

More than that, however, I was beginning to think I was a sucker for him. "Don't." I put my hand up to stop him, but he pressed his chest against it and covered my hand with his own. I stared at how small mine was in comparison, and a shiver tickled down my back and around to my breasts. My breathing faltered as he took another few steps into me until there was barely any space between us. He was so tall and I was so not, I had to tilt my head back to meet his eyes.

His burned. They burned for me in a way no man's ever had.

How was I supposed to resist that?

And yet I knew I had to. I scowled up at him. "You should go."

In answer, he pressed the entire length of his body against mine and heat flashed through me. Excitement rippled in my lower belly. Tingling started between my legs. My nipples hardened.

Angry at my body and him, I shoved at him, but it was like trying to shove a concrete wall. "This is totally inappropriate," I hissed.

He grabbed my hands to stop my ineffectual shoving and gently but effectively pinned my hands above my head. My chest thrust up against him, and I gasped as my breasts swelled.

Eyes dark with knowing and intent, he bent his head toward me.

"Don't." I shook my head, hating the bite in my tone, but carrying on nonetheless. "I'm not playing cavewoman to your caveman."

His lips twitched. "Shame that. Do you often deny yourself what you want?"

"No, but I think with my head, not my vagina."

He laughed, his warm breath puffing against my lips.

I loved when he laughed. I loved when I made him laugh. He needed laughter more than anything. The sound thrilled me, making my belly squeeze with pleasure. And I realized it wasn't just my body betraying me but my heart too.

As if he'd seen the thought in my eyes, he let go of one of my hands so he could press cool fingers against my breast, over my heart. I gasped at the dizzying sensation of being touched so intimately. He asked, "Have you ever thought about thinking with this thing?"

"As far as I'm aware, my left breast isn't much of a thinker," I evaded.

He grinned. "You know what I mean, Pixie."

"Don't call me that."

Expression turning thoughtful, he said, "I thought we were friends."

"We were. But then you pinned me to a bathroom wall."

"Thanks for the reminder." He took hold of my free hand again and pressed it back to the wall with the other. At the flash of anger in my eyes, he said, "If you were really pissed off about it, you'd be struggling."

I flushed. "It would be futile. You're a giant."

"I'd let you go. You know I would. I'd hate it. But I'd let you go … if you didn't want this?"

We looked silently at one another, his face so close to mine, I could see little flecks of yellow gold in his green eyes.

In those moments, I forgot where I was. Who I was. And what the right thing to do for him was.

And I didn't even realize I was straining toward him until he brought it to my attention. "Why are you fighting this when you want it?"

Why *was* I fighting this again?

"Nora?"

I closed my eyes, shutting him out, which allowed the memory of why I was fighting this to return to me. "Because—"

His mouth crushed down on mine, silencing me. Surprise turned to instinct. I kissed him back, meeting his tongue with my own, straining against his hold on my wrists but not to get away. To wrap my arms around him. Run my fingers through his hair.

Heat flushed through me like I was covered in fuel and he'd started a fire at my feet. It lashed like lightning until I was surrounded in a blaze.

Too hot. Too needy. Too everything.

I wanted to rip off my clothes.

I wanted to rip off his clothes.

And then he broke the kiss to pull back and stare at me in triumph.

If he'd been anyone else, if it had been any other moment, I'd have called him out for being smug.

Instead, I remembered exactly why we should not be doing this.

Whatever he saw in my expression made him loosen his grip on my wrists. I lowered them, but he didn't step away.

He waited, his hands resting gently on my small shoulders.

Something in his eyes made my defenses crumble. Tenderness rushed through me and I found myself caressing his cheek, feeling his stubble prickle my skin. Sadness doused the fire. "She's gone," I told him gently. "Not even I can distract you from that."

Unbearable, bleak anguish fought with the desire in his eyes and he slowly slid his hands off my shoulders and down to my waist. With a gentle tug I fell into him, clutching at his chest.

He tore through my soul with the whispered, tortured words, "But you can try."

chapter 1

THERE WAS A PART OF ME THAT DIDN'T WANT TO GO HOME. THE SMELL of fast food clung to my nostrils, and I worried that over time, I'd never get the smell off my skin, out of my hair. And yet I still didn't want to go home. "Have a nice day," I said to my last customer, handing them their burger and fries.

I stepped back from the counter, drawing Molly's eyes. She was at the drink machine, filling up a supersize cup with soda. She made a face. "Why did I agree to overtime?"

Smirking at her, I wanted to shout, "I'll cover for you!" Instead I reminded her, "Because you're saving to buy that piece-of-crap car from Laurie."

"Ah, yeah. Dreaming big."

I chuckled. "Bigger than me. I'm still hauling my ass around on these." I pointed at my legs.

"Yeah, and that ass will continue to defy gravity because of it."

"It defies gravity?" I peeked around at it. "Seriously? And here I thought it was nonexistent."

Molly grinned. "Oh no, you have an ass. It's cute as a button like the rest of you. It's a sweet little heart-shaped butt."

"You are paying way too much attention to my ass."

"It's called compare and contrast," she argued, pointing at her ass. "Your whole ass could fit into one of my butt cheeks."

"Uh...could I have my order now?"

We glanced over at her customer, a sullen freshman who was staring at us like we'd crawled out from under a rock.

"I'll see you tomorrow," I said to Molly, but before I disappeared around the corner, I leaned back and called out to her, "Oh, and I would kill for your ass. And your boobs. Just so you know."

My friend beamed at me, and I wandered off toward the locker room, hoping I'd made her day a little better. Molly was her own brand of cute, but she worried way too much about her weight.

Grabbing my stuff out of the lockers in the back of the building, I tried to shake off the guilt I felt about wanting to remain here serving fries rather than go home. It said a lot. About me or my life, I'm not sure. I wasn't even sure there was a difference.

Working part-time at a fast-food place was not what I dreamed I'd be doing with my life after I graduated. Yet I'd known it was coming. While everyone else was making plans to go to college or travel, I was among the very few who couldn't do any of those things. Eighteen. And trapped.

My closest friend was Molly. She got me the job since she'd been working here for the past two years on weekends. Now she was full-time. Although she'd joked about it, Molly had never dreamed big. I didn't know if it wasn't in her, or if she was lazy or what. All I knew was that my friend hated school. She seemed content to work fast-food and live at home because she never thought about the future. She was always living in the now.

I, however, thought about the future all the time.

I liked school.

I was *not* content here.

A feeling of claustrophobia crawled over me but I shoved it back. Sometimes it could feel like I had fifty people sitting on my chest, mocking me. Pushing through it, I grabbed my purse.

Time to go home.

Calling bye to Molly as I passed through the front of the restaurant, I inwardly flinched when I saw Stacey Dewitte sitting with a bunch of friends at the table near the door. She narrowed her eyes at me, and I looked away. My neighbor was a few years younger than me and once upon a time had been under the illusion that I was something I was not. I didn't know who was more disappointed in me working at the fast-food place: Stacey or me.

Needing this day to be over, I pushed the door open, oblivious at first to the two guys messing around, playfully wrestling outside.

Until one shoved the other and he hit me with enough force to send me sprawling to the dusty road with a thud.

I was so surprised to find myself on the ground, it took a moment for the pain to hit, to feel the ache in my left knee and the sting in my palms.

I was suddenly surrounded by noise.

"Oh fuck, am really sorry."

"Ye awright, lass?"

"Let me gee ye a hand up."

"Dinnae ye bother, I'll get her, ye fud."

A strong hand gripped my bicep, and I found myself gently pulled to my feet. I looked up at the guy holding me, held in the spot not only by his hand but by the kind concern in his dark eyes. He didn't look much older than me—tall, with the wiry, lean build of youth.

"Here's yer bag. Sorry aboot that." The guy with him handed me my purse.

Understanding his words but confused by the way he'd said them, by their alien accent, I blurted, "What?"

"Speak properly. She can't understand ye." The guy still holding my arm nudged his friend. He looked back at me. "Are you okay?"

His words sounded careful now, slower and pronounced. I gently pulled my arm from his grip and nodded. "Yeah."

"We're really sorry."

"I got that. Don't worry. A scrape on the knee won't kill me."

He winced and looked down at my knee. My work pants were covered in dust and grime. "Bugger." When he looked up, I could tell he was going to apologize again.

"Don't." I smiled. "Really, I'm fine."

He smiled back. It was cute and lopsided. "Jim." He held out his hand. "Jim McAlister."

"Are you Scottish?" I asked, delighted by the notion as I shook his calloused hand.

"Aye," his friend said, offering me his hand too. "Roddy Livingston."

"I'm Nora O'Brien."

"Irish-American?" Jim's eyes danced with amusement. "You know, you're one of only a few people we've met in America who guessed where we're from. We've gotten—"

"Irish," Roddy supplied. "English. And dinnae forget Swedish. That was ma favorite."

"I apologize for my countrymen," I joked. "I hope we haven't caused too much offense."

Jim grinned at me. "Not at all. How did ye know we were Scottish?"

"A lucky guess," I confessed. "We don't get a lot of people from Europe visiting our small town."

"We're on a road trip," Roddy explained. He had a full head of wavy ginger hair, and he was taller than me (most people were) but shorter than his friend.

Where Roddy was of medium-height but a burly build, Jim was tall and built like a swimmer. He had tan skin, dark hair, and thickly lashed, dark brown eyes.

And he was staring at me intensely the entire time his friend explained where they'd visited so far. I flushed under Jim's perusal, having never been the entire focus of anyone's attention like this before, let alone a cute Scottish guy.

"Actually," Jim cut off his friend when he said they were leaving here tomorrow, "I was thinking we should stay a little longer." He said the words to me, giving me a cute-boy smirk as he did so.

He was flirting with me?

Roddy snorted. "Oh, aye? After a five-minute meetin'?"

"Aye."

Completely caught up in the idea of a foreigner delaying his departure from Donovan to see me again when we'd barely said a few words made me grin. It was silly and adventurous, and it appealed to my secretly romantic nature. It was so outside my humdrum life. I guess that's why I threw caution to the wind. "Have you been to the lake yet?"

Jim's whole face lit up. "No. Are ye offering to take me?"

"Both of you." I laughed, reminding him he had a friend. "Do you like to fish?"

"I do." Roddy suddenly looked much happier about the idea of staying.

"I don't. But if *you're* there, nothing else matters."

Charmed, I flushed and he took a step toward me, startling me. It seemed to surprise him too, as if he hadn't been in control of the movement.

"Fuck, if I'm gonnae feel like a third wheel the entire fuckin' time, then naw." Roddy turned mulish.

Jim's expression clouded but before he could say something that might cause an argument, I intervened. "You knocked me on my ass," I reminded Roddy. "You owe me."

He sighed but the corner of his mouth tilted up. "Fine."

"I need to get home," I said, taking a reluctant step back.

Jim tracked my movements, and I felt a little like a deer caught in his line of sight. He really did stare at me so determinedly. All of a sudden, I didn't know whether I should feel thrilled or wary.

"Where will we meet?"

My shift didn't start until the afternoon the next day. I'd have to lie to my parents and tell them I'd had no choice but to take on overtime. "Here. At nine a.m."

"Nine a.m.? I dinnae—"

Jim clamped a hand over his friend's mouth and grinned at me. "Nine is great. See ye then, Nora O'Brien."

I nodded and turned on my heel. My neck prickled, feeling his eyes on me the entire time I walked south down Main Street, which ran through the center of Donovan, about four miles long, split into north and south. Most businesses in Donovan were located on the north end, from Foster's Veterinary Surgery at the very tip beyond the elementary and high schools. We had lots of small businesses in Donovan—Wilson's Market, Montgomery & Sons Attorneys at Law, the pizza place—and then there were the recognizable chains like the gas station, the little red and white building I worked in, and so on. South Main Street was mostly residential.

I walked down North Main and then turned right onto West Sullivan where I lived in a small one-story, two-bedroom house that I tried to keep looking as nice as possible. It took me fifteen minutes to walk there from the fast-food restaurant, and I sighed on approach because the grass was getting a little long on our small lawn. Ours was one of the smallest properties in the neighborhood, most being two-story houses with pretty porches. We didn't have a porch. The house was a light gray, rectangular box with a darker gray over-hanging roof. It had pretty white shutters at the small windows, though, and I painted them every year.

Despite Donovan being the kind of town where every building was spaced out so there was room to breathe and lots of light, our house hardly got any out front because of the big-ass tree planted in our lawn. It blocked nearly all the light trying to shine in through my bedroom window.

"You're late." My mom sighed heavily, brushing by me as I stepped into the house. I watched as she grabbed her coat from the hook on the wall, and yanked it so hard the hook came with it. She sighed again and cut me a look. "I thought you were going to fix that."

"I'll do it tonight." I kicked off my shoes.

"He's eaten, and he's watching the game." Mom shrugged into her coat, and her voice lowered. "He's in a shitty mood."

When was he ever not in a shitty mood? "Right."

"There's some leftovers in the fridge for you."

"I've got overtime tomorrow," I said before she could leave.

Her expression tightened. "I thought you weren't going to take on overtime? We need you here."

"And we need this job. If I don't do overtime, they said they'll get someone who can," I lied, for the first time ever. An ugly ache pressed on my chest at the deception. But the excitement of being away from here with a boy who looked at me as if I was something special was too big a feeling for that ugly ache to contend with.

"Christ," Mom snapped. "I'm working two fucking jobs as it is, Nora. You know I ain't got time to be here."

I bit my lip, my cheeks flushing. I felt awful.

But selfishly, not awful enough.

"Fine. We'll need to ask Dawn to check in on him from time to time." Dawn was our neighbor—a stay-at-home mom who was kind to us. "You'll be finished by six?"

I nodded.

"I don't have overtime yet this week so I'll be done by two tomorrow."

"What about tonight?" Mom was a bartender at Al's five nights out of the week, and a part-time waitress at Geena's five days a week.

"I'll be home by one-thirty."

Dad usually fussed when she got home, which meant she probably wouldn't get to sleep until around three in the morning, and then she was back up again at seven for her shift at the diner at eight.

It didn't have to be that way. I could've worked full-time during the day while she did nightshift or vice versa, and we would've made it work. But she didn't want to be here anymore than I did. She'd worked constantly my whole life.

I watched her leave, remembering how much it used to hurt.

It didn't hurt so much now. In fact, I worried I was beginning to feel numb about it.

"That you, kid?" my dad yelled.

I found him in our living room, his wheelchair set up in front of the television. His eyes were glued to the screen, and he didn't look up once, even when he snapped, "You're late."

"I know. Sorry. Need anything?"

His lip curled at the television. "Do I need anything? God decided long ago that I needed less than every-fucking-body else."

Inwardly I sighed, having heard him say the same thing over and over since I was eleven years old. My eyes dropped to his left leg. Or what was left of it. Seven years ago, it had been amputated at the knee.

"Drink?"

"Got one." He flicked me an irritated look. "I'll call you if I need you."

In other words, get lost.

With pleasure.

I found the leftover pasta Mom had stuck in the fridge and dumped it on a plate. I'd eat it cold. I stared at the kitchen door, left open in case he hollered.

Before everything went to hell, I could barely remember a time when my dad yelled at me. Now he was always yelling about something.

Surprisingly, he didn't call for anything, and I was able to eat my cold pasta in peace. After doing the dishes Mom had left for me, I got out my tools and screwed the coat hook into another part of the hallway wall. I filled the previous hole with Spackle.

After showering, I got Dad another beer. "Last one for today," I reminded him. The doctor said he shouldn't have more than two in any twenty-four-hour period.

His eyes snapped up at me in outrage. "If I want another beer, I'll have another fucking beer. I got nothing. I just sit here rotting away, looking at your lifeless fucking face, watching your mom's ass walk out the door more often than walk in, and you want to take away the only pleasures in life I have. I'll have a fuckin—don't you walk away, girl!"

When he threw a tantrum, there was nothing else for it. Sometimes when he spoke to me like that, I wanted to cut him off by screaming continuously in his face. If I didn't run out of breath for five whole minutes, it still wouldn't equate to the many times I'd felt that man's spittle on my cheeks.

I didn't close my bedroom door the whole way in case he called for me again. The TV got louder. Much louder. Still not enough for me to walk back out there and ask him to turn it down.

Having gotten good at drowning him out, I turned and faced my sanctuary. My bedroom was small. There wasn't a lot in it except a bed, a small writing desk, and a closet for the few clothes I had. There were a few books, not many. I got most of my reading material from the library.

Most.

Not all. Like the stuff hidden in my room.

I crouched down and pulled out the old shoebox I'd hidden under my bed and gently lifted it onto my bedspread. I savored opening it, like it was a treasure chest. Calm moved through me at the sight of my stash. I had a bunch of secondhand plays and poetry books in there, books I'd bought online and hidden so my mom wouldn't see what I'd "wasted" my money on.

I didn't think they were a waste. Far from it.

Pulling a pile out, I stroked the peeling cover of *The Crucible*. Underneath it was *Dr. Faustus* and *Romeo & Juliet*. Underneath those, *Twelfth Night*, *Othello*, *Hamlet*, and *Macbeth*. I had a thing for Shakespeare. He made even the most ordinary feelings, un-extraordinary thoughts, sound so grandiose. Better yet, he spoke of the most complex, dark emotions in a way that was beautiful and absorbing. I wanted so badly to see a live production of one of his plays.

I wanted so badly to *be in* a live production of one of his plays.

No one knew that. Not even Molly. No one knew I had wild dreams of being an actress on the stage. They'd laugh at me. And rightly so. When I was a kid, I'd been part of an amateur theater group, but had to stop when Dad couldn't take care of himself anymore. That was the extent of my experience on the stage. I'd loved it, though. I loved disappearing into someone else's life, another world, telling stories that held the audience enthralled. And the way they'd clap at the end. Just clap and clap. It was like a giant hug in place of all the hugs my mom had forgotten to give me.

I slumped against my bed, berating myself for that thought. Mom wasn't a bad person. She kept a roof over my head, food in my belly, shoes on my feet. She didn't have a lot of time for me. She worked hard. That was my mom's life. I shouldn't be angry at her for that.

A roar from the crowd at the game my dad was watching made me flinch.

Now, for him … I don't know if what I felt was anger.

Maybe more like resentment.

It was horrible to resent him. I knew that. Sometimes I thought maybe I wasn't a very nice person.

I put everything back in the box, closed it, and tried to shut out the ache in my chest and that horrible gnawing feeling I'd had in my stomach for a long time now. To help, I grabbed a book I'd checked out and got comfy on my bed.

For a while, I was lost in a story about another world and a girl who was in a prison that made mine look like a constant vacation. Finally, I glanced at my watch, and reluctantly put my book down.

Back in the living room, I found my dad with his head bowed, sleeping. When I switched off the TV, his head flew up and he looked around, disoriented. When he was like this, sleepy and confused, he seemed so vulnerable. It made me sad to remember how my dad used to be.

He'd never relied on anyone before the wheelchair. That's why he was so pissed off all the time. He hated being dependent.

"Hey, Dad," I gently touched his shoulder, and he blinked up at me. "Time for bed."

Dad nodded, and I stepped out of the way. Walking behind him slowly, I followed him into my parents' bedroom. Mom always helped him change into bottoms he could sleep in so I didn't have to. Dad removed his shirt, leaving only his T-shirt. Once, his shoulders had been broad and his biceps strong from working construction. They'd lost a lot of definition over the years.

He was still strong enough to help me get him into bed.

"Warm enough, Dad?"

"Yeah."

"Night, then."

"Nora." He grabbed my hand and I felt my stomach sink, sensing what was coming. "I'm sorry."

"I know, Dad."

His sad eyes pleaded with me to understand. "I get so hacked off and I don't mean to take it out on you, baby girl. You know you're the best thing your mom and I ever did, right?"

Tears threatened and my throat felt tight and hot. "I know," I whispered.

"Do you, though?" His grip tightened. "Love you, baby girl."

I fought back the sting in my nose and blew out a shaky breath. "Love you too, Dad."

It wasn't until I got back to my room and into bed that I pressed my mouth into my pillow and sobbed.

I hated the nights he reminded me of what I'd lost.

Life would've been so much easier if I didn't have the memories of a dad who'd given me all the affection my mom hadn't. He was free and easy with hugs and kisses, and he'd filled my ears with his grand plans for my future. I was going to college—I was going to take over the world.

And then everything changed.

For as long as I could remember, my dad worked his ass off, which was one of the reasons I didn't understand why Mom worked so much. Dad owned the largest construction company in the county. He had lots of guys working for him, and we lived in a nice big house he'd built on the outskirts of Donovan. However, he had diabetes. As his company got more successful, Dad got more stressed. He stopped avoiding the wrong foods and alcohol until finally, he got gangrene in his leg and they had no choice but to amputate below the knee. I was eleven. Just a kid.

Dad lost work and Kyle Trent bought his company off him for a pittance and turned it into a success again. The Trents even bought our old house. I had to assume it was mortgaged up to my parents' ears because there was no money from it as far as I knew.

Mom started working more. Somehow, I ended up being my dad's caretaker. It wasn't an easy job, but he was my dad. His life was hard and so was my mom's, so I did what I had to do to help. It meant, however, that I was tired a lot and I didn't have the same time to dedicate to school. Yet I was determined I was going to keep up my grades. Even when Dad became a different man and crushed my dreams of the future. He made it clear college was no longer an option for me. I reminded myself there was still community college.

Someday.

If I ever had time.

I muffled my cries against my pillow, gripping my thin duvet tight in my hand. I mourned my future. Dad had spent my first eleven years building it up into something amazing. But mostly, I mourned my dad. I grieved for my hero who'd kissed away my tears, hugged away my fears, and treated me like I was everything that was important to him.

When I was little, having a loving father in my life was fact, as how it should be. And when he was suddenly gone, replaced by someone bitter, sad, and vulnerable, I felt like I'd been untethered from my safety post, left to float up and away into the sky, unshielded from the storms ahead.

I cannot tell you how scary that feeling is. Sometimes I think it would've been better to never have had that.

Because I wouldn't miss it so damn much.

Shuddering from the pain, I wrapped my arms tight around myself and tried to calm down.

I thought of the boy I'd met today and how he'd looked at me like I was something special.

Like the way my dad looked at me on days the man he used to be fought through.

Slowly, my shuddering eased and the guilt I felt over lying to my mom about tomorrow went with it. I needed a day outside of the norm. A day to breathe full and free. Just one day. Just one memory to carry me through the following days when breathing would be that little bit harder.

chapter 2

THEY WERE WAITING FOR ME THE NEXT MORNING, STANDING NEXT TO A new Mustang. I ran a hand over the hood. "Where did you get the car?"

Jim moved around to stand next to me, so I had to tilt my head back to meet his eyes. "We rented it."

"Nice."

"It took us a while to get used to driving on the other side of the road."

I laughed, imagining them turning the wrong way down streets. "I bet."

"So," Roddy crossed his arms over his chest, "are we goin' tae this lake or what?"

"He's a little grouchy," I said to Jim.

"He's not a morning person."

His friend grunted. "Like *you* are."

"When a bonny lassie is waiting for me, I am." Jim winked at me and put a hand on my lower back, guiding me to the car.

I felt a moment of uncertainty. "Uh ... you guys aren't serial killers, right?"

"Bit late to be askin' that now," Roddy huffed. "Get in, woman."

"Wow. He really isn't a morning person."

"How's yer knee?" Jim asked, looking at my legs as I got in the car.

"Fine. I have a little bruise, that's it."

"That was just an excuse to check oot her legs," Roddy said as Jim slid into the backseat behind him.

He was rewarded with a slap across the back of the head.

Roddy perked up a little once we reached the lake. The country park and lake were situated in the northeast of town on the south bend of Donovan Lake. I'd decided to take them there because it was mostly surrounded by trailers—some permanent homes, other vacation homes—and it meant there were a lot of families hanging out there during the summer. It was a safe place for me to get to know two guys I'd only just met.

We took a small rowboat out with fishing rods, and Roddy fished while Jim quizzed me. Or Jim tried to.

"Ye'er barely giving me anything." He laughed. "Most girls love talking about themselves."

"There's not a lot to say, I'm afraid."

"Okay. Well, I know ye work at that burger place. Is it full-time, part-time, a summer thing?"

"Who knows." I shrugged, and he laughed, seeming delighted by my vagueness.

I didn't intentionally mean to be mysterious; I genuinely didn't know what my future held at this point.

"Have ye lived here all of yer life? Do ye live with yer parents? What do they do? What do ye want to do with yer life?"

The rapid-fire questions made me smile. The sun was beginning to rise higher over the trees, so I slipped on my cheap sunglasses, glad to have another shield over my thoughts. "Yes and yes. My mom works two jobs—she's a bartender and a waitress. My dad doesn't work because he has really bad diabetes. And I don't know. I guess I want to do something that helps people." *Or be a stage actress.*

Jim slowly smiled. "See? That wasn't so hard."

"What about you? Where in Scotland are you from? Do you live with your parents? What do they do? What do you want to do with your life?"

"We work construction in Edinburgh." Jim gestured to Roddy,

who was staring sleepily out at the water, seeming happy to enjoy the peace and the gentle heat of the morning sun. "I live in a place called Sighthill in Edinburgh, with my mum and sister." He paused. "My dad passed away a few months ago. Heart attack."

Sympathy panged in my chest at the little catch his voice. And then Roddy changed my entire perception of him by reaching back to pat his friend's knee in consolation. Jim patted his friend's shoulder in thanks.

"I'm so sorry."

Jim nodded.

Awkwardness fell over the boat as I tried to think of an appropriate new topic. I didn't want to feel like I was blowing past his pain, but I got the impression he didn't want to talk about it any further.

"So, why a road trip?"

He threw me a grateful smile. "I got some money from my dad's pension, Roddy and I turned twenty-one, and we decided to blow it all on a US road trip. We've talked about doing it since we were kids."

"You're twenty-one?"

"Aye." He narrowed his eyes. "Please tell me ye'er legal."

I laughed, blushing. "I'm eighteen."

"Thank fuck," he said, smiling. "Ye would have broken my heart if ye'd said no."

"Yer chat-up lines are gettin' worse, mate," Roddy grumbled.

"It's not a chat-up line." Jim smacked him playfully across the back of the head again, but Roddy didn't flinch this time. Jim looked back at me. "It's not."

I studied him. "Why are you being so charming? You don't know me at all."

"Exactly what I said last night. And this morning."

Jim rolled his eyes. "Roddy. Shut up."

Roddy grunted.

"Well?" I persisted.

"I don't know." He stared at me in that intense way of his. "There's something about ye."

His friend turned to me, shading his eyes from the sun with his hand. "What he's really sayin' is that he fancies the fuck out of ye, he's thinkin' only with his dick, and if ye dinnae dae somethin' to make him see ye'er just a lassie like any other lassie, I'm stuck in Eerie-fuckin'-Indiana for the rest of the summer."

I caught most of what he'd said. And blushed even harder.

"Roddy, if ye dinnae shut up, I'm throwing ye overboard, mate."

"Well, it's the truth. Ye dinnae even ken each other."

"Which is why we're sitting in a boat gettin' to know each other."

"I'm just sayin'… move it along a bit so we can get oot eh' here."

"I've got a better plan." Jim started to row the boat back to dock.

"What ye doin'?" Roddy complained. "I was enjoyin' the lake."

"Really? I couldnae tell with all the bloody complaining ye were doin'."

"Oh, c'mon, I was only jokin'."

But Jim kept rowing us back. He dumped the oars, stood up, and held his hands out to me. I let him pull me up onto the dock. And then he turned around and pushed the boat away with Roddy still inside it.

Roddy scrambled for the oars. "What ye doin'!"

To my surprise, I suddenly found my hand gripped in Jim's large, stronger one. "I'm going with Nora somewhere I can get to know her in peace. And *you* can fish. We'll come back and get ye in a bit."

"Aw, aye, nice!" Roddy called, drawing attention from several people. "Dump me, yer long-time friend, for a lassie ye just met."

"Temporarily, Roddy. And only cause ye'er a pain in the arse."

I snorted as Jim grinned down at me. And then he tugged me along after him. "Are you sure he'll be okay out there?"

"He's fine." Jim laughed. "I'm giving him what he wants. All that pissing and moaning was so we'd bugger off and leave him alone. Trust me."

"Oh. Okay."

"So, where to?"

"This way." I led him off the dock and onto the gravel pathway that wound around the woods edging the lake. To my surprise, we walked in comfortable silence until I found what I was looking for. An empty bench at the edge of the lake, a few minutes from any trailer or other boats. Some privacy. "This way we still get to enjoy the lake."

Jim grinned and took a seat. "It's stunnin' here."

"Yeah, I like it." I sat down and because I was wearing shorts, I could feel the warmth the wood had soaked up from the morning sun. In the height of summer, around two, three o'clock, you couldn't sit on these benches without burning the skin off your thighs. This time in the morning, the heat was as pleasant on my skin as the low sun in the sky was. "I don't get here often enough."

"Why not?"

"I work a lot."

"So ..." Jim relaxed, one leg bent, the other straight, his arms along the back of the bench. He squinted at me in the sun as he sat sprawled out and twice my size. "Will ye answer any of my questions now?"

I tilted my head in consideration. "Depends on the question."

"Let's start with the easy stuff. Favorite color?"

"Whoa, there," I teased. "That's a little personal."

Jim chuckled. It was a nice sound. "My favorite color is Hibs green."

"I don't know what color that is."

"Hibernian green. Hibs are an Edinburgh football team. Soccer."

"I don't know a lot about soccer. My dad is a huge Colts fan, though."

"I love American football."

"Really?" I was surprised. "I thought you guys had rugby?"

"We do ... but American football is more exciting to me. Don't get me wrong, rugby's hardcore. But your football is so strategic. My sister hates sports but even she will sit and watch an NFL game. I'm a Patriots fan."

"Shhh," I teased, glancing around us. "Don't say that too loudly around here."

Jim grinned. "I won't." He tugged playfully on my ponytail. "Tell me something else about ye. What's yer favorite song?"

Instantly, a memory of my dad and a few guys on his crew jamming to Bon Jovi flitted through my mind, causing a wave of nostalgia and an ache in my chest. I was ten, and Cory Trent, for some reason I'd yet to discover, had told everyone in our class that my mom had told his mom I wet the bed. Which was a total lie. I had my best friend's mom drop me off at the house Dad was fixing up a mile from our own. It was unusual for him to get work in town—his crew was usually booked out somewhere else in the county. I'd thanked God for him being so close that day because I'd been devastated by everyone treating me like a pariah at school.

He'd emerged from the house when one of the guys called out to let him know I was there. As soon as I saw him I burst into tears, and he swept me up into his arms. After I told him what had happened, he was really mad at Cory. Then Dan, his foreman, had turned up the radio and a few of the guys and my dad cheered me up by doing an awful impression of Bon Jovi.

I'd known then I had the best dad in the world.

Which made it worse that I'd lost him not long after that.

"'Livin' on a Prayer.'"

At his silence, I sneaked a peek at Jim—he was shaking with laughter. I narrowed my eyes. "Okay, I'm not answering any more questions if you're going to mock me."

"No, no!" He laughed, putting a hand on my shoulder. "I'm sorry. I just wasn't expecting Bon Jovi."

"Oh? What's your favorite song, cool guy?"

"'All These Things That I've Done,' by the Killers."

I wrinkled my nose. "Okay. That *is* cool."

The bench shook as he laughed again and suddenly, he reached up to take hold of an arm of my sunglasses. He gently pushed them up and settled them on top of my head so he could see my eyes. "You are so adorable."

It was a compliment I'd heard before, and in the past, it had bugged me. I was only five three and, although in the last couple of years I'd finally developed curves, I was petite. I had large dark eyes with really long lashes that made them look even bigger. Whenever anyone described me, it was as "cute" or "adorable." I didn't want to be cute or adorable. I wanted to be more.

But Jim made "adorable" sound like more. I blushed. "I'm not really."

"You are," he insisted.

I peeked at him again and blushed harder under his intense scrutiny. "You're looking at me."

"Aye. It's hard not tae."

I squirmed, not sure how to respond. I'd never been in a position where I was supposed to flirt back. "Are all Scottish guys as flirty as you?"

Jim shrugged. "I didn't think I was being flirty. I was just saying what I was thinking."

"Obviously, it's one and the same when it comes to you," I teased.

He slid closer to me, and I sucked in a breath, feeling nervous butterflies wake in my belly at his nearness. "Favorite movie?"

Realizing he wasn't going in for a kiss, I didn't know whether to be disappointed or relieved. "I don't know … *Moulin Rouge*."

"Another surprise." He raised an eyebrow. "I haven't seen it, but it's not what I would have guessed."

"What would you have guessed?"

"Actually, I have no idea." He grinned. "My favorite movie is *Red*."

"I don't think I've seen that."

"It's fucking hilario—shit, sorry." His cheeks flushed. "I'm trying no' tae swear around ye."

Making an effort to be a gentleman was sweet—very sweet—but I also wanted Jim to be himself. The red in his cheeks gave him a vulnerability I hadn't expected, and I realized that maybe underneath the bravado, I made him nervous too. The thought was a little exhilarating. "You said you work construction?"

He nodded.

"I'll bet you curse a lot, huh? My dad used to own a construction company. As much as he tried not to, he cursed all the time. So did his crew. It doesn't bother me. Sometimes..." I dropped my voice an octave, "*I* even curse. The horror."

He pushed me playfully. "So much for trying to be a gentleman."

I grinned. "Just be you." And before he could start asking me questions I wasn't sure I was ready to answer, I said, "Why did you and Roddy come to Donovan of all places?"

Jim stared at me, as if trying to decide something. Finally, he relaxed against the bench and turned to look out at the lake. His attention to it brought mine to the fact there was a man and two little boys in a boat, laughing and carrying on as they rowed past. I hadn't even been aware of the noise I was so lost in our conversation.

"My dad," Jim suddenly said. "His name was Donovan."

I sensed like I had before, that it was hard for Jim to talk about him. "You don't have to ..."

He glanced back at me. "Roddy avoids the topic completely. Mum starts crying if I mention him. And the truth is talking about him to people who knew him is hard."

Compassion for this boy engulfed me, and I smashed through my usual reserve and placed a hand on his knee in comfort. He looked down at it, seeming surprised and more than a little lost.

"Sometimes..." I heaved a sigh around the sudden constriction in my chest, "it's easier to talk about it with someone who didn't know him or love him because you don't have to worry or deal with their grief, just your own. You can talk about him without having to think about how it'll affect the person you're talking to." I lifted my hand off his knee but turned to face him, my left knee almost touching his hip. "You can talk to me about him. If you'd like ..."

Jim seemed half unsure, half in wonder. "It's a little heavy for a first date."

"This is a date?"

"Aye, it's a date."

I laughed at his insistent tone. "Then I guess we get to decide how we want that date to go. I'm a really good listener, Jim. But we don't have to talk."

He raised an eyebrow, a smirk curling the corners of his lips, and I shoved him for his indecent thoughts. "You know what I meant. God," I huffed, rolling my eyes. "Men."

His laughter settled and he shimmied closer to me on the bench, so my knee *was* touching his hip. Seriousness came down over his gaze like a theater curtain, slow and steady, as he studied what felt like the entirety of my face. Before he lowered his eyes to my hair, I realized we had almost the same color of eyes. Almost black in low lighting but when the sun captured them, they glowed warmer, like dark mahogany.

Jim curled a finger around a strand in my ponytail and played with it as he began to talk. "My dad's mum was Irish, my grandfather Scottish, and as my dad would tell it, they were both fiercely proud of their heritage. They passed away when I was four. Car crash." His eyes flicked to mine for a second, as if to check my reaction, before they drifted back to watching his fingers play with my hair. "When my dad was born, my grandad suggested to my gran that they call him Donovan McAlister. Donovan was my gran's maiden name.

"So, Roddy and I were on the I-70, heading toward Route 66 in Illinois. From there we were going to drive the whole thing. We stopped for gas, and I saw a help-wanted ad on a bulletin board there. For a supermarket in Donovan." He gave the lake a sheepish smile. "Fuckin' stupid, I know...It...I felt like we needed tae come here."

"That's not stupid," I reassured him.

Jim turned to give me another one of those searching looks of his. "No...I'm starting to think it wasn't."

I squirmed under his intensity, unable to hold his gaze because he overwhelmed me. As cool as he was, as much as I liked his accent and thought he was cute, I wasn't prepared for Jim McAlister or the way he looked at me like he'd been struck by lightning.

"What was your dad like?"

"He was the funniest guy I knew." Jim's voice was filled with a mix of humor and grief that made my chest ache for him. "And he had time for nearly everybody. If someone needed help, it was never a problem, it was never too much. I was his best pal."

His smile trembled, and a bright sheen appeared in his eyes. I reached for his hand and held it between both of mine, and it seemed to strengthen Jim, the sheen disappearing, his smile relaxing. "He taught me that family always comes first. That family is more important than how much money I make or fame or any of that shite. He made me feel like it was awright no' tae be ambitious about career but tae be ambitious about life. About finding the right girl and startin' a family."

I had never heard a boy talk of those things before, or at least prioritize those things. I also noticed his accent thickening as he reminisced about his dad. Like he was relaxing with me. "He sounds like a good man."

"Aye." He nodded but something cooled in his expression. "But he wasnae perfect, and everyone seems to have swept that under the rug."

"What do you mean?"

"Mum, specifically. Don't get me wrong. He loved her but he was a bit of a selfish bastard when it came to her. He never took her anywhere or spent much time wi' her. He always went out tae the pub wi' his mates but left Mum at home. Then he got pissed off if she wasnae there when he got home. Like she wasnae supposed tae have a life without him ..." He shot me a quiet look I didn't understand until he spoke again. "And he cheated on her and from what I heard, it wasnae just sex. He fell in love wi' someone else. My parents nearly split up. In the end he chose Mum, but I don't think she ever really forgave him."

"I'm sorry."

"But she acts now like he was a saint." Anger had edged into his words. "I ... just ... I loved my dad, and I forgive him for no' being perfect because none of us are ... but I want tae remember my dad, no' the glossed-over version of him, ye know?"

I nodded, squeezing his hand.

"Does that make me a bad person?"

"God, no."

Jim exhaled slowly and looked back out at the water. I studied his profile, noting the tension had eased from his jaw, from his shoulders. As he watched a bird skirt low over the water and fly off into the trees, he said, "I'm glad I met ye, Nora O'Brien."

"Yeah?"

He looked at me again and then gently removed his hand from between mine but only so he could slide it around my shoulder. "I'd like to stay a little longer, if that's okay."

"Sure, I still have a few hours before I need to get back for work."

"No," he laughed softly, shaking his head. "No, I meant ... I'd like to stay in Donovan a little longer. Beyond today."

Suddenly, I knew what he was asking, and despite feeling intimidated by the desire in Jim's eyes, I was also intrigued by his foreignness. He came from a place so different from Donovan. I'd seen it on TV and in movies, but I still couldn't imagine what life was like in the city he'd grown up in. Part of me didn't even care. What I mostly cared about was that it was so far away from Indiana, so mysterious and tantalizing, like an adventure waiting to happen an ocean away from my plain little life. And Jim was a part of that.

I nodded, not quite ready to let go of him, either.

chapter 3

Since I was twelve years old, I've hated the antiseptic smell of hospitals.

It woke up the angry knots in my stomach.

Regardless, every month, without fail, I jumped on a bus and went through a ninety-minute journey to Indianapolis to the children's hospital there. I'd been doing this for the past five years, not counting the year before when my mom let me visit more often.

It wasn't often my mom gave me a break from life but the year I was twelve, she did.

Now I think she thinks I'm a lunatic. We've argued about my monthly visit, but I won't back down on this one. She's finally stopped trying to get me to.

"Hey, Nora." Anne-Marie approached as I strode down the corridor toward the common room on the hospital's third floor. "You get prettier every day, sweetheart." She wrapped her arm around me and gave me a squeeze.

I smiled fondly up at the nurse I'd known since I was a kid. "So do you."

She rolled her eyes at me but didn't let go. "What did you bring with you today?"

I held up the book in my hand: *The Witches* by Roald Dahl. "Not too scary, right?"

"No," she assured me.

Relieved, I grinned. The only thing that made me forget about those hard knots in my stomach was the knowledge that for a couple of hours, I was going to make the kids in that common room forget the tubes sticking into them, the respirators and oxygen tanks, and their total lack of energy.

I tried to choose books and plays that weren't too adult for the younger kids but were funny enough I could make them entertaining even to the older ones.

Anne-Marie opened the door to the common room. "Hey, guys, look who's here!"

I stepped into the room and was met by smiles, waves, and a collection of "Hey, Nora," some exuberant, some tired but welcoming. Kids of all ages and illnesses stared up at me. Some in wheelchairs, some resting in chairs, some playing a computer game, others board games, some bald, some wan with dark circles under their eyes and a sickly tinge to their young skin, and some I was happy to see looking healthier than they had the last time I saw them.

"You ready to be scared?" I asked, grinning at them as Anne-Marie threw me a wink and left us to it.

What I loved about these kids was that unlike most their age, they stopped playing with their phones, or their iPads, or the computer console in the corner, and gave me their full attention. All because I wasn't there to ask them how sick they were feeling today, or if they felt better, or if they were tired of being tired. I was just there to take them somewhere else for a while.

We settled in, and I stood in front of them, preparing to act out this entire book if we had time. I'd read the book a few times before coming to the hospital and decided how each character would sound. Some small. Some big. I transformed in front of the kids from reserved, exhausted Nora O'Brien into a character actor. I didn't know if I was good. Or awful. All I knew was that these kids loved it. And it was freeing.

"The most important thing you should know about REAL WITCHES is this," I said in a faux English accent that made them smile and lean closer. "Listen very carefully ..."

———

GLANCING AT THE CLOCK, I REALIZED OUR TIME WAS UP, BUT I WAS almost finished. Finally, I acted out the last sentence and closed the book.

Silence reigned and then Jayla, a pretty eight-year-old girl with leukemia, started clapping. The others joined in, although Mikey, a fourteen-year-old with kidney disease, rolled his eyes. "It's supposed to be scary."

"It was scary," Jayla insisted, scowling at him.

"Yeah, to babies like you." Mikey curled his lip at me. "You're too hot to be the witch."

"The witch was beautiful," Annie, a thirteen-year-old from Greer, a town a few miles from Donovan, argued.

"Yeah, until she was revealed to be a hag. It wasn't real when she did that scene." He gestured at me.

"Don't call me hot, Mikey. It's weird."

He grinned at me. "Stop being hot, then."

"She can't stop being hot, silly," Jayla huffed and rolled her eyes at me as if to say, "Boys."

I laughed and crossed the room to kiss her forehead. "I'm glad you enjoyed it, sweetie."

She beamed up at me and then shot Mikey a smug look, making me laugh harder.

Mikey ignored her, giving me what I think was supposed to be a smoldering look. "How come Jayla gets a kiss goodbye and I don't?"

"Don't be creepy, Mikey." I headed toward the door.

"What? So, being on the transplant list doesn't even get me a sympathy make-out?"

I snorted. "Not from me."

"That blows." He thought about it a minute and turned to look at Annie, seated next to him. "What about you?"

She made a face. "I'm no one's second choice, Michael Fuller."

As entertaining as they were, as much as I'd love to spend every day with them, I couldn't. "I have to catch my bus, guys. Thanks for hanging out with me."

"We'll see you next month?" Jayla asked, hope shining in her big blue eyes.

"Unless you're out of here and back home, which I hope you will be, yes, I'll be back next month."

Those hard knots suddenly came back into focus as soon as I said my goodbyes and closed the common room door behind me.

"Is Anne-Marie around?" I asked, passing the nurses' station.

A nurse I didn't recognize shook her head.

"Will you tell her Nora said goodbye and I'll see her next month, same time?"

"Of course."

Like magic, as soon as I stepped outside and breathed in hot, thick city air strong enough to obliterate the hospital smell, the knots in my stomach disappeared.

I caught the bus back to Donovan and spent ninety glorious minutes reading. It was heaven, despite the fact that the air conditioning above my head appeared to be broken and sweat trickled down my back and pooled in my bra.

The familiar gloom I usually felt upon my return to Donovan wasn't there, and I knew it was because my life wasn't the same as it had been last month. The script for my life had been sitting on a dusty, worn-out coffee table only for Jim McAlister to come blasting into the room, throwing the papers into disarray. The script was all messed up now.

And I think that's what I liked most about him.

Thinking about him as I got off the bus, and the last week of trying to sneak off and find time with him, I thought I almost imagined the sound of his voice saying my name.

When I turned around, he actually was standing outside May's Coffeehouse with a to-go cup in his hand. I glanced toward the small parking lot and saw Roddy sitting on the hood of the Mustang.

Jim and I walked toward each other, and he looked perturbed.

Guilt suffused me, making me blush.

"I thought ye were working," he said, nodding toward the bus I got off.

I didn't know what to say. I hadn't intended to tell Jim about my volunteer work at the hospital because it felt ... well, it felt too personal. Like I'd have to explain why.

And I didn't want to. I wasn't ready to talk about that.

However, I could see by the irritation growing in his eyes that I either explained partly or I'd damage our friendship. "I was. Well ... not working but volunteering. At a kids' hospital in Indianapolis."

"Why didn't ye just tell me that?"

I kicked at a stone by my foot, hiding my eyes, and thus the truth, from him. "It sounds ... so Girl Scout," I grumbled.

Jim laughed and gently chucked my chin, so I had no choice but to look up at him. "It's adorable. Ye'er fuckin' adorable."

"Stop calling me adorable." I grabbed his hand but didn't let it go. "What are you and Roddy up to?"

"Well, I'm about to dump his arse so I can spend time with ye."

I giggled. "You are such a good friend."

"I'm the worst. But right now, I could give a fuck because I've been here a week and I still haven't kissed ye ... and I need to do something about that."

The breath whooshed right out of me. "Oh."

Jim gave me a slow, mischievous smile. "I'll take that as a 'Yes, Jim, let's dump Roddy.'"

I shrugged, pretending nonchalance. "Why not?"

Laughing, Jim threw his arm around my shoulders and started walking us toward Roddy and the Mustang. "Roddy, I'm dropping ye off at the motel, mate."

Roddy made a face of disgust and flopped back on the hood of the car. "For fuck's sake."

———

"IF THAT KID DOESN'T STOP THROWING YOU DIRTY LOOKS, I'M GOING TO stick this ice cream in her face," Molly huffed as she came up beside me to pour diet soda into her customer's cup.

I sighed. The kid Molly was referring to was Stacey. She was in here with her crew almost every time I was working a shift. "Don't."

"What's her problem, anyway?"

"It's Stacey *Dewitte*," I said, so quietly it surprised me Molly even heard me.

"Shit. *That's* Melanie's little sister? I didn't even recognize her." Molly glanced over her shoulder, presumably at Stacey. "Why does she hate you? I thought you and Melanie were tight?"

"She doesn't hate me. She's just … disappointed, I guess."

"In what? You don't have to put up with that shit." Molly put the lid on the cup. "You don't—ooh, your boyfriend's here."

I followed her gaze. Jim and Roddy were walking into the restaurant. Smiling at them, I finished packing the to-go bag for my customer and took it over to her at the cash register.

"Have a nice day," I said.

She moved away, and suddenly Jim was at my counter. He gave me a grim look that put me on alert. For two weeks, he and Roddy had stuck around Donovan, often going for short road trips when I was working or busy, but making their way back to town.

For me.

Whenever Roddy was with Jim, he complained constantly about still being here, but Jim was determined to spend time with me, and I continued to enjoy his company—a break from the monotony of my life.

"What's up?" I asked.

But before Jim could answer, my attention was stolen by Stacey walking toward the exit with her friends. Her expression was sullen, but I saw the sadness in the back of her eyes too.

And I felt ashamed for disappointing her.

"Who is that?" Jim pulled my focus back.

"That is Stacey Dewitte," Molly interrupted, putting her hand on her hip. She noted Roddy staring at her impressive chest and scowled at him. "Think again, Scottie."

He crossed his arms and smirked at her. "Sweetheart, if I wanted ye, yer knickers wid be aroond yer ankles like that." He snapped his fingers.

Molly made a face and turned to Jim. "What did he say?"

"Ye don't want to know." Jim fought not to smile. "Ye were saying ... that kid?"

I opened my mouth to deflect, but Molly apparently was a fount of information today. "Melanie Dewitte's little sister. Melanie was Nora's best friend growing up." She squeezed my arm. "She died of cancer when they were twelve."

I wanted to throw her comforting hand off me and yell at her really freaking loudly. If I'd wanted Jim to know about Mel, I would've told him myself.

"Fuck." He reached for my hand. "I'm sorry, Nora."

My smile trembled. "Thanks. It was a long time ago."

"Stacey's acting like a brat, though, Nora. You don't need to put up with that."

"She's not doing anything." I shot Molly a shut-up look; she rolled her eyes and wandered back to her register.

"So, what brings you handsome and not-so-handsome fellas in today?" Molly changed the subject. "The fair Nora, obviously."

"Obviously." Jim stared at me, and I caught that bleakness in his dark gaze again.

"What's going on? Is your family okay?"

"My family is fine ... but ..." He glanced over at Roddy.

His best friend sighed. "Nora, if we stay here, we'll never be able to finish oor road trip. We'll run oot eh' cash afore then. We need to leave."

My pulse suddenly started racing as my eyes flew to Jim. "What? Now?"

"In the morning. First thing. When do ye finish here?" It occurred to me while Jim seemed sad, I was panicked. "I'd like to spend some time with ye before we go."

Before we go.

Shit. It was ending.

Once Jim and Roddy left, everything would return to normal, and I'd feel trapped, unwanted, and depressed all over again. Somehow this guy had become my lifeline.

"I'm supposed to get home after my shift ..." My mom would kill me if I didn't turn up and she had to call in sick to work. Yet I couldn't find it in me to care. As selfish as it was, I wanted to soak up what time I had left with the boy who had crashed into my life and allowed me to breathe again for the first time in a long time. "But it's fine. We can hang out. I finish at five."

Jim exhaled and nodded. He studied me solemnly, and I noted he looked a little pale and tired beneath his tan. "We'll be back in a few hours."

Molly waited until the boys were gone. "That fucking sucks."

I nodded, pretending to busy myself tidying up the condiments tray by my register. I felt her move closer to me.

"Have you guys ...?"

Looking at her, I almost laughed at the expression on her face. Her eyebrows were at her hairline. "You know ..."

"What?"

She made an "o" with her left thumb and forefinger and then stuck her right forefinger in and out of it.

"Ugh, Molly." I grabbed her hands and shoved them down so the customers wouldn't see.

"Well?" she asked through her laughter.

The truth was no, Jim and I hadn't had sex. We had kissed a few times, and he'd fondled my boobs, but that was it. And he'd said upfront he wasn't going to push for sex because he wanted me to know I meant more to him than that.

Part of me was relieved because I wasn't sure I was ready to lose my virginity to Jim, or to anyone, for that matter. Another part of me was scared. Jim confused the hell out of me because I wanted him near, I liked the fact that he felt like an escape from a life I was unhappy with, and I loved that he made me feel like I was someone special. But I was also wary of giving another person that much power over my emotions.

Once upon a time, I thought the sun rose and set with my father. Look where that had gotten me.

"No," I finally answered Molly.

"You should do it tonight," she advised. "If he's leaving. I'd love to be able to tell my grandkids I lost my virginity to a cute Scottish guy passing through town. In fact, I still might. A lie is better than Kenny Stringer behind the bleachers."

"You're going to tell your grandkids how you lost your virginity?"

"Sure, if they ask."

"And Kenny Stringer? Behind the bleachers? Really?"

Molly wrinkled her nose. "We were fourteen." She shuddered. "I'm surprised I even gave sex a shot again after that."

Wait a minute … something niggled at my memory. "You told me you lost your virginity to Cory's cousin Caden in the eleventh grade."

"Well, I didn't want to admit the truth. To be fair, though, Caden was the first boy who was actually any good at it."

I shook my head. "I'm not you, Molly. I can't just sleep with someone."

"But it's his last night here. I bet he's expecting it."

Butterflies raged war in my belly at the thought. Surely not? Jim had said he didn't want to push for that … then again, he'd said that without thinking about the fact that he was leaving. We both knew his departure was coming but we'd ignored the reality of it.

Now that reality had come home to roost, maybe Molly was right. Maybe Jim would want to have goodbye sex.

I worried my lip with my teeth.

"Nora."

The butterflies were making me feel sick.

"Nora."

My knees started to quake a little.

"Nora!" Molly snapped her fingers in front of my face. "God, you're white as a sheet. Shit. You don't have to do anything you don't want to do, okay?"

I nodded, dazed. "Molly, I'm not ready …"

"Then don't." She squeezed my shoulder. "You don't owe this guy anything."

———

JUST AS I FINISHED MY SHIFT, I SAW THE MUSTANG PULL INTO THE parking lot. Although Molly's reassurance had helped some, my anxiety hadn't fully dissipated. I was worried about disappointing Jim. As much as I was fighting it, he'd come to mean a lot to me.

"You're done." Molls grinned at me. "Have fun!"

I gave her a shaky smile and hurried into the back to grab my purse. Unfortunately, I didn't have a change of clothing so I was going to have to hang out with the guys in my uniform. There was no way in hell I was going home to change because my mom would insist on me staying to watch Dad.

Just once … just this once, I wanted to be reckless and irresponsible and totally selfish.

Jim and Roddy were grabbing burgers to go as I came out from the back.

"We got ye something to eat," Jim said, nodding to the to-go bags.

I wasn't a huge fan of having to eat the food I'd been serving all day, but it was sweet of them. I smiled my thanks.

Jim, Roddy, and I had just walked out of the restaurant when the sight of a tall blond getting out of his GMC truck made me falter.

"Shit," I muttered.

Cory Trent.

Jim's hand rested on my lower back. "What's wrong?"

"Nothing, let's go." Unfortunately, we had to walk by Cory and his cousin Caden.

Even before Cory's dad bought my dad's company, he'd been a giant asshole to me. His assholery had only worsened when he asked me out our senior year and I shot him down. That had not gone over well with Cory, who thought he was God's gift to women everywhere.

Word was he was spending the summer before college in Palm Springs where Caden's mom had moved after his parents' divorce.

Apparently, not all summer.

"Well, well, well," Cory called out as he strode toward us.

He wore board shorts, flip-flops, and a green polo shirt, and swaggered like he was the big man in town. Give a boy a little money and popularity and he turns into a dipshit.

Or at least this one had.

In saying that, he'd pretty much been a dipshit since preschool.

"Cory," I sighed.

Jim must have sensed something in my body language or maybe it was the lascivious and angry way Cory was dragging his eyes over my body. Whatever it was, I felt the boys on either side of me go on alert, and Jim stepped a little in front of me.

Cory's eyes flicked to him and then back to me. He sneered. "How the mighty have fallen, huh, Nora?"

"What's yer problem?" Jim asked, a warning in his voice.

Raising an eyebrow, Cory looked at Jim before turning to snort at his cousin. "Who's the fucking foreigner?"

"Guys, let's go." I tugged on Jim's sleeve and took a step forward when Cory was suddenly in my face.

"What's the rush, O'Brien? Don't you think it's time you admit you made a mistake?" His eyes dropped to my breasts, and I wanted to cover them … or kick him in the balls. Actually, I wanted to do both.

Not that there was any need because suddenly Jim was there. He planted a hand on Cory's shoulder and shoved him. Hard. "Back off."

Cory shrugged his polo shirt back into place and scowled at us. "Nice to see you get what you deserve, Nora. You always thought you were better than everyone else. It seems now you know that's not true, you're finally opening those bird legs of yours."

"Ye might want to shut up, mate," Jim warned.

"Oh, I wouldn't get all worked up about this one," Cory said. "She may act like she's something special but she's not." Caden stood there grinning like a dumb sidekick. "Ain't that right, Nora? You know I only asked you out because I felt sorry for you, right? It would have been a pity fuck. Pussy is still pussy, after all."

Something instinctual inside of me must've known how Jim would react, and if it hadn't been for my fast reflexes, Jim would've been on Cory before I'd even blinked. As it was, I moved as Jim sprung forward and used all my strength to wrap my arms around him to pull him away.

"Forget him. He's not worth it." I gently nudged Jim toward the car, throwing Roddy a "help me" look.

Roddy skirted around me and put a hand on his friend's back to push him while I shot Cory a filthy look over my shoulder. I was used to his abuse, but it was humiliating to hear him say that stuff in front of my new friends.

"Use her, fuck her, and run, man, that's my advice," Cory said. "That bitch will only leak loser all over you."

Jim swung back around but he was too late.

Roddy had already dropped our food on the lot, took three strides back to Cory, and punched him so hard, Cory's knees buckled. There was silence as Cory lay flat out on the lot, rolling his head from side to side, dazed, as blood trickled out of his nose.

Caden put his hands up as Roddy glared at him. "Hey, man, I didn't say shit."

Without saying a word, Roddy strolled back to us, glowering. He grabbed the bags of food, opened the car door, and got in.

I looked from Cory on the ground to Jim, a mean look of satisfaction on his face.

"What just happened?"

"Get in the car so we can eat!" Roddy's muffled yell sounded.

Jim broke out into a wide grin. "He likes ye."

My gaze flew back to Cory, who Caden was finally helping to his feet. "Apparently so."

———

WE WERE PARKED OUTSIDE THE GUYS' MOTEL ROOM ON THE OUTSKIRTS OF town. Roddy sat on the sidewalk, finishing his burger, while Jim and I sat on the hood of the Mustang eating ours.

No one had mentioned Cory or the fact that Roddy had come to my defense. In fact, no one had said much of anything while we ate. There was an awkward, heavy silence.

"Well," Roddy crumpled up his now empty brown bag and stood up, "as scintillating as this conversation is, I'm goin' tae hit the sack." He walked over to the car and stopped right in front of me. "Get off the hood."

I did so instantly. Roddy was more than a little intimidating.

And then to my shock, I found myself wrapped in a bear hug. He lifted my feet right off the ground and I had no choice but to hug him back, a surprised giggle bursting from between my lips.

When he put me back on my feet, he gave my waist one last squeeze. "Ye'er a sweetheart, Nora. Dinnae let any bastard tell ye different." He winked at me, and I blushed.

"Thanks, Roddy."

"Aye. Well." He gave me a stoic nod and then walked off toward the motel room.

Realizing that was his goodbye, I called out, "Bye! Have a great trip!"

He threw his hand up in a wave without looking back and then disappeared inside the room.

When I finally turned back to Jim, he wore a wounded look that caused a pang of pain across my chest. I shimmied back onto the hood beside him. "Hey, what's wrong?"

"What's wrong?" He raised an eyebrow. "I'm leaving, that's what's wrong."

"I know." Glum, I pushed the rest of my burger away and looked at the open road in front of us.

"Ye never told me about Melanie," he said suddenly.

I tensed, my shoulders hunching toward my ears at the unexpected subject change. "She never came up."

"I'm sorry ye lost yer friend."

"Thanks."

"Ye haven't told me much about yer parents, either."

I looked at him out of the corner of my eye and found him studying me with a scowl. "What do you want to know?"

"If they're good to ye. What I'm leaving ye to if I go."

"*If* you go?" My head whipped around to stare at him, bewildered. "Jim ... you don't have a responsibility to me."

His dark eyes smoldered suddenly. "Believe me, responsibility is not what I feel for ye. At least it's not the major thing I feel for ye. I ..." He ran a shaky hand through his hair. "Fuck, I don't know what I'm trying tae say. It's just, ye'er special, Nora. Ye'er fuckin' special and when that asshole said those things tonight, I wanted tae kill him. That's why Roddy did it, punched him, not only because he didnae like hearing that guy say that stuff about ye, but because he knew I would have done a lot fuckin' worse tae him if I'd gotten near him."

"Cory is an idiot and not worth your time or your concern. He asked me out senior year and expected me to swoon at his feet like every other empty bimbo who was stupid enough to sleep with him. It hurt his macho pride when I turned him down."

"That's not ... I'm no' worried about him. I'm worried about *you*. Ye deserve more than to be stuck in this dinky wee town, in a shit job."

"I'll be okay," I gritted out. I knew the reality of my situation. I didn't need Jim pointing out how crappy it was.

"I don't want ye tae just be okay." He grabbed my hand, pulling me toward him. "I want yer life to be fucking fantastic, Nora. I think I want that more than I want it for myself."

I tugged against his hold as he overwhelmed me again. He was always overwhelming me.

Jim wouldn't let go of my hand. "What does that mean?" he whispered to himself.

"I don't know," I whispered back.

And then he was kissing me.

I knew from the fumbling around I'd done with my one and only boyfriend, Steven, when we were in the tenth grade that Jim was a million times better at kissing. His lips were soft yet commanding, and his kisses were nice. Steven's had been wet and sloppy. Not nice. Not that I had to put up with his fumbling for long. We broke up once he realized how little free time I actually had.

Thoughts of Steven died as Jim slid his arms around me and he pulled me against his chest. As we kissed, one of his hands caressed my hip, while the other drifted upward to gently squeeze my right breast.

I liked when he did that. It caused a fizzle of something low in my belly. But my mind was much too at play still, and as Jim's kisses became rougher, harder, I worried that Molly was right.

I broke away from him, pressing against his chest to push him back. Embarrassed, feeling young and inexperienced, and concerned there may be something lacking in me, I couldn't meet his eyes. "I can't have sex with you."

Jim was quiet for so long, my heart hammered.

Finally, his fingers slid under my chin and he forced me to look up at him. In his expression, I found hunger but I also found kindness. "I'm not expecting sex, Nora. I told ye ... ye mean more tae me than just a quick shag. And anyway," he glanced around, smiling ruefully, "we're out in the open and Roddy took the room."

I laughed softly as relief moved over me. "I'm sorry. I'm not ready." Or there was something wrong with me, and it would take a miracle to turn me on enough to want to have sex.

"Of course." He cuddled me into his side. "Let's hang out and talk. Tell me more about yer mum and dad."

And because he'd been so sweet to me, always, and I'd never see him again, I gave him a little more of me than I had before. "We're not close." I relaxed against him. "My dad and I used to be, but he changed when he got ..." I hadn't told Jim about my dad's leg and weirdly felt like it wasn't my story to tell. My dad was so touchy about it, like he was ashamed of it. I didn't know if that was to do with losing a limb or because if he'd been more careful, he might have been able to prevent its loss.

"Yer dad got…?"

"Sick," I decided on. "When my dad got sick, he pushed us away."

Jim's arm squeezed around me in reaction. "And yer mum?"

"She's not a bad person. She … she doesn't know how to be close to me, I guess. And she works all the time. Always has."

"And ye'er left tae look after yer dad?"

I nodded.

I felt his breath on my ear as he whispered, "That's too much for someone who's just starting out. Yer parents should be sending ye out into the world, not keeping ye here, looking after them. Ye deserve more than that, Nora."

I smiled sadly. "What else are family for?"

He grunted like he didn't agree with me.

"Are you looking forward to the rest of your trip?" I asked, trying to change the subject.

"Roddy is." He sounded so disheartened. "I'm going tae miss *you* too much. I … really, really care about ye, Nora."

Emotion immediately clogged my throat as I realized our time together was ending. Panic waited in the wings of my mind. "I'll miss you too."

Hearing my voice crack, Jim pulled me into a hard hug, bowing his head in the crook of my neck. I felt him shudder.

My arms tightened around him, and as we held each other as close as two people could, I tried not to give into the fear that by letting Jim go in the morning, I was letting go of the future I was meant to have.

chapter 4

JIM DROPPED ME OFF AT THE HOUSE. I'D DECIDED THERE WAS NO POINT IN hiding him from my mom anymore, considering he'd be gone in the morning.

I studied Jim curiously as we pulled to a stop outside, watching to see what his reaction was to our small house, surrounded by those so much bigger. But he barely even acknowledged it. He said, "This is you?"

"This is me."

He nodded and rubbed a hand over his head, looking anywhere but at me.

"Jim?"

He shook his head, and his hand curled so tight around the steering wheel his knuckles turned white. "I think ye should just go, Nora," he choked out.

Hearing the emotion in his voice, realizing he couldn't meet my eyes because he had tears in his, I felt a deluge of tenderness. It was hard not to be affected by how much this boy had grown to care for me in so little time. I didn't exactly have people lining up to care about me, and I wasn't going to take his affection for granted.

That rush of fondness, of gratitude, made me reach for him. I touched his cheek, the one he had turned from me, feeling the prickle of new stubble against my skin. Gently, I forced him to look at me, my eyes stinging when I saw that he did, in fact, have tears in his.

And something more.

Something that somehow managed to frighten me and call out to my longing at the same time.

"Jim," I whispered, wondering how it was possible that he could feel so much for me when he didn't know me at all.

He jerked me to him, his lips crashing down on mine, and at first, I couldn't react because it was a punishing kiss that scared me a little. All I could do was stroke his cheek, trying to soothe him. It seemed to work, and his kiss grew slower, sweeter, and I enjoyed it more.

He cut off, breathing hard, and pressed one last kiss to my lips.

One last kiss to my nose.

And one last kiss to my forehead.

Tears pricked my eyes at the sweetness of it.

"Please, just go," he begged suddenly.

Feeling guilty and I didn't even really know why, I did as he asked, grabbing my purse and fumbling for the door handle. I was about to shut the door and let him drive off when I decided he deserved more. "Jim." I bent down to look at him, but he was staring stubbornly ahead. "These last two weeks ... I'll never forget them. I've felt alone lately, but you showed me it didn't have to be that way. Thank you." I closed the door before he could say anything because as soon as the words were out of my mouth, I felt incredibly vulnerable.

Cursing myself for saying too much, I hurried up the pathway and let myself inside.

I could hear Dad's football game before I even opened the door.

Mom's jacket was hanging on the new hook I'd put up, her shoes underneath it.

Pushing Jim out of my mind, I braced myself. It was time to fall back into my life and be at peace with how things were for now. That began right then because I was sure my mom was going to kill me.

I kicked off my shoes, my eyes narrowing on the open doorway of my bedroom. Light spilled out into the hallway. "Mom?" I said, walking toward it.

The sight of her sitting on my bed made me falter in the doorway.

She looked up from her lap and glared at me. "I had to call in sick."

"I'm sorry."

Mom scoffed, "No, you're not."

Not knowing what to say, I stood there, waiting for the explosion. It didn't come.

She stood up and made her way over to me. I got my height from my mom, our eyes at the same level.

Our eyes were the same color and shape.

Except hers were cooler, harder, and weary. One of the things I feared most was waking up one morning, looking in the mirror, and seeing my mother's eyes looking back at me.

"You think I don't know about the guy in the Mustang?" She rolled her eyes. "Jesus, Nora, I thought you were smarter than that. Instead, you're running around town with some Irish boy, lying to me about doing overtime."

"He's Scottish," I muttered.

"Who gives a fuck? He's a man and all he's going to do is use you, get you pregnant, leave, and saddle us with more responsibility we don't need."

"One, I didn't sleep with him, and two ..." I felt panic clawing its way back inside of me, and suddenly, it wasn't my mom exploding. It was me. "He's gone! Okay? Gone!"

My mom didn't even flinch at my uncharacteristic burst of emotion. She studied me carefully, and then quietly replied, "I think that's probably for the best. Don't you?"

I laughed, an ugly, hard sound. "This family stopped knowing what was 'for the best' a long time ago."

"What's that supposed to mean?"

Exhausted, I shrugged. "Nothing. It doesn't mean a damn thing."

Eyes narrowing, my mom closed what little space was between

us and whispered, "You listen to me and you listen hard … the sooner you stop living in your head and those fucking books of yours, the better. This is life. And it ain't a bad life. It's small, it's simple, and you got to work hard, but there are people out there who have absolutely nothing. We got something. And you walking around acting like you're better than this, ain't right."

Her words were so similar to what Cory had said, I flinched like she'd slapped me.

Remorse cut through the hard in her eyes, and she sighed. "I'm not trying to hurt you. I just don't want you to be miserable waiting on something to happen that ain't ever going to happen.

"If we had more money, things would be different." She patted my shoulder, which was as close to affection as my mom ever got. "We don't. And we've got to live with the blessings we have and be grateful we have any at all."

Guilt suffused me, and I wondered if I really was a spoiled, ungrateful little brat. I released a breath and nodded. "You're right. I'm sorry I didn't come home tonight. It won't happen again."

She eyed me like she didn't believe me.

"What?"

"Nothing," she mumbled. "I'm going to bed."

But before she slid by me, her eyes darted back to my bed. To under my bed.

My heart jumped in my chest, but I waited until she'd gone before I closed the door and pulled the shoebox out from under the bed. Opening it, I sucked in a breath.

As soon as I turned eighteen, I used what little savings I had to apply for a passport. I didn't know what made me do it or how I thought I'd ever get the chance to use it. I just knew I had to have it. It was like a little blue book of hope and dreams in my hand, and knowing it was in this shoebox, hidden under my bed, made it easier to get through each day in a life I didn't want to lead.

Because it symbolized possibility.

I kept the passport at the very bottom of the pile. Hidden. Yet, somehow it had made its way to the top of the pile.

Glancing over at my bedroom door, I realized my mom had snooped and found my stash.

She'd found the passport.

Suddenly, her warnings to be grateful for what I had made sense.

And as much as I wanted to listen to her advice, to take what she said as wisdom, there was a rebellious voice inside of me telling me my mom should want me to dream bigger than she did. That it was wrong of her not to.

At war with myself, I changed into my pajamas and got into bed, mind whirring as the events of the day played over and over in my head.

My last thought before I drifted to sleep was of Jim and how much I envied him his freedom.

THREE WEEKS LATER ...

"DAD, MOM WANTS ME TO PAY SOME BILLS. WILL YOU BE OKAY IF I GO out for a little bit?"

"I'm not an invalid," he huffed, watching the TV. "Oh, wait. I am."

I sighed. "I'll take that as a yes."

"You can take that as I'm watching the game and I can't hear it over your yammering." His voice rose toward the end of the sentence.

Not deigning to respond, I grabbed my purse and gladly escaped the house. Walking down West Washington I saw our neighbor, Dawn, putting her daughter, Jane, into her car seat. I waved.

"Oh, hey, Nora," she called, smiling at me. "We're heading out to the mall. Need a ride anywhere?"

"No, I'm going to May's to use her computer." May's Coffeehouse was also an internet café and you could pay to use a computer there. We had a computer but it stopped working six months ago and we hadn't gotten around to getting it fixed. And we couldn't afford a new one. We had Wi-Fi, but my cell phone was this cheap, outdated thing and it was frustrating trying to pay online bills with it. It was easier to go to May's. Plus, it got me out of the house.

"Oh, sweetie, you can use ours," Dawn said. "We'll run back into the house with you real quick. We're in no rush."

Dawn Reese and her husband Paul were two of the nicest people I'd ever met. They were the kind of neighbors that would do just about anything for anybody, including putting up with my pain-in-the-ass family. I smiled gratefully. "That's so kind of you, Dawn, but I ..." How did I explain I wanted out of the house and away from my father?

Dawn got a knowing look in her eyes. "You know what? May has faster Wi-Fi anyway."

Giving her another appreciative smile, I nodded. "Have a nice day at the mall."

We waved, and I walked on.

My thoughts drifted to Jim and Roddy, wondering where they were. I knew from our conversations that they flew back to Scotland in a week's time. A sharp ache cut across my chest and I rubbed it absentmindedly. When he was here, Jim's openness and his feelings for me had been intimidating. But over the last three weeks, I'd longed so much to see his face that I started to wonder if maybe I'd fallen in love with him.

I missed his smile.

And I missed the way he looked at me.

Like I mattered.

Like I really, really mattered.

I missed his kisses.

And despite how uncertain I'd been at the time, I now found myself regretting not having slept with him. Jim cared about me. My first time should've been with someone who cared about me like Jim did.

I was such an idiot.

Regret tasted bitter on my tongue and tears burned my eyes.

Strangely, I found myself missing Roddy as well. He was quite belligerent for such a young person, but he was funny too. Plus, I wouldn't soon forget him swatting Cory like he was a bug on a windshield. That made my whole summer.

"Are ye seriously just going to walk by me?"

I froze.

Turned to my right.

And stared. Stunned.

The Mustang was parked in the parking lot where I worked. Roddy was standing by the driver's side door, wearing sunglasses so I couldn't read his expression. And Jim was braced against the hood, his hands on his hips, grinning at me.

I'd been so caught up in my thoughts, I'd walked right by them.

Joy rushed through me, lifting the heavy weight that had settled over me since they'd left.

"What?" I smiled in amazement. "What are you doing here?"

Jim's answer was to jog toward me, laughing, and when he reached me, he wrapped his arms around me and lifted me right off my feet.

I gasped in surprised, locking my arms around his neck to hold on. Jim crushed me to him, kissing me as my feet swayed off the ground. He groaned and squeezed me so tight it hurt. "Jim," I gasped.

He eased his hold, wonder and gravity whirling around his dark eyes. "I came back for ye."

My fingers bit into his shoulders in shock at the pronouncement. What did that mean?

Reading the question in my eyes, he lowered me to my feet but didn't let go. He bent his head toward mine, his words almost a whisper they were so gruff with emotion. "I've missed ye so much. Like, it's not a normal amount of missing considering how long we've known each other. But I feel like I've known ye my whole life, Nora. And yet I feel like I don't know ye at all … and all I want in this life is tae know everything about ye. I want tae be the person who knows ye better than anybody. The thought of some other guy getting that chance physically hurts. And I know ye might think I've lost my mind but when Roddy and I were in Vegas, all I kept thinking was if I could get Nora here, I'd marry her in a heartbeat and take her home with me."

Shocked to my core, I could only stare at him as a thousand thoughts flew around in my head.

Of course, there was a huge part of me that thought he was nuts!

But there was also a part that believed he was utterly sincere.

"I love ye." He gave me a nervous smile. "I've fallen in love with ye. Ye'er not like any girl I've ever met. Ye seem older than eighteen, ye'er kind, funny—I can never work out what ye'er thinking, which drives me crazy in the best way, and ye care about people. And it doesn't hurt ye'er the most beautiful girl I've ever seen in my life."

His lovely words got caught in the jumble in my head.

The thing that kept pushing itself front and center was the memory of Jim telling me I deserved more from life. He was a guy not only offering to love me, truly love me, but he was offering me more out of life.

He was offering me an escape.

I can't explain how much the thought of that gripped me. It was like this monster that had been hiding inside of me for a long time and suddenly, someone opened its prison. It was selfish and self-absorbed and hungry. And it was single-minded.

"Are … are you asking me to marry you and move to Scotland?"

Jim nodded, looking pained. "Ye think I'm insane, don't ye?"

"Yes. Absolutely. I do."

His grip on me loosened, his gaze lowering "I understand."

"But …" There was a part of me that wanted to say yes, which was just as insane.

Jim's eyes flew back to mine, hopeful incredulity alight in them. "What?"

Even though I felt like I might throw up, I also felt a rush of adrenaline. I hadn't felt that in a long time. It made me feel alive. Really alive. "Can you give me today to think about it?"

"Today?" He nodded quickly. "I can do a day."

"Okay." My whole body trembled. "Okay." I couldn't believe I was even considering it. "Come back tonight, midnight. Park up the street from my house. I'll give you my answer then."

Jim let out a shaky exhale. "I can't believe ye'er even considering it. Roddy told me I was insane, but I... no matter what, I couldnae go back home without telling ye that I loved ye."

Fear and hope were strange bedfellows—I felt lightheaded. I swayed a little, and Jim reached out to catch me. "Ye all right?"

"It's just a lot." I laughed and it sounded a little hysterical. "Um ... okay ... I'm going to go think. Tonight?"

"Tonight." He nodded.

And then he kissed me soft, sweetly, and murmured, "I'd do anything for ye, Nora. Protect ye, love ye, give ye anything. I promise."

———

SOMEHOW, I PAID THE BILLS MOM WANTED PAID BUT I BARELY REMEMBER going through the motions. I barely remember speaking to May or saying hello to people I'd known my whole life.

And I barely remembered getting on the bus or sitting on it for fifty minutes. But there I was, standing outside the entrance to the Donovan County Cemetery. The only way I knew how to describe what I was feeling—it was like someone had picked me up and shook me around so hard, my insides were all jangling.

Palms slick, I curled them into fists and pushed myself to stride through the entrance. I hadn't visited in a year. Ever since I knew for definite that I was going to be stuck in Donovan.

After a five-minute walk, I found her.

> *In loving memory of*
> *Melanie Dewitte*
> *1993 - 2005*
> *A beloved daughter, sister, and friend*
> *Forever in our hearts.*

Like always, tears stung my eyes and nose. Glad there was no one else around in this part of the cemetery I walked over to her grave and sat down beside the black headstone.

"Hey, Mel ..." My voice was watery, croaky. "I'm sorry I haven't visited in a while."

There was silence, and then a gentle gust of wind blew a decapitated rose across Mel's grave. I laughed. Roses were my favorite flowers. Mel knew that. "I'll take that as an angry hello. And I deserve it. I'm sorry." I smoothed a hand down her headstone and laid my cheek against it, letting my tears fall. With Melanie, I could be honest about my feelings. "I just didn't want to disappoint you. You should see the way Stacey looks at me. God, your sister thinks I'm a loser. And I feel like a loser. I know, I know, you don't think I am. But I've let you down, Mel. I promised you I'd get out of here, that I'd find a stage somewhere and have this amazing life. Not just for me but for you. I promised you I'd make it extraordinary, that I'd do it for both of us." I shuddered trying to control myself. "It was all taken from you. Everything. But I'm still here ... and I'm working in a goddamn fast-food restaurant, taking abuse from my dad."

That gentle wind tickled through my hair comfortingly, and as with the rose, I liked to think it really was my best friend. I closed my eyes, wishing I could hear her voice, but somehow over the years, her voice had disappeared from my memory. I could still see her face, picture her laughing, but as hard as I tried, and God, I tried, I couldn't hear her anymore.

"I miss you," I whispered. "I miss someone knowing me. Really knowing me. Better than they know themselves. I don't have that anymore, Mel ... And I know it's selfish to sit here and say that to you, but like always, you're the only one I can talk to." I swiped at my cheeks and sniffled. After a moment of silence, I confessed, "I met someone. A boy. He's from Scotland." I grinned, knowing how much Melanie would have loved that. "I think he might be a little crazy because he says he loves me and he's only known me a few weeks. In fact, he doesn't even really *know* me." I frowned, searching for my feelings. "I missed him so much while he was gone that I think I must love him. But it's a gamble, right? A huge risk. He wants me to marry him." I laughed. "I know, I know, you'd tell me I was crazy. You think I'm nuts for even thinking about getting married at eighteen. We always said we'd never be that kind of girl, that we'd make our dreams come true first before we thought about falling in love.

"But he wants me to go to Scotland with him. *Scotland.* I've never been farther than Indianapolis."

For a while, I sat in silence, digging for the courage to say to her what I could never say out loud to anyone else. "If I stay here, I don't get that amazing life I promised you I would have for the both of us. If I do the crazy thing and marry a guy I don't even really know, I at least get the chance to get out of here. To find what we always wanted. But that means risking so much. Giving up my family—and as crappy as they can be, they're still my family, and they need me. And it's a risk. If Jim is who I think he is, that's great because I love having him in my life. But what if he's not? What if he turns out to be something completely different, something worse than what I already have?

"I'm like the most selfish person ever for even considering this, right?"

I closed my eyes and trailed my hand down the side of her head-stone. "But if I say no … I'm afraid of who I'll become here, Mel. I feel like I'm drowning. And nobody cares. Nobody but Jim. And I love him for it. Surely that counts for something? Surely that counts for everything?"

A gust of wind abruptly blew over me, and the jangling in my body stopped momentarily.

"Yeah." I gave a wobbly smile. "That's what I thought you'd say."

———

"DAD, TIME FOR BED."

Like always, my dad had nodded off in front of the TV, and my voice startled him awake. He frowned at me but nodded, and like always, I walked behind his wheelchair as we made our way into my parents' bedroom.

Mom hadn't come home from her shift at the diner. She'd called me to tell me she was working overtime at Al's. I'd cried when I got off the phone with her because as much as we weren't close, I'd wanted to see her one last time. I'd have to make do with writing her a letter. It was an explanation. It was an apology. And it was an appeal for forgiveness.

Dad helped me get him into bed, and he shifted on his side, giving me his back.

"Dad."

He grunted.

"Dad."

"What?" he huffed.

Before I could stop them, tears welled inside of me and spilled down my cheeks. I struggled to speak, to say the words without him hearing the tears in them. I licked at the salt on my lips and exhaled. "You know I love you, right?"

In the dim glow of the hallway light, I saw him tense.

And then he relaxed ever so slowly. He didn't turn to me. He stared at the wall. And then in a tone that broke my heart, one filled with regret and grief, he whispered, "I love you too, baby girl."

My body shook with the effort not to sob, and I fled the room without saying goodnight. Goodbye.

I grabbed my jacket off the hook in the hall, slipped on my shoes, and checked my backpack again to make sure I had everything I needed. After visiting Mel, I'd come back to Donovan and emptied out my savings and bank account. I left most of it in the envelope with the letter to my mom and dad and placed it on my pillow.

The rest I was taking with me, even though it would probably only last our time in Vegas.

I double-checked I had my passport and quelled nausea that rose inside of me.

Finally, the clock on my cell said it was midnight.

As I slipped out of the house on West Washington Street, I wiped at my tears, not wanting Jim to think I was too torn up about going with him.

I caught sight of the Mustang down the street as Jim climbed out of it. We hurried toward each other, my heart pounding so hard in my chest, I thought it might explode.

And then I was in Jim's arms and he was holding me tight, suppressing the hard shaking he could feel rattling through me. "Shh," he whispered, pressing a kiss to my hair. "It's all going tae be okay now."

I had to hope Jim was right because we were leaving for Vegas and I was about to bet everything I had on him.

chapter 5

TUCKING THE POLO SHIRT INTO MY WORK PANTS, I LOOKED AT MYSELF for barely a second in the mirror to make sure I was neat and tidy. I hated seeing myself in the uniform. With an inward sigh, I clipped my name tag above my left breast. I was just smoothing my hair back in its long ponytail when Jim appeared in the mirror behind me.

He looped his arms around my waist and settled his chin on my shoulder to stare at me in the mirror. His hair was mussed, his cheeks stubbly, and he gave me that cute lopsided grin.

Two years ago, my infatuation for him would've made me lean back into him, cover his hands on my belly with my own. Yet something had changed inside of me in the three years we'd been married. Maybe changed wasn't the right word.

Maybe the word I was looking for was realization.

"I wish ye didn't have tae go in for another hour. I don't start until ten this morning. You and I could get a lot done in an hour." He squeezed me closer and gave me a wicked smile.

I was still attracted to my husband. So that was something. But it got churned up in all my other feelings, or non-feelings rather, and it made me pull out of his arms. "Sorry, can't."

As I walked into our small, open-plan sitting room/kitchen, I felt him following me.

"I wish tae fuck I knew what was going on yer head," he bit out impatiently. "But I never do."

Not wanting an argument before work, I looked over my shoulder at him as I shoved my feet into my comfortable black shoes and teased, "I thought that's what you liked about me."

Hurt flickered in his dark eyes before he hid it from me. "It was sexy at first. Now it's a bad joke."

Guilt flared across my chest in an ache, and I got defensive. "You knew who I was when you married me, Jim."

"Aye." He nodded, turning angry. "I just thought after three years of fucking marriage, ye'd let me in once in a while."

I thought of last night and the way I'd let him in on our couch. I looked at it pointedly.

If anything, it made him angrier, although there was heat in his eyes too. "Oh aye, baby, ye'll let me fuck ye anyway I want ... but God forbid I try tae cuddle ye."

We stared at each other like two opponents, wishing and wondering why we had to have this same conversation every few weeks. It felt like we'd been doing this battle for at least a year.

"Is this about college?" he snapped.

My guilt momentarily faded and was replaced by frustration. I grabbed my purse and strode toward the door. "I haven't got time for this."

"Well, make time." He was fast, suddenly towering over me, his hand pressed against our front door.

"What do you want me to say?"

Jim suddenly gentled and reached out to cup my cheek. "Baby, ye know we don't have the money for it. Tae get into school here, ye'd have tae pay for open university tae get the qualifications ye need ... and ye don't even know what ye want tae do with yer life."

"I know I don't want to be stacking shelves in a supermarket." I hadn't left the US to be right back where I'd started!

Guilt tightened his features. "Look, I'm working hard, and in a few years, I might even make gaffer. It'll be more money, and you might not even have to work at all. We'll have kids by then, and ye can be here with them."

The thought made me shudder inside. "I don't want to put that kind of pressure on you. Especially since it's not about you making more money, Jim. It's about me making more money, doing something with my life that I'm proud of, and right now, I'm not qualified to do anything."

"I don't look at it like ye'er putting pressure on me. I want tae give ye a good life, so ye dinnae have tae worry about working. We're a team."

He never heard me. As much as I tried to make him listen, he never really heard me. But I didn't want to argue about it. "I know that."

He looked at me warily. "Do ye?"

———

TWO WEEKS LATER WE WERE BACK TO NORMAL, STICKING OUR HEADS IN the sand and pretending our marriage was fine. But our marriage wasn't fine. It was littered with broken promises.

On our wedding day, I'd promised to love and cherish my husband, believing that I did and I would.

And when he'd asked me to marry him, Jim promised that with him, I'd do and have everything I wanted. That wasn't true. Edinburgh was expensive, and although education wasn't as expensive as back home, it was still out of our financial reach. There were ways, but it would mean struggling along for a bit. It was possible, though. Of course, it was. But Jim didn't support the idea, and without his support, I couldn't do it.

I don't know if it was childish resentment, or if the sad fact was all I'd ever felt for my husband was naïve infatuation, but one morning I woke up and realized I'd broken my promise to love him. I did love Jim … but I wasn't *in* love with him. I'd married my friend, not my best friend, and as it turned out, there was a pretty damn big difference.

In truth, I knew we were heading for a collision but the thought scared me almost as much as the idea of *this* being my life forever. Sometimes it felt like I'd swapped countries, not situations, but that wasn't true. At least with Jim, I had a supportive family and a group of friends who made me smile.

Despite being shocked and wary of me when I'd first arrived in Edinburgh, Jim's mother, Angie, and his older sister, Seonaid, came to care for me. They had little choice, I suppose because, for those first few months, we lived in their cramped three-bedroom house in Sighthill. Sighthill, I discovered, was about twenty minutes west, outside of the city center.

I didn't care for the area where Jim grew up. It was the city center that I fell in love with. It was hard not to. There was the amazing architecture, of course—the neoclassical and Georgian buildings in New Town were gorgeous. When I first walked around New Town, I could imagine myself in Regency dresses, acting out a Jane Austen novel.

Then there was the castle. Edinburgh Castle sat on an extinct volcano between Old and New Town, a mammoth king perched upon his throne, watching over his kingdom. More than anything, I would've loved a home with a view of that majestic building, but Jim and I would have to quadruple our annual income and then some to afford a place anywhere with a view like that.

Edinburgh was beautiful. Scotland was beautiful. It was everything I'd imagined and more.

Old Town was charming as well, but in a different way to New Town. The university was there, and of course, that held my interest. And my longing.

There was also the Royal Mile, a Reformation-era street with cobbled roads and dark, atmospheric alleyways.

The city was more than its looks. New Town was where the money was, with beautiful apartments, lawyers, accountants, and psychiatrists, high-end shopping malls, cocktail bars, five-star restaurants, and luxury boutique hotels. It was aspirational, and appealed to that secret part of me that wondered what life would be like if money were no obstacle.

Old Town was more complex. It was casual, down-to-earth, arty, pretentious, fun-loving, serious, quirky, and staid. It bustled with students, and I think maybe that was why it was a jumble of every vibe you could think of. And I loved it because it meant no matter who you were, there was a place for you there.

As for Leith, an area down by the Shore, I liked it too. It was down by the waterfront, a mishmash of money and not so much money. Luxury apartments were built by the water, there were Michelin-star restaurants, cosmetic surgery clinics, and the Royal Yacht *Britannia*. But there were also pubs that didn't look like they'd seen a good scrub in a while, and a mall with stores for people with lower to middle incomes. I'd gotten a job at a supermarket in Leith, and Jim made okay money at his construction job. Although we were saving most of our money to buy a house, and it was a push on our income to do so, Jim wanted a nice place for me and rented us a one-bedroom apartment a mere fifteen-minute walk from the shore, and my job at the supermarket.

Soon after we moved in, Seonaid got a place a block from us. Until I saw his sister's name in writing, I thought it was spelled Seona because it was pronounced *see-oh-nah*. Apparently, there was a mild controversy around her name, as most people thought it should be pronounced "Shona." She left school at sixteen, and under advisement from her mom, deliberately softened her accent so it sounded more anglicized, and started working in a hair salon. She'd worked her butt off to eventually get a job in this fancy hair salon in New Town. She was making what Jim and I made combined and could afford a nice place on her own. I liked having her near as she'd become my closest friend here.

Any free time we had, we usually spent with Roddy and Seonaid. Sometimes we were joined by Seonaid's friends and guys Jim and Roddy worked construction with. But more often than not, if it was an impromptu pub visit, it was just the four of us.

Just as it was a Sunday a few weeks after Jim and I had argued about the future. Again.

We'd met up with Seonaid and Roddy at Leith's Landing, a pub right on the shore. On a sunny day, we loved sitting outside by the water. But I'd come to find that sunny days were almost a rarity in Scotland, and if I missed anything more than I missed my family, it was the Indiana summers.

"Oh, what an arsehole," Roddy huffed, chugging back more of his lager as he watched the huge TV screen behind Seonaid's head. There was a soccer game on, and although Jim and Roddy had been commenting on the game for the last thirty minutes, I wouldn't have even been able to tell you who the hell was playing.

Soccer made my eyes glaze over and my hearing switch to mute.

Despite Jim having his arm around me, I thought I had ceased to exist as I usually did when the guys were watching soccer. Seonaid had been telling me about an actress whose hair she'd cut during the week. She couldn't tell me who but we were having fun playing the guessing game.

It surprised me then when Jim suddenly turned to me and said, "I booked us intae a lodge in Loch Lomond in two weeks' time. Friday tae Sunday. Thought ye might like it."

I looked into his familiar-as-my-own face. Jim had an ability to disarm me and trigger my guilt. Despite knowing how we liked our coffee, which sleeping position made us snore, what foods gave us gas, and how much toilet paper we each went through in a week, my husband didn't know me. But then he'd make me feel guilty over my despair by doing something sweet that almost made up for it.

Since I'd moved here, Jim had tried to show me parts of Scotland whenever we had time. Usually, during the summer we'd take time off work and rent a caravan (like a camper van that was permanently situated in a holiday park) or stay at a lodge somewhere. So far, Loch Lomond was my favorite place. There was something about being surrounded by hills and tranquil water that made me feel at peace for a while. And peace was a hard thing for me to grasp on to.

"Yeah?"

Jim pressed a soft kiss to my lips. When he pulled back, he studied me, a small crease between his brows. "I think we need a wee break away together."

My ugly subconscious wanted to argue that a weekend break to Loch Lomond wasn't going to solve our problems, but like Jim, I hoped for a miracle. "It sounds great."

"What are you whispering about?" Seonaid said loudly across the table.

I grinned. "None of your beeswax."

She smirked. "Is it about uni?"

Her question immediately made me tense against Jim, and his arm locked tight around me. He cut his sister a scowl. "What are ye talking about?"

Seonaid frowned and looked at me. At the sight of my wide eyes, ever-so-slightly shaking head, and clenched jaw, she raised an eyebrow. "Um ..."

Jim looked down at me. "What about uni?"

"Nothing."

He cursed under his breath and turned back to his sister. "What about uni?"

Seonaid's gaze slid back and forth between me and her brother; clearly, she decided not to listen to me. "I looked into Edinburgh Uni's admission and turns out Nora could get in."

"What?" Baffled, Jim stared at her.

"Edinburgh University," Seonaid said slowly. "Nora could get in."

"How the fuck could Nora get into Edinburgh Uni?" Roddy suddenly said without looking away from the game. "It's one of the top twenty universities in the world. Fourth in the UK."

Seonaid snorted. "How the hell do you know that?"

Roddy tore his eyes away from the screen to give her a droll look. "I ken ye think I'm a thick fuck, but I *can* read, ye ken, Cee-Cee."

"I don't think you're a thick fuck. Just a lazy one." She grinned unrepentantly.

His lids lowered ever so slightly. "I'm not lazy when it matters."

No one could mistake the innuendo in his voice. Seonaid rolled her eyes and turned back to Jim. I'd soon discovered that Roddy was the only one who called Seonaid Cee-Cee (a nickname she thought didn't even make sense and was ridiculous, but that she allowed nonetheless). There was something between them I couldn't quite put my finger on. Jim seemed oblivious to it. Either that or he was pretending (something he was good at) nothing existed between his sister and best friend but friendship. I wasn't sure that was true. Perhaps on Seonaid's part, but I wasn't convinced on Roddy's. He flirted with her all the time, but he was so blunt, dry, and sarcastic, I think Seonaid assumed it was all banter. Plus, she was four years older, so I don't think it even crossed her mind that the guy who'd grown up with her kid brother might fancy the pants off her.

"How … wait …" Jim lowered his arm from around my shoulders and turned to me. "How can ye get intae Edinburgh Uni? And tae study what?"

Dreading an argument, especially after our last one in which Jim made it clear school was not an option, I shook my head. "It doesn't matter."

"It does matter."

"Wait," Seonaid leaned across the table, "are you telling me you haven't told him about your amazing SAT scores?"

"SAT what?"

I could hear the agitation in his voice and wanted to kill his sister. "Seonaid, leave it."

"No, don't leave it," Jim huffed. "Tell me."

"SAT's are like our highers and advanced highers," Seonaid explained. "You need a good score to get into university. If you're from the States and want to go to Edinburgh, you need a score of at least an 1800 along with two AP classes at grade four. Nora got a 2100 on her SAT's and has three AP classes at grade five."

"I dinnae know what the fuck that means," he snapped.

Seonaid huffed. "It means your wife is incredibly fucking smart. Something I'd thought you'd surely know by now."

Jim stared down at me like he'd never seen me before. "Why didn't I know this?"

"That I'm smart?"

"I know ye'er smart, for Christ's sake."

Did he? Really?

"Ye'er always reading." He shrugged.

"Well, as Roddy just proved, even numbnuts can read, Jim," Seonaid said.

"My nuts are no' numb," Roddy replied. "One lick would prove that tae ye."

Jim cracked him across the head with the palm of his hand.

Roddy shot him a look out of the corner of his eye. "Too far?"

Ignoring him, Seonaid reached for her brother's hand, eyes bright with excitement. "Can you imagine Nora at Edinburgh Uni? No one in our family could even have imagined getting into Edinburgh! Mum would be so bloody proud if Nora got in."

My pulse raced at the thought of attending the university, of being among those students I envied every time I passed them in their university hoodies, soaking up knowledge along with like-minded people who enjoyed learning. And making Angie and Seonaid proud would be icing on the cake.

He looked at his sister like she was speaking another language.

And then his voice turned accusatory as he turned to me. "Tae study what?"

"Psychology," Seonaid spoke for me again.

Jim's eyes narrowed. "Why the fuck would ye study psychology?"

"Uh, I don't know," Seonaid got defensive, "maybe so she can go into clinical psychology, or education, or health, or further education, or fucking anything that will actually mean something to her."

Jim glowered at her. "Would ye mind letting my wife speak?"

Seonaid cut him a dirty look before settling back and taking a gulp of wine.

Silence fell over the table.

"Well?"

I sighed. "Jim, it's a moot point, isn't it?"

"Do ye know how expensive it is?"

"Because I'm a UK resident now, it's less than a few grand a year." After two years of marriage, I was able to apply for permanent residency so the fees were *considerably* less for a Scottish student.

"A few grand? Aye, and tae do what? That's oor money for a house," he argued. "We talked about this."

Anger, embarrassment, and guilt flooded me, flushing my cheeks. "I know. That's why *I* never brought it up."

After studying me, Jim seemed satisfied I was telling the truth, and he relaxed. Marginally. His arm slid back around my shoulder, but its weight no longer felt comforting. It felt oppressive, like a claim.

I looked across the table at Seonaid to find her frowning at her brother. She shot me a look of concern. "Jim—"

"Seonaid, I love ye, but this is none of yer fucking business."

The awkward silence that fell over the table seemed even more pronounced in contrast to the noise of the pub—from the groans and cheers shouted at the TV screen and the happy Sunday chatter at the bar, and around the tables scattered throughout the large room.

But if there was anything Roddy was particularly good at, it was breaking an awkward silence.

"Ye ken what is yer business, Cee-Cee? How lonely I was in ma bed last night."

Despite the tension radiating off Jim, I almost spat my beer out in laughter.

Amusement glittered in Seonaid's dark eyes. "As long as you have your right hand, Roddy, you'll never be lonely."

Jim shook against me with light laughter, and I laughed loudly, possibly more out relief that he was letting the last conversation go.

Roddy grinned at her. She was the only one who ever made him really smile like that. "I'm ambidextrous, sweetheart."

"A wanking insurance policy." She raised an eyebrow. "So life did throw you a bone after all. Pun intended."

Chuckling now, Roddy opened his mouth to retort when his gaze suddenly drifted over Seonaid's shoulder, and the smile fell right off his face. He grabbed his lager and before taking a long swig, he announced, "The arsehole just arrived."

Seonaid's latest lover, Fergus, was walking toward our table. Seonaid threw Roddy an exasperated look. "Be nice."

He ignored her, staring determinedly at the television, something I knew he would do as long as Fergus was around. Roddy was never nice to any of Seonaid's boyfriends, and she'd had a few since I'd been here. How it hadn't occurred to her that Roddy's flirtatiousness might actually be hiding real feelings, I did not know.

Or maybe she was in denial too.

Or it could be that she had a particular type and Roddy wasn't it.

Sympathy for my friend made it hard for me to truly like Fergus. That and the fact that Seonaid was always attracted to really good-looking guys who knew they were good-looking and were fuckwits about it.

Roddy was far too rough around the edges to compete looks-wise with those guys, but despite his claims earlier, Roddy was never short of a girl or two. He had a brusque standoffishness that seemed to work for women. They sensed what I already knew—that beneath that rough, abrupt, cocky exterior was a very kind, loyal man. It drove them crazy and appealed to the feminine instinct to be the one woman who could bring that side of him to the surface.

"Hey, babe," Seonaid stood up to hug and kiss Fergus.

He settled at the table with us. "Hey, all. How is everyone doing?"

Jim and I responded.

Roddy did not.

Fergus barely paid attention. "I can't stay long, baby," he said to Seonaid. "Jack asked me to help him move today."

"Oh." Seonaid's expression fell. "We haven't seen each other all week, though."

"I know ..." He kissed her softly. "Don't nag, baby, eh?"

I wanted to kick him in the balls.

Apparently, so did Seonaid. "I'm not nagging. Did that sound like nagging to you?" she asked us.

Roddy side-eyed her but didn't respond.

Avoiding the question, Jim shrugged and looked at the TV.

"Drinks?" I said, trying to break the awkwardness. "Anyone?"

"Another lager," Jim said.

Roddy lifted his empty glass. "Same here."

"Wine." Seonaid sighed, realizing no one wanted to get involved in another couple's spat.

"I'll have a Tennent's. Thanks, Nora." Fergus spun around in his seat to see what game was on. "What did I miss?"

I left the table as Jim filled him in.

Instead of standing at the bar waiting to get served, I hopped up onto a bar stool. Because of my height, I tended to get ID'd more, which was frustrating since the legal drinking age here was eighteen. Even though Gareth, the bartender, knew me, I still hated feeling like a little girl standing at that bar.

Gareth was busy serving someone else, and as I sat there stewing on the conflict between my husband and me, I slowly became aware of a prickling sensation in my scalp. Following the feeling, I turned my head ever so slightly and scanned the room. At first, I couldn't discern why I'd felt like I was being watched … and then my eyes connected with his.

The noise of the bar dimmed to a murmur as we stared at one another, this stranger and me. From the distance across the bar, I couldn't tell what color his eyes were, but they were focused. Intent. On me.

He was older. Tall, broad-shouldered, looking crammed into the booth he and his companion were in. The woman sitting in the booth behind him looked tiny in comparison.

He was utterly masculine in a way that caused my breath to falter. Square, strong jawline, expressive mouth, unshaven, and a moody countenance. There was a crease between his brows and sexy laugh lines around his eyes.

I flushed, quickly turning back to the bar.

My back felt hot beneath my long hair as if the stranger's stare was still burning into me.

"Nora, I'll be with ye as soon as I can," Gareth called, looking apologetic.

I gave him a reassuring smile because the pub was always busy on Sundays.

"Nora, is it?"

The stool next to me shifted, and I reluctantly looked at my new neighbor. A lanky guy, maybe late twenties, early thirties, grinned at me from the stool while another stockier guy stood at his side. They each had a pint of Guinness in their hands and were leering at me in a way I knew and dreaded.

I flicked a glance across the room at my table and relaxed marginally at the sight of Jim laughing with Seonaid, not paying attention to the bar.

"Let us buy ye a drink, Nora," the lanky one said.

"I'm okay, thanks."

"Aw, c'mon." His grin was lopsided, and his pupils told me he'd had more than a few pints today. "We dinnae bite. Unless ye ask, o' course."

More firmly, I replied, "No thanks," and looked away.

Not even a second later, I felt his hand brush my back as it came to rest on the edge of my stool. I glanced at him, shrinking away at finding he'd trapped me against the bar.

"I'm Lewis." He nodded to his friend. "This is Pete. And we both decided ye'er the sexiest wee thing we've seen in ages."

"I'm also married." I held up my ring finger. "So ..." *Fuck off.*

Lewis dismissed this information. "Who cares."

"I fucking care."

Anxiety suffused me as my eyes flew behind Pete to find my husband, looking furious. "Jim, it's fine."

Jim shoved Pete out of the way and stepped up to Lewis. "Get yer fuckin' hand off her stool before I rip it off and shove it up yer arse."

"Jim," I pleaded.

"What's yer problem, mate?" Lewis slammed his Guinness down on the counter and slid off the stool. He was taller than Jim but not as built, yet it didn't seem to matter.

He was drunk.

And my husband was overprotective.

"Jim," I warned, slipping off the stool and placing a hand on his chest. "Just leave it. They're drunk. They didn't mean anything."

Jim pushed my hand away hard enough to make me stumble back and then he threw the first punch.

After that, everything was a blur.

Shouts and cries, both outraged and encouraging, filled the air as Jim and Lewis went at each other. It wasn't a fair fight because Jim was nowhere near as drunk, and he was bigger, but Lewis was dogged.

After Jim hit him hard enough to throw him back into the bar counter, Lewis barely took a moment to shake his dazed head, and then lunged at Jim like a bull, catching him around the middle.

I saw him driving Jim toward me, but there were stools and a pillar in my way. My reflexes weren't fast enough.

They knocked me right off my feet.

Pain ricocheted up my right wrist as I hit the floor hard. There was a blur of movement and sound above me, and one deep voice cutting through, "For fuck's sake."

Strong hands gripped me under my arms, and I found myself lifted to my feet like I weighed no more than a hummingbird. I caught a glimpse of my rescuer's face as his large body moved; a jolt of awareness rocked through me. It was the stranger who'd studied me earlier.

Suddenly, he had his arms around Jim, pulling him away from his opponent, while his companion did the same to Lewis.

"Enough," he announced calmly, his voice cutting through the entire room.

Roddy shoved his way through the crowd to get to Jim. To anyone else, Roddy looked unaffected but I knew him better. And like me, he was annoyed at my husband.

It took him a moment, but Jim jerked out of the stranger's hold. He pointed his finger at Lewis. "Ye stay the fuck away from my wife." He then gestured at me, and I wanted the floor to open up and swallow me whole.

I glared at my husband as I tried to ignore the penetrating stare of the stranger.

"Right. Out." Gareth pushed past people to get to Lewis and his friend.

"How come we need tae go?" Lewis huffed, wiping the blood from his nose. "He hit me first."

"Because I know him. I dinnae know you. All I know is Jim's never caused a problem in ma bar before ... until you. So you and yer pal can get the fuck out, or I'll throw ye out."

The stranger's friend let Lewis go, and with much grumbling and empty threats, they staggered out.

Roddy said something to Jim that made him scowl, but I couldn't hear what. As everyone settled down, fixing upturned chairs and sitting at their tables, I was aware of the stranger and his friend taking a seat at the bar. I didn't dare make eye contact with him again. Not only because I was humiliated, but because I was genuinely concerned Jim might overreact if he caught me looking at another man. Worrying about that was another problem in our marriage. I knew it was.

My whole body was stiff, and my wrist throbbed as I gazed in reproach at my husband. He stared back at me, seeming defeated.

I wanted to cry.

Jim hadn't always been as possessive, as territorial as he was now. It'd worsened over the years, and I didn't need that psychology degree to know it stemmed from insecurity.

I feared my husband sensed my true feelings.

The reproach abruptly fled, replaced by guilt.

"Are you okay?"

I jerked out of my melancholic thoughts to find Seonaid right in front of me, her hands on my biceps. I looked up into her concerned face. "I'm fine."

"You hit the floor hard. Mr. Hottie," she nodded to the stranger at the bar, "got to you before I could."

The throbbing in my wrist intensified and I winced, lifting it. "I went down on my wrist."

Anger suffused Seonaid's face, and she glanced over her shoulder at her brother. Whatever he saw on her face had him finally moving toward me.

"Ye okay?" he asked quietly.

"No, she's not. She's hurt her wrist."

"It's fine." I cradled it to my chest.

"Jesus," Jim winced, sliding his hand around my waist, "I'm sorry, Nora. I'm so sorry."

I nodded. I was too exhausted to berate him like I wanted to.

"Let's get ye home, get yer wrist wrapped up."

The mood was obliterated anyway, and I was sure the whole pub would breathe a sigh of relief once we left. "Okay."

"Do you want me to come?" Seonaid asked.

"No, we don't." Jim shot her a back-off look, and she raised her hands in defense.

"Okay. I'll get your purse for you." She wandered back to the table and I saw her say something to Roddy. Fergus, oblivious to anything not related to him, sat playing with his phone.

Jim kissed me softly, murmuring against my mouth, "I'm so sorry."

I nodded again, anxious fluttering flaring to life in my belly as I thought about the much bigger conversation I feared on our horizon. As Seonaid walked back toward us with my purse, I used the moment to surreptitiously check out the stranger at the bar.

Our eyes met again. This time he was so close, close enough to hear my conversation with Jim, close enough I could see curiosity in his beautiful green eyes. He'd been so calm and authoritative, breaking up the fight. He'd barely even had to say anything.

I still had the phantom imprint of his hands under my arms, and my eyes dropped to those hands. A shiver rippled through me, making me feel a strange mix of guilt and pleasure. He had big hands, large knuckles, slim fingers. Elegant hands. My gaze lingered longer than I'd meant, taking in his extremely fit physique delineated by his black thermal.

It wasn't only his height and general attractiveness that made the stranger stand out. He reeked of money. Despite the simplicity of his clothing—a thermal and jeans—he reeked of money. When he'd picked me up, I'd gotten a whiff of cologne so sexy ... earthy but fresh. Like wood, and amber, mint leaves, and apple. It smelled expensive.

Maybe it wasn't the clothes or the cologne that gave the impression of money. Maybe it was the confidence, the ownership of the room, like wherever he went, this guy was the one in charge.

Maybe it was an age thing, I reminded myself. He was probably in his mid-thirties.

Seonaid suddenly blocked him from view, giving me a knowing smirk. "Your purse."

I blushed, glancing at Jim to make sure he hadn't noticed my ogling (he hadn't), and gave my sister-in-law a hug.

As Jim slid his arm around my back and led me out of the bar, I glanced over my shoulder one last time to find the stranger watching me. He lifted his drink, and I nodded my thanks, holding his gaze until Jim had led us out of sight.

chapter 6

It wasn't the alarm that woke me up for work the next morning.

It was Jim's tongue.

A languid, luscious feeling low in my belly pushed through me, moving me toward consciousness. A delicious tension tightened and swelled inside me, forcing me awake with a gasp. Confusion reigned for a few seconds. I was lying in bed with my pajama top bunched around my neck, breasts bare.

And then I felt the tongue on my clit.

"Oh God," I groaned, looking down to see Jim's head between my thighs.

He looked up at me from between his thick lashes but continued to love me with his mouth.

My head flew back from the sensation as he played me expertly.

Fingers curling into the sheets, I shoved my surprise aside and enjoyed his pursuit of my orgasm. My hips undulated against his mouth, wanting more, always reaching for more.

After three years, Jim had this part down pat.

It didn't take long for the orgasm to ripple through me in pulling waves, and before I was even through it, Jim was braced over me. He thrust inside while I was still swollen tight from climax, and I gripped onto his waist, wincing at the slight burn.

As my release faded, I watched my husband as he threw his head back, eyes closed tight, teeth gritted, hips pumping against mine. I lifted mine to meet his thrusts, feeling a stirring of pleasure, but nothing like what I felt when he put his mouth on me.

We'd discovered I couldn't come with penetrative sex. I would never tell Jim this but I felt too disconnected when he was moving inside me. Jim didn't seem to mind. He was happy with a regular blow job. In return, he always got me off with his mouth first before he got himself off inside me.

"So. *Good*," Jim grunted out, groaning hard as his hips stilled for a second and then jerked in spurts as he came.

After he rolled off me, he threw his arm over his eyes as his chest moved up and down in short, fast movement. I glanced at the alarm clock to discover I only had ten minutes until I needed to get ready for work.

What a nice way to greet the day, I thought, and turned on my side, tucking my hands under my head to stare at Jim as he came down from his orgasm.

Once his breathing evened out, I whispered, "Well, that was new."

Jim lifted his arm from his eyes and grinned at me. "New good?"

It was a little disconcerting to wake up with his mouth between my legs but definitely good. "Yes. Duh."

He chuckled and rolled into me, his hand sliding down over my bare ass. "I wanted to make up for yesterday. I was an arsehole."

I touched his bruised cheek, unable to meet his eyes. "Just promise not to do it again."

"I promise." He kissed me. "Nora?"

"Mmm?"

"I want ye tae stop taking the pill."

He might as well have thrown an ice-cold bucket of water over me. Shivering suddenly, I pulled out of his arms and sat up. Cold sweat broke out under my arms, across my palms, and my heart rate increased. "What?"

Please tell me I didn't hear right.

"I think we should start trying for a baby."

What the ever-loving fuck?

"Nora?"

He'd lost his mind!

"Nora?"

"Have you lost your mind?" I whipped around to glare at him.

A mulish expression fell over his face and he threw back the covers to bounce out of bed. As he pulled on a pair of clean underwear and jeans, he bit out, "I want kids, Nora."

"I'm twenty-one," I argued immediately.

"So?"

"So?" Now I threw myself out of bed because if I didn't, I think I might have killed him. Moving around the room gathering my clean underwear and work clothes, I said, "I'm not ready to have kids."

"Why not? I never wanted tae be one of those older parents who doesnae have the energy for their kids." He followed me into the bathroom. "Twenty-one isn't that young."

"If you really think that, you and I are living on two very different planets right now, Jim," I warned. "I'm not ready to have this discussion with you."

His expression darkened. "Now? Or ever?"

Fear gripped me.

And I suddenly saw my fear mirrored in his eyes. "Nora, I love ye. I want kids with ye."

"I am too young to be a mom. And a child is not the answer to our problems."

His eyes flashed. "That's no' what this is."

"Oh, that's exactly what this is." It was him trying to trap me for life.

The thought made me flinch, like I'd smacked into a pane of glass, not realizing it was there.

It was him trying to trap me for life.

Something must have given the thought away. Jim staggered back, looking pale. "Is it that ye dinnae want kids or ye dinnae want kids with me?"

Feeling nauseated, I lifted a trembling hand to my forehead and focused on my feet. "You sprung this on me. That's not fair."

"I want a baby," he said, toneless. "Ye need tae stop taking the pill." He walked out of the bathroom as if the discussion were over.

It took me a minute to process what he'd dared to say to me. To *demand*. And then a fire lit inside me and I rushed out of the bathroom after him. "Don't you dare dictate to me, especially about my own body!"

He whirled in the doorway of our bedroom, eyes blazing. "Aye, well, ye promised that body tae me when ye married me, so I have some say in it tae. This is the only way we can keep our relationship moving forward."

His possessiveness felt like a vise around my rib cage and the words were out before I could stop them. "No, it's a desperate attempt to keep me."

An awful silence swept into the room, like cold snow suddenly falling upon a hot desert.

We looked at one another, opponents waiting for the other to make the first move.

"Why?" he said, his voice thick, cracking. "Why would I need tae keep ye? That would only be true if I felt like I was losing ye."

Unable to see the anguish in his eyes, I lowered my eyes back to my feet.

"And if we're being honest here, Nora, I've felt like I've been losing ye for a while. Sometimes I wonder if I ever had ye or if ye only used me tae get out that dump of a town back in the States."

Pain scored across my chest, the guilt, the shame, the fear overwhelming. I stumbled back toward the bed, sensing my legs couldn't hold me up under the weight of the horrible truth.

"Yet I dinnae care," Jim whispered, "I dinnae care, Nora, because I love ye that fucking much. I dinnae care that ye stopped saying 'I love ye' back tae me months ago. All I care about is waking up next tae ye every morning and falling asleep every night with ye in my bed.

"I don't want tae be the arsehole who cannae trust his wife tae talk tae other men. I dinnae want tae worry about coming home one day tae find ye've packed up and left, like ye packed up and left yer family before me."

Suddenly, he was on his knees in front of me, his arms around my waist. And he looked up at me with such a terrible love, I felt something crack inside of me. "Ye don't have tae love me, Nora. Just keep caring about me, like I know ye do, and promise tae stay. For good. Stay with me. Choose me. Choose me. Choose us as a family ... including kids."

This time as we looked at each other in silence. His expression was one of longing and mine was of guilt. Because I'd give anything to be able to return the depth of his love.

Anything.

But you can't force love.

He stood up, and as he did, he leaned down to kiss me softly. When he pulled back, he whispered, "Otherwise we cannae go on like this. Tonight, I want yer answer."

———

Tonight, I want yer answer.

I flinched, almost dropping the cereal box I was stacking on the shelf at work.

I dinnae want tae worry about coming home one day tae find ye've packed up and left, like ye packed up and left yer family before me.

"Shit," I breathed, and then bit my lip, remembering where I was.

I glanced around but there was only one woman down the other end of the aisle, not paying me any attention.

The truth was I hadn't felt such turmoil since I'd left my parents in the first place. I'd taken a risk running away with Jim, hoping the love I felt for him was enough and that with him, I'd find a better life. Instead, I'd found a not-so-dissimilar life to the one I'd led in Donovan, and a husband who didn't get me, didn't know me, and yet loved me all the same. Or whatever version of me he thought he knew. He loved me to the point it was breaking him. Because we both knew now what I'd felt wasn't love when we met.

It was naïve infatuation. And infatuation dies if it isn't nurtured into love.

"Fuck," I muttered.

This relationship was making me hate myself.

And I already pretty much hated me before Jim and I got to this point. Because leaving my parents had not been easy at all. I'd emailed my mom a number of times once I'd arrived in Edinburgh, but she never responded. After six months of emailing and no response, an email bounced back because the email address was no longer in use.

Although I was the one in the wrong, I couldn't help feeling deeply hurt by my mom's refusal to talk to me. I let that hurt simmer too long. About a year after our marriage, I wrote my mom a letter, but a month later, it was returned to me unopened.

Molly and Dawn, my only contacts, were no longer living in Donovan. Not long after I left, Molly returned my apology email to tell me that I'd inspired her. For a while we exchanged emails but soon we stopped, both busy with our new lives. Last we talked was about eighteen months ago, and Molly was living in San Diego with her boyfriend Jed. He owned a bar, he hired her as a bartender, and they thought they hated each other because they argued so much, but it turned out there was a fine line between love and hate.

I feared staying with Jim would draw him over the line. Right into Hateville.

There was no way you could stay with someone and not have them love you back the way you loved them, and not have that turn to poison.

I'd been selfish enough, surely. I couldn't let Jim do that to himself. I couldn't do that to Jim.

Yet I was scared too. Scared to be without him here. Scared I'd lose Seonaid and Roddy and Angie.

But they were his first.

The truth was I didn't know if I was capable of love. Maybe everything that happened with my dad and Mel had closed me off, made me disconnect. Did that mean I'd be better off staying with Jim if it wasn't possible for me to love him that way? Or was that even more selfish than staying with Jim out of guilt?

"Excuse me, I've been looking all over the place and I can't seem to find syrup."

The speaker sounded like a gravelly Ewan McGregor, an accent that was more anglicized and refined than Jim's. The deep, coarse lilt jolted me out of my thoughts, and I turned around to face the customer.

And my jaw nearly hit the floor.

Recognition lit the stranger's green eyes. "You."

"You," I repeated.

The stranger from the bar. The one who picked me up off the floor and stopped the fight.

"Small world." He smirked.

"Apparently."

We stared at one another and I found myself completely arrested by him. Standing this close, he was overwhelming in his masculinity, towering over my five feet three by more than a foot.

The stranger cleared his throat. "Syrup?"

Flushing at my ridiculous staring, I nodded. "Sure. This way." I passed by him, keeping my distance, but I got a whiff of his great-smelling cologne.

I heard him follow me, and my every nerve zinged with awareness. Why did he have to see me here? In this stupid uniform? I was suddenly very much aware of how unflattering it was on my petite frame.

"So, where in the US are you from?" he asked as he fell into step beside me with his longer strides.

"Indiana," I replied.

"I like Indiana."

"You've been?" I asked, surprised.

He nodded, giving me a small smile that was far, far, *far* too sexy. "It's not in an alternate dimension."

I laughed, hating how nervous it sounded. I didn't want this man to think he intimidated me. Even though he did. "Clearly, you've never been to Donovan."

His tone was amused. "I can't say I have."

If he ever visited Donovan, the women there would never let him escape. I bit my lip to stop from laughing at the thought.

"Syrup." I stopped at a shelf and gestured to it. "All kinds."

Instead of looking at the shelf, the stranger looked at me. His gaze dropped to my hand. "How's the wrist?"

He'd noticed that, huh? A little thrill rushed through me again at the thought of having his attention. "It's okay. Thanks for intervening yesterday."

"I can only imagine those guys must have crossed the line with you for your husband to react that way."

Yeah, sure, that was it. I couldn't tell if he was being passive aggressive or really just assuming what anyone would. It drilled it home even further how badly I was changing my husband and I suddenly felt defensive. I didn't want to talk about this with a stranger with the fancy watch and lilting, cultured Scottish accent that gave me tingles in my lady places. He probably thought Jim and I were like those melodramatic couples on the *Jerry Springer* show, so far outside his social sphere it wasn't funny.

"Can I help you with anything else?"

If he was surprised by my sudden abruptness, he didn't show it. "No, just the syrup." He reached by me to grab a bottle off the shelf.

I gave him a tight-lipped smile and turned on my heel to leave him to it.

"You're awfully young to be someone's wife, no?"

I stilled at the curiosity in his voice.

It didn't make sense to me that he would notice me in a bar, let alone be curious enough to quiz me in my workplace. Yet, I was curious about him too. If only for the fact that I'd never had such a visceral reaction to a stranger before. I spun slowly on my heel, and gave him a raised eyebrow. "Excuse me?"

The stranger smirked, apparently enjoying my irritation. "What I meant to say was, you're awfully smart to have married so young."

I crossed my arms over my chest, flummoxed. "How do you know I'm smart?"

He gestured to his eyes. "I can see it."

"You can just see I'm smart?" I was not convinced. I gestured around me. "Really?"

"Many a smart person has worked in a supermarket. And you look too weary for someone your age. I've been around, met a lot of people; weariness in youth usually means they've been around too and are older than their years."

That stunned me because the truth was, I *felt* older than my years. On the defense again, I huffed, "No one can know that about anyone by just looking into their eyes."

"You have very expressive eyes."

Nervous of his proximity and the attraction I felt, I took a step back, watching him warily. "You don't know me. You're a perfect stranger."

"I know." He gave me a wicked smile that made my belly flip low, deep down in that sensual place inside of me. "And unfortunately, as long as that ring stays on your finger," he pointed to my gold wedding band, "that's the way I'll stay."

Flattered, intimidated, turned on, I covered up my many emotions with snark. "Aren't I a little young for you?"

"Ouch." He laughed, grabbing his chest. "Straight to the ego."

I grinned. "Well?"

He studied me, almost in that same intense way Jim used to. Except back then, Jim's intensity made a part of me wary. I didn't feel wary with this stranger. I felt a bizarre, overwhelming need to launch myself at his mouth.

"Yesterday morning," he mused, rubbing a thumb over the lips that had me so hypnotized, "I would have agreed that twenty…"

"Twenty-one," I supplied.

"That twenty-one was definitely too young for me."

My breath caught. "And today?"

"I'd bet everything I owned that this particular twenty-one-year-old isn't like many her age. Pity," his hot gaze swept over me, making me shiver with want, "that she's a little too married."

Pity, I wanted to reply.

I smirked at him. "You're smooth, I'll give you that. Arrogant, but good."

He tilted his head, green eyes bright with amusement. "Arrogant? How so?"

"Because I get the feeling if I weren't married, you'd expect me to be in your bed by the end of the day. Expect it like it was your due."

The stranger seemed to consider that. "Maybe," he finally murmured. "I guess we'll never know."

And just like that, his words caused an unexplainable, crushing sadness to crumble down on top of me.

Even more bizarre, the stranger seemed to sense it, his own regret darkening his expression. With a grim, tight-lipped smile, he took a few steps back. "Good luck with life, girl from the bar."

Good luck with life, stranger from the bar.

But I couldn't get the words out. They were stuck.

Finally, his tall figure disappeared around the corner of the aisle, his footsteps slowly fading away.

I exhaled on a gasp.

What the hell was that?

Feeling shaken by the strange encounter, I backed down the aisle, trying to remember what the hell I'd been in the middle of doing.

Then a thought hit me. A decision, really. And I stumbled to a stop in the middle of the international foods aisle. A man, a stranger, had elicited a reaction in me that Jim had never been close to producing. As I'd stared into that man's eyes, I wanted to know who he was, what he did, what made him tick. Everything about him. I realized that I'd felt about the stranger how Jim must've felt about me when we met.

I didn't know that's what I was supposed to feel back then.

I hadn't been able to see past the hope Jim represented.

However, I knew now. And I was an adult. I didn't have ignorance or childish naïveté to fall back on as an excuse for my mistakes.

Jim deserved to find someone who would love him the way he deserved to be loved. He didn't deserve to be driven crazy by unrequited love, and I didn't deserve to feel at fault for his possessiveness.

I had to let my husband go.

The decision made me want to throw up.

"Nora."

Recognizing the voice, I spun around, confused to find Jim's mother standing in front of me. "Angie?"

She stared at me instead of speaking, and as she did so, the kind of dread I'd experienced when Melanie told me she was dying rushed over me. Angie was pale, her blue eyes filled with devastation.

"Nora?" My name trembled on her lips.

No.

No.

NO!

"He's gone," she sobbed suddenly, the noise harsh, sharp, horrifying.

"No." I shook my head, stumbling away from her.

She silently pleaded with me, begged me.

"Angie ..." Nausea rolled up inside of me. "Please."

She sobbed harder. "He's gone. My baby's gone."

part 2

chapter 7

As the bus traveled from Sighthill to Princes Street, I looked out the window, watching people as we slowly moved west toward the city center. I liked to people watch. I liked to imagine what their lives were like beyond the moments I witnessed. The bus stopped in traffic, and I noted an elderly couple walking down the busy street, holding hands, shoulders brushing, murmuring to each other with smiles on their faces.

Were they childhood sweethearts? An example of an epic love that you heard about, but never dreamed of experiencing? Sixty years, and still as in love as ever.

Or were they widowers, divorcees, who stumbled upon one another later in life, finally finding the love of their lives and enjoying it rather than regretting the years that had gone by without the other?

I smiled wistfully as the bus inched along, leaving the older couple behind.

"It's bloody roastin'!" a woman across the aisle jolted me out of my musings as she shouted to the driver. "What aboot opening some windies, eh?"

This wasn't entirely true. Although Scots and I had a differing opinion on what constituted hot weather, even I knew this month had been mild. And wet.

"Look, just because ye'er menopausal doesnae mean we aw have tae pit up wi' it, awright?" a guy sitting behind her said.

Groaning inwardly, I hurried to put my earbuds in to block out the coming argument.

I was grateful to get off the bus, happy to walk on the paved sidewalk on Princes Street and follow it alongside Edinburgh Waverley train station. As Hozier's *Take Me to Church* blocked out the sounds of the traffic and the bustle and chatter of the people passing me, I felt an ease settle over me. I loved being in the city. I loved escaping to it from my tiny one-bedroom apartment in the ugly gray council building a block from Angie's house.

I guess that's why I took the job in Old Town and didn't get something closer to the apartment. Angie argued I was wasting bus fare. But I needed the escape.

Walking up the steep, curved street that led up onto the Royal Mile, as I passed my place of work I peered inside. Leah, the owner and my boss, was smiling and chatting with a customer. The mannequins in the window displayed vintage-style dresses and sweet cardigans. The boutique clothing store, called Apple Butter, was small but always busy because of its prime position on Cockburn Street (pronounced Co-burn, which is a relief because, seriously, who would name a street after something that happens to a guy when he jerks off for too long?). The road itself was cobblestone, much like the Royal Mile, and sitting on wide, high-heel-friendly sidewalks were independent, boutique-style stores selling jewelry, antiques, and clothes. There were also pubs and cafés, and a tattoo parlor.

I climbed swiftly up the steep hill, following the curve of it away from Apple Butter. Today was my day off and I had somewhere else I needed to be. The truth was I could catch a bus to my actual destination. But I liked the walk through the city, through Old Town.

Not far from the university buildings, I stopped in at my new go-to coffee place and headed straight for the bathroom. Once inside, I changed into dark green leggings, a dark green shirt with frayed short sleeves, and a jagged hem. I folded my jeans and sweater neatly, shoved them into my backpack, and stilled when I looked into the mirror.

The sight of my cool, hard, weary eyes frightened me.

My fear had come true.

Those were my mom's eyes looking back at me.

I fingered the hair at the nape of my neck, wondering if she'd recognize me now.

I remembered the morning I got it cut.

"What have you done?" Seonaid stared at me in shock.

I felt numb to her shock. To any shock. "I cut it."

She rushed at me, touching a short strand. "You didn't just cut it. You massacred it."

It was true. My long hair was no longer. I'd asked the hair stylist to give me a pixie cut. "Are you annoyed I cut it, or annoyed because I didn't have you cut it?"

"We both know I wouldn't have done it." Seonaid shook her head at me, tears filling her eyes. She cried all the time. Enough tears for the both of us. "He loved your hair."

"Well, he's not here anymore."

"Nora ..." Her face crumpled and suddenly I was in her arms.

I hugged her back, my arms as tight around her as they could be, and whispered soothing words as she sobbed, hard, shuddering, wracking sobs.

"We need to go," I whispered finally. "We need to get Angie."

Reluctantly, Seonaid stepped back, wiping the pools of mascara from the corners of her eyes. I stopped to stare in the full-length mirror that hung on the wall by the front door. Jim had put it there for me when we first moved in. Straightening my black dress, I looked at myself, feeling disconnected from the image in front of me. Who was that young woman in the widow weeds with hair so short it made her eyes too big? Too big and blank, like all the emotion had been leached out that morning in the supermarket. I recalled crumpling to my knees in Angie's arms in the international foods aisle. I remembered crying so hard I thought I'd never be able to breathe again. My tears then seemed to have taken all my grief with them as they splashed onto my clothes, onto Angie's shoulder.

Now I felt ... nothing.

I blinked, coming out of the memory. My hair was still pixie short. But I was no longer numb.

The feelings that overwhelmed me some months after Jim's funeral were too much. Whatever strength had kept me moving, kept me going, wrapped up in the steel of nothingness, dissipated over time. Until the feelings started to seep through the diminishing steeliness. I didn't want to deal with them because I was afraid of who I'd be once processing them was over.

So, how did a young woman go on after the husband she was planning to divorce died suddenly of a brain aneurysm at the tender age of twenty-four?

I straightened my costume, grabbed my backpack, strode out into the coffeehouse, and stood in line to order an Americano to go, all the while the staff barely blinked at what I was wearing. After a few months of the same routine every week, the baristas were used to me.

Coffee to go, I strode out into the world, unsurprised when no one paid attention to me as I strolled down the street past the university buildings. This was why I loved this part of Edinburgh, and the city in general. People were used to everyone marching to the beat of their own drum, and barely took notice of anyone dressed out of the ordinary.

I cut across The Meadows, the park behind the university buildings where, on sunny days, you could find people having picnics, playing soccer and other sports, and kids laughing and playing in the play area. The sky was overcast today, but it didn't matter—it was Festival month. The Edinburgh International Festival, or the Fringe, I'd come to learn, completely engulfed the city during August. Streets were crammed full of tourists, and billboards, walls, and storefronts were covered in leaflets for stand-up comedy shows for famous comedians and ambitious newcomers. There were plays, one-man shows, concerts, book festivals, art events, and film premieres from all over the world. Jim used to hate it. He hated how we couldn't get a seat in our favorite pub or restaurant in the city center, or how you couldn't walk a beat without tripping over tourists. The only thing he did like was the pop-up beer gardens that appeared everywhere.

But I liked the Fringe.

I liked the energy and the vibrancy, the smells, and the noise.

I liked how easy it was to disappear in the crowds.

And The Meadows set up with tents and crowded with people was a much easier sight for me than the one that greeted me weeks before. Students, everywhere. Sitting with their backs against trees with textbooks open around them. I'd always looked away quickly because the longing inside me was a betrayal. I had no right to the feeling.

Before long I'd arrived at the red brick, late-nineteenth-century building that housed the children's hospital. I passed through the accident and emergency department, and took the stairs to the same floor I took the stairs to every week.

Seonaid's friend, Trish, was a nurse supervisor and the only reason I was able to dress as Peter Pan and visit the kids here. After Jim died, after it became harder to deal with the mess of emotions left behind, all I could remember was the measure of peace I used to feel visiting the children's hospital back in Indianapolis. The joy it brought those kids when I turned up to entertain them made me feel like I was doing something worthwhile. Although I'd written to Anne-Marie to explain my sudden absence, I'd never stopped feeling guilty about abandoning those children.

I'd tried to explain it to Seonaid and was met with resistance at first.

"No." Seonaid shook her head stubbornly. "You won't have time."

"How so?"

"Because you're going to apply for university."

I didn't want to talk about that. A block of ice settled in my stomach. "No. I'm not."

Seonaid flinched at my tone. "Nora ..."

"Do you think your friend, Trish, would talk to me about it? Let me visit the kids once in a while? A volunteer entertainer?"

She looked at me like she was half afraid I was losing my mind. "A children's entertainer?"

"Yes."

"And you used to do this back in the US?"

"Yes."

"And Jim knew about it?"

"Yes."

"Why didn't you mention it before?"

"What's the big deal? And I'm mentioning it now, aren't I?"

"The big deal is the timing, Nora," Seonaid insisted. "It's been ten months. Not a long time in the grand scheme of things ... but you need to start moving on with life. Going after the things you've always wanted. Like an education."

"This is what I want," I said. "Are you going to help me out or not?"

Despite not understanding it, at all, Seonaid did put me in touch with Trish. And Trish, although surprised a twenty-two-year-old would be interested in being a children's entertainer, gave me a shot, despite my lack of professional credentials.

I have to admit to being secretly pleased when she gushed about how brilliant she'd thought I'd been when I acted out chapters from the first *Lemony Snicket* book.

"Trish said you were amazing." Seonaid looked at me suspiciously that night. "Like really bloody good. She's surprised you're not in an acting program."

The praise settled deep in my bones, alighting an ages-old longing and ambition. I didn't show how much the words affected me, though. "That was kind of her."

Seonaid narrowed her eyes, studying me as if she were trying to uncover all my secrets. "I worry about you, Nora," she whispered.

"Don't." I gave her a small smile. "I had the best time with the kids today. I feel better than I've felt in a long time."

"Good," she murmured, but the concern in her eyes remained.

"Ye'er here," Jan, the staff nurse, said as she approached me in the corridor en route to the children's common room. As supervisor,

Trish was usually busy on the days I visited, so Jan was the one who I dealt with mostly.

"As promised."

Jan grinned at me. "I've never met a more dedicated volunteer."

I wanted to smile but after my last visit, I was worried I'd be told not to come back. "And the parents are okay about me visiting?"

A parent had been here last week and had been, as was their right, full of questions about my business at the children's hospital. She hadn't been impressed to learn I wasn't a professional children's entertainer, but someone a member of staff knew. She insisted on sticking around to watch me, and I'd had to shove my nervousness aside, and pretend to be Peter Pan telling stories to kids who needed to stop growing older and sicker for a while.

"Mrs. Stewart thought ye were very good with the children," Jan reassured me. "She was miffed she hadn't been told about yer visits, which is fair enough. I thought all the parents had been made aware of ye, but she must have slipped through. Anyway, she's happy to let Aaron continue to participate in yer visits."

Relieved, I exhaled. "Good. I love my time with the kids."

Jan shook her head at me, grinning. "Ye either have the biggest heart of any young woman I've ever met, or ye'er hiding from something when ye come here."

I sucked back my next exhale like she'd slapped me.

Rubbing my arm in comfort, she said, "I think it's a bit of both. And no matter ... the results are the same. Ye'er doing a good thing."

My tension melted as I realized she wasn't going to press me about my reasons, but led me toward the common room and announced me to the kids.

Poppy, a little girl who had kidney disease and was treated with four-hour dialysis three mornings a week, beamed at me. "Nora." She gave me a tired smile, and I grinned, peace moving through me rapidly, my whole body relaxing. The day I visited was a dialysis day for Poppy and despite how exhausted she was after treatment, she'd insisted to her mom that she be allowed to stay and listen to my readings. Jan always set her up in a big comfy chair with a lap blanket, and her concerned mother collected her at the end of my visits. Although Poppy's mother was concerned about leaving her kid after treatment, and rightly so, she understood that her little girl needed to feel like there was more to life than her kidney disease.

And some American chick dressed as Peter Pan, acting out stories, took her away from that for a little while.

Why the Peter Pan costume, you ask?

"What the hell have ye done?" Roddy said as I approached him in the church at Jim's funeral.

"What?"

"Yer hair?" He glowered at it.

"I cut it."

"Aye, ye dinnae say. Ye look like fuckin' Peter Pan."

"She looks bonny." Angie gave me a kiss on the cheek, her eyes welling up, her lips trembling. "She'd look like an angel no matter how she wore her hair. Jim would think so too."

"Jim would lose his heid." Roddy grunted. "He loved yer fuckin' hair."

That's why I cut it off. "I felt like a change."

"Peter fuckin' Pan," Roddy grumbled as we shuffled into the front pew together.

It made sense to me, not only because of the hair, but because of everything the boy who couldn't grow up represented.

I smiled, taking in the room. Seven kids today, all of whom I recognized from last week. "Hey, guys," I marched into the room with a swagger a la Peter Pan. "You ready to go on another adventure?"

"Uh ... Peter?" Jan said, sounding amused.

I looked over my shoulder. "Yeah?"

Jan approached me and spoke in low tones. "There's someone else who wants to visit with ye today. Would ye mind? Her name is Sylvie. Her mum, Nicky, was a nurse here and Sylvie got used to being around us. Nicky passed away not too long ago. She lives with her uncle but her dad sees her when he can. She was supposed to be with her dad today but he had a work emergency and Sylvie asked to be dropped off here. It's becoming a regular occurrence. We don't mind. It's the wee lass we feel for."

It sounded like a terribly sad situation. I understood those. "It's definitely no problem."

She disappeared to fetch Sylvie and I grinned at the room, my fists on my hips, my feet braced apart. "Are you all ready?"

"What are ye reading today?" Aaron quizzed from his place on the couch. He was holding an iPad in his hand, but his attention was on me.

"Oh, I'm taking you on the best adventure today. Just you wait."

After talking to the kids for a minute or so, one of the double doors opened and Jan walked in with her hand on the shoulder of a tall, pretty girl. She wore her white-blond hair short, so the ends tickled under her chin.

My breath lodged in my throat.

Jesus Christ.

She looked like Mel.

"Nora—I mean, Peter, this is Syl—"

"Sylvie Lennox." The girl stepped out from under Jan's hand. "I'm ten and I stay with my uncle Aidan in Fountainbridge. We stay right on the canal there."

All I could do was stare, not just because she reminded me so much of Mel, but because she was so much younger than I'd first thought. Ten years old. And yet, there was an otherworldliness about her. Experience. Losing her mom.

"Hey Sylvie. I'm Peter Pan."

"No, you're not," she said quite seriously as she walked over to me. She slowly lowered herself to the ground and crossed her legs. "Jan called you Nora. And you look more like a Nora than a Peter. Plus … Peter Pan is fictional. And a boy."

Enchanted by her and her cultured Scottish accent, I lowered myself to my haunches and grinned. I whispered, "Why not pretend? Everyone else here prefers Peter to plain old Nora."

Sylvie appeared to give this serious consideration. And then she nodded. "Okay. But I want to know Nora too."

A lightness danced across my chest, chipping away at the layers of aching weight. "You got it."

I stood up and faced the rest of the group who waited patiently for me to begin. "Last night, I went on the greatest adventure. I traveled all the way from Neverland to this magical place called Indiana. There I met a girl called Melanie and she took me on a really cool journey filled with heroes and villains." I pulled out a book from my bag and showed it to them. "Now I'm going to take you on the same voyage."

"So … did you fly back to Neverland this morning? And then fly back again?" Poppy squinted at me in confusion.

"I did."

"But … how is it possible?" Aaron, a ten-year-old recovering from leukemia said, suspicious.

Sylvie piped up, "Because time stops in Neverland."

"Exactly right, Sylvie. Remember, guys, I told you that in Neverland, dreams are born and time is never planned."

"I wish we lived in Neverland," one of the youngest kids, Kirsty, said.

"How do you get to Neverland?" Poppy asked.

"You have to fly there," Sylvie said. "With pixie dust."

I grinned down at Sylvie. Someone had clearly read *Peter Pan* or at least seen the movie. "Exactly."

"But *how* do you get there? Where is it?"

"Up there. In the sky." I pointed upward. "Second star to the right and straight on till morning."

"Okay, we get it. Nora, just tell us what adventure Melanie took ye on?" Aaron asked, shuffling forward on the couch to peer at my book.

I laughed at Aaron's reluctance to play along but gave him what he wanted. I opened Roald Dahl's *Matilda* and gave them my cheekiest smile. "Let's find out, shall we?"

We were halfway through chapter three when Sylvie's hand shot straight up.

I stopped reading and mock scowled at her. "Not enjoying the adventure?"

"Yes," Sylvie said, nodding vehemently. "But I wondered ... can I be Miss Trunchbull?"

In the few months I'd been visiting the hospital, not one of the other kids had asked to read with me. Something stirred inside me. Affection. Immediate affection that made no logical sense. But I felt it as I gazed down at this girl, stunned by the feeling.

"Of course." I held out my hand and Sylvie grinned at me, taking it, allowing me to pull her to her feet.

From there we began reading together, and I had to try to stifle my delighted laughter at Sylvie's brilliant and dastardly Miss Trunchbull. She had all the kids laughing at her horrible villain, and my time with them flew faster than ever before.

Jan came in to let me know time was up, and the kids groaned, pleading for me to stay.

"Peter Pan has to get back to Neverland. If he stays away too long, Tinkerbell misses him," Jan said, coming into the room to take Sylvie's hand. "Time to wait on your dad, sweetheart."

"Wait." Sylvie tugged on her hand and hurried over to me as I packed my book into my bag. She leaned over to ask, "Will you sit with me while I wait for my dad?"

"Now?" I looked over at Jan who nodded. "Sure."

"Great!"

After I said goodbye to the other kids, I followed Jan and Sylvie back to the nurses' station. "I'm going to change first."

Sylvie looked up at me like a little adult. "Okay. I'll wait right here." She gestured to two waiting room seats backed up against the wall.

Curious over the little girl who reminded me so much of Mel, I hurried to change into my jeans and shirt, and returned to her.

Her whole face lit up at the sight of me. "Nora."

I smiled because you would've thought she hadn't seen me in weeks. "Hey, you."

"Where are you from?" Sylvie asked quite abruptly.

"I'm from America. Do you know where that is?"

"I've been." Sylvie sat up taller, expression brightening. "Uncle Aidan took me and Mum to Disneyworld a few years ago. Is that where you're from?"

"No. I'm from the Midwest. Indiana."

"Like in your story about the girl? Melanie?"

"Yeah. Did you enjoy today? You seemed to know an awful lot about Peter Pan."

"My mum read it to me. It was her favorite book. Uncle Aidan still reads it to me from time to time." She looked at me with those serious eyes. "She died. Last year."

It was too much. Too much for any kid. It was moments like these I wanted to kick and scream and rail at the Fates, because how the hell was it okay that a child should be destined to lose her mother before she even reached her teens? I bit down the emotion and said, "I'm so sorry, Sylvie."

She swallowed hard, like she was trying to hold back emotion. Being brave.

Only ten years old and being brave.

"I live with Uncle Aidan now, and I have a teacher who comes to the house to teach me school. A lot." She rolled her eyes. "But not on the days Daddy can see me. I stayed at Daddy's last night but he had to work today and Uncle Aidan is in London because he makes music with famous people."

It sounded like she didn't have a heck of a lot of stability and I wondered what the two men in her life were thinking. She should be in school, not being homeschooled, and she shouldn't come in second to a job and be dumped on her mom's old colleagues. Irritation made my blood hot, but I hid it for Sylvie's sake.

"Uncle Aidan says he'll take me traveling with him when I'm older." Her eyes were bright with obvious hero worship. I noted the way she appeared to light up when talking about her uncle in comparison to her dad.

"You were so good today, reading the part of Miss Trunchbull. You're a very talented actress."

Sylvie beamed. "Really? You too! The kids really believe you're Peter Pan."

I hid my smile at the way she referred to the other kids, as if she weren't one. "Well, thank you."

"I can't wait to tell Uncle Aidan about you ..."

I listened, giving her my full attention and knowing it was what she needed as she sat and told me about life living with her uncle Aidan.

Not too long later, a harried-looking guy came hurrying around the corridor, his shoulders slumping in relief at the sight of Sylvie. I went on alert as Sylvie stopped talking. The guy was of average height, slim, and was good-looking in a dark, Irish Colin Farrell kind of way.

"Sylvie." His eyes flicked to me, suspicion in them.

"Daddy ..." Sylvie gave him a halfhearted wave.

"Who is this?" He dropped to his haunches in front of his daughter. I noted the dark circles under his eyes and the sweat on his forehead. The man looked exhausted and worried for his daughter, and I felt a little bad for prejudging him.

"This is Nora."

"Cal," Jan said, marching down the corridor. She did not look happy. "You were a while."

He winced and stood up, shooting her an apologetic look. "My meeting ran over. I'm sorry." His eyes flicked down to me again.

Jan gestured to me. "This is Nora. She's a children's entertainer. Sylvie asked her to wait with her."

"Oh. Right." His expression eased somewhat. "Nice to meet ye."

"Likewise."

"Right, then. Thanks again, Jan."

Jan gave him a tight-lipped nod.

"Come on, Sylvie."

Sylvie immediately turned to me. "Will you be back next week?"

My heart ached for her. "I will."

"Daddy, can I come back next week?"

He grabbed her hand and she reluctantly got up. "Sylvie, this is a hospital. We can't keep imposing."

"Nora doesn't mind."

"Sylvie." His voice contained warning.

Her eyes lowered in dejection, and she shot me a sad look. "Bye, Nora."

Strangely, the words felt sharp and ragged as I forced them off my tongue. "Bye, Sylvie."

As I watched her hurry to keep up with her father's quick steps, sadness for the girl pressed heavily upon me.

"She lives with her uncle Aidan full-time," Jan said. "When her mum was alive, she had full custody because he," she nodded down the hallway with a sneer on her mouth, "wasn't ready to be a dad. When he finally decided he was, he was too busy with his work to really be one. Guardianship naturally passed to her brother Aidan. He started homeschooling Sylvie when Nicky got sick and hasn't wanted to interrupt her routine since she lost her mum. I think it's time, though."

"Yeah, she should be with other kids her age," I agreed.

"He's doing the best he can, I suppose."

"You sound like you like him."

To my surprise Jan flushed. "Let's just say ye'd be hard pushed to find a woman who didn't like Aidan Lennox."

chapter 8

I FOUND MYSELF THINKING CONSTANTLY OF SYLVIE OVER THE NEXT FEW days. Whether I was a moth to the flame of someone's personal tragedy, or if it was because she reminded me of Mel, I didn't know. Or maybe it was because there was something about the kid and her grown-up seriousness that tugged at my heartstrings. Whatever the reason, she was on my mind, and I was hoping I might see her again a week later as I was busying myself to leave the flat for the hospital. I wanted to make sure the kid was doing all right.

As I was finishing my coffee and picking up my backpack to go, there was a knock on my door. Hurrying quietly over to it, I got up on my tiptoes to squint through the peephole. My stomach dropped at the sight of Seonaid and Angie on the other side. I glanced behind me at my small apartment. The kitchen was one counter along the back wall with an oven, sink, cupboards, and a small fridge/freezer. It was directly opposite the sitting room, which was only big enough for two small couches, a tiny coffee table, and a television. Directly ahead of the front door was the door to the bedroom, big enough for a bed, and it had a built-in-wardrobe for the few clothes I had. There was a tiny, seen-many-better-days bathroom off the bedroom.

It was tidy and clean, but grim and depressing, and miles away from what Jim had been striving for.

"We heard you moving around, Nora. Open up," Seonaid said.

With no other choice, I turned the multiple locks on the door and pulled back the chain. As soon as the door was open, Angie and Seonaid barged in. Seonaid looked annoyed and Angie concerned. Jim's mother shook her head, gesturing for me to shut the door. "Jim wid hate that ye'er livin' here. I wish ye'd rethink and come stay with me until ye'er on yer feet."

"You know how much that offer means to me, Angie, but I need to take care of myself." I walked around them, feeling their eyes burning into me as I grabbed my backpack, making it clear I was on my way out. Jim's family and friends had been so kind to me over the last year. They hadn't stopped acting like I was a member of their family. But being around them was too difficult for me.

"You're going out?" Seonaid scowled. "We dropped by to ask you to come out for brunch with us. We both have the day off."

"I can't." I said apologetically. "I'm volunteering at the hospital."

"Volunteering being the operative word," Seonaid said. "Go another day. We haven't see you in ages."

Guilt over avoiding them gnawed at me. I realized that the wall I'd put up between me and Jim's family and Roddy had hurt them, but I couldn't bear to hear them talk about how lucky Jim was to have had me in his life; how he got to at least have that kind of amazing love before he died. The guilt wrecked me, carved me up inside because they didn't see the ugly truth. They persisted in trying to keep me a part of the family and I allowed them to, because part of me needed the punishment their presence provided.

"I can't. Jan is expecting me."

Angie's face fell. "Surely she can dae without ye this once. I've no seen ye in weeks, Nora."

"I know." I squeezed her arm as I passed them, heading for the door. "I'll make it up to you. But I promised the kids I'd be back this week and I can't make promises to sick kids and not keep them, you know."

"I think volunteering at the hospital is wonderful, but I dinnae want yer whole life to be about it. Assure me it's no." Angie said, looking worried.

I'd opened the door, wishing I could escape without answering, because I didn't have the answer she wanted. So I lied. "It's not. I promise. But it is worthwhile. It takes the kids out of the reality of their situations for a while and it makes me feel good for now."

They seemed to reluctantly accept that as they walked out of my apartment, disappointed I was choosing the hospital over them again. They also seemed to sense there was more to my volunteering than the need for charity. I wondered how they could be so suspicious of my motives now, but have never clued in on the fact that all was not sweetness and light between Jim and me. I remembered the way Angie had touched my face in sympathy when she'd seen I'd cut off all my hair. She thought she understood why because everyone had heard Jim say at some point or another how I was never to cut my hair, that he loved my hair. But Angie didn't really understand why I did it.

My long hair *wasn't* a painful reminder of Jim, of losing him. It was the agonizing reminder that I'd started to lose myself when I'd followed him to Edinburgh to escape my life. Once there, once I'd realized I didn't love him like he loved me, instead of being honest, I'd stayed with him and played the part of the wife he'd wanted, and in doing so lost myself entirely.

———

SYLVIE WAS BACK. HER FATHER ONCE MORE HAD SOME BUSINESS THING come up, and he'd dropped her off at the hospital for a few hours, despite the fact he'd said they couldn't keep imposing. After I'd finished reading to the kids, with help from Sylvie once again, my precocious new young friend asked me to have lunch with her in the cafeteria. She'd even tried to buy my lunch, much to my amusement.

"So why here?" I said, nosy, as we ate mac and cheese. "Why doesn't your dad drop you off at your uncle's?"

She sighed, as though she had the weight of the world on her tiny shoulders. "Uncle Aidan is really busy. I know it. But he would hang out with me instead of doing his work. It's not fair. Daddy kind of promised Uncle Aidan it wouldn't happen again, but ..." She shrugged. And then she smiled. "But *we* get to hang out so it's cool."

I was still concerned by the instability in Sylvie's life, but I smiled. "It is."

"I told Uncle Aidan all about you and how you let me read with you." She grinned. "Did I tell you Uncle Aidan knows famous people?"

Trying not to laugh, I nodded. "You might have mentioned it."

"He's a music producer and composer," she said. "That means he works on famous people's music with them and also he writes, like, music for films and stuff. You know, like, music without words."

That was pretty swanky and impressive. "Like score music."

She nodded her head vigorously. "He has all these instruments and computer stuff. He's really clever."

"He sounds really clever."

"Yeah, and," she continued on, as excited about her subject as ever, "Uncle Aidan had a room painted blue and purple in the flat and all these pretty things put in it with a big bed just for me. My tutor Miss Robertson said I'm a really lucky girl."

"Yeah." I smiled, growing nosier about her life by the second. "And does Miss Robertson teach you a lot?"

"Uh-huh. She comes to the house Mondays, Tuesdays, and Fridays. And we work all day," she groaned. "It's not like school at all. It's harder because I'm the only kid in the class. I can't get away with anything."

She sounded so beleaguered it made me laugh. It was good to know she was receiving a fine education but I still think it was about time this kid got back to school and had some normality in her life.

Suddenly, she giggled, making me smile. "What is it?"

She leaned across the table and whispered, "I think Miss Robertson fancies Uncle Aidan."

I chuckled at her mischief. "Yeah? You trying to play matchmaker?"

Sylvie wrinkled her nose. "Nah. Uncle Aidan has been all over the world and he's dated some of the most beautifulest ladies I've ever seen."

Feeling put out for Miss Robertson, I reminded her gently, "Beauty is only skin deep."

"Mum used to say that too." Sylvie nodded. "But I don't think she told Uncle Aidan that."

I burst out laughing before I could stop myself. Her uncle sounded like quite the character.

"Do you have an uncle?" Sylvie asked suddenly.

Sobering at the mention of family, I shook my head. "No." Neither of my parents had siblings.

"Are your mum and dad in America?"

"They are."

"They must miss you."

The thought was a deep ache in my chest. Too deep. Too painful. "What about you? Is Uncle Aidan your only other relative?"

"My nana and grandad live in England so I only see them every now and then. My dad doesn't have parents. He was in foster care when he was growing up."

"What is your dad's job?" I found it telling that Sylvie was so excited to talk about her uncle Aidan and his career, but she'd yet to offer up much on her father.

"He's an engineer." She said. "I don't know what that means."

"It means he's very smart."

She nodded. "I suppose."

I frowned. "Sometimes adults get busy, huh?"

A surprisingly mulish expression appeared on her face. "Uncle Aidan always makes time."

The hero worship she had for him was off the charts. I almost felt sorry for her dad. And basically anyone who was competing for her affection. Her uncle sounded like an experienced, cultured, intimidating, mythical being.

Uncle Aidan was clearly a superhero and not of this planet.

———

THE NEXT WEEK SYLVIE WAS THERE AGAIN, THIS TIME HAVING BEGGED her uncle to drop her off at the hospital to take part in the reading and sit with me a little while. I couldn't stay as long with her, however, because I'd promised Seonaid I'd meet her for lunch. Leaving Sylvie in the capable hands of Jan, I took off reluctantly. Despite how ill-at-ease Seonaid could make me feel, I also needed her, and that's why I wouldn't put so much space between us that it would damage our friendship.

We were meeting at her favorite coffee place, The Caffeine Drip, in New Town, a good thirty-minute walk on an average day. It became forty-five minutes during the Fringe, as I tried to maneuver my way through the crowded streets. The temperature was warm but the dark clouds above and the humidity suggested a storm was coming. By the time I got to the coffee shop, my clothes were sticking to me and I was thankful for my short hair.

"You've put weight on," Seonaid said, hugging me.

I raised an eyebrow as I pulled back. "Is that good?"

She gave me a reassuring smile. "You were looking a little thin."

The truth was I did have more of an appetite lately. I didn't know if it was the kids, or if meeting Sylvie had put things into perspective for me, but I was feeling a little more aware. Like I'd been unconscious for a while, but something was stirring me awake.

"I feel fine."

"Good." She scrutinized me.

I was grateful when the friendly waitress appeared to take our order, breaking my friend's gaze. Once the waitress was gone, I attempted to guide the conversation away from myself. "How's work?"

"Usual." She shrugged. "Busy."

Seonaid loved talking about her work, which meant she was deliberately trying to steer conversation back to me.

Crap.

"And how's ..." I scrambled to remember the name of the guy she'd been dating recently. When Jim died, Fergus had been less than supportive. It was too much for him and he broke up with Seonaid just when she needed him the most. Although it was awful, I think it was the best thing that could've happened to Seonaid. It woke her up to the kind of men she'd been dating. From then on, she'd decided to only date nice guys, no matter how sexy they were or weren't to her. She tried online dating, and had unfortunately gone through a stream of really nice guys who didn't turn her on.

"Frank," she supplied with a sigh. "Frank is gone. Frank could not find the clit so bye-bye, Frank."

I gave a bark of laughter. "Poor Frank."

"Hey, Frank was ten years older than me. If he hasn't found the clit in the twenty-odd years he's been having sex, then Frank is either lazy or clueless. Neither appealed to me."

Smirking, I nodded. "Got it."

"Anyway, despite Frank, I'm enjoying online dating. I've met some interesting people, and made friends with the guys who I didn't connect with sexually."

"I'm glad." I was not glad for the speculative look in her eyes.

"So, I was thinking maybe you could set up a profile on the dating site I use."

And there it was.

"I don't think so."

"It would get you out of the house."

"I don't have a house."

"Flat. It would get you out of that dinky, depressing little flat you hibernate in."

"I don't hibernate."

"Going to work and volunteering at a hospital does not equate to socializing."

"I disagree."

"Nora, please think about it. I don't want to push, but I'm worried about you. It's like you're refusing to move on."

The waitress reappeared with our food. Once she'd left, I looked at my plate, my annoyance and guilt fighting with one another. I picked up my fork and knife, my fingers curling tightly around them in irritation before I could use them to cut into my panini. Unable to look at her for fear she'd see the emotion roiling in my eyes, I said with quiet sternness, "I'm not online dating. You don't want to push me, then don't push me."

Awkward silence fell over the table as we made a show of eating. Finally, unable to bear her hurt silence anymore, I queried, "How's Roddy?"

Apparently, it was the right thing to ask because Seonaid blew out a beleaguered breath. "He's messing around with the new barmaid at Leith's Landing. I don't know what he sees in her. She's as dull as dishwater. All she does is pout and giggle."

"And give him sex with no strings attached." I nudged the hornet's nest.

Seonaid's eyes narrowed. "That's what he thinks. But I can see she's trying to wrangle him into a relationship. I swear to God if he even thinks about settling down with that spoon, I will end him."

"Why do you care who he settles down with?"

She gave me a *duh* look. "It's Roddy."

"Surely, we should be happy for him, no matter who he ends up with?"

"I'd quite like to hear you say that to him the next time he complains about one of my boyfriends."

God, I wanted smack their heads together. Could two people be more blind about how they felt for each other?

"Fair enough."

"So …" She studied me in that thoughtful way of hers. "Tell me about the volunteering."

"What do you want to know?"

"I want to know that you're not surrounding yourself with children who aren't going to be here in a year's time."

Understanding her concern, I gave her a reassuring smile. "Some of the kids are pretty sick but most aren't terminal. Some of *those* poor kids are too ill to sit in a room and listen to me tell stories or play games. I'm fine. In fact, this one kid isn't even sick," I said, grinning as I thought about Sylvie. "Her mom was a nurse there …" I went on to tell her about Sylvie and her guardian, the epic Uncle Aidan.

"He sounds hot," Seonaid decided.

I snorted. "How can someone sound hot?"

"Well, for one, he clearly has money. The apartment she described in Fountainbridge … not cheap. Also, she says he works with famous people and has dated beautiful women. Pretty people usually stick together."

"Not true. There have been many unattractive famous men who have ended up with beautiful young women."

"I'm not saying he's probably typically good-looking. Seemingly unattractive men can be so charismatic, they're hot."

Chuckling, I shook my head. "Why does it matter if he's hot or not? The important thing is that this great kid has had the crappiest thing in the world happen to her and she's so strong but he's clearly blind to that. He keeps her locked up in that flat with a tutor instead of sending her back to school where she belongs. And she hero-worships him so much, she's not going to complain about not being at school with her friends. She lost her mom—she won't want to do anything to push him away."

Seonaid nodded. "I see your point. I do. But you don't know the whole situation, you only know what you've gotten from the kid. Try suddenly becoming guardian to a kid who lost her mum to a long-term illness and has a flaky father. Wouldn't you wrap that kid up in cotton wool too? Being overprotective in this situation isn't really a bad thing. Give the poor guy a break."

Her advice percolated and I found myself frowning. "I didn't mean to be judgy. I *just* … I really like the kid. I'm worried about her."

"I can see that." Seonaid cocked her head in thought. "Maybe you should try to meet the uncle—get a feel for him. You know, so you can rest assured she's in good hands."

Knowing exactly why she wanted me to meet the uncle—and it wasn't purely for Sylvie's sake—I shook my head, trying not to laugh. "You're indefatigable."

Seonaid's brows drew together. "All I heard was the word *fat.*"

"It means dogged. Persistent. You never stop."

She adopted an innocent expression. "I don't know what you're talking about."

"I'm talking about you trying to match me up with every man I come in contact with."

"That's not true." She waved her fork at me. "I have never tried to set you up with Roddy. I'm not that cruel."

"Hey," I waved my fork right back at her, "I'd be lucky to be Roddy Livingston's girl."

"Yeah?" She smirked at me. "If you feel that strongly, maybe you should pick up a phone and I don't know … call him once in a while."

Well, I walked right into that one. "I call him," I hedged.

"Then hang up and when he calls back, you don't answer."

Flushing at my stupidity, I asked quietly, "Did he tell you that?"

"Aye. He did. And this is Roddy, Nora. He doesn't think, 'aw, wee shame, Nora's having a tough time connecting with her dead husband's best friend who also happens to be her best friend.' He's thinking, 'If she doesn't fucking cut the bullshit, I'm done.'"

I blanched at the thought of losing Roddy. "I'll call him."

She reached over and grabbed my hand. "He can't say it because it's Roddy and admitting any real feelings would send him into septic shock, but he loves you. When he lost Jim, he lost a brother. You're like a sister to him, more than I ever was. Don't … don't hurt him, Nora."

Tears suddenly burned in my eyes and I dropped my gaze. "He's the last person I want to hurt." I couldn't explain to her how difficult it was to be around Roddy. How it brought all the memories flooding back to that time when I should have let Jim McAlister walk out of my life and find someone who could love him the way he deserved.

"How about this? You, Roddy, and I meet for a drink at Leith's Landing?"

"Won't the barmaid you hate be there?"

She sneered. "Yes. But I'm willing to put up with it if it makes it easier for you to spend time with Roddy."

"It's because he reminds me so much of Jim," I hurried to explain, not wanting her to know the real reason.

Seonaid nodded. "I get it. So? Next Sunday?"

"Yeah, okay," I agreed, hating the swarming kaleidoscope of butterflies that erupted in my belly at the thought.

chapter 9

IT WAS SURPRISINGLY EASIER THAN I'D ANTICIPATED TO GET THROUGH A few hours at the pub with Roddy. Seonaid made it easy by distracting him constantly with her digs at the barmaid he was dating, even though the girl wasn't working, and therefore unable to defend herself.

However, I knew from the lack of any real emotion when talking about the barmaid that Roddy wasn't in as deep as Seonaid feared. He was too busy exchanging mock barbs with the woman he actually cared about to give much thought to the barmaid.

My friends' funny dynamic put me at ease and I got through hanging out with Roddy, assured I could do it again. And if Roddy had been pissed off at me, he never showed it.

That week I'd also had the privilege of spending more time with Sylvie, who had talked her uncle into letting her join the group again for my readings. I also introduced some games that day, and Sylvie served as my little helper. This time she and I couldn't sit and talk because I'd agreed to have lunch again with Seonaid. At the despondent look on Sylvie's face when I told her I had to leave, I knew I wouldn't schedule lunch after my visits at the hospital again.

During our time with the kids, Sylvie expounded on the awesomeness of her uncle Aidan to everyone. I think some of the kids were a little tired of hearing, "Well, my uncle Aidan says," but others had fallen under her spell. She'd transformed her uncle into a godlike creature, to the point where I think she had some of the younger kids believing he was an actual superhero. I let her. What was the harm? More than ever, those kids needed to believe in miracles and superheroes. Wasn't that what was I doing there? Spinning them stories of magic and escape?

The Wednesday after my Sunday drinks with Roddy and Seonaid, I found myself in the untenable position of wanting to say no to Sylvie and not being able to. Somehow, she'd gotten her hands on a Twister game board and had talked the kids into playing.

I hadn't thought it was a great idea, and Jan wasn't too sure, either, but Sylvie won by announcing only she and I would play, and the kids would take turns spinning the wheel. It actually turned out to be a pretty good idea because we ended up in such awkward positions, in fits of giggles, that we had all the kids laughing and trying to cheat by placing us in even more ungainly positions!

I was in the middle of begging Poppy not to cheat with the Twister spinner when a deep, masculine voice sounded from behind me at the door.

"What is going on here?"

Unable to turn to see who it was, I heard Jan's voice. "The children's entertain—"

"Uncle Aidan!" Sylvie squealed in my ear, making me flinch. "I'm moving but you can't move!" She unwound her leg from mine and was gone.

"How is that fair?" I asked. I wanted to move. I had my ass in the air and the mysterious Uncle Aidan was right behind it.

I bowed my head trying to see through my legs but all I saw were his and Jan's feet and then Sylvie's as she rushed him.

"Come play, Uncle Aidan," Sylvie begged excitedly.

"I think I'll just watch." His voice rumbled, sounding amused. He had a great voice. A beautiful lilting, cultured Scottish accent. And my ass was in his face. In green Peter Pan leggings that did nothing to hide the shape of my body, I might add.

Great.

I looked super professional right now.

"Oh, please," Sylvie begged. "Please."

"No, sweetheart. You go back to the game. I'll be here when you're done."

"But I want you to play with Nora—I mean, Peter Pan."

I almost choked. It was time to get up before Peter Pan was made to play Twister with a strange man. The thought sounded so perverted, I had to swallow a giggle.

"Please, please!" the other kids suddenly started begging.

Sylvie began instructing him on the position she'd been in.

"Guys, leave Sylvie's uncle—" The squeak of the plastic mat halted me mid-sentence.

And then I felt his heat, followed by the smell of expensive cologne. It was earthy but fresh. Like wood, and amber, mint leaves and apple.

Oh, dear God.

Slowly, I lifted my head and found myself staring into green eyes that were bright with amusement. *Familiar* green eyes with flecks of yellow gold.

"You must be Peter Pan," he said, laughter trembling on his lips.

Lips I remembered well.

In fact, I remembered those broad shoulders too, that square, unshaven, strong jawline and expressive mouth. I remembered the sexy laugh lines around his eyes. It all belonged on a very tall, well-built guy who had once picked me up off the floor of a pub and then flirted with me the following day in a supermarket on what would turn out to be one of the worst days of my life.

Uncle Aidan was the stranger from the bar.

Small goddamn world.

Realizing I hadn't spoken, I managed a croaky, "Hey."

Our faces were too close together, and his long leg was currently entangled with my short one.

"Right hand green, Peter Pan!" Sylvie announced.

I wrenched my gaze from his to the mat. The nearest green spot would mean climbing her uncle like a monkey. Part of me wondered if she'd cheated. I shot her a suspicious look and watched her shake with giggles.

"Oh, crap," I muttered under my breath.

I heard the rumble of laughter and my eyes flew back to his. There was a challenge in his, but not recognition. He didn't remember me. Why would he? I was just a girl he briefly met once.

"I'm not doing it."

His eyes grew round with mock innocence. "But that would be cheating."

"Cheating?" Sylvie heard. "No cheating."

"No cheating, Peter Pan!" Poppy cried out from her chair.

Soon all the kids were buzzing with laughter and conversation as I stared at the man who was already too close for comfort.

There was no way I was doing it. It wouldn't be appropriate. I moved toward him as if I was going to do it and I let my left hand and foot slip. I flipped at the last minute, crashing down on the mat on my back.

"Oh no, I fell! I lose!" I threw my hands up in the air.

I heard his laughter before his face appeared upside down above mine. My breath caught as he smiled down at me. "Liar."

"It's called pretending." I grinned up at him. "There's a difference."

Instead of smiling back at me, he suddenly frowned. "Have we met?"

Although I didn't like to admit it, I was gratified that he'd felt a flicker of recognition. It was more than a little humbling that I had recognized him immediately, but he had no idea who I was. "No," I lied. What was the point in reminding him? If he remembered me, he'd only have questions about the wedding ring I no longer wore.

Suddenly, Sylvie was kneeling over me. "You meant that."

I sat up. "Prove it."

She thrust a book at me. "You have to read now. I want Uncle Aidan to hear all the voices you do."

Embarrassment threatened to freeze me in place. It was one thing to act out a story for a bunch of kids, even a parent or two, but for

Aidan Lennox? Mr. Sexy Stranger from the bar/worldly music producer/composer/only dates beautiful women/gave up the bachelor life to care for his dying sister and then adopted his sister's kid?

This guy wasn't for real, right?

I jumped spryly to my feet and turned to watch him get all six-plus feet of his large build up off the mat with more grace than a big guy should be able to pull off. He towered over me, making me feel like one of the kids. I wondered how odd we looked standing together.

Aidan took a seat and Sylvie sat on the floor between his legs. The kids looked at me expectantly, so I had to force myself to block him out.

I did this for the kids.

Stranger from the Bar wasn't going to mess up what I had here with them because he was an intimidating hunk of man candy.

At first, I couldn't help but be aware of the masculine gaze focused so intently on me. Despite his earlier amusement, I could feel him studying me, trying to work me out. I understood it, of course. His kid was spending time with me, and he wanted to see what I was all about.

Eventually, however, the joy of acting out the story took over. Every time I'd look up from the page and see Poppy's wide eyes and enthralled expression, or Aaron's unusual stillness that gave away his interest, or Aly's smiling, encouraging face, or Sylvie's admiration, I was pushed on, all inhibitions forgotten at my feet.

Soon, Jan reappeared to tell us time was up. Like always and to my gratification, the kids groaned their displeasure. "I'll be back next week, guys."

Aaron approached me slowly and then stopped, shifting from foot to foot as he looked anywhere but at me. "I won't be here next week."

Please be good news. Please. "Oh?"

"I'm better." He shrugged, finally looking at me. "I'm going home."

Gladness suffused me. "Aaron, I'm going to miss you, kid. But that's the best news ever."

"Aye." He nodded. "Thanks. You know, for ..." He gestured around the room.

He reminded me so much of Roddy in that moment, I had to stop myself from pulling him into a hug. I brushed my fist against his shoulder. "See you around, kid."

Aaron grinned, seeming relieved I wasn't going to get all emotional on him. "Bye."

As soon as he left my side, Sylvie dragged her uncle to me. I smiled at her, even though Aidan made me nervous. Gathering my things, I said, "You heading out?"

"Uncle Aidan said we can have lunch with you in the cafeteria. Please, Nora, please."

My stomach dropped at the thought as she looked at me with such adorable pleading, my chest actually ached. She had that magical ability to turn you to mush. You know, like puppy dogs had.

My eyes flew up to Aidan's, but his expression was neutral. I couldn't make out what he was thinking.

When I looked back at Sylvie, I found I couldn't deny her. "Of course. Let me grab my stuff."

They left to wait outside, and I took the time to gather my things and say goodbye to the kids. I squeezed Poppy's hand as I passed and she rewarded me with the world's sweetest smile.

Aidan and Sylvie were at the nurses' station talking to Jan, but as soon as Sylvie saw me, she impatiently pulled Aidan away. I waved at Jan, and then fell into tense silence beside uncle and niece. The silence, however, was only on mine and Aidan's part. Sylvie filled the hallways with her excited chatter. I knew why I was drawn to Sylvie—she reminded me so much of Mel. She was opinionated but kind, strong and brave, and she'd been through so much, I found I couldn't help but want to protect her. Moreover, as a child she was literal and uncomplicated. She didn't want to pry into my reasons for dressing up like Peter Pan and telling stories. She didn't know about my dead husband, or grill me about moving on with my life. In Sylvie, I found peace from the world outside.

However, I didn't know why Sylvie was so drawn to me. I would've thought it was my storytelling but she seemed more interested in Nora than Peter Pan.

As if to prove my point, she gestured to a restroom up ahead. "Do you want to change your clothes, Nora?"

My lips twitched at her suggestion. "Embarrassed by my cool threads?" I tugged at the ragged hem of my costume.

Sylvie wrinkled her nose. "A little."

"Sylvie," Aidan admonished, but I could tell by the small smirk he wore he thought she was hilarious. Lucky for him, I thought she was too.

"I'll change, Your Highness." I gave her a mock bow that made her laugh.

Inside the restroom, I found my fingers trembling as I undressed and pulled on my skinny jeans and T-shirt. I was all too aware of Aidan. More than that, I was worried he didn't like Sylvie spending time with me. His stare was unnerving and unwavering, as if he were analyzing my every word and movement, trying to work out if I was good enough to be around his niece.

I hated that feeling.

I met them outside, squirming inwardly as Aidan's eyes flickered down my body and back up again. Without meaning to, my hand went to my hair, my fingers rubbing against the short strands at my nape in a self-conscious movement. For the first time since cutting it, I felt a pang of regret.

Jim hadn't been the only one who'd liked my hair.

I liked my hair.

Being short with slender curves and a propensity toward wearing jeans and shorts, my hair had made me feel feminine. I'd loved that I could wear it down, curl it, braid it, throw it up in a messy bun. Anything. It always made me feel pretty.

Huh.

I guess I hadn't really realized that about my hair until right then. Somehow, I thought I'd kept it long for Jim but I hadn't. Not really.

It should've taken me, just me, to realize I didn't like my freaking hair short. Not a guy! Certainly not this guy.

Deciding right there and then I couldn't care less what Aidan Lennox thought about my looks, I threw my shoulders back and walked. They fell into step beside me.

"Uncle Aidan said I can get mac and cheese again if they have it."

Mac and cheese *always* sounded good. I might have had butterflies, but I could eat around them. Maybe carbs would crush the little bastards. "Sounds great."

That was it? That was all I was going to say? Why were words deserting me?

Thankfully, Sylvie continued to chatter as we entered the cafeteria, and as we waited in line for our food. Aidan paid for my lunch and when I thanked him, he waved my words away.

Irritation bubbled under my skin but I let it go. He'd gone from teasing me back at the common room with the kids, to stoic silence and a blank expression I quite frankly wanted to smack off his face.

I liked being able to read people.

"So, Nora. What's your surname?" Aidan said as soon as we took a seat.

"Surely your private investigator can find that out," I cracked.

He smirked. "I'd rather not have to pay him to find out something you can tell me."

Weirdly, I didn't think *he* was joking about having a PI.

"It's O'Brien," I said, even though technically, it was still McAlister.

"Uncle Aidan thought you were brilliant, didn't you, Uncle Aidan?" Sylvie piped up before shoving a huge forkful of macaroni into her mouth.

There was that annoying smirk again. "Very entertaining."

My eyes narrowed, not knowing whether he was being condescending. "Thank you?"

"Where do you work?" he asked abruptly.

"A shop," I said.

He looked unamused by my vagueness. "Aye, would I know it?"

"Probably not." I turned to Sylvie. "The mac and cheese is good, right?"

"Not as good as my mum's but it's okay. Can you make mac and cheese?" Her eyes lit up at the thought.

"It's not my specialty, I'm afraid." I'd learned to cook growing up because I had to, but it wasn't something I'd ever really enjoyed.

"What is your specialty?" Aidan questioned.

He was intimidating me with his interrogative tone but I refused to let him realize that. "I'm killer with a takeaway menu. I can order in five seconds flat."

Reluctant amusement flitted across his expression. "You don't cook. You work in a shop. And you volunteer at a sick kids' hospital. Not a lot to go on there."

Trying to steer the conversation away from me, I replied, "Do you cook?"

"I dabble."

"Uncle Aidan is a great cook," Sylvie said.

Surprise, surprise.

"He learned a lot from traveling, didn't you, Uncle Aidan?"

He gazed down at her fondly, and I realized he hadn't touched a drop of the soup or any of the salad in front of him. To be fair, the salad looked like it had been foraged a month ago. "I did."

Not really wanting to know but needing to keep the conversation off me, I asked, "Where have you traveled?"

"Your neck of the woods. A lot. China, Japan, Australia, New Zealand, Russia, most of mainland Europe, Scandinavia, Israel, Poland, Bulgaria, South Africa ..." I knew that list went on.

I suddenly felt very young, uncultured, and inexperienced, and it prompted me to ask, "What age are you?"

Aidan raised an eyebrow at my somewhat abrupt question. His eyes drifted over my face, seeming to linger on my mouth before moving back up to meet my stare. The blood beneath my cheeks warmed at his perusal. "What age are you?"

Realizing I would have to give him information to receive information, I was honest. "Twenty-two."

He frowned in thought. "Are you sure we haven't met? You remind me of someone."

"I don't think so."

"You haven't told her what age you are." Sylvie stared innocently at her uncle. "Nora told you."

He grinned at her. "Is that how it works?"

"It's only fair."

"She's right," I agreed.

Aidan leaned back in his chair, pushing his uneaten tray aside. "I'm thirty-four."

"He's old," Sylvie teased.

Twelve years older than me. Twelve more years of experience. Of traveling the world.

God, I must appear like some silly, weird kid to him, hanging around hospitals pretending to be Peter Pan.

"Old?" He pressed a hand to his chest like she'd wounded him, reminding me of that moment in the supermarket. How could he not remember me? The air between us had been so charged.

There was tension still between us now. But it was different. Back then, he'd looked at me with curiosity, maybe even a little fascination. Now he was careful with me. Reserved.

Understandable. Because now I was involved in his kid's life. I wasn't just some girl in a supermarket he might have found a little attractive.

"Not that old," Sylvie amended, grinning. She had cheese sauce around her mouth, and I watched as Aidan folded up a napkin and leaned over to gently wipe it. Sylvie took it from him to finish the job. A pang echoed in my chest at the ordinary but sweet gesture. His expression may have been guarded with me, but every time he looked at his niece, he didn't hide the fact that he adored her.

My curiosity about him grew. "Sylvie said you're a music producer?"

He nodded, his countenance changing when he looked at me. It was like he had an emotional portcullis that lifted when he turned to Sylvie and slammed shut when he addressed me. "That's right. That's where the traveling came in. I don't travel as much now." He looked at Sylvie who was sopping up the last of her macaroni with bread. "For obvious reasons."

"What instruments do you play?"

He frowned.

I shifted uncomfortably. "What?"

"Nothing." He shook his head. "That's not what people usually ask."

"Really?" I made a face. "When you tell people you're a music producer, they don't ask if you can play an instrument or two?"

"The first thing most people ask is who I've worked with."

Understanding dawned. "They want to know about the famous people?"

He nodded.

Did that mean he wanted to brag about the famous people? Because that was not an attractive quality in anybody.

"I don't really care," I told him, straight up. "They're merely people with more Instagram followers than most."

"Is that right?"

I wondered if I'd insulted him. "Not to say that they don't deserve their fame ... or that you don't work hard," I scrambled to explain, "I just ... I mean, I'm more impressed with the actual music than the fame ... part. Or ... I'm not explaining it very well."

"You're explaining it fine. I don't care about the fame part, either. I like working with talented people."

"Like David Bowie," Sylvie said.

David Bowie? I think my jaw hit the table. "You know who David Bowie is?"

"Uncle Aidan loves his music."

My head spun as I looked at Aidan like I'd never seen him before. "You worked with David Bowie?"

He grinned at my awe. "No. I've had the pleasure of his company a few times. I met him through his producer. I was a little younger than you, just starting out."

The knowledge that Aidan spent time in the company of not just famous people, but FAMOUS people suddenly sank in. I went from being overwhelmed by the guy to completely intimidated. In my head, I'd known since the moment Sylvie started talking about him that her uncle was older, experienced, worldly. And even back then, over a year ago when we first met, I knew he'd reeked of class and money.

But it was more than that.

He was smart and driven and the most successful individual I'd ever met in real life. He'd gone from this amazing life with these apparently gorgeous women and an astounding career, to changing it so he could look after his dying sister and then look after her kid. He hadn't run from that. This man had made a choice and was sticking with it.

And *I* was dressing up as Peter Pan to entertain kids and bury myself in fantasy so I didn't have to face reality.

I pushed back my chair and the feet squealed against the linoleum. "I just remembered I have somewhere to be. I'm so sorry."

"You haven't finished your lunch," Sylvie said, disappointment ringing in her words.

Even though her sad face pained me, I gave her a small smile as I stood. "I'm sorry, sweetie. I have to go. Thanks for hanging out with me again."

She immediately got out of her chair and threw her arms around my waist. A lump formed in my throat as I hugged her back. For some reason, guilt welled inside me and my eyes unwillingly flew to Aidan.

His expression was grim.

"Thanks for lunch," I said politely.

He barely nodded as Sylvie finally let me go.

I brushed her cheek with the back of my hand, my tenderness for her only increasing by the minute. "I hope I see you again, Sylvie."

She nodded vigorously. "Definitely."

With another affectionate smile her way, and total avoidance of her uncle's gaze, I left.

I needed to.

He made me feel small, and I didn't mean physically. Before meeting him, I was okay with my life choices. And you know what? I was only twenty-two years old! Maybe when I was his age, I'd be worldly and sophisticated too.

For now, however, I wasn't. The two of us couldn't be more different and even if I wanted to let my guard down with him, he'd never understand. So it was up to him. He could let Sylvie come back, or he could decide not to. But I was done being grilled and made to feel insignificant under his intense scrutiny.

chapter 10

I'D LIKE TO SAY SYLVIE AND AIDAN WEREN'T ON MY MIND FOR THE REST of the week but they were. It had been a long time since anyone had judged me. That I knew of. Not since Indiana.

Jim's family and friends had accepted me, and even when they were frustrated with my choices, I never felt like they were appraising me. They were simply concerned.

I felt under a microscope with Aidan.

And it pissed me off!

It lit a fire in me that I wasn't expecting. I couldn't get his cocky, knowing, judgy little smirk out of my mind.

But with it came more guilt because, as angry as Aidan made me feel, as little as his larger-than-life presence made me feel, there was also attraction there. There had been from the moment I'd met him. Before Jim was gone. The kind of attraction I'd never felt for my own husband.

I hated myself for that.

Sylvie wasn't a part of those feelings, however. She was something else. For Sylvie I still worried, and even though it would bring Aidan inevitably back into my life, I didn't want to say goodbye to the kid. I wanted to see her safe and happy and back at school with friends. I wanted to know that she was going to be all right.

That was why then when I walked into the hospital the following week, I was relieved to see Sylvie—but anxious as well because she was accompanied by Aidan. They were standing at the nurses' station, Sylvie with a book in one hand while gripping Aidan's hand with the other. Jan was nowhere in sight, which would account for the young nurse who was leaning across the desk, smiling dreamily up at Aidan while he talked.

I guessed it was hard for her not to.

He wore black jeans, black boots, and a plain black crew-neck T-shirt that was loose at his waist but tight on the biceps. Because they were impressive biceps. I swallowed hard as my steps slowed. How could he make something as simple as jeans and a T-shirt seem expensive?

He looked like a bodyguard on casual Friday.

A bodyguard protectively holding the hand of his little girl.

Heterosexual women who met him were screwed.

Or wishing they would be soon.

I rolled my eyes at the thought, shaking myself out of the Aidan-induced stupor.

It had taken me twenty-two years, but I finally had my first real crush. Oh God. Worst *someone* ever!

Sylvie glanced up from her book and did a double take. "Nora!" she cried happily and let go of Aidan's hand, hurrying toward me. She grinned, holding up the book. It was *Coraline* by Neil Gaiman. I'd told her a few weeks ago that I'd read it around her age and loved it.

"Are you enjoying it?"

"*Yeah*," she said, like it was obvious. "Will you read it to the kids?"

I loved how she continued to not include herself in the category of "the kids."

"I thought today we'd actually start with *Harry Potter*, if that's cool with you?"

"Ooh, I love *Harry Potter*."

"Is there a muggle alive who doesn't?" My focus was drawn from her face upwards as I felt Aidan approach.

He gave me a nod. "Nora."

Goosebumps prickled along the back of my neck at the sound of my name on his lips. Feeling ridiculous about the reaction, I tried to prove to myself I could handle this guy. "Aren't you a little old for storytelling?"

Sylvie giggled while Aidan gave me a droll look. "Attacking my age. How unoriginal of you, Peter Pan."

"Oh, I wasn't attacking your age," I said, walking around him, "I was attacking your maturity level. But hey, who am I to judge? You want to listen to a little *Harry Potter*, that's okay with me."

"I'll have you know, *Harry Potter* appeals to a very broad age range."

Somehow, I doubted he was among them. "That's true." I pressed a hand to the common room door, stopping before I entered to look over my shoulder at Aidan. "But I'd be surprised if it appealed to a man like you."

He stunned me by leaning into me to put his hand above mine on the door. I sucked in a breath at his nearness, his chest so close to my face, I'd only have to move an inch and my lips would meet his T-shirt. His heat and scent overwhelmed me, and my gaze stuttered on its way up to his face.

Smirking smugly down at me, as if he knew how he affected me, he murmured just loud enough for me to hear, "You don't know what appeals to a man like me, Pixie." He pushed the door open before I could respond; I stumbled into the common room like a klutz.

I knew my cheeks were an embarrassing shade of pink.

Thankfully, the kids' warm welcome meant I didn't have to look at Aidan again. As we settled in, and I opened *Harry Potter and the Philosopher's Stone*, I was more than aware of Aidan standing at the wall by the door, his arms crossed over his broad chest making his muscular arms bulge. I was betting that was deliberate.

Exasperating, distracting man.

However, I understood he was here for a reason. Sylvie wanted to see me and hear me tell stories, and he wanted to make her happy. But he didn't trust me. I guess he had no reason to—he didn't know me. Could I fault him for that? Not at all. And if he was going to continue to be around, I was going to continue to crush the insecurities that arose around him and pretend I didn't feel like an unsophisticated country bumpkin.

When the reading was over for the day and I'd chatted a little with the kids, Aidan approached me while Sylvie talked with Poppy. I braced myself for whatever would come out of his mouth next.

And I hated the way I had to crane my neck to look up at him. Jim had been tall but this guy was like a goddamn rugby player.

"Are you an actress or a film student?" he asked as I shrugged on my backpack.

Flattered that he would think I was either, I shook my head. "Neither. Just a shop girl."

"No," he said, his expression thoughtful and intense, "definitely not just a shop girl. You're talented."

Amazed, I didn't know how to respond.

Aidan continued before I could. "You draw people in, make the story come alive. That's hard to do merely standing there, reading a book aloud. I'm begrudgingly impressed."

Begrudgingly?

I scowled up at him but before I could respond, Sylvie interrupted. "Lunch again. Please?"

And as always, it was difficult to say no to her.

Honestly, I didn't want to. I, of course, wanted to spend time with Sylvie. But as much as Aidan flummoxed me, I also unwillingly gravitated toward him. Which made me want to run in the opposite direction. Confusing, I know!

"Sure, sweetheart. Nora and I are going to step outside for a minute to have a private conversation. You stay here."

While my heart raced at whatever was about to be said in this "private conversation," Sylvie frowned up at him. "Why?"

He gave her a stern look. "Well, it wouldn't be private if I told you, now would it?"

"I like her." Her words held a surprisingly hard edge. She

appeared to sense the undercurrent between me and her uncle in that way that adults liked to pretend kids couldn't.

"I know." He cupped her face, giving her a reassuring smile. "We'll only be a second."

I tried to give her a reassuring smile of my own as I followed her uncle into the corridor, but that was hard to do when I suspected I was about to be confronted. Adrenaline shot through me, making my hands shake.

Out in the corridor, I followed Aidan to a quiet corner and looked up at him expectantly.

Expression grim, he folded his arms over his chest and announced, "Sylvie is growing too attached to you."

Confused, I mirrored his body language. "Too attached?"

"It isn't wise."

"I'm not sure I understand." Surely if this was about trust, that would take time. You couldn't automatically trust someone. You had to give them time to earn it. I knew I needed time to earn his trust regarding Sylvie. How could he not see that?

Aidan looked quickly peeved. "Because she's already lost too much. I don't want her attaching herself to something temporary."

"But I'm not going anywhere," I argued.

"Right now, you're not. But you're only twenty-two. How long is this little volunteer phase of yours going to last?" His green eyes were hard. "I don't want Sylvie at this hospital. She should never have been dumped here in the first place."

I realized then that part of his anger was really toward Sylvie's dad, but that didn't mean his words didn't sting.

"Some of these children are seriously ill and she's befriended them," he continued, exasperated. "I don't want her to lose any more than she already has. And, as noble as it is to give your time to these kids, I'd like to know what it is exactly you get out of these visits?"

I wanted to tell him that he didn't need to know why. But he was the parent of a kid I spent time with, so of course he needed to know why.

"It's not about me," I answered, my tone brittle with tension. "If being with me— listening to me telling them a story—gives a child some happiness in a time when they are pretty sorely lacking that emotion, then it's worth any sadness I might feel when I have to say goodbye to them." I gestured to my ridiculous costume. "I don't do this for me. I do it for them." I turned abruptly and strode back toward the common room before my explanation transformed into anger.

If I wouldn't allow Seonaid, my goddamn best friend, to question my motives, I certainly wouldn't stand for being questioned by Mr. Big Shot.

I collected Sylvie, not wanting her to be punished for my argument with her uncle, even if I wanted to run as far away from him as possible. Instead, I sat in the cafeteria with them both, refusing to look at him, and engaging Sylvie in constant conversation.

The whole time, I felt his eyes on me. I hated it.

Because once again, he made me feel small.

And this time it *was* his fault.

chapter 11

THE KIDS LOOKED UP AT ME EXPECTANTLY AS I LOOKED BACK AT THEM with a hollow feeling in my chest. I'd dreaded this moment. For the past week, I'd talked myself into believing this moment wouldn't happen. Yet here I was, back at the hospital dressed as Peter Pan, and there was a face missing in the small crowd.

Sylvie.

Acute disappointment held me frozen in place as I tried to think of what I could've said or done to reassure Aidan instead of pissing him off. My only hope was that Sylvie had been enrolled back at school and that was why she wasn't here.

"Peter?" Aly asked expectantly.

Her voice drew me out of my stupor, and for the first time, I noted Aly was tucked under a blanket on a chair. Only last week, she'd been sitting on the floor with the other kids, well enough to move around on her own.

Aly's leukemia was worsening.

I shook myself, suddenly annoyed. Sylvie had been through hell and back, but she was healthy and safe, which was more than I could say for the kids I'd come here to entertain. For whatever reason, I'd let myself get too attached to Sylvie Lennox. It was time to let go.

I grinned at Aly, like I didn't see how sick she was because she really didn't need the reminder. "Are we all ready for more *Harry Potter*?"

Before they could respond, the doors to the common room swung open, and my breath caught as Aidan Lennox's gaze locked on mine.

"Don't start without me!" Sylvie rushed into the room from under the arm he had bracing the door open.

Relief flooded me as she grinned excitedly and then flopped down on the floor at my feet. She rolled her wrist, mimicking the royal wave, and said cheekily, "You may continue."

Trying to suppress my laughter, I placed my left foot behind my right and bent my knee, lowering into a graceful bow. "Your Highness."

Sylvie giggled and cupped a hand around her mouth to whisper, "You're doing it like a girl."

I cupped my hand around my mouth and whispered back, "I think they know I'm a girl."

"Well, now they do."

Lips pinched together to stop my laughter, I glanced up at the door to find Aidan watching us carefully. I let my gratitude shine out of my eyes and his expression softened. He acknowledged my silent thank you with a nod, and then he closed the door, leaving me alone with the children.

Offering me his trust.

———

I DON'T KNOW WHAT AIDAN DID WITH HIS TIME WHILE I ENTERTAINED the kids, I only know that when Sylvie grabbed my hand and led me out of the common room, Aidan was striding down the hall toward us, his phone to his ear. He zeroed in on us and I heard him say, "Like I said, if he wants to do this, he needs to come to me … Just tell him. Look, I have to go. We'll speak later."

His features were strained as he stopped before us and slipped his phone into his pocket. Concern for him prompted me to ask, "Everything okay?"

He studied me, so intently I swear my breath caught in my throat.

"Aye, thanks." He looked down at Sylvie. "Did you have fun?"

"Yup! We've nearly finished the first book. Can I have mac and cheese now?"

Aidan sighed, amused. "You're going to turn into one giant plate of macaroni." He looked at me. "That's all she ever wants me to cook."

"I can see the attraction," I said, smiling up at him. Then I saw the speculative look in his eyes and realized what I'd said. I flushed. "I meant the appeal. I can see the appeal. Of mac and cheese."

And just like that, I think my knickers melted under extreme heat because Aidan Lennox's rugged features relaxed into the sexiest goddamn smile I'd ever seen in my life.

No person could possibly be safe from that smile.

"Would you like some?"

My pulse skyrocketed at the deep rumble of his words, and the words themselves.

Uh.

Yes, please.

Wait. What? Was he flirting with me. "What?"

Aidan's grin grew. "Some mac and cheese. Would you like some? For lunch?"

Oh God. Open up the floor and let it swallow me whole! I blushed. "Uh, sure."

"Why has your face gone red?" Sylvie asked as we began to walk toward the cafeteria.

I flushed even harder. Aidan chuckled. "My face hasn't gone red."

"Pink, then," Sylvie amended.

"It's hot in here."

"It's not that hot."

"Kid," I said, laughing through my pain. "I'm not pink, red, or any shade in between. I am perfectly normal."

Sylvie's eyebrows pinched together. "You dress up like a storybook character every week. I don't know if that's normal."

Aidan burst out laughing and I scowled at him. That only made him laugh harder. "She's got you there," he said, his words gravelly with amusement.

I looked down at Sylvie, clearly delighted that she'd made her uncle laugh. I mock glowered at her. "You, Sylvie Lennox, are way too smart for your age."

"Good," Aidan replied for her. "She makes up for all the idiots who are way too dumb for their age."

Unsure if that was a personal dig, I raised an eyebrow. "And am I one of those idiots?"

"No." Aidan opened the door to the cafeteria and gestured for us to go in before him. Sylvie hurried through first, and as I moved to follow her, my eyes were drawn up to her uncle like iron to a magnetic field. "You're something else entirely, Pixie."

Our eyes locked and I stalled. "Pixie?"

"Aye. There's something …" He shook his head and then dropped his free hand to my waist to nudge me forward.

I didn't move. I tensed at his touch, afraid I'd either melt back into his arm or forward into his chest. It was astonishing to me that someone who was practically a stranger could affect me so much. "There's something?"

"Nothing," he replied gruffly, forcing me to move as he guided us both into the cafeteria after Sylvie. "You just remind me of a pixie in that daft outfit."

I glanced down, realizing I'd forgotten to change out of my costume, and when I looked back up to follow Aidan and Sylvie to the food counter, I was aware of people regarding my outfit with curious looks.

"You know, we don't have to eat hospital food," Aidan said to Sylvie as I approached. "We could invite Nora to eat lunch with us anywhere."

"I like the mac and cheese here," Sylvie replied, eyeing it hungrily. I wondered where she packed it all away in that tiny body of hers. "So does Nora."

I let her speak for me because I wasn't sure I was ready to venture out into the real world with Aidan. In here we were in our weird little bubble; I felt protected by that bubble. If we stepped outside, all the differences between us would only be amplified. In here, we were just two people who cared for Sylvie and I could get past my insecurities around him.

Before he could beat me to it, I paid for our lunches.

"You didn't have to do that," he said as we followed Sylvie to an empty table.

"You paid last time."

"I can afford to."

At his blunt reply, I answered, irritated, "I can afford to buy you lunch, Aidan."

He studied me in that intense way again, making me squirm as I took the seat across from him. "Independently wealthy?"

I glowered at his sarcasm. "Yes. I'm a princess from a far-off land, disguised as a nobody so I can live my life in freedom from the restraints of life as a monarch."

Sylvie stared at me wide-eyed.

Aidan scoffed. "Do you ever stop telling stories?"

"That would be cool, though," Sylvie said wistfully. "I wish I was a princess."

"You are a princess," Aidan said matter-of-factly, like it was stupid of anyone to think otherwise. Sylvie beamed from ear to ear and then dove into her macaroni.

He made her so happy.

Lit up her entire world.

His gaze flicked from her to me and he tensed. Whatever he saw in my expression seemed to catch him by the back of the neck and hold him frozen, unable to look away from me.

A current rippled in the air between us, and a shiver caressed the back of my neck, tickling down my spine, around my back, and across my breasts. I sucked in a breath, feeling my nipples harden.

So inappropriate!

I flushed, looking down at my plate, mortified.

Realizing there was not only silence from Aidan but from Sylvie,

I chanced a look at her and found her glancing from me to her uncle, her little brow creased in confusion.

Aidan cleared his throat. "So, Nora, any chance you're going to tell us anything real about yourself anytime soon?"

Glad to think of anything but my attraction to him, I pondered his question. "Um ... I like macaroni and cheese."

Sylvie huffed. "We already knew that."

"I'm from the US."

"And that!"

"Okay, okay." I tapped my chin, pretending to think. "I know. I'm twenty-two."

She shook her head at me. "And that, silly."

"I know something about you," Aidan suddenly said.

"And what's that?"

"You don't know when to stop pretending."

His words were like a punch to the gut. "That's not true," I whispered.

Seeming confused by my reaction, Aidan leaned across the table. "I never meant anything by it, Pixie. I was only kidding."

Mortified, I gave him a sharp nod, and studied my food. The silence around the table made me feel guilty. "I love Shakespeare."

"Shakespeare?" Aidan said.

I looked up at him. "Shakespeare."

"What's Shakespeare?" Sylvie asked.

"Not a what, a *he*. He wrote plays," Aidan supplied, his eyes not leaving mine. "A little too old for you, sweetheart. You'll learn Shakespeare when you're a teenager."

"Why do I have to wait?"

"Because he deals with stuff that's a little too grown up for you."

She seemed to accept this and returned to her mac and cheese.

"So," Aidan turned his attention back to me, "the comedies or the tragedies?"

"Both."

"Favorite?"

I couldn't understand why he appeared so genuinely interested in my answer but I did know it made me want to tell him. "Comedy: *Twelfth Night*. Tragedy: a toss-up between *Hamlet, King Lear* and *Othello*. I can't choose."

"So the tragedies are really your favorite, then," he said.

Thinking about it, I guessed they were. I shrugged.

"Have you ever starred in a production?"

The question ripped open a longing, a dream, making me inwardly wince. I shook my head, looking down at my uneaten plate.

"Nora?"

"So, who else have you worked with?" I asked, trying to sound nonchalant.

Aidan didn't hide his irritation or the disappointment in his expression. "Nora—"

"He doesn't like to talk about it," Sylvie piped up.

I frowned at her. "You told me about Bowie."

"But he didn't really work with him."

This kid. I grinned at her. "That's true." My eyes flicked to Aidan, studying me again like I was under a microscope. My smile fell.

And just like that, so did the uncomfortable silence.

————

IT HAD BEEN CLEAR THAT AIDAN WAS ANNOYED WITH ME FOR AVOIDING his questions. I'd given him something of myself and then immediately shut down again. I wasn't stupid—I could see how that was annoying. But I was almost afraid of what I would say if I kept talking. It had been hard for me to trust Jim enough to give him what he had of me, and I guess it wasn't hard to deduce that my lack of trust in men came from the situation with my dad. I feared having my heart broken again. And somehow, instinctually, I just knew that giving Aidan even a little of me and having him reject it would hurt more than any other man's rejection.

Thankfully, Sylvie was there to pick up the slack and she kept us entertained during lunch. I didn't run away this time, even though I wanted to. We finished eating and I walked them out of the hospital. Aidan offered to drive me home but I insisted I liked to walk, not wanting him to see where I lived.

We parted ways, and as I watched them drive away in his black Range Rover, I felt more than a pang of regret. I'd been rude to Aidan. If he would stop peppering me with personal questions, I wouldn't have to be rude. But the damn guy seemed intent on figuring me out.

A few days later I was at Apple Butter working—eyeing a preppy ivory cardigan with a little gold bicycle stitched above the left breast, wondering if Leah would let me pay for it over time—when the door opened and I turned to find Roddy stepping into the store. He wore a gray T-shirt covered in dust and grime, jeans that were in much the same condition, and construction boots on his feet. He'd obviously come from work.

I put the cardigan back and hurried over to him, my pulse starting to race. Roddy would only be here if there was bad news. "What is it? What's wrong?"

He frowned at me. "Nothin'. It's lunchtime. Thought ye could get off now so we can grab lunch together. Ye ken, now that ye'er no avoidin' me."

Although I blushed at being called out on it, I was too relieved that nothing was wrong to care about his dig. I played it off, rolling my eyes. "Wait here."

Glancing around the store at all the pretty, feminine clothes, Roddy replied dryly, "Aye, like am gonnae venture any further in."

Chuckling, I hurried through the archway that led to the small accessories department to find Leah on her knees, reorganizing a jewelry stand. "Leah, can I take my lunch early?"

"With the man with the very deep voice?" She peered up at me, a curious smile on her face.

"He's just a friend."

She leaned back on her heels to see past me, disappointment dimming her expression when she didn't catch sight of him. "Is he as hot as his voice?"

"Far sexier than that," Roddy's voice rumbled through to us, making me snort.

Leah laughed. "Ooh, I like him."

"You're practically engaged," I reminded her.

She pouted in response and then waved her hand at me. "Shoo, then. Go have your lunch break with the man with the delicious voice."

After thanking her, I grabbed my purse from the back and ushered Roddy outside before my boss decided to come and check him out.

"So, this is a surprise," I said as we strode up Cockburn Street.

"We're workin' on flat renovations off the Mile," he explained.

After deciding to grab something as close by as possible, we found a table at the Royal Mile Tavern for some pub grub. Our talk was small as we ordered food and waited, and there was silence when our fish and chips arrived because Roddy never spoke until he'd had a few big bites of food. Once he got the "I'm no longer a hungry caveman" look on his face, I said, "So, are you still dating your barmaid?"

Roddy smirked. "Her name is Petra."

"Petra? Where is she from?"

"She's Croatian."

"Huh. Seonaid never mentioned that."

He grinned at his food. "Seonaid wouldnae."

I sometimes wondered if he dated a certain type of woman simply to piss Seonaid off. "Is it serious?"

"When is it ever?"

"Don't you want it to be? Eventually?"

Roddy sighed heavily, and I knew the conversation was making him uncomfortable. Roddy did not do feelings. "One day, maybe."

"Does Petra know it isn't serious? Because Seonaid thinks she's angling for it to be."

This time he huffed, throwing me a drop-it look. "Aye, she kens."

Thinking of my predicament with Aidan, I wondered if maybe Roddy might be able to help me out. "So, how do you avoid telling her anything personal without coming off rude and pushing her away completely?"

His response was a stony expression.

I smirked. "I'm actually looking for some advice."

"About fuck buddies?" His eyebrows nearly hit his hairline.

I flushed, mortified that Jim's best friend would think I'd come to him for advice about having sex with a new guy. "No. God, no!"

"Why the 'God, no!'? It's okay if ye want tae move on, Nora."

Even though he appeared to genuinely mean it, I ignored the comment. "No, it's not that. It's just there's this kid at the hospital and I've grown fond of her, but her guardian—her uncle—he's pestering me with all these questions about myself. I get it, because I'm spending time with the kid once a week, but I'm not comfortable divulging information about myself to this person. We have lunch after my time with the kids, and he interrogates me. I'm trying to avoid it but I'm coming off totally rude. I thought maybe you might have some advice on how I can be vague without making him want to stop Sylvie—his niece—from spending time with me."

He studied me thoughtfully. "What age is he? The guardian?"

"Thirty-four. Why?" A knowing glint entered his eyes and I shook my head. "It's not like that." Even to my own ears, it sounded like a lie. But it wasn't. Aidan Lennox was not attracted to me like I was attracted to him.

Roddy's gaze drifted over my face. "He tryin' tae spend time wi' ye?"

"His kid is, so he is."

"He doesnae have tae, though."

"She lost her mom. His sister. He's protective."

"Aye. But anyone can dae a wee bit diggin' tae get pertinent information about the person spendin' time wi' their kid. He doesnae need tae have lunch wi' ye and ask ye."

Roddy had it all wrong. "It's not like that."

"Nora," he seemed aggravated, "it's you, so I'd be surprised if it wisnae like that. Ye want tae ken why Petra kens it isnae serious wi' us? First, I told her if she wanted in ma bed, it wis temporary. And from that point on, I never ask her any questions about herself other than 'Did ye have a gid day at work?' 'Dae ye want a drink?' and 'Dae ye want me tae fuck ye harder?'"

I scowled at his bluntness. "You're a real prince, Roddy."

"Whit I'm sayin' is, a guy doesnae ask a woman about herself unless he really wants tae ken. And he usually only really wants tae ken because he also wants tae ken what she sounds like when she comes."

This was Roddy unfiltered, without Jim there to smack him across the head for talking like that in front of me. Weirdly, it was nice that Roddy could be his wonderful, uncouth self around me, and it be okay. That we could be truly comfortable with each other.

I immediately felt guilty for enjoying it.

Roddy misunderstood my expression. "Ye'er allowed tae want that, Nora. Tae move on. There's nothin' wrong wi' lettin' this guy get tae ken ye. Answer his fuckin' questions if ye want tae."

"It's not like that," I insisted. "Aidan is older, cultured, experienced. I think he looks at me as this strange kid he's worried *his* kid is spending time with."

My friend's gaze dropped to my chest in an undecidedly friendly way before moving back up to my face. "He doesnae see ye as a kid."

"How do you know?" I huffed at his arrogance.

"Because I'm a man. I ken these things."

Exasperated, I shook my head. Coming to Roddy for advice was a bad idea. His blunt honesty and male perspective had only confused me.

I changed the subject. "Seonaid is dating someone new. Zach. He's your age."

He stared determinedly at his food, although he couldn't hide the flex of his jaw muscle as he ground his teeth. After a few seconds, he gritted out, "Another *nice* guy?"

"No, I think she's taking a break from nice guys. Zach is for sex. Lots of stamina, that one." I smiled to myself as I watched his fingers curl tightly around his fork and knife. Maybe it was mean of me, but

Roddy Livingston was the most straightforward guy I'd ever met. There was absolutely no excuse for him not to tell Seonaid how he felt about her. If he didn't want other guys sleeping in her bed, then he needed to man up and do something about it.

Suddenly, I was staring straight into Roddy's angry eyes.

Guilt punched out my smugness. "Roddy—"

"I ken what ye'er doin'," he seethed. "So let's make a deal right here and now. I won't push ye tae move on fae Jim, and ye won't push me aboot Seonaid, and that means no rubbin' who she's fuckin' in ma face. I get enough o' that fae her."

I didn't want to agree to that. I wanted to know why he felt like he couldn't tell her how he felt. Couldn't he see that there was possibility there? Didn't he see how jealous she got of Petra and the women who had come before her?

Yet, I couldn't prod at the subject because that would give him license to prod at my relationship with Jim and all my hang-ups because of it.

I nodded, apology in my eyes, and watched him relax.

"So," he said after a minute of silence, "Angie wants us aw tae have Sunday lunch together soon. Ye up for it?"

I couldn't go on avoiding Angie forever. It wasn't fair to her. At least this way, I'd have Seonaid and Roddy there as buffers between me and her rose-tinted view of my relationship with her son.

"Sure. Sounds good."

chapter 12

I WAS IN THE MIDDLE OF MAKING THE KIDS LAUGH AS I READ THE FIRST chapters of the second *Harry Potter* book when the common room door creaked open and Aidan appeared, throwing me an apologetic look. My pulse skittered at the sight of him, but I continued to read on, even as he got in Sylvie's eye line and gestured for her to come to him. She did so reluctantly, and then I heard her say, "But I want to stay."

That stopped me. I lowered my book. "Everything okay?" I called over to them.

Aidan straightened from being on his haunches, his hand on Sylvie's shoulder. "Sylvie's dad is on his way. He's got the rest of the day off and wants to spend time with her."

"Oh." Disappointed I wouldn't have my lunch with her, I nodded. "Well, of course."

"But I want to stay," Sylvie said, looking as disappointed as I felt.

I walked over to her and gave her a reassuring smile. "I bet your dad has a great day planned for you. And we'll see each other soon."

"Can't I stay until the end?"

I looked up at Aidan and if I wasn't mistaken, he was annoyed. Not at me but at Sylvie's dad. He shook his head.

"I think your dad is on his way right now, sweetie."

Her lip trembled and I thought my stoic little Sylvie might cry. However, she shook it off in a gesture that was so adult, it was unsettling. As though she were used to shaking off sad things and moving on quickly. "Okay. Next week?"

Again, I looked to Aidan for confirmation. He nodded and I smiled down at her. "Next week."

She hugged me and then took her uncle's hand. "Bye," I said to him too. He gave me a frustrating nod of acknowledgment, and nothing more.

I bit my lip at the feeling of deflation that came over me when they left. Even though I knew better, I'd let Roddy's opinion get to me. I'd started to think maybe he was right and Aidan had other reasons for wanting to get to know me. Maybe the sexual tension wasn't all one-sided.

However, the fact that he could walk away from the few hours we spent together every week without seeming disappointed at all knocked me back down to earth.

I longed for Sylvie and Aidan like they were something I was addicted to.

Sylvie seemed to feel the same.

Aidan, however, probably really did see me as the slightly nutty young woman his kid had developed a surprising attachment to.

With them gone, I tried to get my head back in the game. I threw all my energy into acting out the book in my hand. I was good at pretending, so none of the kids were aware of my sadness as they laughed, gasped, and leaned in close to hear more about Harry and his friends.

After Jan came in to wrap up our time together, I said goodbye to everyone and got permission from Jan to use Aly's bathroom to change in. Aly had her own private room, one that she was in more and more the sicker she got. I didn't know how much longer she'd be attending my readings. That sweet kid was going to get worse before she got better.

I changed in her bathroom before Jan brought her back in, and then said goodbye to the nurses. The city had emptied of festival-goers, and I was contemplating buying a smoothie from the nearby

Meadowlark Café when the sight of Aidan standing outside the hospital drew me to a stop.

He was on the phone and hadn't seen me approach yet. What was he still doing here? Where was Sylvie?

I'm not going to lie—I thought about hurrying by him before he noticed me. I was unnerved by the way my heart galloped away from me anytime he was in the vicinity.

But he looked up, our eyes locked, and the whole world stood still. All I could hear was the rushing of blood in my ears.

And then Aidan telling whoever was on the phone that he had to go. He slipped his phone into his back pocket and walked over to me, stopping inside my personal space. I had to tilt my head to maintain eye contact.

"What are you still doing here? Did Sylvie's dad come get her?"

Aidan nodded. "Aye. Thought I'd wait for you, though. See if you wanted to grab lunch."

Shocked, I could only stare at him in reply. And then Roddy's voice was in my head, telling me that Aidan was clearly interested in me. I couldn't understand why someone older, sophisticated, gorgeous, and successful would be interested in me. And yes, I knew that didn't say much for my self-esteem, but it was how I felt.

Before meeting him, I felt like I'd lived more years than I had. I was weary and tired and life had felt too much like a fight.

Then Aidan came along and he made me feel like I hadn't seen anything of the world at all.

We were very different people, and I had no doubt wanting him was a bad idea ... but my heart was racing, my skin was tingling, and there was a flurry of excitement in my belly. I felt alive. Awake. For the first time in forever, I felt anticipation fizzing inside of me and I didn't want to lose that feeling yet.

"That sounds good."

I wasn't sure but I thought I saw relief flicker in his expression. But then it was gone and I only saw tension. "Are you sure you're okay? Is it Sylvie's dad?"

"This way," he said instead, and I followed him to his SUV.

He opened the passenger door for me, something no guy had done for …well, ever … and I stood a little stunned by the gentlemanly action and how much I liked it.

"Nora?"

I looked up into his questioning eyes and hid my reaction with a smirk. "Just wondering if it's smart of me to get into a car alone with a strange, older man."

Aidan fought a smile. "You had to get that 'older' comment in again, didn't you?"

Laughing, I stepped into the SUV, and he closed the door gently behind me. The car was spacious and luxurious inside. I'd never been in a Range Rover before and marveled at the comfort and style. It smelled of new leather too.

So, this was how the other half lived.

The driver's door opened and unlike tiny me, Aidan slid into his seat. His seat was pushed way back to allow room for his long legs. Once he was clipped in, he put the car into drive and my eyes locked on his hands as they relaxed against the steering wheel. Like the rest of him, his hands were big, but they were definitely musician's hands. Long-fingered, big-knuckled, but elegant somehow. A deep flip low in my belly made me squirm in embarrassment.

How could a guy's hands turn me on so much?

"Cal is trying to spend more time with Sylvie."

Jolted out of my sexual meanderings, I focused on his words because they were important. "Do you think that's a bad thing?"

"No." But his grip tightened momentarily on the steering wheel. "No."

"Something about it is bothering you."

We stopped at a red light, and Aidan looked at me. "I want stability for her. I worry that change right now could hurt her."

"Change, how?"

"Seeing her dad more. Right now, he gets her two days every second week. But lately he's been calling whenever he's free and asking to see her."

I wasn't sure it was a bad thing that her dad was getting his head out of his ass and making an effort to see his kid, but I understood where Aidan was coming from. It was only a year ago that she'd lost her mom. "Maybe you guys should talk about it."

"Aye, maybe."

Silence fell over the car and I could tell he was lost in his thoughts about it. Wanting to leave him to muse, I watched traffic. And then I realized we were driving out of the city center. "So ... where are we eating?"

"There's a pub right on the promenade at Portobello Beach. It's a nice day. I thought we should enjoy it while it's here."

That was something people said a lot around here. Scottish summers were mercurial beasts, with more rain than anything else. So when the sun came out, we appreciated and made the most of it.

"Sounds good."

With Jim, I'd been comfortable with him from the start. Silence fell between us and I'd never felt the need to fill it. Similarly, with Aidan, the silence between us didn't bother me. But the atmosphere between us wasn't comfortable. I was too aware of his every movement, watching him out of the corner of my eye as he drove us east to Portobello.

"Sylvie cares about you," Aidan said suddenly.

Warmth filled me at the thought. "I care about her. I won't hurt her, Aidan."

He glanced at me, his expression sincere. "I know that now, Nora."

Relief moved through me. "Thank you."

"I just want her to be okay."

"It would be expected if she wasn't," I told him. "She lost her mom. You can protect her from everything, but you can't protect her from that loss, and thinking that you can is only going to make you feel like you've failed somehow. And you're not failing."

He was quiet so long, I thought maybe my presumption had pissed him off. But he said, "How did you get so wise?"

When it comes to loss, I know what I'm talking about. I didn't say it out loud. "Born that way, I guess."

Not too long later, Aidan parked on a street facing the water. The sun glinted off the waves in the distance and I could see the promenade was busy with people eating lunch, walking their dogs, or just hanging out. The salty sea air immediately put me and everyone else in a good mood. It was a little past one o'clock so people were on lunch breaks, but with how busy the beach was, you'd think it was a weekend day.

"Do you think we'll get a table?" I said. He insisted on opening my door and taking my hand to help me down.

Warm, calloused skin slid over mine and I drew in a breath at the sparks of electricity that danced up my arm. My eyes flew to his. Our eyes locked.

Did he feel it too?

As if I'd asked the question aloud, he squeezed my hand and closed the door once I was out of the car. To my shock, he kept holding my hand, leading me down the street toward the promenade.

"I called ahead," he said. "I know a guy who works at the pub."

I hurried to match his long strides, my heart banging hard inside my chest as I stared up at him. Feeling my gaze, he looked down and gave me a quizzical smile.

"What is it, Pixie?"

I decided to be honest. "You're holding my hand."

His smile transformed into that sexy one that cut me off at the knees every single time. "So I am."

He didn't let go.

I bit my lip to stop the girlish giggle that wanted to escape. "Is there a reason for that?"

"So you don't fly off to Neverland, of course." He winked.

I laughed. "Cute. Very cute."

Aidan stopped to push open the door to the pub, his beautiful eyes filled with laughter.

I let him lead me inside. There was an area, a few steps up from the bar on our right, with tables at bay windows overlooking the water. The place was packed, no tables free at all.

"Uh ..." A young woman with bright blue eyes and short, white-blond hair glanced at the seating and then back at us. "It's about a thirty-minute wait right now."

"Where's Giggsy?" Aidan asked.

"Right here, mate." We turned to watch a guy walking down a passageway by the bar. When he reached us, his eyes flicked to Aidan's hand in mine and he shook his head laughing. "They get younger every time."

"Fuck off, Giggsy."

"Nice. And here I've been enduring bleeding ears from these buggers," he thumbed behind him at the bar staff, "to reserve you a table last minute on the promenade." Without saying another word, he strolled away and Aidan followed. He led us up the platform to a set of French doors that opened out onto the promenade, and to my delight, to one of only four tables set out there, looking over the water.

A sweet breeze blew up off the North Sea offering a light relief from the rare hot September sun. Gulls cried out as they flew high in the sky above us.

"There you go." Giggsy gestured to our table and Aidan held out a chair for me. "What a gentleman." His friend clapped him on the shoulder. Aidan rolled his eyes and Giggsy mock frowned at me. "Please tell me you're legal."

While I was mortified by the idea that I looked *that* young next to him, Aidan sighed heavily. "Have you got a death wish?"

"I can't help myself. They get hotter and younger while mine get older and nag a lot. How do you do it?"

My irritation with this man grew by the second, not only because he kept referring to Aidan's love interests like they were products on a conveyer belt, but because he was talking about me without even looking at me. Like I didn't matter. *Sexist ... Grrr!*

Giggsy grinned down at me. "Can I get you a drink, sweetheart?"

"Water, please. Although if I wanted to, I could have a beer. For nearly five years."

"American?" He turned to Aidan again. "Very nice. A different state from the last one, I imagine. Are you collecting states now? You're my hero, mate."

"Oi!" I snapped my fingers, drawing his attention back to me. "I'm not Aidan's latest piece, so stop categorizing me as one, and stop talking about me like it doesn't matter I can hear you. It's disrespectful. Didn't your momma teach you manners?"

I have no idea where the angry outburst came from. Maybe I wanted Aidan to know I wasn't some bimbo to decorate his arm, in case that's where his own thoughts were going.

Giggsy looked a little shell-shocked. He murmured to Aidan he'd get his usual and be back to take our order. I looked determinedly out at the water, unable to meet Aidan's eyes.

"I'm sorry about Giggsy."

I watched a couple walk hand in hand down the beach, each carrying their shoes in their free hands. "Don't worry about it."

"Nora, look at me."

I did so reluctantly.

He appeared concerned. "I didn't ask you out to lunch as a lead-up to sex. You're definitely not my *latest piece*. I wanted to spend some time with you."

Confused, I could only stare at him, hoping somehow to magically figure him out. If he didn't want me to be a fuck buddy, but he wanted to hold hands and spend time together ... well ... shit. What did that mean?

Then something occurred to me.

And I didn't know how I could've been so blind.

Maybe ... maybe Aidan was lonely. "How are you?" I suddenly blurted. "We've talked a little about Sylvie and how she is after her mom passed, but we haven't talked about you. Are *you* okay, Aidan?"

I could tell he was surprised by the question. He stared at me, almost as if he couldn't believe I was real. I didn't understand his reaction but I couldn't ask about it because Giggsy came back with our drinks and to take our order.

It was too hot for a heavy lunch so I ordered light, as did Aidan, and I waited after Giggsy left to see if he would answer me.

Finally, he did. "You want the truth, Nora? Something I've never told anybody? I resented it. Nicky, my sister, being sick. Dying. Expecting me to take care of Sylvie. I'm a selfish bastard who actually resented her for it. I had no fucking clue what was ahead of all of us or what she'd go through in the end. I couldn't see any of that for my own selfish inability to see past my fucking career."

What he didn't know was that I understood that resentment. "But you did see past it eventually."

As if my lack of judgment took him aback, Aidan studied me thoughtfully. When he spoke, his voice was low and gravelly with emotion. "Our parents are not strong people. They could never handle the bad stuff. They hated that Nicky was a single parent, and once they moved down south, they made very little effort to come see Sylvie. They weren't strong enough to be there for my sister. They only came at the end. After I watched cancer eat my sister alive. I watched her stay strong and brave and selfless to the end, caring only about me and Sylvie and what was to become of us. Those months changed everything."

"How long was she sick?"

"About four months." He gave me his profile, looking out at the water, and I saw the pain he kept hidden most of the time. "It was the end of January last year. She called me while I was in New York and asked me to come home. She wouldn't tell me why but I knew that it had to be bad for her to ask me. When I got home, she told me while we were alone. That she had cervical cancer." His eyes flew back to mine, blazing with anger and grief. "Nicky was a bloody nurse. She *knew*, Nora. She knew and she was so paralyzed by fear she couldn't face it until it was too late. She could have lived. She could have survived. But she left it too bloody late."

I reached across the table and grabbed his hand. "I'm so sorry."

He squeezed it. "We told Sylvie together," he continued. "You know how smart she is. She understood. I ..." He swallowed hard, clearly lost in the memory. "I couldn't stand it. I had to leave the room. Listening to her wail like a wounded—" He cut off, letting go of my hand to take a huge gulp of water.

Pain for him squeezed my chest tight.

"Everything stopped. Life as you know, it just stops. I moved in with them, got a full-time nurse, and I hired Olive Robertson to homeschool Sylvie so she could spend as much time with her mum as possible without missing out on school.

"Aye … I stopped resenting Nicky as I watched her die, but you know what's worse, Pixie?"

I blinked back tears at the hollow emptiness in his voice, wondering how I could not have noticed how much pain this man was hiding. "What was worse?"

"I wanted her to die. Because anticipating her leaving was fucking agony. I just wanted her to die." He shook his head, as if ashamed of himself. "Now that she's gone, I can't believe I ever thought that every single goddamn day she had to spend with us, with Sylvie, wasn't a miracle. And I hate myself for wishing those days away."

I was overwhelmed.

It pressed down on my chest, making it hard for me to breathe.

Because I felt like I understood this man more than anyone ever could, and all I wanted to do was wrap my arms around him tight and whisper in his ear he wasn't alone. My heart had been broken before, and right there on the promenade, it broke again. Because I knew that this man and the little girl he loved so much were going to use me up and leave me in pieces.

And I didn't know if I could let them. They could be my repentance, I could let them selflessly take what they needed and leave me shattered, and maybe in some twisted way, I'd find peace. Yet I still had some measure of self-preservation left that made me want to run away. Because people could disappoint you, and sometimes that was okay, but sometimes, like with my dad, it wrecked you so badly it changed you irrevocably. I'd made so many mistakes because of that, and I was afraid that when Aidan inevitably disappointed me, I'd lose what little of myself I still respected.

Aidan's eyes narrowed on me and he said, "I haven't told anyone that."

"Why are you telling *me*?"

"Because I'm being haunted, Nora, and I sense you know all about being haunted."

Horrified that he could see that, I shook my head. "You don't know anything about me."

"Your name is Nora Rose O'Brien McAlister. You were born November 12, 1992, in Donovan, Indiana. You lived there until you were eighteen years old when you eloped with Jim McAlister to Vegas, and then returned with him to Edinburgh. You were married three years before he died of a brain aneurysm. You work at Apple Butter on Cockburn Street and you live alone in Sighthill." He paused as I tried to recover from the shock of him having all that information about me. "I remember you, Pixie. I remember locking eyes with a pretty girl in a pub one day and then lifting her off the floor after her husband got into a fight with a drunk over her. And I remember seeing you again the next day in the supermarket, knowing you were too young and too married, and wanting you anyway. And maybe if it had been six months earlier, I would have been a selfish bastard and tried to seduce you, damn the consequences. But my sister was in a flat above the supermarket, dying, and I'd promised her and my niece I'd make pancakes with syrup."

A tear splashed down my cheek before I could stop it. I brushed it away quickly, impatiently.

"I'm not the kind of man who would allow his ten-year-old kid to spend so much time with a woman and not have her investigated, Pixie. So don't take it personally."

When I didn't say anything—I couldn't speak for fear I'd burst into tears—Aidan continued, his words no longer fingernails picking at my wounded memories, but a knife, slicing them clean open.

"I know your secret, Nora. I know that you really become Peter Pan for yourself, not for the kids. What I can't understand is why an obviously talented, smart, twenty-two-year-old with her whole life ahead of her would volunteer on her day off at a sick children's hospital ... because she *needs* to. Because you do need to, Nora. I see it. Is this more than your husband dying too young? Or did you love him that much you can't see that life still goes on? Whatever it is, like me, you're haunted. And I can't help but need to know ... what the hell happened to *you*?"

Roddy's voice suddenly appeared in my mind. *There's nothin' wrong wi' lettin' this guy get tae ken ye. Answer his fuckin' questions if ye want tae.*

Except I wasn't sure I wanted to. I wasn't ready. Telling him meant finally facing all that guilt I kept buried beneath my costume.

"I'm sorry." I pushed back from the table, nearly overturning my chair. "I have to go."

I left him there.

Alone.

After he'd given me so much of himself.

And I'd never liked myself less.

chapter 13

I SHOULDN'T HAVE BEEN SURPRISED WHEN AIDAN DIDN'T STICK AROUND the next week. He barely looked at me when he picked up Sylvie from the hospital. She'd already told me that Uncle Aidan had a meeting so they couldn't stay for lunch.

However, the aloofness with which he treated me made me suspect Aidan didn't have a meeting at all. He just didn't want to be around someone who could listen to him bare his soul and then abandon him directly afterwards.

I was a coward.

All this time I'd been telling myself that I needed to fill my life with good, do good—like spending time with the kids at the hospital —searching for peace from my guilt. Finally, I'd found two people who maybe I could really help, and I was so terrified that I'd get torn up by them in the process that I was running away.

There was no time for me to apologize to Aidan, and I didn't have his phone number so I could call to make amends. Yet I hated the idea of him hating me more than I hated the idea of getting hurt.

The following Wednesday when I hurried into the hospital, I found Sylvie and Aidan waiting for me.

"You're here." I grinned, relieved, because I'd begun to worry that Aidan would stop bringing Sylvie altogether.

"Yup!" Sylvie grinned. "And we can stay for lunch this time."

My eyes flew up to Aidan's to find him staring stonily down at me.

"That's wonderful."

His expression didn't change and I had to look away because I couldn't stand to see him look through me. "Well, let's go inside."

"I'll be here when you're done." Aidan lowered himself into a chair, his phone out, eyes determinedly on it.

I wanted to apologize right then and there, but the kids were waiting and I didn't want to make my apologies in front of Sylvie. Shoving my concern for him out of my mind, I focused on the kids and their excitement that we were nearing the epic conclusion of the third *Harry Potter* book.

Aware of the time pressing toward the end of my session with the kids, my nerves started to grow wings. I had full-on belly flutters way before Jan came in to tell us our time was up. As always, Sylvie let me say goodbye to the kids before she tugged on my hand and drew me outside to find Aidan. He glanced up at our approach, quickly finished typing something on his phone, and then stood up, slipping his phone back into his pocket. As he smiled down at Sylvie and asked if she had fun, those flutters in my belly were accompanied by that flip of attraction.

I was obsessed with his smile. The sexy crinkles at the corners of his eyes, the slant of cocky mischief, no matter what provoked the smile.

"Lunch!" Sylvie announced, leading the way.

"Let me guess," Aidan said. "Mac and cheese."

Sylvie rolled her eyes. "It's not like it's a hard guess, Uncle Aidan." She threw me a look as if to say, "He thinks he's so smart." I couldn't help but laugh.

But Aidan wasn't laughing. He'd withdrawn into himself as he walked silently behind us to the cafeteria. Sylvie glanced over her shoulder at him every now and then, frowning, followed by a look at me, as if she knew I was the reason he wasn't acting his usual easy-going self.

Even mad at me, however, he wouldn't let me pay for lunch. "You paid last time," he stated flatly.

The awful tension increased and by the time we were sitting with our food at the table in the quiet cafeteria, I could feel my panic building. Whether it was fear that Sylvie would start to question us and get upset, or fear that I was losing whatever connection I'd made with Aidan, I didn't know. Maybe it was both. It was probably both.

"So, is Miss Robertson teaching you anything interesting?" I desperately sought conversation from the one Lennox who still liked me.

Sylvie scrunched up her face in thought. "She's teaching me about the Scottish Wars of Independence. That's pretty cool."

That sounded pretty violent. They were starting kids young on that stuff, huh. "Well, someday you can tell me all about it. My knowledge of Scottish history isn't great."

"You should sit in with Miss Robertson and me," Sylvie said, excited by the prospect. "Uncle Aidan, can Nora share my lessons?"

"No, sweetheart, I'm afraid not."

His emphatic tone told her that his response was final. Her little brows puckered together as she looked between us in confusion.

Hurt by Aidan's cold treatment and knowing I had no right to be, I struggled to say something, anything to break the tension.

My struggle was brought to an abrupt halt when Sylvie pushed back her chair. "There's Jan. I need to ask her something." And like a bolt of lightning, she was across the cafeteria before we could stop her.

We both turned to make sure Jan was in fact there. She was. And whatever Sylvie said made Jan look over at us. She gave us both a reassuring nod and then led Sylvie out of the cafeteria.

What the ever-loving fuck?

Slowing, I turned back in my chair to see Aidan focused on his plate. There was no sign that he was angry about Sylvie deliberately leaving us alone. And we both knew it was deliberate because there was still a full plate of uneaten mac and cheese on the table.

However, Aidan remained unmoved. He appeared cool and remote.

And tired.

Tired and alone.

Feeling anguish for him and a longing I couldn't deny, I realized that since he confided in me that day at the beach, I didn't feel so intimidated by him anymore. He felt more human now, more real, more real to me than very few people ever had. Because for the first time in a long time, I'd connected with someone. I *had* connected with him and I couldn't deny that.

And I think Aidan had connected with me too, otherwise he wouldn't have told me about his pain, and he wouldn't be so angry with me now.

It was time to be brave.

Brave for him.

"Donovan is a small town. It was too small for me."

Aidan's head jerked up.

"At first it didn't feel too small because my dad was this larger-than-life character who promised me that I was going to go out into the world and be somebody. He filled my head with dreams while my mom worked too much to care. Dad had his own construction company and we lived in a nice house compared to most people in Donovan, so it didn't seem implausible that I would *be* someone someday.

"But it changed. My dad had diabetes and his company was so successful, he got too busy and stopped taking care of himself. He ended up with gangrene in his leg and they had to amputate. He had to sell his company for less than what it was worth, we lost the house, and we moved into a small place that was just big enough to get a wheelchair through the doorways." It felt like another life now, and that emotional distance only made the guilt over leaving my parents tenfold. "I was eleven and my mom had to work even more hours to make up the loss of income. Suddenly, I was my dad's care-taker. And he wasn't the dad I'd grown up with anymore. He was mad at the world and he could be a mean son of a bitch." I looked deep into Aidan's eyes and said pointedly, "I loved him, but I resented him too."

Understanding softened his expression, giving me the strength to continue.

"It wasn't easy but I had Mel. She was my best friend growing up. Sylvie reminds me so much of her, it's uncanny. She was the only one who knew about the plays I had stashed away in a shoebox under my bed. She was the only one who knew I wanted to be a stage actress. I did some shows when I was a kid, and I loved falling into the part, and the way it made the audience so happy." I blinked away those memories. "Mel believed I could do it and she got it because she had big dreams of getting out of Donovan too, and becoming a singer in a rock band." I laughed sadly, the sound immediately followed by wet in my eyes. "She died when we were thirteen. Cancer. I used to visit her and entertain her and the friends she made there, reading and acting books out loud."

Aidan sighed, the sound sad. "Nora."

"I know." I blinked the tears away. "Everything all starts to make sense. But it doesn't. None of it *really* makes sense. Losing Mel. Losing my dad. And losing my dream because suddenly my parents were telling me there was 'no money for college, and anyway, who would look after Dad?' I was working at a fast-food restaurant when I graduated. I should've been at the college of my choice. I'd worked for it, I'd earned it, but I never got it. And I was drowning, Aidan. I couldn't breathe.

"Then Jim came along. This Scottish, flirty boy who took one look at me and for whatever reason I will never understand, fell in love. When he asked me to run away with him and get married, I knew it was crazy. But I was convinced that I loved him too, and that with him I could have the life I wanted. The idea of living in Scotland was so exciting. It blinded me. And I left my parents there without facing them. I left them a letter and snuck off in the night. I left them and now they won't talk to me. My letters return unopened. I've never gone back. And Jim ..." I paused, the words getting stuck in my throat.

"What happened, Nora?"

The guilt rose out of where I tried to bury it, and the grief was too much. All I could see was Jim's face as he looked at me on his knees, silently pleading with me to love him, asking me to choose him. It felt like someone was crushing my ribs as the tears let loose, spilling down my cheeks one after the other after the other. "He loved me too much. He didn't want me to have anything that would take me from him. And I was trapped all over again, working a shitty job I didn't care about, lying to myself to keep the peace between us. I wasn't in love with him," I confessed on a sob. "I didn't realize until it was too late. And he knew and he still wanted me. I stole from him, Aidan. Those years with him were stolen. He could have spent those with a girl who would've loved him the way he deserved to be loved. I've disappointed everyone. My parents. Jim. Mel. God, Jim … I hate myself, Aidan. I hate myself for letting his last years on this earth be with someone he knew didn't love him the way he loved her. I can never make up for that. Never." I was crying so hard, it took me a moment to realize Aidan had gotten out of his seat. But then I felt him pull me up out of mine so he could wrap his arms around me. Mine automatically wrapped around his waist and I buried my head in his chest, letting his kindness draw all my tears out.

Even when my sobs calmed, we stood there.

Just holding onto one another so tightly.

chapter 14

"NORA. COME IN, NORA. EARTH TO NORA. DID YOU CHANGE YOUR name or something and I don't know about it? Nora!"

I blinked, jolted from my thoughts, confused to find myself in Apple Butter with an exasperated Leah in my face.

Oh.

I was at work.

Whoops.

"Sorry," I apologized. "I didn't sleep well last night."

"Yes, obviously." She gestured to my face with a pointed finger. "You could use a little eye highlighter to deflect those dark circles. I have some if you want to borrow it?"

Somehow managing not to make a face, I shook my head. "I'm fine, thanks."

Leah cocked her head to the side, contemplating me. "I thought there was something different about you ... are you growing out your hair?"

I touched the strands that were now curling out in a kink at my neck. "Yeah."

"Well, you should go back to your stylist and tell them that. They'll cut into a look you can grow out."

In other words, she thought it looked like shit. "Thanks, Leah."

"Anytime." She beamed, missing my sarcasm. "Anyhoo, I need

to run to the bank so you're watching the store." She snapped her fingers. "No more daydreaming."

"You got it," I promised, relieved when she finally left.

Sighing, I relaxed against the cute powder-blue checkout counter and tried hard not to think of the day before. It proved too difficult. My mind kept going back to that moment when I'd made myself utterly vulnerable to Aidan. After all this time, I'd chosen someone to finally be open with and it had to be a man I knew could shatter what was left of me.

Not that he hadn't been kind.

We'd eventually pulled out of each other's arms, although Aidan had kept his hands on my waist, staring down at me with so much tenderness, it made me want to cry all over again.

I touched my cheek, thinking of the way he'd stroked his thumb across it.

Then his gaze had dropped to my mouth and there was tension between us again, only this time, it was a different kind of tension.

"You okay, Nora?" Sylvie's voice had broken through the moment.

I'd pulled away from Aidan to find Jan and Sylvie standing before us. Jan wore a knowing expression but I could see her concern for me too. Somehow, I gathered my wits enough to tell Sylvie I was okay. I knew she wanted to pester me because clearly, I wasn't okay, but Jan's hand on her shoulder seemed to silence her.

"I have to go, though." I needed time to regroup. Not wanting Aidan to think I was running again, however, I'd looked up at him pointedly. "I'll see you soon, then?"

Seeming to understand I needed a breather, he said, "Definitely."

After saying my goodbyes to Sylvie, I walked out of the cafeteria with Jan.

"We came back earlier," Jan said, "but ye were crying in his arms. Ye'er not all right, are ye?"

I smiled weakly at her. "I will be."

"He cares about ye."

I wanted him to. Desperately. "We hardly know each other."

"Doesn't change the facts." She gave my shoulder a squeeze. "Ye *will* be okay, Nora."

However, that night as I tried to sleep, I couldn't for worrying about how vulnerable I really had made myself to a man I didn't really know. When I was with him, those fears drifted away, but being alone and having time to think about it brought them all back.

And yet … there wasn't only the fear. There was relief.

Relief I never expected to feel.

I'd spewed out all the ugliness I'd ever committed and he didn't run away. He held me and comforted me and looked at me like I wasn't a bad person after all.

My attachment to him was deepening, as my attachment to Sylvie had. And that, I knew, was incredibly dangerous. Just as my attachment to the kids at the hospital, some of whom were terminal. Spending time with them was, at best, an act of kindness, at worst, an act of self-flagellation.

But to let myself fall for Aidan Lennox when he himself was at his most vulnerable was masochistic. He was a man with a huge life beyond me, and as soon as he stopped feeling so haunted, so alone, surely little Nora O'Brien from Nowhere, Indiana would be left behind.

As if my thoughts had conjured him, the door to the shop opened, drawing me up off the counter. My heart beat faster as Aidan walked in. He closed the door behind him and stared across the shop at me.

And I knew that my self-flagellation wasn't over.

I couldn't run away from him.

I didn't want to.

Drawn to him in a way I couldn't explain, I walked slowly toward him, and he to me. We met in the middle of the shop. As soon as I was within touching distance, he put his hand on my waist to draw me even closer. My breath caught as our eyes locked and it took me a second or two to find the ability to ask, "What are you doing here?"

"I wanted to see you. Make sure you're okay."

I rested my hand on his arm, the one that held me close, and nodded. "I think so."

He frowned, reaching up with his free hand to brush his thumb over my cheek in that way that made my knees tremble. "I couldn't sleep last night for worrying about you."

And I saw it. What I'd been trying so hard not to see.

I saw that he wanted me ... like I wanted him.

I was at war with myself, thinking he should probably leave but wanting him to stay. More than anything I didn't want to hurt him. Again.

However, maybe friendship was the key. We could be there for each other without turning it into something that would be incredibly painful when it was inevitably over. Friendship, I could survive. We both could.

"Aidan, I—"

"Ah, good the shop isn't on fire." My boss's voice broke the moment as she strode in.

Aidan's eyebrows were drawn together, as if he knew I was in a battle with myself and the side he wanted to lose was winning.

"Oh, hello." Leah stopped beside us and I gently extricated myself from Aidan's grasp. I scowled when I saw my boss's eyes running over him hungrily. I felt sorry for her fiancé. "I'm Nora's boss—Leah." She held out a hand, grinning flirtatiously. "Are you the man with the delicious voice from the other week there?"

Aidan shot me a scowl. "No, I'm not."

Thank you, Leah. "That was Roddy." I looked up at Aidan. "Jim's best friend."

Before he could react, Leah gave a huff of laughter. "Who knew you were hiding all these gorgeous men, Nora." She wagged her finger at me like I'd been naughty and then turned back to Aidan. "I didn't quite catch your name."

"Aidan." He gave her a curt nod and stepped back, his eyes falling on me. "This isn't over, Pixie."

His determined expression froze me in place as I continued to fight with myself and what I wanted. Because I swear to God, every time that man called me Pixie, I wanted to show him just how naughty I could be.

———

THE HOUSE IN SIGHTHILL BROUGHT BACK MEMORIES OF MY FIRST FEW months in Scotland. Those days seemed so long ago, even though they really weren't. But now they felt like they belonged to another person.

Angie opened the door, her dark hair, now dyed and perfectly in place, her makeup immaculate, her clothes also. She was an older version of Seonaid, and still very attractive. However, there was sadness in her eyes that hadn't been there when we met. She'd lost her husband and then her son.

Pieces of her were just … gone.

"It's so good tae see ye." She enveloped me in a hug so tight, it was like she was afraid I'd float away if she let go.

"You too."

Stepping into the house, I was suddenly smacked in the face with memories of Jim. He was everywhere. And it wasn't because Angie had photos of her family on nearly every wall. I could see him in the stairwell, chasing me up the stairs, and making me laugh in frightened delight when he caught me at the top and pretended to bite my neck like a vampire after we'd watched a stupid horror movie.

I could see him at the end of the hallway, holding his mom tight because she was sad we were moving out. I remembered him telling her that we'd visit all the time and she could come see us whenever she wanted.

"I can't hear his voice anymore," I whispered.

Angie's arm circled my shoulder and she pulled me to her to kiss my temple. "It's okay, sweetheart."

But it wasn't okay. Letting everything out with Aidan had unearthed my emotions, and I wasn't okay.

"There you are." Seonaid came striding out of the kitchen.

"Roddy is about to eat the whole bloody chicken if you don't get in here."

Angie gave me one more squeeze and I plastered a smile on. "Let him try."

Seonaid hugged me as soon as I approached. "He's being a dick. I need backup."

"Being a dick about what?"

"Her latest boy-toy," Roddy supplied as we walked into the kitchen.

"He's not a boy-toy, Radar Ears." Seonaid gestured for her mother to sit down while she got us all drinks. The table was already set, a Sunday roast chicken and all the accoutrements with it. "And don't even say one more word in front of my mum."

"I think Angie wid like tae ken ye'er irresponsibly dating a man half yer age."

I grinned at his teasing, relaxing a little now that he and Seonaid were there to take my mind off the difficult stuff.

"If he were half my age," she slammed a beer down on the table beside him, "it would be illegal."

"Hey, nae judgment here."

Seonaid smacked him across the head and he shot me a pleased grin.

I laughed. "You're giving him what he wants."

She scowled and put a glass of water in front of me before taking a seat beside her mom. "He knows how to push my buttons."

His grin turned wicked and as he opened his mouth to speak, Seonaid raised her fork and shouted, "Don't even say anything dirty, Roddy Livingston!"

I smothered my laughter by taking a sip of water as Roddy shook with silent mirth.

Angie sighed. "Will you pair ever grow up?"

"Oh, I'm all grown up, Angie," Roddy said, shooting Seonaid a pointed look.

To his delight, she blushed.

Interesting.

As interesting as it was, however, she also appeared in need of a rescue. "That picture you sent me of Zach. Wow."

She smiled in thanks, shooting Roddy a smug look before opening her mouth.

This time she was cut off by Angie. "Aye, he's gid-looking all right, but he's a blethering idiot."

Roddy choked on a sip of beer.

"At least the homely ones ye were dating had a brain in their heids."

"Zach has a brain."

"I said in their heids, Seonaid, no their underwear."

While Roddy roared with delight, I tried, for my friend's sake, to hold back my laughter. Seonaid turned to Roddy in outrage. "Like your barmaid is a bloody rocket scientist? I heard her ask you if grenadine was a girl's name."

"That's a language barrier issue."

"Yeah, she seems to understand baser elements of the English language, no problem, however."

"And whit does that mean?"

"It means that when she thinks she's whispering in your ear, she isn't whispering!"

I snorted and Seonaid cut me a look of betrayal. I offered her one of apology and turned to Angie to change the subject. "It all looks delicious."

"Aye, it does, so can we bloody well eat?" Roddy asked.

"Tuck in," Angie said.

Knowing Roddy well, we waited until his plate was piled high before serving ourselves. Although Seonaid grumbled about feminism the entire time we did.

"It's so nice tae have noise back in the house," Angie said wistfully. "I miss it."

Seonaid reached over to squeeze her mom's hand.

"I miss him," Angie went on, and I braced myself. I knew she needed to talk about him, but it was so goddamn difficult to hear. She looked at me and repeated the words she'd said before, words that were a knife in my gut. "But I take peace in knowin' ma boy found the kind of love some of us never find."

"*Ye don't have tae love me, Nora. Just keep caring about me, like I know ye do, and promise tae stay. For good. Stay with me. Choose me.*"

I swallowed a gasp at finally hearing Jim's voice after months of searching for it. There it was. Those words and the longing in them, the hurt he couldn't hide in his eyes as he said them.

Angie had no idea how much pain I'd caused her son.

And suddenly, I realized … maybe it wasn't only me who needed to be protected from Aidan. Maybe he needed to be shielded from me too. Like someone should have safeguarded Jim's heart from me.

My fingers curled tightly around my fork as I looked down at my plate. Finally, I felt at last the battle I'd been fighting within myself since Wednesday was over. For once I had to do the right thing.

chapter 15

"NORA, CAN YOU HELP A CUSTOMER?" LEAH'S HEAD APPEARED AROUND the doorframe, looking into the closet we called a staff room. "Where are you going?"

I pulled on my backpack and strode past her. "Remember I finish at twelve today. It's five after."

"But Amy isn't here yet."

"I'm sorry. I have to get to the hospital."

Her eyes widened. "Oh? What happened?"

Life happened.

"Uh, excuse me..." A girl stood at the counter looking annoyed. "Can someone help me, please?"

Leah turned to help the customer and I took the opportunity to dash out of the store without having to explain myself. I regretted agreeing to do overtime on my day off because I knew Leah would try to extend my hours, even though I had already told her I could only work until noon. As it was, it was going to be a push to get to the hospital in time for my session with the kids at our usual twelve-thirty.

By the time I climbed the hill from the shop and hurried up the old cobbled road of the Royal Mile, I could feel my anxiety building. It was stupid—the kids would be there when I arrived, but I hated the idea of being late. In the weeks I'd been visiting, I hadn't been late once. And I still needed to change my clothes. I'd have to do it when I got there but before any of them saw me.

They called Edinburgh the windy city, and today—behaving like its forces were against me—it lived up to its name. I strode into the wind feeling its icy resistance. A whimsical part of me wondered if the city was trying to tell me something. Would I look on this day in the future and wish I'd listened to it and turned back?

Hurrying, I cut a twenty-minute walk down to fifteen. It would've been less if not for the damn wind. I almost skidded to a stop once I reached the ward, the nurses looking up in surprise when I appeared at their station sweaty and out of breath. There was no Aidan waiting outside with Sylvie. I didn't know what that meant.

"Hey," I puffed out.

Jan and Trish grinned at me. "We didn't know if ye were coming today," Jan said.

I grinned back at Jan. "Only illness or death."

Catching my meaning, she chuckled and came around the nurses' station. "They're all in the common room."

"Where can I change before they see me?"

She shook her head in amusement. "They won't mind."

"I know." I shrugged.

"Alison is in the common room, so her private bathroom will be free."

"Thanks. Two minutes," I promised. I'd been nervous about seeing Aidan and explaining the whole friendship-only thing. Now I was worried he wasn't here at all.

Perceptive as ever, Jan informed me, "They're already here. Both of them."

Relieved, I nodded and darted along the corridor and through Aly's empty private room to her bathroom, the door banging shut behind me.

Yanking off my sweater and jeans, I began to feel the little hum of excitement in my belly, as I always did when I was about to spend time with them. And it *was* about them.

Really.

"It is," I snapped at myself.

I pulled on my green leggings and shirt, about was about to button it closed when the bathroom door suddenly jerked open.

The breath left my body as I froze, looking up at his familiar eyes staring down at me.

He was so tall, his shoulders so broad, he almost filled the entire doorway.

I tried to open my mouth, to ask him what he thought he was doing, but the words got stuck as his gaze drifted from my eyes to my lips, and down. His perusal was long and thorough, from head to toe and back up again. He lingered on the sight of my bra beneath the open shirt, and when his eyes finally returned to meet mine, they were brimming with heat.

His expression was determined.

A mixture of fear and thrill and nervousness burst through me, finally melting my freeze as he stepped into the bathroom, locking the door.

"What are you doing?" I stumbled into the wall behind me.

Amusement danced in his eyes as he moved slowly, predatorily toward me. "I'm thinking that Peter Pan has never looked so sexy."

Unfortunately, I was a sucker for a Scottish accent.

Clearly, or I wouldn't have ended up here, so far from home.

More than that, however, I was beginning to think I was a sucker for him. "Don't." I put my hand up to stop him, but he pressed his chest against it, and covered my hand with his own. I stared at how small mine was in comparison, and a shiver trickled down my back and around to my breasts. My breathing faltered as he took another few steps into me until there was barely any space between us. He was so tall, and I was so not that I had to tilt my head back to meet his eyes.

His burned. They burned for me in a way no man's ever had.

How was I supposed to resist that?

And yet I knew I had to. I scowled up at him. "You should go."

In answer, he pressed the entire length of his body against mine and heat flashed through me. Excitement rippled in my lower belly. Tingling started between my legs. My nipples hardened.

Angry at my body and angry at him, I shoved at him but it was like trying to shove a concrete wall. "This is totally inappropriate," I hissed.

He grabbed my hands to stop my ineffectual shoving and gently but effectively pinned my hands above my head. My chest thrust up against him and I gasped as my breasts swelled.

Eyes dark with knowing and intent, he bent his head toward me.

"Don't." I shook my head, hating the bite in my tone, but carrying on nonetheless. "I'm not playing cavewoman to your caveman."

His lips twitched. "Shame that. Do you often deny yourself what you want?"

"No, but I think with my head, not my vagina."

He laughed, his warm breath puffing against my lips.

I loved when he laughed. I loved when I made him laugh. He needed laughter more than anything. The sound thrilled me, making my belly squeeze with pleasure. And I realized it wasn't just my body betraying me but my heart too.

As if he'd seen the thought in my eyes, he let go of one of my hands so he could press cool fingers against my breast, over my heart. I gasped at the dizzying sensation of being touched so intimately. He asked, "Have you ever thought about thinking with this thing?"

"As far as I'm aware, my left breast isn't much of a thinker," I evaded.

He grinned. "You know what I mean, Pixie."

"Don't call me that."

Expression turning thoughtful, he said, "I thought we were friends."

"We were. But then you pinned me to a bathroom wall."

"Thanks for the reminder." He took hold of my free hand again and pressed it back to the wall with the other. At the flash of anger in my eyes, he said, "If you were really pissed off about it, you'd be struggling."

I flushed. "It would be futile. You're a giant."

"I'd let you go. You know I would. I'd hate it. But I'd let you go ... if you didn't want this?"

We looked silently at one another, his face so close to mine, I could see little flecks of yellow gold in his green eyes.

In those moments, I forgot where I was. Who I was. And what the right thing to do for him was.

And I didn't even realize I was straining toward him until he brought it to my attention. "Why are you fighting this when you want it?"

Why *was* I fighting this again?

"Nora?"

I closed my eyes, shutting him out, which allowed the memory of why I was fighting this to return to me. "Because—"

His mouth crushed down on mine, silencing me. Surprise turned to instinct. I kissed him back, meeting his tongue with my own, straining against his hold on my wrists but not to get away. To wrap my arms around him. Run my fingers through his hair.

Heat flushed through me like I was covered in fuel and he'd started a fire at my feet. It lashed like lightning until I was surrounded in a blaze.

Too hot. Too needy. Too everything.

I wanted to rip off my clothes.

I wanted to rip off his clothes.

And then he broke the kiss to pull back and stare at me in triumph.

If he'd been anyone else, if it had been any other moment, I'd have called him out for being smug.

Instead, I remembered exactly why we should not be doing this.

Whatever he saw in my expression made him loosen his grip on my wrists. I lowered them, but he didn't step away.

He waited, his hands resting gently on my small shoulders.

Something in his eyes made my defenses crumble. Tenderness

rushed through me and I found myself caressing his cheek, feeling his stubble prickle my skin. Sadness doused the fire. "She's gone," I told him gently. "Not even I can distract you from that."

Unbearable, bleak anguish fought with the desire in his eyes and he slowly slid his hands off my shoulders and down to my waist. With a gentle tug I fell into him, clutching at his chest.

He tore through my soul with the whispered, tortured words, "But you can try."

Looking up into his face, one that I longed to see every day, one that incited excitement when I knew I would see it, I understood then that I would never hurt him like I'd hurt Jim. My feelings for him were on an entirely different level, and as guilty as that made me feel, it also reassured me. The only person in danger here was me.

And for him, I was willing to chance the possibility of getting my heart broken.

Drawn to Aidan, drawn to Sylvie, I think I'd known all along that these two people were my repentance for the mistakes I made with Jim and my family. It didn't matter what happened to my heart in the end—all that mattered was that I could be what Aidan and Sylvie needed at this point in their lives. And maybe afterward I'd finally be at peace with myself.

So why the hell shouldn't I let us have what we both wanted?

I threw my hands around his nape and went up on my tiptoes as I pulled his head toward mine. It took only the first nudge and he was bending to meet me. Our lips met in a passionate crash of hunger, and suddenly his hands were gripping the backs of my thighs and lifting me off my feet. I wrapped my legs around his hips as he pressed my back against the bathroom wall, our mouths never untangling for a second. His stubble pricked my skin as the kiss descended from hungry to ravenous—dirty, desperate, and hot as sin.

I'd never experienced anything like it, this heat between us, this want. It was like we knew the only way to feel anything good was to disappear as freely and deeply into one another as possible.

One of his rough, warm hands glided up my bare waist to cup my breast. He gave it a gentle squeeze and then dragged his thumb over the rise of it, pulling the fabric of my bra down. My nipple peaked in the cool air and I gasped when his thumb brushed over it. The noise melted under Aidan's kisses and he groaned, pushing his hips more firmly between mine so his hard, scorching erection pressed against me where I most wanted it.

I whimpered, my fingers curling tight in his hair as my thighs clamped around his hips, silently pleading for more.

"Right, you pair, oot of there!"

The sound of Jan's angry voice was the equivalent of suddenly finding ourselves dumped in snow. We broke apart, my eyes wide with horror and his narrowed with frustration.

"Fuck," he muttered, gently easing me to the floor.

"Did ye hear me?" Jan pounded the door.

"We're coming, Jan." Aidan replied gently.

We heard her harrumph followed by the sounds of her footsteps fading away from the door.

Feeling shaken that I could have lost myself so much in him that I'd forget I was at a freaking children's hospital, I ran a trembling hand through my hair. "I can't believe I did that here."

"Hey." He brushed away my hands as they were attempting to button my shirt. He buttoned it calmly for me. "We lost our heads for a moment. Don't beat yourself up about it."

I forced myself to meet his gaze. "Was that all it was? Us losing our heads *for a moment*?"

Aidan straightened my shirt and pressed a sweet kiss to my lips. "No," he whispered across my swollen mouth. "This isn't over, Pixie. Sylvie's with her dad tonight so I have the place to myself. I want you there."

My pulse skittered at the thought, excitement making my belly squeeze deep and low. "Okay."

"No misunderstandings." His eyes blazed with determination. "Tonight you're in my bed. I'm going to make love to you, and fuck you and come with you until every muscle in your body aches."

A moan of longing bubbled out of me and I bit my lip to halt its sound, but I couldn't halt the wet between my legs.

Satisfied by my nonverbal response, he took a reluctant step back and I felt his eyes on me as I gathered my stuff, putting my clothes in my backpack. I smoothed my hands down my costume, wishing there was a mirror in here. "I don't have stubble burn on my cheeks, do I?"

Aidan shook his head, smirking. "No. But you'll most certainly have it between your thighs by tomorrow morning."

Tingles exploded around my breasts and between my legs, and I felt my nipples harden into points. Heat blossomed beneath my cheeks. "Jesus," I huffed. "I have to go out to the kids ... you couldn't have waited to say something like that to me?"

My reaction made him laugh as he pulled open the bathroom door. "No one will know you're wet except me. Which I love, by the way."

"How do you know I am?" I said, trying to reign in the man's cockiness a little.

"Aren't you?"

"I guess you'll find out tonight for sure."

"Pixie knows how to play," he murmured.

I glanced at him over my shoulder as we walked out of Aly's room and all the pain and grief I'd seen in his eyes minutes earlier was buried. It was now replaced by amusement, desire, and if I wasn't mistaken, happiness.

I had made him happy.

I grinned at the thought. "You have no idea."

Aidan laughed, the sound dying when we stepped out into the corridor to find Jan waiting for us. At her look of displeasure, we both fell silent, like naughty schoolchildren caught doing something very wrong.

"Never again." She wagged her finger at us.

"Never," we promised in unison, and meant it. What we'd done had been totally inappropriate and my only excuse was that this man had the ability to obliterate all thoughts of anything else in the world but him.

Suffice it to say, I found it extremely difficult to concentrate with the kids. It was like trying to run through knee-deep water. But try I did because my time with them was as important as the time I'd now promised to Aidan.

chapter 16

THIS WAS IT.

This was the night everything would irrevocably change between us. I stood by the canal where a narrowboat and a barge were anchored. It was a chilly evening, announcing summer's gradual end, and I wore a cardigan over my dress. I didn't have anything fancy to wear, but since Aidan was attracted to me even when I was wearing a Peter Pan costume, I didn't think it would really matter to him what I wore.

The dress was red with subtle white polka dots. It had a scalloped V-neck that hinted at cleavage, short sleeves, buttons down the front, and a baby-doll silhouette. I wore low-heeled brown leather ankle boots that had seen better days but were my favorite shoes. It was casual. Cute. Not seductive. Tonight was going to be nerve-wracking enough. I wanted to be comfortable.

Plus, I'd calculated how to get to the sexy times with Aidan as fast as possible and this dress was easily whipped off over my head.

It was around seven-thirty so the sun was still in the sky, bathing the apartments around the canal in warm orange and pink. Aidan's building was situated near Fountainbridge Square where the two boats were moored. There was a bar there and a restaurant and shops, so it wasn't like there weren't people milling around. However, there was a stillness about the evening, as if everyone and everything knew something special was about to happen for me.

Such whimsical thinking wasn't like me of late, but with my heart banging away in my chest as I approached the front door to Aidan's building, I couldn't help feeling as if this night *was* just for us.

Something good and thrilling on the horizon of a bleak past we were hopefully moving away from.

To say Sylvie had been delighted when I accepted a ride home from her uncle was putting it mildly. She made it clear it was like her two best friends had decided they'd be best friends too, and all was well in her world. She chattered excitedly in the back of the Range Rover as Aidan drove me home to Sighthill. Since I'd made the decision to do this—whatever this was—I saw no reason to hide where I lived from him. He already knew I lived in Sighthill anyway.

"Has your dad got cool plans for you tonight?" I'd asked Sylvie, recognizing the street we were driving down as being a block from my own.

Sylvie had shrugged. "I suppose."

"He's taking her out for dinner tonight. To the Scran and Scallie. You like it there, sweetheart," Aidan gently reminded her.

I'd wondered what was with her sudden disinterest in the idea of spending the night with her dad.

"It's Daddy's favorite place to eat. Not mine."

At her uncharacteristically petulant tone, I shot Aidan a look. He'd caught it out of the corner of his eye and said, "Are you not happy because Sally is going to be there? Because I told you if you're upset about her moving in with your dad, I can talk to him."

Ah.

Cal had a girlfriend. I hadn't known that. "Has Sally been around long?"

Sylvie had shrugged again so I'd looked to Aidan.

"Yeah. They've been dating for over a year but Sally recently moved in with him."

"Sally's fine," Sylvie said.

Before I could respond, Aidan slowed the car and asked, "Is this you?"

I turned and looked out of my window up at my grim home. My

apartment was part of a block of flats covered in pebble-dash render stained and gray with age. The small patches of grass outside were overgrown in parts and dying in others. A couple of my neighbors had windows that didn't look as if they'd been cleaned from the inside for years.

This was where I lived. I wouldn't be ashamed. Most of the people here were working hard to be able to afford their homes. I was one of them. And my little flat may not have been much but it was clean and tidy and I could afford the rent without help from anyone else.

"This is me. Thanks for the ride."

"Anytime." He'd given me a sexy half smile as he pulled his phone out of the holder in the center console. "Number. Please."

He had been lucky he'd added that please, and my expression told him so, making him laugh as I put my number into his phone. When I handed it back to him, he called me. "Now you have mine too. I'll text you," he said, his gaze meaningful.

I'd nodded, feeling tingles in my good-for-nothing places at the thought of seeing him later in the day.

Turning back to Sylvie, I found her watching us curiously, as if she sensed something was up but was too young to really understand what.

"I'll see you soon," I said, reaching out for her hand.

When she'd taken it, I squeezed hers tight, and then reluctantly let go. Her shouts of goodbye to me and her exuberant waving as I walked down the path to my building had made me smile. The searing glance Aidan had given me before he drove off killed the smile as anticipation enveloped me.

Not long later, I got a text with his address and a time. I texted back a simple "I'll be there" response.

And now here I was.

With my palms sweating.

I pressed the buzzer to his apartment and some seconds later heard his delicious voice, "Hello?"

"It's me."

The door buzzed and I smiled as I stepped inside, thinking that sometimes he was a man of few words.

Aidan lived on the second from the top floor and when the elevator binged open, it was facing his apartment door—he was standing in it, his arms crossed over his chest as he leaned against the doorjamb.

My breath caught as I took him in. He was pure masculine, rugged perfection. Every time I saw him, he grew more attractive. His soulful eyes were focused on me as mine took in the fact that he was wearing a different T-shirt from earlier and ragged jeans. His hair was still wet so I knew, like me, he'd just had a shower.

Shivers tickled down my spine at the reason why. I stepped out of the elevator before the doors closed on me and approached him slowly, still drinking him in, disbelieving really that this kind, funny, smart, and unbelievably sexy man was gazing at me like he thought I was all those things too. His eyes drifted down my body slowly and then rose, lingering over every detail, until they came back to my face.

"I like this dress," he said.

I smiled softly. "You're easily pleased."

Aidan took my hand and led me inside his apartment, but I didn't have a chance to look at it because he was speaking again, distracting me. "No, I didn't used to be." He closed the door, locking it behind us. "I used to be an arsehole." His expression was almost one of wonder as he looked down at me. "A picky, womanizing arsehole."

I tensed, not really enjoying the idea of him and other women. And picky? I remember Sylvie telling me her uncle dated the most beautiful women she'd ever seen.

Christ.

I tugged on my cardigan, wondering what possessed me to wear it.

"Don't." It was as if he sensed my sudden insecurity, sliding an arm around my waist and drawing me to him. My hands fluttered down on his hard, warm chest, and I tilted my head back to keep eye contact. "You're perfect."

"My hair is too short." I touched the strands at my nape. "It used to be long."

"I remember."

"I cut it because of Jim," I told him sadly. "At the time, I was so angry about everything, and he loved my hair and he told me never to cut it, and when he died … I cut it. All of it. I was punishing him for dying. It's so goddamn stupid, I know."

Aidan squeezed my waist in reassurance.

"But I loved my hair too," I said, feeling stupid about the whole thing. "I know it's only hair … but I'm mad I cut it."

He studied me so long, I was almost afraid to ask what he was thinking, but I shouldn't have been. Aidan released my waist with one hand to brush his fingers through the bangs that had grown out past my ears. His fingers curled around my ear, his thumb stroking my cheekbone, and his eyes caught mine with a fierceness that made my belly squeeze. "You could shave it all off, Pixie, and still be so bloody beautiful, I can't concentrate on anything else when you're in the room."

Wow. I exhaled slowly on his name, "Aidan."

His eyes closed as if he was in pain and he dropped his forehead to mine. His cologne washed over me, the heat of him prickling my skin like I'd stepped out of an air-conditioned room into the hot sun. "I want to hear you say my name like that when I'm inside you," he murmured against my lips.

I was happy to oblige and my fingers curled into his T-shirt telling him so.

"But," he snapped back up to full height, "I promised myself I wouldn't fall on you like a sex-starved teenager as soon as you walked in the door. I need you to know this is more than sex for me, Nora."

It was something Jim had said to me when we'd first become friends. At the time, I'd thought it was sweet, special, because the boys at school had made it clear that it would only ever be about sex if I was to give them the time of day. It was strange, though, how two men could say the same thing to me and yet I reacted so completely differently.

With Aidan, it didn't feel *just sweet* to hear those words.

It felt like my heart was breaking from the joy of such a promise from him. I never knew happiness and need and excitement could be painful when you felt them in extremes.

"Me too," I promised in return.

Aidan gripped one of my hands. "Let me show you the flat. We've got a nice view here."

The hallway led out from our left into an open-plan living room and kitchen, and a corridor ran along the side of the kitchen into the back of the apartment. The living room and what could have been a dining area but was apparently a small music studio were situated in the large space at the front of the room with twin patio doors and balconies looking out over the canal and the city beyond.

"This is beautiful," I said honestly. There was a table and chairs on one of the balconies. "It must be nice to sit out there and have breakfast on a sunny morning."

His smile was fond. "Sylvie's favorite thing to do, in fact."

"I love how you love her," I said without thinking.

"More than anything."

I didn't tell him but his love for his kid was one of the sexiest things about him. Smiling, I turned from the view, taking in the baby grand piano, guitars (electric and acoustic), keyboard, and a large desk with a three-monitor computer on it against the far wall that ran right up to the entrance. It was the only wall with exposed brick and that along with the hardwood floors gave the apartment a city-loft feel.

"My studio," Aidan said, rueful. "It used to be a dining area and my studio was in the second bedroom where I had sound-proofing on the walls, but I had to rip it all out and make it a bedroom for Sylvie. There haven't been any complaints from the neighbors yet and I work in an actual studio in New Town, but we'll probably need to move at some point. Get a place that works better for us."

I wandered over to the computer and instruments, amazed that Aidan could sit here and create and write and produce music. "You're so clever."

"For all you know, I'm shit at it."

I snorted and turned to find him grinning cheekily at me. God, his boyish smile was sexier than anything else. "I somehow doubt that."

He shrugged and I laughed, taking that to mean he was *shit hot* at it, and I wandered past him toward the kitchen at the back of the room.

Sleek, white, and shiny, it wasn't my kind of kitchen—I preferred the country cottage look—but it worked in the space. And I liked the island with the stools.

Aidan gestured. "Kitchen. Obviously." He led me past it.

Down the corridor, behind the kitchen was a door on the right. Aidan opened it to reveal a large bedroom. The walls were painted blue and situated in the middle was a bed fit for a princess. It was a mini four-poster with purple gauze curtains draped down the posts from the frame at the top. The bedding was purple with cushions of velvet and Indian silk in jewel tones piled on top. It was the kind of bed a kid could dive into and get lost in. Bookshelves lined the walls, cluttered with books and soft toys, dolls, photos in picture frames, and knickknacks. Opposite the bed was a cabinet with a TV, DVD player, and a computer console. Adjacent to that was a little desk with an iMac. A large wardrobe suggested she had plenty of clothes and shoes, and a purple velvet cuddle chair and matching stool in the corner had an open book draped over the arm.

Sylvie Lennox had lost the most important person in her world, and although he could never replace that, her uncle Aidan had made sure she had everything else she could ever want or need.

Tears burned my eyes as I imagined this man gutting his music studio—something incredibly important to him—and creating a room like this for Sylvie.

"It's perfect," I whispered.

"Aye, well, she deserves it."

I nodded and stepped back outside, because being in there made me more emotional than I'd like.

As if he knew, Aidan closed the door and then pointed down the hall, swiftly changing our focus. "The master suite is down there."

"Oh." I stared down the hall, anticipating walking in there with him. My pulse raced. Up until this point I hadn't been nervous about having sex with Aidan because in our little prelude, it hadn't even crossed my mind to care. We were so caught up in each other.

But now I felt little nervous butterflies join the ones that fluttered around with anticipation. From what I could deduce, Aidan Lennox had been around. Even without the twelve more years of sexual experience than I had, he'd still be more sexually experienced. I'd only ever slept with Jim, and I never got the impression Jim was dissatisfied. Yet that was different, because Jim was in love with me. What if I wasn't enough for a guy like Aidan? What if I didn't *know* enough?

"Wine?" Aidan suddenly asked.

My gaze flew to his and I could see his brow was a little furrowed, as if he was wondering what I was thinking. "Wine?"

"Would you like a glass of wine?"

How did I tell him I wasn't a wine kind of gal?

"No to the wine?"

"Do you have beer instead?"

Aidan grinned and started toward the kitchen. I hurried after him and he glanced over his shoulder at me while he pulled two bottles out of his fridge, popped them open, and handed me one. The cold bottle made me shiver. Or it could have been the heat in Aidan's eyes that had never really eased from the second he'd let me in the door.

"I'm not sophisticated," I blurted out before I could think about what I was revealing. "I'm from a tiny town, I didn't go to college, I married at eighteen, we lived a simple life, I still live a simple life, and I've never been anywhere else but Indiana and Scotland." I let out a shaky breath. "And I drink beer."

I could tell Aidan was trying not to laugh and I didn't get what was funny until he said, "You're fucking perfect."

Jim had thought so too. "No one's perfect."

"You are to me."

"Such a sweet talker."

"Only with you."

And I think I believed him. "Why?" I wasn't looking for compliments, I merely wanted to understand. "I'm not filled with false modesty, Aidan. I really have no clue what Jim saw in me. I know I'm not ugly, but it was like he got struck by a thunderbolt when we met. And then he never stopped loving me. But why? Because he didn't really know me. I sometimes think he loved a version of me he'd made up in his head. And now you. You say you want me too." I gestured to all that was him. "You've seen you, right?"

This time he did grin. "Have you always been this funny?"

"I'm being serious."

At my tone, his amusement fled. "I'm not Jim. Did you have this connection with him?"

I shook my head sadly.

"Then there's the difference. What *I* feel is sparked by what *you* feel, and vice versa. No one can explain attraction, Nora. It's there or it isn't. As for Jim ... I'll never really know what made him fall for you but I can guess. You have a wise, soulful quality, as if you've seen more than most your age. It gives you a maturity I've rarely encountered in someone as young as you. And yet whatever that is, it's mixed with innocence and vulnerability that I don't think you even realize is there. And you're petite, Pixie," his gaze dragged down my body hungrily, "feminine in every way. That fragility, along with your appearance ... well, it makes a certain kind of man want to protect you—it brings out the caveman in him."

I raised an eyebrow, having never regarded myself in that way before. I didn't feel fragile. Vulnerable, yes, sometimes, but not fragile. The thought that men somehow saw me as weak, irked. It more than irked that Aidan might be attracted to me because he thought I needed his protection. "Are you that kind of man?"

"I'm not going to lie—it definitely caught my attention when I first saw you. But as I've gotten to know you? No, that's not the appeal. I've never been interested in dating someone your age. I like my women smart, mature, and intelligent as well as sexy. You're all those things. And anyone who really knows you realizes quickly that you don't need anyone to protect you. You just need someone to listen. To see who you really are."

And he was so right. I thought of my parents and how I spoke and they never really listened, and how Jim was the same. How Seonaid tried but Jim always got in the way.

Aidan was the first person I'd met since Mel who really listened. He was the first person since Mel who I wanted to give all of my thoughts to. Like he'd given his secret thoughts to me.

"I think that's what you need too."

"Exactly."

I took a swig of my beer because I felt too much and I was scared it was all about to come spewing out. My eyes flew around the room, looking for a distraction, and it caught on the piano. Walking around the kitchen counter, I made my way over to it. I reached out to touch its shiny black lacquered surface and then pulled my hand back.

"Do you play?" Aidan asked as he followed me over.

I shook my head and looked up at him. "Will you play something for me?"

He reached for my beer and I gave it up, bemused. Aidan walked back over to the kitchen counter and put them down, and I felt the tension emanating off him as he strode back to me.

Suddenly, I was in his arms and his hands were smoothing down my back and over my ass, pulling me into him. "Later," he promised. "Right now, I'd rather play you."

My heart rate took off as I clutched him, my whole body swelling into him with need. "What about our drinks and not jumping on me like a sex-starved teenager?"

"Here's something you should know about me, Pixie." He bent his head to brush his mouth over mine, just a whisper, a tease. "I can be a selfish fuck when I want something."

My hands slid around his neck. "As long as you're not a selfish *fuck*, I don't care."

His body shook with laughter and his arms tightened around me. "Have I told you lately how much I like you?"

I grinned back. "I like you too."

"And I'm definitely not a selfish fuck," he growled. He kissed me hard and then pulled back. "I promised my head between your legs and I meant it."

A strong ripple of desire flooded my belly, making me wet. "Aidan," I breathed, holding on tighter, fearing my legs wouldn't keep me standing much longer.

He groaned and kissed me, lifting me easily into his arms so I could wrap my legs around his thighs. Kissing me voraciously, he began walking us blindly toward the back of the apartment. Any nervousness I'd felt was, like last time, obliterated by my body's craving for him.

"Oh my God."

The strange, feminine voice filled with shock drew us apart near the kitchen, our heads flying toward the apartment door. It was now open and a beautiful, tall, curvaceous blond was gaping at us in stunned silence as she held a key in one hand and grocery bag in the other.

"Laine." Aidan slowly dropped me to the floor but I kept clinging to him, confused by the sudden appearance of this gorgeous creature. Who the hell was she?

She wore a casual navy and white maxi dress that hugged her generous curves and flat sandals with little crystals decorating the straps; her long blond hair fell around her shoulders in silky, tousled waves, and her makeup was done to perfection. She really was quite something to look at.

And she obviously had a key to Aidan's apartment.

At that realization, I tried to pull away but he held on.

"What are you doing here?" he asked.

Laine closed the door behind her, having apparently gathered her wits after walking in on us. "I wanted to see you and I brought dinner. I'm sorry." She stopped in front of us, giving me a small, apologetic smile that didn't quite reach her eyes. "I didn't think you'd have company. You said in your text that Sylvie was with her dad tonight." After lowering the grocery bag to the floor, she reached out a hand to me and Aidan finally let me go so I could accept it. "I'm Laine, Aidan's best friend."

Aidan's best friend? How come he'd never mentioned her, then?

I could see, despite how put together she was, the faintest of lines around her eyes that suggested she and Aidan were the same age. She reeked of expensive perfume, money, and class. Much like him. Minus the perfume, of course. "Nora. I'm a ... *friend* too."

"Nora is more than a friend." Aidan shot me a displeased look that disappeared when he turned to Laine. Affection lit his expression and I felt an unaccountable jealousy over it. "It's nice to have you home." My jealousy only worsened as he hugged her and her fingers curled into his back.

Hmm.

Best friend, indeed.

"I can leave," Laine said, stepping back from him.

"No, don't. You've been gone a while." Aidan's reply surprised me. Weren't we just about to rip each other's clothes off? And yes, I knew it would be impolite to ask her to leave, especially since they hadn't seen each other for whatever reason, but I couldn't help the fact that my hurt was pricked. He turned to me. "Laine is a film producer for a small production company. She's been filming in New Zealand for weeks."

Wow.

Okay.

So not only was she beautiful, she was successful.

There was absolutely no reason to be threatened by that since apparently, they were just friends. Yet, Laine wasn't looking at Aidan like he was just a friend. And while she may have shaken my hand, I didn't miss the chill in the back of her pretty blue eyes when she did so.

"I brought dessert." Laine lifted the bag. "I like my dessert. As if you couldn't tell." She ran her hands over her generous hips in a self-deprecating way that rang false. Laine must have been five ten. She was all slim waist, long legs, big bust, and full hips.

Basically, she was a walking wet dream and my total opposite in every way. I watched Aidan for any reaction to her but he was looking at me. There was apology in his expression and, if I wasn't mistaken, sexual frustration.

I relaxed marginally, realizing he was being a good friend, but that didn't mean he welcomed the interruption.

Ungenerously, I thought that if Laine was any kind of friend, she would've read the situation and given us privacy. Then I realized she had a key to his apartment and my jealousy returned tenfold.

How could I be jealous of a woman Aidan had been friends with for God knows how long? He and I had only met for real a few months ago. But jealous I was, and I did not like the emotion. Not even a little bit.

Attempting to cover my feelings, I gave him a reassuring smile and watched as he followed Laine into the kitchen to share out the pyramid of profiteroles and wine she'd brought. They worked around each other with ease, silently giving away their comfort with each other.

I swallowed hard, suddenly feeling *I* was the one who was intruding. "Bathroom?" I asked Aidan.

He gestured to me to come to him and I walked over, wanting to tug at my dress but stopping myself from making it obvious that I felt like a young country bumpkin next to Laine's casual sophistication.

Aidan's hand came to rest on my lower back, his fingers touching my ass, as he guided me down the hall to a door opposite the one he'd said was the master suite. He pushed it open, revealing a good-sized bathroom, tiled in a masculine gray slate. It had a large shower, an amazing claw-footed tub, and the essentials of toilet and sink. Aidan lowered his head and brushed a kiss across my lips. He murmured, "I'm sorry about this."

"Don't be," I whispered. "She's your friend."

His hand on my back pressed me deeper to him. "*Just* a friend."

I believed him. It was Laine I wasn't so sure about. Call it female intuition.

After he left me, I closed the door, lost in my thoughts. Maybe I was being unfair. Just because I couldn't understand any woman not being attracted to Aidan didn't mean that every woman was. It wasn't my place to question her motives. Not yet, anyway.

I moved toward the bathroom only to realize there wasn't any toilet paper. Embarrassment filled me. I would have to go out and ask for some. Great. Willing the heat out of my cheeks, I opened the bathroom door and had just stepped into the hall when I heard my name in low tones.

"Yes, that's Nora." Aidan said.

"She's the girl who dresses like Peter Pan, isn't she? At the hospital."

I sucked in a breath, leaning back against the wall, knowing eavesdropping was not cool but was unable to stop. Aidan had told Laine about me but he hadn't told me about Laine? What did that mean?

"I can't believe you're fucking Peter Pan."

"For God's sake, Laine."

"Well, you are. I didn't walk in on something innocent here, Aidan."

"I'm not sleeping with her. Yet."

"She's a *child*."

"For Christ's sake, she's not a child. She's almost twenty-three."

"She looks younger. And she's still a child. I thought you liked women your age—you know, sophisticated and educated. You told me this girl is some American high school dropout. Has this thing with Nicky and Sylvie forced you into an early midlife crisis?"

Aidan's reply was angry. "This *thing* with Nicky and Sylvie?"

"That's ... not ... I'm sorry. That was tactless. But I'm worried about you. You're not yourself right now. You're making decisions I know you will come to regret. This girl ... she's not a good idea, Aidan."

"That's where you're wrong. You met her for two minutes and

think you've got her worked out. You don't know a damn thing about Nora. She's the best idea I've had in years. And if you're going to be judgmental, Laine, you can walk your arse right out this second."

"Jesus, Aidan, I'm sorry."

I ducked back inside the bathroom before I could hear anything else. I was already sorry for hearing too much. Trembling, I closed the door softly behind me and leaned my forehead against it. Laine hadn't come right out and said it but her meaning was clear. I wasn't sophisticated or educated enough for Aidan. Although I wasn't some high school dropout!

For a while I'd forgotten my own insecurities. Even as he showed me around his apartment that I could never imagine being able to afford, even seeing his music equipment, knowing he'd used it to produce music for talented people around the world ... I'd stopped feeling intimidated by him. All I cared about was the way he looked at me. He hadn't made me feel too young or too uncultured for him.

He made me feel necessary.

But how long would that last if his best friend could see how unlikely we were together? I'd known going in that I was someone Aidan needed temporarily, and I'd known that my heart would probably be shattered by the end of it. It was to be my repentance. Right?

However, I suddenly had an inkling of how badly I could be damaged by him if just hearing Laine point out our differences hurt this much. Moreover, seeing Laine hug Aidan familiarly had provoked a kind of jealousy I didn't know I was capable of.

Aidan Lennox was going to leave me in pieces.

I thought I was brave enough to handle it, but maybe I wasn't. Maybe Laine interrupting us before we had sex was a good thing.

Shaken, I hit the flush on the toilet like I'd used it, ran the tap, and then hurried out of there. Wondering if I looked as pale as I felt and hoping I did so it confirmed the lie I was about to tell, I rounded into the kitchen to find Laine and Aidan looking up from the dessert they'd laid out. My stomach revolted at the idea of eating it, turning my lie into a truth.

And suddenly I was more than hurt.

I was angry.

Angry for constantly beating myself up about everything. Some of it was deserved. But wasn't it time I stopped pounding myself with these insecurities? My gaze flashed angrily between them, suddenly not caring if they knew I'd heard.

"I'm sorry," I said, grabbing my purse off the kitchen counter. "I don't feel well. I don't think my stomach is *sophisticated* enough for dessert tonight."

I didn't say goodbye. I hurried straight for the front door, hearing Aidan's curse behind me. And I was almost completely out when his strong hand gripped my bicep, hauling me back around.

Irritation and concern mingled in his eyes as they blazed down at me. "Don't go. I'll tell her to leave."

I yanked my arm out of his hold. "It's fine." It wasn't, but he wasn't the person I was really angry with. I didn't even think Laine was. I was angry with myself. "Spend time with your friend. We'll talk later."

I backed up toward the elevator but Aidan followed me. "I don't want you to go."

"Nora ..." Laine suddenly appeared in his doorway. She no longer wore her sandals and looked way too comfortable for my liking. "I'm so sorry. I'm overprotective of Aidan. We've known each other since we were kids. But that's no excuse."

Her apology made it worse. There was so much history between these two and even if it was platonic, I really was the intruder. She'd been gone a while and wanted to see her best friend only to discover him lip-locked with a younger woman he'd only recently met.

One she didn't exactly approve of.

And even if she'd misjudged me, I got it.

Her words would not have hurt me so much if I hadn't felt them about myself. And the only way to stop feeling that way about myself was to change my life. I knew that.

However, I hadn't forgiven myself for Jim and until I did (if ever), I wouldn't allow myself to have the life I wanted.

It was fucked up.

I was fucked up.

Aidan didn't deserve to get entangled with someone who was this confused, even if it was to gain a temporary reprieve from his own pain. I would never hurt him by walking away from what we'd started here, but Laine's interruption was timely. We needed to get to know each other better before we threw sex into the mix and took whatever was between us to a place we could never get back from in one piece.

"It's fine," I reassured her.

"Obviously it's not." She gestured to me leaving.

"Laine," Aidan looked over his shoulder at her, sounding annoyed, "can you go back inside, please?"

She shot him a hurt look but did as he asked.

Up on my tiptoes, I pressed a kiss to the corner of his mouth in goodbye and he automatically wrapped his arms around me, keeping me there.

I smiled. "Let me go."

He shook his head, his expression broody as hell.

It made me laugh, despite the mess of feelings I was dealing with. "I'm not running away, but you have to allow me to leave, Aidan. I overheard some not very nice things about myself and I kind of just want to go home."

His hold on me tightened ever so slightly but then he slowly let go. "*Promise* me you're not running."

"I promise." I touched his chest, hoping he could see my longing for him in my eyes. Stepping back, I hit the elevator button and the doors binged open immediately. "Call me?"

"Aye, of course." He crossed his arms, disgruntled. "I'll make this up to you."

I nodded and got into the elevator.

Our eyes held and as the door began to close, something like desperation filled Aidan's gaze. "Nora—"

Whatever he was going to say was cut off by the doors closing and the elevator shifting downwards.

I leaned back against it, sighing in relief to get away from the heaviness of the situation. As the elevator doors opened on the ground floor, my phone buzzed in my purse. I fumbled with it as I exited the building and wasn't surprised to find a text from Aidan.

I don't believe any of what she said.

Another text arrived.

You're a fucking miracle.

And then another.

I'm not letting you go, Pixie.

Although I wasn't sure how I wanted things to progress now with Aidan—my mind in a battle with my body—I was sure of one thing.

I texted him in reply: *I don't want you to.*

chapter 17

After I'd gotten off the bus on Princes Street the next morning and was walking past the Waverley Train Station toward Cockburn Street, my phone rang in my purse.

Aidan.

Well, he had said he wasn't letting me go, and I guess that meant I was only getting one night of space to deal with Laine's attitude toward me. Really, it made me think about how other people would view our relationship—his friends, my friends. It kept me awake for a while until I remembered that I hadn't made a habit of caring what other people thought about every decision I made so why start now? After that I fell asleep, determined I wouldn't let Laine pick at my insecurities. So I wasn't sophisticated or cultured and I *was* young. But, despite my mistakes, I wasn't a bad person. I had a good heart, even if it had led me down the wrong paths sometimes. Moreover, I cared about people, even strangers on the street. I was intelligent and self-educated to a point. I worked hard and was a good listener, and I was mature for my age.

These were all qualities to be admired, and it was about time I started to believe in myself a little more.

I only hoped my self-administered pep talk stuck to me like glue while I was in Aidan's world.

"Hey," I answered, putting a finger in my other ear to block out the traffic on the road next to me.

"Just wanted to check in, make sure you're okay."

"I am," I reassured him. "I'm good. You?" What I really wanted to ask was how long Laine hung around after I was gone, but I kept my jealousy to myself.

"Frustrated that our night didn't go according to plan. We both deserved to have it."

Part of me wanted to say there will be other nights but I didn't want to mislead him. "You got to spend time with your friend, though."

Aidan sighed. "Not really. I wasn't in the greatest mood when you left so Laine went home."

"I'm sorry." Was it wrong that I really, really wasn't?

"You have nothing to be sorry for. You weren't the one who was rude."

Oh, dear. It seemed Laine wasn't forgiven quite yet. I was a little gleeful about that. I never knew I could be petty until I saw Laine hug Aidan possessively.

"Anyway, Sylvie's back from Cal's and I was thinking the three of us could have dinner tonight if you're free?"

Relieved, I nodded, even though he couldn't see me. "That sounds great."

"I don't want to chase you off, Pixie. I'm willing to take this slow if that's what you need. Or go as fast as you like. Your call. I don't want to rush you into anything."

Maybe he'd sensed my fear as I got on that elevator last night, or maybe it was him being a nice guy, offering me a more normal pace. Whatever his reasoning, I was grateful. "I think we should slow it down a little."

There was silence on the other end and I felt flutters in my stomach, wondering what that silence meant. Eventually, he said, "We're only slowing down, though, right? Not coming to a halt?"

"Only slowing down. I ..." Nearing the store, I ducked into a quiet alcove. "I've only ever been with Jim. I ... it's not that I don't want to. I just ... I—"

"Nora," Aidan interrupted, his voice firm. "We go at your pace."

"Then let's get to know each other a little better first."

"We can do that."

Feeling unburdened and also amazed that I could be so honest with Aidan and have him actually listen, I grinned. "I can't wait to see you tonight. Sylvie too."

"Me too. Sylvie will be excited."

"Good. I have to go or I'll be late for work."

"Okay, Pixie. My place again around seven? I'll cook. Do you want me to pick you up?"

"No, if you're busy cooking, I can get a bus."

"Let me get you a cab."

I rolled my eyes. "Aidan, I can get a bus."

"A cab is safer."

"I use the bus all the time. I'll see you at seven."

"Fine, but don't … wear anything too sexy. Like yesterday."

I heard the amusement in his voice and chuckled. "You thought the dress I was wearing yesterday was sexy? Really? That?"

"It was sexy," he argued. "There were legs and tits everywhere."

I burst out laughing, startling a girl passing by who hadn't realized I was standing there. I gave her an apologetic smile and turned away. "There was not."

"Everywhere," he insisted, teasing. "Tonight, jeans and a jumper that covers everything below your chin."

"I'll wear what I want."

"Aye," he grumbled. "I thought you'd say that."

"I understand it must be exciting for an old guy like yourself to see twenty-two-year-old legs and tits but you did promise you could take this slow," I teased right back.

Aidan gave a huff of amusement, making the line crackle. "Almost twenty-three. And I didn't get to see your tits. I got to see nipple and fuck, we need to stop talking about this right now. Don't you have somewhere to be?"

Giggling at his disgruntlement, I managed a yes.

"Then get going. Oh, and Pixie …"

"Yeah?"

"Crack another old guy joke and I'll speed things up so fast, you won't be able to walk for days."

My breath stuttered and there was a tense silence between us. Finally, I huffed out, "Well played," and hung up.

———

THIS TIME WHEN THE ELEVATOR DOORS OPENED TO AIDAN'S FLOOR, IT was Sylvie who came flying out to greet me. She wrapped her arms around my waist and hugged me tightly.

"Hey, you." I brushed her hair off her face as she grinned at me.

"Uncle Aidan made lasagna!"

I laughed at her excitement as she led me into the apartment. "I take it you like lasagna?"

"It's my favorite thing after mac and cheese. You like lasagna, right?" I nodded and she beamed. "Knew it!"

"Knew what?" Aidan sauntered around the kitchen counter, drying his hands on a dishtowel. The apartment smelled amazing and my belly didn't know whether to growl hungrily or flip-flop in thrill at the mere sight of Aidan Lennox and the sexy smile he was shooting my way.

"That Nora likes lasagna," Sylvie said.

"That's good news," Aidan approached me, his eyes dancing with laughter, "because Sylvie insisted I make a ton of it." He bent down to press a lingering kiss to the corner of my mouth and my breath caught at his nearness. "Hi, Pixie."

"Hey, yourself."

I think he heard my breathiness because his smile turned cocky.

Sylvie had no reaction to any of this other than to smile at me and insist, "Come see my room."

Instead of telling her I'd already seen it, I let her have her fun and followed her into the blue and purple space that was all Sylvie. I oohed and aahed over it like I'd wanted to yesterday.

"The best part—" Sylvie reached for a guitar case I hadn't seen braced against the side of one of the posts on her bed. "Uncle Aidan's teaching me. Do you want to hear?"

"Of course." I sat down on her bed while she got the guitar out. It was a small blue acoustic covered in purple star stickers. When Sylvie started to sing and play Bruno Mars *Lazy Song*, my jaw nearly hit the floor. Her sweet young voice was sweet and clear, and she played the guitar well. She was pure joy.

When she was finished, she looked at me expectantly.

I burst into applause and we both jerked around when it was joined by another. Aidan stood in her doorway clapping. His eyes moved from Sylvie to me and I shook my head in wonder. "She's amazing."

"I know."

"Do you think so, Nora?"

I turned back to her. "You're so talented, kid."

She smiled shyly. "Uncle Aidan won't let me record anything."

Looking over my shoulder, I watched as Aidan strolled slowly into the room and over to her. Gently extricating the guitar from her hands, he told her gently, "You're too young. Now be a good girl and go set the table."

She made a face. "We don't have a table."

"You know I meant the counter."

With a beleaguered sigh, Sylvie did his bidding, leaving us alone in her room. I watched him as he put her guitar in the case. I tentatively said, "Maybe she *should* be doing something with her talent?"

He placed the guitar back against the wall and sat down next to me on the bed, his leg pressed against mine. His hand came down on the top of my thigh, like he couldn't be near me and not touch me. "Like what?"

I hadn't come to his apartment tonight with the thought of broaching the subject of Sylvie's education, and I certainly didn't want to overstep but I was worried about her. It trumped my fear of pissing off Aidan. "Like a choir. At school. Where maybe she should be again?"

Aidan's hand tensed on my leg but he didn't move it. "I home-schooled her so she could be close to her mum, and then I thought it best to let her have time to adjust to life without Nicky."

"It's been over a year, Aidan," I said gently. "I know this might not be any of my business, but Sylvie lights up when she's with the kids at the hospital. Maybe it's time you put her back in school and let her have some normality again."

"It's not that I haven't thought about it. I just don't want to put her through too many changes in a short period of time."

"This would be a good change. Talk to her. She's a smart kid, and we both know she knows her own mind."

He exhaled heavily. "I'm fucking this up, aren't I?"

"No!" I cupped his face in my hands, rubbing my thumbs over the thick bristle on his cheeks. My eyes got lost in his as I found myself wanting to wipe away every fear or concern this man had. "You are doing magnificently."

His lips quirked at the corner. "Magnificently?"

I smiled. "Magnificently."

Quite abruptly, his mouth was on mine and heat flashed through my body as I clung to him.

"Uncle Aidan, the oven is beeping!"

Aidan released me with a groan. "What are you doing to me, Pixie?" He stood up swiftly, running a hand through his hair. "No fucking control," he muttered before storming out of the room.

I didn't know whether to be overjoyed he wanted me so much or worried that his lack of control meant we'd be speeding things up despite my request for slow. Because it seemed that as soon as that man got his mouth on me, I was ready to get naked.

Not too long later, we ate sitting on stools at the kitchen counter. I was amused when Aidan pointedly put Sylvie between us. She made us laugh as she chattered about the day she'd spent with her dad at the zoo.

"He tried to pretend like the penguins didn't scare him but they so did." She giggled, screwing up her face. "How can you be scared of penguins?"

"Clearly, he's seen *Batman Returns*," Aidan murmured.

"Huh?" Sylvie said, echoing my thoughts.

"It's a movie." Aidan shrugged. "With a very scary penguin man in it."

"Oh. I don't think I want to see a movie with a scary penguin man in it."

"I wouldn't let you see that movie, even if you wanted to, sweetheart."

Before she could argue—because telling a girl she can't do something only makes her want to do it more—I asked, "So, you had fun with your dad?"

She nodded, smiling, and it was the first positive answer I'd gotten from her regarding Cal. "Yeah. It was good."

"That's great, sweetie."

"Listen, Sylvie." Aidan turned to her, looking very serious. "How would you feel about going back to school?" I didn't know why he decided to talk to her about this while I was present, but I knew it meant I'd earned his trust.

She stared up at him for a second and I didn't like the hint of anxiety I caught in her eyes. "Won't ... won't you be sad without me?"

Understanding dawned and I saw it did for Aidan too. "I'm happy when you're happy, sweetheart. And if going back to school would make you happy, I'll be over the moon."

She glanced at me, seeming unsure, and I gave her a little nod of encouragement. Turning back to Aidan, she nodded. "I want to go back."

Aidan grinned and Sylvie's whole being appeared to relax. All this time she hadn't wanted to say she'd like to go back to school because she thought her uncle would be sad for her to leave him during the day. Oh, this kid! I wanted to hug her so tightly.

Her uncle wrapped his arm around her and pulled her deep into his side for a cuddle. "Then we'll get you back to school."

After that, Sylvie was a bundle of excitement, barely sitting still to eat dessert, and not giving us a chance to digest it when she shot over to Aidan's computer. "Uncle Aidan, let Nora hear the music for the dancers."

"Sylvie, we've just eaten."

"*I'll* let her hear, then."

"You know," he slipped off his stool, walking quickly toward her, "not to touch the computer."

She grinned cheekily at him. "It made you come over, though."

I snorted and then tried to cover the sound of my laughter as Aidan shot me a look. "Sorry," I mouthed, but he shook his head, a small smile playing around his gorgeous lips.

"Is it this one?" he asked Sylvie as he clicked on something.

"Yeah."

I hopped off the stool and wandered over to them but before I reached them, music flared into the room, halting me.

I didn't know a lot about music, only what I liked to listen to. Aidan's was instrumental. It started slow, melancholic, with violins and cellos. And the piano. And the oboe. Goosebumps prickled along my skin as the tempo picked up with drums and the strings grew more wailing and violent. Then suddenly, joined by an electric dance bass, it became soaring, rushing, and made my body wanted to fly around the room.

Eventually, it trailed off to a whimper and my eyes flew to Aidan's. Something darkened in his expression, something like longing, and I knew it was mirrored in my own. "That was stunning," I whispered, in awe of him.

"Thank you," he said, his voice a little hoarse. He cleared it. "It's for an international dance group called The Company. I know one of the directors and she asked me to write the music for their upcoming show."

I'd heard of The Company. I'd seen them on television. They were amazing! "Aidan, that's wonderful. Your music is wonderful."

He gave me a boyish smile that made me almost forget Sylvie was in the room.

But then she pleaded, "Play the piano for Nora, Uncle Aidan, please!"

"Maybe later."

"You'll forget later." Sylvie pouted.

Since I'd been longing to hear him play the instrument from the moment I saw it in his apartment, I said, "Actually, I'd quite like to hear you play if you wouldn't mind?"

Aidan shook his head, but he smiled. "Ganged up on."

Anticipation held me frozen in place as he slid onto the piano bench. "What would you like to hear?"

I was about to ask him to play an original piece when Sylvie demanded, "Goodbye Yellow Brick Road."

To my confusion Aidan tensed, the amusement dimming in his eyes. "Sweetheart…"

Sylvie leaned on the piano with her elbow and cupped her face in her hand. "Please," she said with big beguiling eyes.

I didn't understand Aidan's reluctance, or the sorrow that passed fleetingly across his expression, before he smoothed it away and started to play. The ballad was familiar to me only because of Angie. The Elton John song was one of her favorites. Sylvie's choice was surprising, not only because it was way before her time, but because it was a melancholy tune about a man who gets what he always thought he wanted only to feel like it's a life that doesn't belong to him, and then longs for a simpler time. A simpler life.

It was a little grown up for Sylvie.

Although I liked the song, it never made me emotional the way it appeared to make Angie when she listened to it. However, watching Aidan's fingers dance effortlessly across the keys, taking in the way he studied Sylvie in concern I felt goosebumps prickle my skin.

Something passed between uncle and niece that I didn't understand, but it was weighed down with so much emotion I could only guess that the song had some significance in regard to Nicky.

When the music came to an end, silence fell over us all.

I wanted to reach out and draw both of them into my arms.

Before I could offer comfort, however, Sylvie drew up from the piano and announced, "I'm going to go practice on the guitar so I'll be so good, Uncle Aidan *has* to put me in a song."

She dashed out of the room, her earlier bittersweet expression apparently replaced with determination, and Aidan and I shared a tender look.

"She's pretty awesome, huh?"

His gaze drifted to where she disappeared. "She's Nicky. As long as I have Sylvie, I haven't lost my Nicky. Goodbye Yellow Brick Road was Nicky's favorite. She asked me to play it for her a few hours before she died."

Emotion burned in my throat for him and I blinked away tears, looking out at the view over the canal so he wouldn't see that I was a total watering pot.

"Can I get you anything else?" he asked.

It sounded like there was innuendo in his voice, quickly drying up my tears. I shot him a chiding look. "No, you may not."

He laughed. "I didn't mean it like that. Dirty girl."

I bit my lip to hold back my smile but it was impossible around him. "I'll have water, please."

Less than a minute later, I had a bottle of water in my hand and we were seated on the corner sofa with much-needed distance between us. The sounds of Sylvie's guitar and her sweet voice played soundtrack in the background.

I thought of last night and how close we'd gotten to making love. "Why didn't you mention Laine before last night?" I blurted out.

Aidan frowned. "Didn't I?"

"Nope."

"She's been gone a while so I guess she never really came up. Last night you got to see a shit side of her. I'm sorry. She's actually a really good person. She's just protective of her friends and family."

Hmm. Protective indeed.

"How long have you known each other?"

"Since we were kids. Teenagers."

"And you're just friends?" I'd decided there was no point pussy-footing around it. If Aidan had a fuck buddy, I needed to know about it.

Something flickered in his eyes before he said, "Just friends."

Suspicious, I cocked my head, studying him. "Were you always just friends?"

He sighed. "We dated when we were kids. Sixteen. Seventeen. We broke up but we stayed friends. There's nothing to be jealous of. Believe me."

They'd dated when they were kids. Had he dumped her and she'd never gotten over him? I could be completely off-base but for someone who was "actually a really good person," but she'd actually been a really huge bitch last night. And people were only bitchy when they were pissed off, territorial, etc.

I heard Aidan when he talked to me. I listened. He'd made it clear he wanted something more between us than sex. He wanted a relationship. However, he hadn't mentioned whether we were exclusive, and as much as I was working on my insecurities, I still had my doubts about being able to keep his attention.

Rather than stew on those thoughts, I decided to be honest. "I know we're taking it slow and you're probably not used to that … so I … are you seeing anyone else, Aidan?"

His expression darkened. "No."

At his blunt, annoyed response, I scowled. "I'm not accusing you of anything. I'm trying to get a clear picture of what's going on between us because I'm not the kind of woman who can share." That became very obvious to me last night.

"Laine's a friend," he bit out. "Just a friend. And there are no other women in the picture."

"Why are you getting annoyed?"

"Because I thought it was pretty fucking obvious how I feel about you and you're making me feel like you don't trust me."

I felt a whoosh in my belly at his words, like the feeling you get when the roller coaster you're on plunges down the biggest dip on the track. "I do trust you. I'm just …" I looked away.

"You're just?"

"Not used to feeling jealous," I said.

Aidan was silent, and I continued to look out the window, afraid I'd put him off completely. Did I seem childish, naïve, possessive?

"At least you're jealous of the living, Nora," he said. "I'm fucking jealous of a dead man."

My head whipped around to him, shock slackening my features. He was tense, uncomfortable, but he held my eyes.

"I've never cared enough before to be jealous. I'm not the type. But I've been jealous of Jim from the moment he led you out of that pub. I was jealous of him in that supermarket when you brushed your hair off your face and I saw his ring on your finger."

"You didn't even know me then."

"No, but I wanted you. And it pissed me off that you were so young and you were already married. It didn't seem right. Or fair. But I understand now that I know you. I would have stolen you away too, made you mine so no one else could have you."

As beautiful as that sounded, I was also choked with guilt and sadness. "Don't feel jealous of Jim, Aidan. I loved him for three years but I was never *in love* with him. He had female friends, some who flirted with him, and I never batted an eyelash. I never feared one of them taking him from me. Toward the end, I wanted it to happen. I wanted him to fall in love with someone else and leave me so I didn't have to be the bad guy anymore.

"Laine curled her fingers into your T-shirt when she hugged you, and it was enough to make me want to throw a beer in her face. And that was before she insulted me." I gave him a wobbly grin, not quite meeting his eyes, my fingers trembling around my bottle of water at my confession.

"Nora, look at me."

His voice was thick with emotion and that more than his demand made me respond. "I've never wanted anyone the way I want you. Aye, I want you in my bed, so much it's painful, but it's more than that. I just want you. Here. Talking with me. In my life. Knowing I can pick up the phone and call you or touch you whenever I want. Never have I felt that way with anyone. We clear?"

We were so clear, my body reacted. My nipples hardened, tight points beneath my bra, shivers cascaded down my spine, and I wanted some part of him between my legs more than I wanted most things in this world.

The sound of Sylvie's faint voice in the background, however, kept me from launching myself at him. So much for going slow. "We're clear."

"We should probably talk about something else," he grumbled, shifting as though uncomfortable and I guessed he was as aroused as I was.

Knowing Sylvie would douse the fire somewhat, I said, "How adorable was it that Sylvie didn't want to go back to school because she didn't want to make you sad?"

Aidan shot me a grateful look. "Aye, she can be sweet when she's not full of cheek."

I laughed. "She's smart."

"Too smart."

"Remember you said there's no such thing," I argued.

He grinned. "So I did."

"Are you talking about me?" Sylvie suddenly appeared in the hallway by the kitchen.

Aidan looked over his shoulder at her. "Why would we be talking about you?"

"I heard my name."

"We were talking about you going back to school."

"Yeah?" She hurried over and threw herself on the couch between us. "When do I go back?"

And just like that, her presence calmed the tension between Aidan and me.

Later that evening as I lay in bed, having gotten home via the taxi Aidan insisted I take, I thought about this epic thing between him and me. It was epic. I didn't even know it was possible to have so much feeling for one person. To be pulled toward him like it was completely out of my control. To want to see him every day and bury my skin against his and let the fire consume us.

And to know that he felt the same way only emphasized the power of my attraction.

I knew the smart thing to do was to take things slowly, to really get to know each other beyond the natural chemistry between us. But my God, it was going to be so much harder to slow down that I'd thought.

chapter 18

"SO, WHAT IS IT YOU REALLY WANT TO DO WITH YOUR LIFE?"

I was caught off guard by the abrupt question. Aidan and I had ordered and as the waiter walked away, I settled into my chair to enjoy our first evening alone together in a while.

He leaned his elbows on the table, ducking his head to stare into my eyes in that intensely focused way that made me feel like the only person in the world. "I mean, if you're happy working at Apple Butter, great, but you're smart, Nora. I can't imagine it's enough for you."

I shifted, feeling a little uncomfortable to be under this specific microscope. "Hitting me with the hard questions tonight, huh?"

His eyebrows rose. "I didn't realize it *was* a hard question."

In the last four weeks, we'd seen as much of each other as we could. I didn't think it was enough for either of us but I still had my work, the kids, Seonaid, Roddy, and Angie while Aidan was juggling a number of projects and Sylvie had returned to school a little over a week ago. That had been an adjustment for the two of them.

Cal wanted to spend more time with Sylvie so Aidan had agreed to let her stay with him Friday nights and Saturday during the day. He'd also jumped on the chance for us to have a date but I'd made certain, to his visible frustration, that he knew it didn't necessarily mean we were speeding things up. I had work in the morning.

The restaurant he'd decided on was The Dome on George Street.

I'd never eaten here but the inside was even more impressive than the outside. It had Greco-Roman architecture with a Corinthian portico entrance. Inside the main dining room was a central bar with tables and chairs spread out from around it. But the eye-catching part was its domed ceiling with stained glass inserts and specialist lighting.

I'd borrowed a Ralph Lauren little black dress from Seonaid. It was figure-hugging and ended at the knees on her but at the calves on me. The black stilettos I'd gotten on sale to match gave me height but they weren't the most comfortable. I was glad we were sitting down for most of the night.

As well as letting me borrow her dress, Seonaid had trimmed and cut my hair into a style that it would grow out of better.

Altogether, I wasn't looking myself. Older, sexier, and I didn't miss how taken aback Aidan was when he helped me out of my coat. His eyes had dragged down my body and back up again and at the sensual look he'd given me, I'd wondered if perhaps the dress was a mistake.

"Is it, Nora? A hard question?"

Yes, it was an incredibly difficult question. My guilt over the things I'd done hadn't gone away because I'd met Aidan and Sylvie. In fact, even though they were supposed to be my repentance, I often thought the guilt may have worsened. Aidan gave me so much more than Jim ever had, and I'd known him all of a few months.

I was still confused, still unsure, and still not ready to face my own future. And I didn't want to talk about it. "I'm happy at Apple Butter," I lied.

"With your SAT scores, I somehow doubt that."

My what? How did he ...? "What?"

"It was in the file my guy gave me when I had him look into you." He said it so blasé, like it was normal to look into people's private lives.

I'd known about it, of course, but I hadn't known it had been detailed enough to provide my SAT scores.

"You could get into the finest universities, if that was what you wanted," he said.

"That costs money, Aidan."

"We'll find a way."

My heart fluttered at *we*, but my agitation didn't leave me. "Just leave it."

Another eyebrow raise. "Why don't you want to talk about this? You've been honest with me up until this point—why stop now?"

I looked around at the low-lit room where couples and friends and families enjoyed great-looking meals. If Aidan didn't cease and desist on this subject, he was going to ruin my appetite. "We're out for a nice meal. Don't turn it into an interrogation."

"I've never needed to before. You've been upfront with me until now."

He sounded so disgruntled, he leaned away from the table, a scowl between his brows, his full lower lip pinched by the upper. I grinned, trying to ease the sudden tension between us.

"You look like a petulant schoolboy."

Aidan's lips parted in annoyance. "I've never been accused of petulance in my life."

"There's a first time for everything." I cocked my head, enjoying teasing him. "You look like someone has taken away your favorite toy."

Our food arrived so Aidan couldn't reply. I looked down at the highlander chicken on my plate, covered in whiskey sauce accompanied with smooth, creamy mash. The perfect dinner for a cold October evening. "This smells amazing."

He didn't say anything. He started to eat and I realized my teasing hadn't dissuaded him from my evasion or his annoyance with me.

I dug in because there was no way I was letting his mood spoil my dinner. Moaning around the first bite, I kicked my feet a little in food joy. Aidan's gaze flew up from his plate and I saw the crack of a smile. I wiggled my butt in my seat as I took another bite, and he outright laughed.

"Good?"

I nodded around my mouthful, my eyes wide. Swallowing, I said, "So good."

"You're like an excited pup." He shook his head, still smiling.

"I like good food."

"Then we'll make sure you have more of it in the future."

We shared a warm look and I relaxed as the tension eased between us.

———

IT WAS SILLY OF ME TO THINK AIDAN HAD GIVEN UP ON THE SUBJECT. HE was a man with a very successful career who had somehow managed to make the upturning of his life work for him.

He was determined.

Persistent.

Dogged.

Of which I was reminded while he was driving me home. Our evening had been filled with casual conversation as we learned little things about each other and talked about our week. We also discussed Sylvie and how quickly she'd adapted to being back at school.

But we were only in his car a few minutes when he said, "I don't like the fact that you feel like you can't talk to me."

Surprised by the turn in conversation and by the untruth in his statement, I frowned at him. He quickly glanced at me before looking back at the road. "Glare at me all you want but you're the one hiding something."

"I'm not hiding anything."

"You don't want to talk about your future and that's a pretty big fucking deal, Nora."

"What do you want me to say?"

"I want you to tell me what you want from your future."

I want what's sitting in the seat next to me. But I didn't confess that. "I'm not sure."

"What about the theater? You told me you wanted to act when you were a kid. Clearly that hasn't changed. I've seen how you are when you're Peter Pan. You become someone totally different for those kids. It's amazing to watch."

I flushed at the compliment. "Thank you. That's sweet. But it doesn't mean I want to act."

"It doesn't mean you don't."

"Argh, you are an annoying man sometimes."

He grinned. "I think we're getting somewhere."

"Aidan."

"Pixie."

My stomach flipped at the thought of telling him the truth. "You don't want to know what's going on in my head right now."

"That's where you're wrong."

"*I* don't want you to know what's going on in my head," I amended.

The atmosphere changed abruptly and I could see the muscle in his jaw flex.

"Aidan?"

"We'll drop it, then."

I'd hurt his feelings. Shit. "Aidan ..." I exhaled, the sound heavy and shaky. "I don't want you to think I'm any more messed up than I already am."

"You're not messed up."

I laughed but it was hollow-sounding and it made him glance at me in concern. I reached over and squeezed his arm gratefully. "You're kind to say that, but we both know I'm living in limbo right now. And I want to be able to tell you that I'm ready to get out of it, but I'm not sure I am. A while ago, when Jim was alive, I talked to Seonaid about college here and we found out that I could get into Edinburgh to study psychology. It would only cost a couple of thousand and I knew Jim and I could afford it if we put our house-buying plans on hold. I started to imagine what life would be like as a student and was already looking into the amateur theater groups.

But the first mention of it to Jim, a mere casual comment, he completely shut me down."

"Why?" Aidan sounded as confused as I'd felt at first.

Until I'd realized the truth. "He knew, Aidan. He knew I didn't love him like he loved me and he was scared that if I went to college, I wouldn't need him anymore. He was scared he'd lose me. But stopping me only pushed me away even further."

"So why haven't you done it … now that he's …"

"Now that he's gone?" I finished for him, the words sounding bitter even to my ears. "Guilt."

"Guilt?" Aidan pulled up in front of my building, switched off the engine, and turned to me. I could see something like anger brewing in his eyes. "Guilt?" he repeated.

Knowing not to tell him was to push him away, I forged ahead with the truth. "I don't deserve it. I told you before … I stole years with Jim. Why should I get to have the things I want?"

"Jesus Christ, Nora." He ran a hand over his face, looking shell-shocked by what I'd said.

I waited, anxious to know what that meant.

Suddenly, something seemed to occur to him and he looked at me sharply. "If you really feel that way, like you don't deserve to move on, then why are you here? What am I to you?"

I whispered, "I couldn't stay away from you if I tried. You? You're everything, Aidan."

It was as though the words winded him and then that fierce determination blazed across his face as he reached over to unclip my seat belt. Shoving it out of the way, he wrapped his arms around my waist and hauled me across the center console into his lap.

My foot caught on the steering wheel and I laughed as I tried to get comfortable. "You could've just asked me to come closer."

He didn't laugh. He kissed me.

I sank against him, opening my mouth and kissing him back, deepening it. I loved the way his fingers tightened on my hips, almost bruising as they gripped me with need. I cupped his face, loving the scratch of his unshaved cheeks against my hands, and I spread my legs across his lap so I could press deeper against him. At the feel of Aidan's erection nudging me, I gasped into his mouth and ground into him. His groan reverberated through me and I tilted my hips, liking the waves of pleasure rocking through me as I rubbed against him.

Suddenly, I found myself pushed away and I blinked, confused for a second until I saw the impatient desire on his face. "Please tell me we're done with going slow. I need you, Nora," his voice was low, hoarse, "so fucking much."

The flames of want licked hungrily at me too and I couldn't turn him away. Four weeks was slow enough. "I don't have much in my apartment, but there is a bed."

He immediately threw open his door and I tried to slip off him and outside as gracefully as possible. Aidan was right behind me, his arm around my waist, not letting me go, as he reached into the car for my purse and then shut the door behind him. I took my purse in one hand and his hand in the other, hearing the beep of his car lock and vaguely wondering if it was a good idea to leave his car there, but caring more about getting him upstairs and naked.

Inside the building, I turned into him, not able to wait even a second for one more kiss. He granted my wish and we stumbled against the bottom of the stairwell wall as I lost my footing in the stupid stilettos.

I groaned into his mouth as one large hand smoothed down my ass and gripped it, pulling me into him so his raging hard-on pushed against my belly, while the other hand cupped and squeezed my breast. "Oh God—" I broke the kiss, feeling more desperate than I'd ever felt in my life. "I feel like I'm on fire."

"Tell me about it." He pulled away and gently nudged me upstairs. "Lead the way, Pixie, before this happens in the stairwell."

The tingling between my legs intensified at the image of us going at it here, and I found I rather got off on the idea of Aidan and I having risqué sex. Hmm. I filed the thought for later and hurried up the stairs. We couldn't even speak we were so focused on getting to my apartment and to my bed. And I couldn't even care he was going to see where I lived. I only cared about getting this man inside me. Finally!

I practically skittered around the corner into my hall and then stumbled to a halt at the sight of a person sitting outside my door.

What?

Shit.

Seonaid looked up at me, her eyes red-rimmed, her cheeks pale. I felt Aidan's heat at my back, along with the press of a possessive hand above my ass. Seonaid's eyes grew wide as they flew to him, and she quickly got on her feet. She gave me a shaky smile. "I can leave."

"No," I said immediately. My friend looked like she hadn't slept for days. "What's going on?"

She ran a hand over her messy ponytail, looking uncomfortable and embarrassed. "I'll come back."

Realizing how rude I was being, I turned to Aidan, who looked confused, frustrated, but also a little concerned. "Aidan, this is Seonaid." I'd talked about her with him and his eyes lit with recognition. "Seonaid, this Aidan." I'd only confessed to Seonaid last weekend about Aidan after realizing I needed to borrow something to wear for my date. I'd tried to play it down and would've been successful too if her appearance here was anything to go by. Seonaid would never have come here if she thought I was sleeping with Aidan, since she was such a huge advocate for me moving on. But her witnessing Aidan and I panting down the hall had blown that evasion out of the water.

Right now, I didn't care.

Something was up with my friend.

"Nice to meet you." Aidan held out a hand to her.

She took it, giving him a tremulous smile. "You too."

"Look," he put his hand on my shoulder, drawing my attention back to him, "I'm going to head home, let you catch up with your friend. Call me?"

Feeling guilty for getting him all hot and bothered, I gave him an apologetic smile. "You sure?"

"Of course." He leaned down and pressed a soft kiss to my mouth and when he pulled back, he murmured against my lips, "But we pick up where we left off, Pixie."

I grinned. "Agreed."

He gave me one more quick kiss, like he couldn't help himself, gave Seonaid a nod of goodbye, and walked away.

I stared after him, regretting we'd been interrupted, even though I was worried about Seonaid. When I looked back at her, she winced apologetically. "I'm so sorry."

"Don't be." I grabbed her arm and led her to my door, fumbling in my purse for the key. I let us in, locking it behind us. "Now, what's going on?"

"Oh fuck, Nora," she groaned, her hands on her head in despair. "I had sex with Roddy."

chapter 19

"You what?"

Seonaid groaned at my expression and slumped down onto my sofa. "Oh, I've fucked up, haven't I?"

Stunned and confused, and still trying to come down from sexual frustration, I moved into the kitchen to put the kettle on. "Why don't you start from the beginning?" *How the hell had this happened?*

"Fuck, fuck, fuck."

"Seonaid."

"I don't know… Fuck!"

I waited patiently for her to speak. The kettle started to boil and whine loudly, so she waited, likely using the time to gather her thoughts. We looked at each other across the small space. At the fear darkening her blue eyes, I felt anxious. What did this mean for our friendship? If Seonaid and Roddy started avoiding each other, would that mean our threesome would crumble over time? Would Roddy and I eventually stop talking altogether if he no longer spoke with Seonaid? And how would Angie react to that?

As difficult as it was at first, I'd started to feel like I was getting my friends back and was able to do so without the grief or pain constantly attacking me. More than that, however, Roddy and Seonaid needed each other. I hope they hadn't screwed that up.

She waited while I made us tea and brought it over. She clasped her mug tightly in her hands, shivering as heat rushed into her.

The apartment was cold and would be while the central heating booted up. We kept our coats on, looking at each over our hot mugs of tea. "Well?"

Seonaid gave me a grim look. "A man came into the salon yesterday with his girlfriend and I swear to God, Nora, he was Jim's spitting image. I've been trying," her lips trembled as tears filled her eyes, "I've been trying so hard to keep it together for you and Mum, but something happened when I saw that guy … I felt haunted for the rest of the day. And I really wanted to be around someone who loved him as much as I did, someone who could handle my sadness. So I went to Roddy." She shot me a teary, apologetic look, and I felt guilty that she felt I couldn't handle her grief. "I told him what happened and he … he held me while I cried. And then we had a few beers together and …" She shook her head, disbelief written all over her face. "We'd been talking together on the couch and then somehow, we were all over each other."

Engrossed, I urged, "What happened next?"

"We had sex on the couch and before I could even think about what the hell we'd done, he picked me up and took me to his bed." She said it like she was horrified but her expression conveyed anything but horror. "And we went at it again. Like animals." She shivered and bit her lip and I had to stop myself from laughing.

Clearly, Seonaid had enjoyed herself.

So, what was the problem?

"Afterward, I couldn't believe what the hell we'd done!" She threw her hands up and stood, spilling tea over her mug without realizing. "How the hell could we have done this? We're Roddy and Seonaid! Friends! My little brother's best friend."

"You've slept with men younger than Roddy," I reminded her.

"Not the point." She whirled around, eyes blazing. "We screwed up one of the most important relationships in our lives."

"Does Roddy feel that way?" Somehow, I doubted it.

"Look, I'm not stupid, okay. Roddy has fancied me his entire life so it was obvious he was pretty fucking satisfied with himself." She made a face. "But I can see what he can't."

"And what's that?"

"That sex between us only messes things up. I can't have casual sex with Roddy."

"What if he doesn't want to have casual sex?" He definitely didn't.

"Of course it's casual sex. It's Roddy."

Oh dear God, how could she be so blind? "I'm pretty sure Roddy sees you as more than casual sex."

"Exactly. He cares about me. Like I care about him. So being fuck buddies—no matter how amazing the sex was, and oh my God, it was annoyingly *amazing*—will only damage how we feel for each other. He's a bloke, so he can't see that far ahead, but I can."

"Maybe it would turn into something more?"

"Nora," she huffed my name in exasperation, "it won't. That's what I'm trying to say. But Roddy ... he doesn't get it." Slumping down again, her eyes watered. "He's really mad at me right now. I think I may have acted like what we'd done was disgusting and somehow managed to hurt his feelings. You know ... the ones he pretends he doesn't have."

My chest ached for Roddy because I knew she'd more than hurt his feelings. She'd given him everything he'd ever wanted and then taken it away, as if what they'd done was shameful. I knew Seonaid hadn't meant it and I could see how remorseful she felt, but I was still hurt on Roddy's behalf. "He cares about you, Seonaid. You need to tell him everything you told me."

"I want to sweep it under the rug and hope that things return to normal. I can't lose his friendship, Nora."

"Then go to him. Tell him that." It might not be what he wanted to hear but at least he'd know he was important to her.

Seonaid was quiet, and then she looked up at me from beneath her long, wet lashes. "Sorry I interrupted your evening."

At her pointed comment, I shifted a little uncomfortably. "About that—"

"You are allowed to have sex with other men, Nora. I'm happy for you."

"I wasn't anticipating it happening. I mean..." I flopped back against the couch. "I lose my head every time I'm around him."

"Does that mean you two are already...?"

"No. I mean, we're definitely heading in that direction and have been." I gave her an apologetic look. "I didn't want to talk about it yet."

"I get it." She kicked off her boots and curled her feet up on the couch. "You didn't mention he's older than you. Or that he is seriously, seriously hot."

I laughed nervously. "Too hot."

"No such thing."

"Is the age difference that noticeable?" I asked, worried.

"Only that he's older than you. How? How old is he?"

"Twelve years older."

"Ach, that's nothing. That means he knows what he's doing in bed."

I grinned. "Yeah, I'm pretty sure he does."

Her smile fell as she studied me carefully. "You have feelings for him?"

"He needs me," I evaded. "He and Sylvie need me. And you? Are you sure you don't have feelings for Roddy?"

"I lost Jim. I can't lose Roddy," she evaded right back.

OVER THE NEXT FEW DAYS I TRIED TO CALL RODDY TO SEE IF HE WAS okay but he was avoiding my calls, which meant he absolutely wasn't okay. My plan was to drop in at Leith's Landing on Sunday to see if I could catch him there and assess his situation for myself.

However, before Sunday could be reached, I made my way over to Aidan's to have dinner with him and Sylvie. I didn't know how we were going to get through another evening without it ending with us ripping our clothes off but I knew we both wouldn't want to have sex with Sylvie in the apartment.

He needed to get a bigger place with thick walls and many doors between his and Sylvie's room.

No one answered the buzzer at the front entrance so I hit a few of his neighbors until someone let me in. Aidan's apartment door was unlocked so I pushed in tentatively, wondering where they were. I had a bad feeling in my gut I couldn't explain.

"Guys?" I called as I walked into the apartment.

Aidan stood outside on the balcony, staring out at the view, his hands in his pockets. Although I couldn't see his face, his posture was rigid. That and his lack of greeting at the door put me on alert. I looked behind me but there was no Sylvie. When I stopped to listen, however, I could hear the faint sound of music playing from her room.

I moved over to the patio doors and pulled it open. Aidan's head turned slightly but he didn't look at me. He was so remote.

I stepped out onto the balcony and placed a hand on his back. I studied his profile, willing him to look at me, and finally he did. What I saw in his expression made my body lock in fear.

There was raw anger and grief. "Aidan?"

He shook his head and looked back out at the view and my insides jangled with nerves.

"Aidan, please, tell me what's going on."

"I'm afraid if I speak," he bit out, "that'll I do something stupid. Like ... fucking kill him."

Dear God, what the hell was going on? "Okay, you're freaking me out."

Instead of answering, he whipped around and marched back inside the apartment. I hurried after him, closing the door behind us and locking out the cold. He'd been standing out there in nothing but a thermal henley and jeans.

"Where's Sylvie?"

"In her room. Listening to her idol's new album. Clueless. The way I want her to stay."

"Aidan, you have to talk to me."

His answer was to grab my hand and lead me down the hallway to a door I'd only peeked in. It led us into the master suite. A spacious room decorated in dove gray and accented with navy. Masculine, tranquil. He had a huge bed and bedside tables, a big comfy armchair, and not much else. Off the master suite I saw an open door to a dressing room, and opposite the bed another door leading to a private bathroom.

He closed the door behind us and then suddenly hauled me into his arms. I wrapped mine around his waist as he bent his head to the crook of my neck and held me. To my ever-mounting concern, I felt tremors run through him and I tightened my embrace, as if that could somehow ease whatever had done this to him.

After what felt like forever, he pulled back, cupping my face in his hands and staring at me like he wished I could ease his pain too. But what pain? What was going on? "Aidan?"

"He's taking her from me." His eyes glistened as his anger hit me full force. "Cal's taking Sylvie."

Stunned, horrified, confused, I could do nothing but stare at him as I tried to work out what the hell he could mean. "What? No. Wh —Aidan, that's not possible. I thought that wasn't possible. You have guardianship. Full custody."

He shook his head, scrubbing his hands over his short beard like he wanted to rip the thing off in frustration.

I didn't understand. Hadn't Jan told me Nicky had full custody and she'd left Sylvie to Aidan's legal care?

"There was never anything legal about the custody arrangements between Nicky and Cal," he gritted out. "They agreed that she would have full custody and he would see Sylvie whenever he could. When Nicky died, he didn't even question that she'd asked me to take care of Sylvie."

Anger was building in my gut. "So why now?"

Aidan caught my flare of fury and fed off it, his face darkening. "Well, according to him, he always wanted to but he didn't want to put Sylvie through too much change. She'd been living with me for months with Nicky. But now … now the fucker is getting married and he wants to give Sylvie a more stable environment to grow up in. His fucking words."

"There has to be something we can do."

"I've already spoken to my lawyer. She wasn't …" He looked away, his throat working as if he was trying to hold down emotion. His voice hoarse, he said, "She wasn't hopeful. But she says we can try. That there's evidence to prove he's been an unstable parent in her life." Aidan looked back at me, his fear right at the surface. "We have to try, Nora, because he's … he's moving to California." He flexed his hands, eyes burning with unshed tears. "He's moving my wee girl away from me."

I let my tears fall on his behalf, shaking my head. No. Cal couldn't do this to him. I wouldn't let him. "No." I shook my head. "No."

Aidan pulled me into his arms, kissing my hair, wrapping me up so tight. But in the end, it was me comforting him, whispering words of fierce assurance that nothing on earth would stop us from keeping that little girl with him.

———

SINCE NICKY HAD NEVER FILED WITH THE COURT FOR FULL CUSTODY, since there was never any legal mention that Cal hadn't been around when Sylvie was little, and since he'd provided financial assistance even if he hadn't provided emotional assistance, Aidan's lawyer gave him the bad news less than a week later.

I'd called him every day as soon as I got off work, and I'd wanted to meet him after my volunteer session on Wednesday but he'd told me he was bogged down with work and the legal situation and we'd talk later. Trying not to feel useless, I told myself I understood, but what I really wanted was to be there for him.

On Thursday after work, I called him as I walked down Cockburn Street toward my bus stop. Just as I was about to hang up, he answered.

And I knew by his tone that it was bad news. "Where are you?" I said.

"At the flat."

"I'm coming to you."

"No, Nora, I ... I had to tell Sylvie today and she's not good, I think—" He was cut off at the sound of Sylvie's petulant cry in the background. "I want Nora!"

Wanting to be there that instant, I said, "Let me come over, Aidan. Let me be there for you both."

He was quiet and then gruffly agreed. Not wanting to delay, I did what I usually couldn't afford to do and grabbed a cab. During the short journey, I tried not to think about the fact that Aidan wanted to push me away right now. How could he not understand that the thought of him losing Sylvie crippled me? They'd stolen my heart. It was theirs. And now it was breaking for them.

This time when I stepped out of the elevator, Sylvie was there. She rushed me, knocking me back on my heels, and I let her cling to me, holding her tight as she cried quiet tears.

Once I got her back in the apartment, Aidan took her hand and led her away to clean her face, murmuring to her all the time that everything would be okay. When he came back, he was alone. "She needs a minute."

I was bristling with fury. "I don't understand how this is happening."

"This is happening because Nicky stupidly believed that the arsehole would always put his career before Sylvie. That there was no fucking need for legalities," he hissed. "And I stupidly fucking let her convince me."

"Is it this woman?" I asked. "This Sally person. Do you think she's got something to do with it?"

"Oh, she's got everything to do with it," he said, lowering his voice. "She sat in the meeting with our lawyers today looking so fucking smug. If he wasn't getting married, he would've buggered off to California without Sylvie."

I glanced toward the back of the apartment, remembering the few times I'd met Cal. He seemed to care for Sylvie, but what did I know.

"He upped his visitation over the last year deliberately." Aidan shook his head, seeming exasperated with himself for not seeing it. "Everything he's been doing since Nicky died has been calculated."

"He should've told you."

Aidan's eyes flew to mine and the heartbreak was too much for me to bear. "Aye."

We both knew, without saying it, that if Cal had told Aidan his plans from the start, Aidan would've had time to prepare. He wouldn't have spent the last year planning his future as Sylvie's father.

Tears threatened to spill and I reached for him but he waved me off. "I can't," he told me gruffly. "I have to keep it together for Sylvie."

I nodded. "She seems to understand what's going on."

"I think she could've coped with the idea as long as she was staying in Edinburgh, seeing me, seeing her friends. But dragging her off to fucking California ..." He trailed off, shaking his head. "He's a selfish bastard."

"Didn't the lawyers think the same?"

"As far as the law is concerned, Cal is her father. It's on the birth certificate. He's provided financial assistance for her upbringing, and he's getting married and settling down. I'm merely her bachelor uncle with a less-than-stable career. My lawyer said it was so fucking cut and dry, it wouldn't even make it to court. I'd have to prove that something sinister was going on with Cal, and there isn't. And in any case, they'd likely put Sylvie through all these interviews with social services and traumatizing shit I couldn't put her through. As for Cal taking her abroad, she said it was unfortunate that his job is taking him to the US, but—and I fucking quote, 'The child should remain in the custody of her birth father, especially in light of the recent loss of her mother, and a judge would see it the same way.'"

"Aidan."

"And I know they're right. Rationally, I know that. I could even get on board with letting her go to him eventually, but why the fuck does he have to take her so far away from me? Eh? Why would he do that to a kid he proclaims to love when she's already lost so fucking much?"

I tried to hold on to my anger, for his sake, to be the calm in his storm, and it took every ounce of control to do so. Still, I whispered, "Because he's selfish."

"I'm okay now." Sylvie's voice brought our heads around. She stood by the kitchen counter, her cheeks pale with red splotches from crying. Her eyes were red-rimmed but clear, and she wore a resolute look on her beautiful face that made me want to bawl like a baby. "Can we order pizza, Uncle Aidan?"

"We can order anything you want, sweetheart."

I wanted to scream.

I wanted to scream, throw a tantrum and curse the world for its utter fucking merciless unfairness!

However, I didn't.

I pasted on a shaky smile and joined them in the sitting room as Aidan called to order pizza.

We could do this. For Sylvie, we could pretend for a little while that everything was going to be okay.

chapter 20

I LOOKED AROUND AT THE FAMILIAR LIVING ROOM, CONFUSED. THE TV faced out at the room from a walnut cabinet it had sat in as long as I could remember, a huge couch positioned in front of it, with a glass coffee table I hated because it needed dust and fingerprints removed every five minutes.

There was a photo framed on the wall above the television. The picture was taken when I was about nine years old. I'm in my dad's arms and Mom is leaning into us. We look like a close family. Maybe we even were back then.

"There you are."

I spun around, shocked to hear my dad's voice, and even more shocked to see him pushing himself into the room in his wheelchair. He hadn't changed a bit since I'd left.

"Dad?"

"I've been looking for you everywhere," he snapped. "Where have you been?"

"She won't tell us." Mom walked into the room behind him, shrugging into her jacket. "And I don't have time to stick around and listen to her excuses."

"They're no excuses." Jim brushed by her.

My heart stopped. "Jim?"

He gave me a sad smile. "Ye look like ye've seen a ghost."

"You're here? How are you here?"

Ignoring my parents muttering between themselves, Jim strode right up to me and cupped my face in his hands. "I'm always here, Nora."

"Pixie?"

I spun around, out of Jim's touch, reeling at the sight of Aidan and Sylvie standing by the fireplace. "How?" *How did they get there?*

"I thought you were with us, Pixie?" *he asked, expression grim. Then just like that, Sylvie disappeared. I cried out her name and Aidan looked at the spot she'd been standing in.* "With me," *he whispered.* "I thought you were with me."

"I am!" *I cried, wanting to rush to him but I couldn't move. I couldn't budge.* "Aidan!"

"Calm, Nora, I've got ye." *I glanced over my shoulder to see Jim looking down at the floor. I followed his gaze, terror suffusing me to see skeleton hands had burst through the floor. They had an unearthly grip on my feet, locking me in place.*

"No!" *I screamed, trying to pull away.*

"Shhh," *Jim hushed me, wrapping his arms around my upper body to pull me against him.* "Ye cannae leave me, Nora. Ye owe me."

"Jim, please," *I sobbed.*

"Pixie?"

I looked over at Aidan to find him glaring at me in hostile disappointment. He lifted a hand and my fear grew as finger by finger, his hand disappeared. "Aidan!"

"Nora! Nora, what's happening?"

My eyes flew back over my shoulder to see my mother and father wearing twin looks of horror as they watched their own limbs start to disappear. "Nora!"

"Jim, let me go!" *I screamed, struggling to get to them.*

"There's nae point, Nora. Ye'll never reach them all in time. It's better ye stay with me than tae choose."

"That is choosing!" *I shrieked in outrage.*

"Then choose me. Finally, fuckin' choose me. Ye owe me."

"Jim ..." *I leaned into him.* "I'm so sorry. Please, I'm so sorry."

"Pixie."

Aidan was disappearing. "No." *I fought against Jim, hitting and shrugging and punching but he held me supernaturally fast.* "No!"

"I wish I'd never met ye, Pixie."

"Aidan, no!"

"Too many ghosts between us," *he whispered.*

And then he was gone.

"AIDAN!"

"Nora, wake up. Nora." I was jolted abruptly and horribly awake, my eyes flying open. I took in the blurry face above my own and winced against the light, completely discombobulated.

Where the hell was I?

"You fell asleep on the couch. We all did."

"Aidan?" I attempted to blink the weariness out of my eyes and pushed up off the couch, groaning as pain shot up my neck. Oh yeah, I'd definitely fallen asleep somewhere other than a bed.

Aidan's face came into focus and I realized he was kneeling beside the couch in front of me. His hair was wet and he'd changed clothing. "I let you sleep."

I bent my aching neck from side to side and yawned. "I'm sorry."

"Don't be." He gave me an affectionate smile and reached out to push my hair off my face. "I think we all needed it."

I glanced around his sitting room and frowned. "Where's Sylvie?" Last night after pizza, we'd had a movie marathon to take our minds off reality. I didn't remember falling asleep.

"I woke up about two hours ago, put her to bed, had a shower."

"What time is it?"

"It's only eight o'clock. I know you start work at ten so I was going to wake you soon, but you were having a nightmare ..."

I frowned, trying to remember. "I was?"

He touched my knee, expression concerned. "You kept crying out my name. Like ... you'd lost me or something."

"I can't remember," I whispered, reaching down to take his hand. "But it does sound like a nightmare."

He kissed my knuckles. "Breakfast?"

I nodded. "Let me help."

In the end, I managed to convince him to sit his gorgeous butt on a stool while I puttered about his kitchen making omelets. We whispered to each other as I worked, attempting to keep the noise level down so as not to wake Sylvie.

"You look good in my kitchen," Aidan said in a low voice, giving me a soft smile that did nothing to wipe away the sadness in the back of his eyes. I wished I had the power to make everything better. I'd take making him smile as a small win, though.

"Your kitchen is nicer than mine."

"I wouldn't know."

I grinned cheekily at the reminder. "I'm still sorry about that."

"Your friend needed you."

"Yeah, she did. But that doesn't mean I didn't need you."

"Need Uncle Aidan for what?"

I jumped, nearly dropping the spatula.

Sylvie had appeared out of nowhere, standing there in her pajamas, yawning and rubbing her eyes sleepily.

"Do you want breakfast, sweetheart?" Aidan promptly asked, getting off his stool to go to her. Even though she was past the age for it, he swept her up into his arms like she was six years old and carried her over to a stool.

Sylvie yawned again. "Cereal."

"Coming right up."

While I finished fixing our breakfast, Aidan poured out Sylvie's Cheerios and slid a glass of orange juice in front of her.

We ate in silence, but whether it was out of tiredness or the weight of knowing how temporary this moment was, I didn't know. However, I soaked it up and I knew from the way Aidan kept throwing her glances that he was taking in every moment with his niece while he could.

"Did you sleep over, Nora?" Sylvie suddenly asked, peering around her uncle at me.

Not wanting her to get the wrong idea, I said, "We all fell asleep on the couch."

She frowned and Aidan supplied before she could ask, "I woke up earlier and put you to bed."

"Oh. Okay. Last night was fun." She gave us a tired smile.

"Yeah," Aidan said, smoothing a hand over her bedraggled hair. "It was."

I looked away before I did the unthinkable and burst into tears.

Sylvie's gaze moved from her uncle to me and then back to Aidan. "Can we do something today? All of us?"

"Nora has to work, sweetheart."

Clearly disappointed, she slumped in her seat.

"I don't have to," I blurted out.

Aidan raised an eyebrow. "You don't?"

"No. Maybe—" I coughed dramatically. "Yeah ..." I coughed harder. "I'm definitely coming down with something."

He grinned. "Is that so?"

"Yeah, but don't worry, it's not contagious. I can still hang out with you guys."

"Yay!" Sylvie beamed. "What should we do?"

"Well, first Nora will need to phone her boss and explain about this mysterious noncontagious illness."

I shoved him playfully and jumped down off the stool. "Where's my purse?"

"It's not even nine o'clock yet. Will she be in?"

"Yup. Leah's usually at the store by eight thirty."

The buzzer for the apartment sounded as I found my purse and I looked over at Aidan in surprise. It was a little early for visitors. He frowned as he got off his stool to answer it. "Could be Laine," he said. "She's back from that job in Paris."

I had no idea what job in Paris. I'm sure Aidan had probably mentioned it but I tended to switch off when Laine was mentioned. She still wasn't forgiven for saying those humiliating things about me.

However, it wasn't Laine.

"Aidan, it's Cal," the masculine voice crackled over the buzzer.

Aidan froze for a second and then reluctantly pressed the entrance button.

"Uncle Aidan, what's Daddy doing here?" Sylvie said, slipping off the stool and hurrying over to him. Even though she was tall for her age, she'd never looked so young standing there in her Hello Kitty pajamas and slippers with her short hair a mass of tangled, golden silk. Her little face was pinched with worry.

"I don't know, sweetheart. I guess we'll find out in a minute."

After Aidan opened his apartment door, the three of us stood together. It occurred to me we were like soldiers on a front line, awaiting an enemy attack.

It wasn't how we should have felt about Sylvie's dad but it was how we'd been made to feel. If he'd only been honest with Aidan from the start, this whole damn thing might not have been so messy. Instead, there was a whole lot of resentment waiting for him in this apartment.

A fist appeared first to knock on the open door, and then Cal stepped inside, his smooth expression tightening as he took us in, standing with our legs braced and our arms crossed over our chests.

Following in behind him was a tall, attractive brunette. She wore an expensive-looking, tailored herringbone coat that fitted her slim figure to perfection, black leather gloves, and black heeled boots. Dangling from the elbow of one arm was a black Kate Spade handbag.

Her striking light gray eyes took us in and her pretty mouth pursed in displeasure.

Cal gave his daughter a weak smile. "Morning, baby doll."

"Hi, Daddy. What are you doing here?" She looked up at him with too much suspicion and concern for a little girl.

After a moment of uncomfortable silence, Cal cleared his throat and spoke to Aidan, although he didn't look him in the eye. "We need to talk. In private."

"About what?"

Cal sighed heavily. "In private, Aidan."

"And I asked, about what?"

His tone was the equivalent of the patio door sliding open and letting in the October morning chill.

Cal looked down at Sylvie. "Baby doll, why don't you take Sally and show her your room?"

"No." Aidan shook his head.

Cal scowled. "Sally, take Sylvie and get her washed and dressed."

Sally made to move forward but Aidan held up a hand, warding her off. She was smart enough to stop. He spoke without taking his eyes off Cal and his fiancée. "Pixie, *you* take Sylvie into her room."

And so I took a reluctant Sylvie away from whatever was happening out there, feeling uneasiness crash over me.

"What's happening, Nora?" Sylvie's mouth trembled as she gazed up at me with limpid fear in her eyes.

"I don't know, sweetie." My voice shook, probably only intensifying her worries, but I had a horrible feeling in my gut. "Let's get you dressed."

I had gotten her into the bathroom and she was brushing her teeth when I heard Aidan yell, "Over my dead body!"

Sylvie whimpered as my eyes grew wide.

What the hell was going on?

"Let's hurry up, sweetie."

"Nora?"

"It's okay."

"Don't you fucking dare!" Aidan roared.

"Don't you talk to her like that!" Cal yelled back.

"This is my home. Get the fuck out!"

"Not without Sylvie."

I felt her little hand curl around mine, bringing my startled gaze down to her. "Clothes on, Sylvie," I whispered, hurrying her into clean underwear, jeans, and a sweater.

The yelling continued from the front of the apartment but I couldn't stay in the bathroom with her forever, and I hated that Aidan was out there with no backup for whatever the hell was going on.

Holding tight to Sylvie's hand, we hurried back out to them to find Aidan still in a face-off with Cal and Sally. "What is going on?"

Cal turned to me, his expression pleading. "Unfortunately, my new boss wants me over in San Francisco a few weeks earlier than we'd planned. Sally and I are leaving in ten days and that means Sylvie is too. We thought it best to come get her now, so we can adjust as a family for a few days before we head to the States. We have to talk with her school and get her transferred to a local school over there. It makes sense if she's with us while that all happens. Most of her things can be sent for once we're over there."

"No!" Sylvie shouted immediately.

Cal's face fell. "Baby—"

"No!" She ripped her hand from mine and fled. Her bedroom door slammed shut behind her.

Incredulous and furious, I shot her father the dirtiest look in my repertoire. "Don't you think a little warning would have been nice?"

"We didn't get any warning—" Sally began but I cut her off.

"I meant for Aidan and Sylvie. You couldn't have picked up a phone and called Aidan to explain? I'm assuming you found out about this before this morning?"

He nodded.

"When?" Aidan bit out. The muscles in his biceps bulged with tension as he held them across his chest, as if trying to contain himself.

Again, Cal wouldn't meet his eyes. "Yesterday morning."

"You dirty bastard." Aidan moved for him but I gripped his arm to halt him. "You knew about this at the meeting with our lawyers yesterday?"

When Sylvie's dad didn't reply, Sally sighed, as if we were causing a fuss for no reason. "We knew that you would try to stall everything and we don't have time for that, Aidan. It was best to do it like this."

"It was callous to do it like this," I retorted.

"This is really none of your business."

I glared at her. "This man and that beautiful little girl *are* my business."

"Aidan, please," Cal said, his expression seeming genuinely remorseful. "You're right. This wasn't the best way, but none of this is going to be easy on Sylvie. I thought it was better to rip the Band-Aid off. I've been weak, too afraid to ask for what's mine. But she *is* mine and I want her home with me. Now."

At Aidan's continued silence, Sally threw her hands up. "For goodness' sake, she belongs to Cal. Legally. We will call the police if we have to."

"Sally," Cal warned.

She huffed. "It's true."

He seemed to plead with her to be quiet. "This is her uncle, not her goddamn kidnapper."

"Just give me today with her," Aidan said, the words hoarse. I stepped closer into him, hearing the pain in his voice, even if these selfish assholes were too deaf to hear it.

"I wish I could, I do, but we've got too much to get done. And it'll be hard no matter when we do this. Let's get it over with. And anyway, you travel all the time to California. You'll see her soon."

Fury threatened to explode out of me. "You can't even give him one day to say goodbye to his kid?"

"Not. His. Kid," Sally enunciated coldly. "Now move out of our way or," she held up her phone, "I will call the police."

When Cal didn't say anything to stop her this time, I reluctantly stepped aside and guided a rigid Aidan out of the way too.

Cal strode by us, his cheeks flushed, whether with embarrassment or anger, I couldn't say. His bitch of a fiancée marched at his back, throwing me a smug look I wanted to wipe off her face. How could it be that Sylvie was going to be raised by that cow?

Powerlessness held me immobile, unable to say anything to soothe Aidan, who I think had disappeared too deep inside himself for me to reach anyway.

"No!" I heard Sylvie sob. "Daddy, no!"

"Tell me what you want to take with you, darling," Sally said in a surprisingly placating voice. "You don't want to leave anything behind you love."

Uh. What about her uncle, you stupid asshat!

"Daddy, no, let me stay," she cried so hard. Tears burned my eyes, my throat so tight, it was painful.

A few minutes later Cal walked out of the room with a tearful Sylvie in his arms; a far more subdued Sally followed with a small suitcase of Sylvie's in hand.

"Uncle Aidan!" Sylvie shrieked and struggled to get out of her dad's arms. Visibly distressed, Cal lowered her to the ground and she threw herself at her uncle.

Aidan caught her in his arms, holding her so tight, his eyes closed in obvious agony. Sylvie clung on fiercely, begging him not to let her go. "Shhh, baby girl, shhh," he said, voice trembling. "It'll be okay."

But nothing he said could quell her tears and after five minutes of Cal quietly asking her to come back to him, her father lost his patience and hauled her out of Aidan's arms.

"NO!" she screamed, holding her arms out to Aidan as Cal strode away. "Uncle Aidan! Nora! Uncle Aidan! Nora! NO!"

I sobbed, looking down at my feet, unable to watch, wishing I couldn't hear that little girl scream all the way out into the hall.

And then to my absolute horror, I heard Aidan cry out and looked up in time to watch his knees give way. I reached for him, falling to my knees too, wrapping my arms around him. He fell against me, one fist curled tight in my shirt, the other in my hair, and I listened to him struggle to breathe through the tears he'd tried so hard to hold back.

chapter 21

I CALLED IN SICK TO WORK AFTER ALL, BUT IT WASN'T TO SPEND A bittersweet day with two of my favorite people. It was to take care of one of them.

Devastated was too underwhelming a word for how Aidan felt. I was devastated for him. The remembered sounds of Sylvie's pleas would pierce through our silence, making me wince every time, and I could only imagine that sound was on a constant loop in Aidan's mind too. Grief and exhaustion from having so little sleep the night before hit him and he passed out on the couch.

While he was out, I called in sick and set about looking through his fridge and cupboards to see what I could make him to eat when he woke up. Finding the ingredients to make a quick pasta salad, I thought about Sylvie's bedroom as I worked. All of her things would have to be packed up and I'd rather I be the one to do it than him.

My eyes flew over to him every ten seconds, like I was afraid he'd disappear too. His large, long body was sprawled out on the couch as he slept. A big, strong guy who worked out five days a week and was one of the most potently masculine men I'd ever met.

It gutted me to see him knocked down like this.

As I chopped tomatoes, I began to seethe, wondering what the hell could be wrong with a person that they'd be so selfish as to cause the scene that I'd witnessed this morning. I worried for my sweet girl growing up with a man and woman as selfish as Cal and

Sally. It wasn't that I was blind to the truth. Sylvie was Cal's daughter and it was his right to raise her. But I hated how it was always on his terms. He was too busy with his career to be around much when she was younger, but now that he'd finally decided to grow up, he demanded his parental rights—to hell with how much of a wrench it would be, not only for Aidan but for Sylvie.

My phone buzzed on the kitchen counter and I hurried to answer it so it wouldn't wake Aidan. It was Seonaid. "Hey," I whispered.

"Nora? Why are you whispering?"

"Aidan's sleeping."

"Oh." She sounded sly.

I flinched. "No. Not *oh*. Something happened."

"Aye, I popped around Apple Butter to see if you wanted to grab a quick lunch and your nutty boss said you were sick?"

I felt tears choke me and I found I couldn't quite get the words out.

"Nora? What's going on?"

"You know how I told you Sylvie's dad wanted full custody."

"Yeah."

"He came and took her this morning. No warning, nothing. Him and his witch of a fiancée barged in here and literally ripped her out of Aidan's arms. There was nothing he could do." I sniffled, swiping angrily at my tears. "There was nothing I could do for him."

"Jesus fuck," Seonaid bit out. "That's bloody awful."

"They're taking her to the States and they couldn't even give him a day. One goddamn day to spend with her. What is wrong with these people? And they're going to be responsible for raising her. I'm so worried for her, Seonaid."

"Oh, babe, I'm sure her dad will take good care of her. He's a prick but he's her dad. And he hasn't been horrible to her, has he?"

"Other than today? No," I admitted reluctantly. "He loves her. But he's so selfish."

"I'm so sorry, Nora. I'm so sorry for Aidan. Is there anything I can do?"

"Thank you, but no. I'm going to stick around here today, make sure he's okay."

"Well, call me if you need me."

I told her I would and we hung up. Aidan shifted on the couch and I tensed, hoping I hadn't woken him. He didn't move again, though, and I continued preparing lunch so it would be ready when he did wake.

A little while later, I was sitting at the counter with a hot mug of tea to warm the chill deep in my bones when Aidan groaned and sat up slowly. I watched him, pretty sure my heart was in my eyes, as he raked his hands through his disheveled hair. Then he rubbed them over his face, his shoulders slumping as if he'd just remembered what he was waking up to.

Sensing my gaze, he glanced over and I tensed at the dull sadness in his eyes.

"I made some lunch for you, if you're hungry," I said, my voice sounding small in the large space.

He shook his head. "I'm fine."

"Aidan ..." I bit back tears and he looked away, the muscle in his jaw flexing. "Maybe we should call someone or ... I don't know."

"There's nothing to be done," he said, his tone flat, empty. "Whether it happened today, tomorrow, or a week from now, it wouldn't have been any easier."

Anger flashed through me. "But you would have known it was coming. It was despicable the way he did that! For you and Sylvie. God—"

"Nora, please," he snapped, eyes burning with feeling now. "I was there, for fuck's sake. I don't need to relive it."

Hurt, I clamped my lips closed and reminded myself this man was going through hell. I could forgive him for a bad attitude today of all days.

"What can I do?"

"There's nothing to do."

And he meant it.

For the next few hours, Aidan sat looking out his patio door window, his thoughts a million miles away. His body might as well have been too because he was giving off serious stay-back vibes. So I did. A few times his phone beeped and he replied to whoever it was, yet he never said a word.

But I wasn't leaving him.

Toward dinnertime, I somehow managed to get him to agree to eat the pasta salad I'd whipped up. He was sitting at the counter, eating and staring sullenly at the same kitchen cupboard door when there was a knock at the door. It was a warning knock, not a request for entry, because the next sound was heels on the hardwood floor, and suddenly Laine was standing looking at Aidan.

What was she doing here?

And then I saw her tortured expression and I knew. She was the one he'd texted earlier. My stomach sank as I wondered if he'd asked her to come. I looked at him and he stared back at Laine with the same empty chill in his eyes he'd given me, which shouldn't have reassured me but did.

"I know you said not to come," Laine said softly. "But I had to make sure you were okay. Are you? Okay?"

She didn't look at me.

Not once.

"Stupid fucking question, no?"

Laine winced. "You know what I meant." She took off the gray winter coat she had on and walked over to the couch to lay it and her handbag on it. Then to my annoyance, she unzipped her boots and placed them neatly behind the couch. Turning to face us in skinny jeans and a stylish cream sweater that probably cost more than what I made in a month, I felt my insides twist with petty jealousy.

It was wrong, when all that should have mattered was that Aidan was surrounded by people who loved him, but I didn't like her. Maybe if she hadn't insulted me in every way possible, I might have grown to get over my jealousy.

Laine looked at Aidan's back with longing she didn't even bother to hide.

Yeah ... even if she hadn't been a bitch to me, I probably

wouldn't have been able to get over the fact that she was in love with him. Because clearly, she was. Right?

Finally, unable to avoid my gaze any longer, she looked at me. "You look tired, Nora. Have you been here all day?"

"The three of us fell asleep last night watching movies," I told her, wanting her to know how close I'd grown to Sylvie and Aidan. "I was here when Cal and Sally came for Sylvie."

At my visible distress, Laine's eyes widened with concern. "How is Sylvie?"

Aidan tensed beside me and I placed a comforting hand on his arm. He ignored it. I squeezed him anyway and let go. "We don't know. She wasn't good when she left."

"No, I bloody imagine not. I could kill Cal!" Laine marched past us and into the kitchen. I watched warily as she reached up and pulled open one of the cupboards. Grabbing a bottle of barely touched Macallan whisky, Laine shut the doors, opened the glasses cabinet, pulled out two glasses, and placed them in front of Aidan. He pushed his plate out of the way and waited patiently as Laine poured out two glasses.

He took the one she offered and she kept the other for herself. Then she looked at me. "You should go home, Nora. Get some rest. I can take it from here."

Oh, I bet you can!

I tried my best to mask my reaction because now was definitely not the time for a jealous hissy fit. "I can stay."

"You look like you haven't slept in days," Laine said, like she actually cared about my well-being. "Aidan, tell her to get some sleep."

Aidan took a swig of whisky and shot me a look out of his dead-ened eyes. "It's fine, Pixie. Go home, get some rest."

Confused, I could only stare at him as he reached for the bottle to pour himself a fresh glass. Was I being politely dismissed by him too? Did he really not want me here? Was I an idiot to think he'd need me over a woman he'd been friends with for years?

I wanted to make sure Aidan was okay, but I also didn't want to stay where I wasn't wanted. "I can stay if you need me. I'm fine, really."

"I plan on drinking this fucking miserable day to an end," he said, his voice hoarse. "You don't need to see that. Go home."

My pride pricked, I immediately slipped off the stool beside him. Fine. If he didn't need me, if he felt like he could unravel with Laine but not with me, let him. Whatever he needed. I wasn't sticking around, feeling like an unwanted little girl.

She didn't even offer me a glass of whisky. Like I wasn't legal.

So I gathered my things, put on my coat and boots, and left his apartment without giving Laine the satisfaction of looking back.

Just as I stepped out of his building and tears of frustration threatened to escape, my phone rang. It was Seonaid again. I cleared my throat, not wanting her to hear I was upset. "Everything okay?"

"That's what I was calling to ask. I wanted to check in. See how Aidan's doing?"

I smiled grimly, thinking sometimes I failed to appreciate what a great person Jim's sister was. "Uh … well … I think I was practically kicked out."

"What?" she snapped.

Her instant anger on my behalf was gratifying. "His friend Laine … she turned up, got out the whisky, and made it clear it was time for the grown-ups to be on their own. Aidan's too fucked-up to care. He told me to leave, to go home, get some rest. I don't know if he meant it or if he wanted me gone too."

"No, Nora, I don't believe that."

"I don't know."

"Where are you now?"

"Just leaving. I'm going to find a bus."

"Okay. Well, let me know when you get home."

As it turned out, I didn't need to let Seonaid know when I got home because she was already there waiting for me. At the sight of her standing outside my door, everything I'd been holding back for Aidan's sake burst forth. My friend wrapped me in her arms and somehow managed to get my key out of my purse and get us into the flat while she hugged me.

"Oh, babe ..." She settled me on the sofa and bustled around in my kitchen, putting the kettle on. "I'm so sorry. I know how fond you are of Sylvie."

"I didn't even get to hold her, to hug her or tell her goodbye!"

Seonaid flew back to my side to hold me until finally, after what felt like forever, I had no more tears inside me. Eventually, I curled up in the corner of the sofa with a mug of tea in my hands and I whispered, "I feel weary, Seonaid. I'm only twenty-two and I feel so goddamn weary."

Seonaid studied me thoughtfully. Her next words shocked the hell out of me. "Maybe if you stopped punishing yourself for crimes you didn't commit, you wouldn't feel so bloody weary."

I gaped at her. "What?"

"Don't you think I know why you started volunteering at the hospital, why you avoided me and Mum and even Roddy for so long? I mean, if it hadn't been for me, you would probably have stopped talking to us altogether."

Stunned, I opened my mouth but I wasn't sure what to say. To deny it would've been to lie to her, and she deserved better than that.

Seonaid leaned toward me, her kindness shining out of her eyes. "I know you didn't love Jim the way he loved you. He knew it too. We spoke about it. You were a kid. You made a mistake marrying him, but you didn't intend for it to be a mistake. And you can't go on punishing yourself for that. I loved my brother, dearly, but he loved you selfishly, Nora. He wanted to keep you all to himself, and that was a disaster waiting to happen. But you ... you, babe, can rest assured that even knowing you didn't love him the way he loved you, you gave my brother some of the happiest years of his short life."

Tears slipped quietly down her pretty face and she gave me a sad smile. "If you're punishing yourself for that, stop. Do you honestly think if you were this horrible person who ruined my brother's life that I would still be here? That I would love you as much as I do?"

A sob burst out of me before I could stop it, and the tears I'd thought had dried up welled out of me again. I threw my arms around her, holding on for dear life. The relief I felt shook me to my soul, because this was Seonaid, the person Jim loved best.

"I'm sorry," I sobbed, holding on to her like she was a life raft. "I'm so sorry."

And for the second time that day, my friend soothed the grief out of me.

———

SOMETIME LATER, EXHAUSTED, I LAID CURLED UP ON THE COUCH, MY palms beneath my head. I looked across the small space at Seonaid curled up on the opposite couch, seemingly daydreaming with glazed eyes to my wall.

"I love them," I confessed.

Her eyes flew to mine in surprise. "Who?"

"Sylvie and Aidan." I forced back fresh tears that threatened, tired of their salt on my skin. "I'm in love with him, Seonaid. It hurts to be this far from him while he's going through this. It hurts so fucking much. I've never felt like this before. And I went into this thing with them knowing I'd get my heart broken. But I thought that was what was meant to happen. That I was supposed to help them through losing Nicky, be someone they could count on, use me up and move on from me better for it. Now my heart *is* breaking and I can't stand it like I thought I could. Sylvie's gone. I don't know if I'll ever see her again. And Aidan … this was the test, right? And he doesn't need me. I don't blame him because what can I offer him? I've nothing to offer a man like that. I'm merely some shop girl who doesn't have the balls to get over her dead husband and pick up the pieces of her life—instead, I hang out at a children's hospital like some pathetic widow."

"That is enough," Seonaid hissed, her eyes flashing angrily at me.

I flinched at the fury in her voice and slowly eased into a sitting position.

"You are not even twenty-three years old yet, Nora. You're smart, you're funny, you're beautiful, and you have all the time in the world to pick up the pieces of your life and make something of it. And you will. I know, deep in my gut, you will. You're special, Nora. It's what drew Jim to you and I'm sure it's what captured Aidan's attention. He'd be lucky to have you. Any man would. And he's just had the second-worst fucking day of his life months after the worst fucking day of his life. Stop putting yourself down and be what he needs. Go back there tomorrow, this Laine bitch be damned, and remind him that *you* are his best friend."

———

WITH SEONAID'S WORDS OF ENCOURAGEMENT BUOYING MY CONFIDENCE, I headed to Aidan's the next morning. To my frustration, it was Laine who answered the door buzzer and let me into the building.

She was waiting for me at the apartment door and I felt a flare of panic when I saw she was wearing the same clothes she'd been wearing the night before. Her makeup was washed off and although she looked tired, it was clear she didn't need a lot of makeup anyway. Her grim, pitying expression made my panic mount.

"Come in." She gestured me inside, placing a comforting hand on my shoulder as I stepped into the apartment.

I barely heard her close the door behind me because I was stunned by the sight in the living room. Or rather, the lack of a sight.

All of Aidan's music equipment, the instruments and computers, were gone.

Just gone.

The space was entirely bare.

"What's going on?"

"Nora … I don't know how to tell you this, and I'm sure I'm the last person you want to hear it from considering my past terrible behavior …" Laine's sympathy made we want to scream at her to spit it out. "Aidan's gone."

My knees trembled, as though the floor had shifted beneath my feet. "Gone? What do you mean, he's gone?"

Anger flickered in Laine's eyes, frustration maybe. "Yesterday after you left, he suddenly started making arrangements to leave the country. He took a job in LA so he can be close to Sylvie, but it meant leaving early this morning." She gestured to his space. "He managed to wrangle a company that could get his gear together last minute and he's got someone over there looking for a place for him."

No.

What?

I gaped at her in disbelief. The panic I'd felt earlier spread over my lungs so I was finding it hard to breathe. "He wouldn't ... he just left?" Without saying goodbye, without explaining? *No.*

Aidan.

The genuine sympathy in Laine's eyes gutted me.

Shredded my insides. Or what was left of the tatters in there.

"Nora, I hope what I'm about to say will help in the long run, even if it doesn't feel like it now. But ... this would've happened, even if Sylvie hadn't been a factor. Believe me. I've been in Aidan's life longer than any woman and he is the ultimate bachelor. It doesn't mean he doesn't care about you—I'm sure he does—but he can be a real arsehole to women. I love him but it's the truth. He makes them all feel like his best friend, like he's never felt anything like it before, and maybe he even believes it for a while. I think he does. But only for a while. And then he gets bored and moves on. I was surprised he was with you so long until ... well," she winced in the damned sympathy again. "He told me you two never actually slept together, which is probably why you lasted longer than any of the others. Anticipation. Like I said. He can be such a bloke.

"But one I care about. Because he's not a bad soul. In fact, he's a very good man, and I know you saw that in the way he was with Sylvie. So please try to forgive him, Nora. He didn't mean to be this cruel to you." She gestured to the empty space in the sitting room. "He just needs Sylvie more than he needs anyone else. I'm sure you can understand that."

Feeling like I might be sick while still clinging to the hope that there had to be some kind of terrible mistake, I pushed past her, heading for the door. "When does his flight leave?"

"In about twenty minutes. You'll never make it to the airport, if that's what you're thinking!" she called after me as I fled the apartment.

No, I couldn't make it to the airport in time. I fumbled for my phone in my purse. However, I could try to stop him from getting on that flight and find out what the hell was going on in his head.

Cursing when I discovered I couldn't get a signal on the elevator, I burst out of it as soon as it hit the ground floor and pressed the call button.

"This is Aidan Lennox. Leave a message."

"No!" I yelled in frustration when I got his voicemail. My hands shook as I quickly shot him a text message.

Where are you? What's happening? Is what Laine said true?

Not even a minute later, my phone buzzed.

My pulse raced when I saw it was a reply from Aidan.

I'm more sorry than I can say. But I have to be where Sylvie is. You deserve better. Goodbye, Pixie.

Somehow, and I don't remember how, I blindly found my way home to Sighthill. And although I left little pieces of shattered me on the sidewalk and bus and roads I crossed over, it wasn't until I got inside my flat that the howling grief blew me into tiny fragments I was afraid I'd never glue back together again.

part 3

chapter 22

"'CONCEAL ME WHAT I AM—'"

"Stop!"

I looked up from my English assignment at Quentin's sharp direction. He glared at the small stage where Eddie and Gwyn were rehearsing the end of act one, scene two of *Twelfth Night* by William Shakespeare. Eddie was playing the Sea Captain, and Gwyn was Viola. As Viola's understudy, I should've been paying more attention but I was trying to finish a paper due at the end of the week. And honestly, I knew this play like the back of my hand.

Quentin glowered at Eddie. "Stop looking at her tits while she's speaking. You're the captain, her guide, her support! You do not perv on a young lady, you licentious hound!"

I covered my mouth to stop my snort. When I joined the *Tollcross Amateur Theatre Company* last September, I'd been somewhat intimidated by its quintessentially melodramatic, Welsh-born director Quentin Alexander. However, over time I'd gotten more comfortable with him, especially because he made me laugh without even trying to.

"They're right there," Eddie complained, gesturing to Gwyn's rather impressive breasts. She wore a tight sweater with a low neckline showcasing her badass cleavage. "Tell her to dress more appropriately."

Gwyn sneered at him. "You do realize everything that just came out of yer mouth is the reason feminism was born, right?"

"Man up," Quentin snarled in his upper-crust accent that sounded more English than Welsh. "You querulous wretch. Say the line without looking at her tits or I swear to the gods of Shakespeare, I will get myself another captain."

Licentious hound, querulous wretch. My lips trembled as I tapped my pen against them. Quentin was on fire today.

"I don't have to take this kind of abuse," Eddie huffed.

"Then get off my stage."

He didn't get off his stage. They started the scene over and I looked back down at the assignment.

"I assume you know the lines ... since you're not paying attention?" Quentin murmured. I startled to find him standing above me.

I gave him an appeasing smile. "Every single one."

"What are you doing?" He nodded to the refurbished MacBook in my lap and the notebooks scattered on the chair beside me.

"English lit paper."

"Well, at least it's productive, which is more than I can say for whatever it is Amanda is doing." He nodded behind me and I looked over my shoulder to see my fellow understudy Amanda giggling at whatever Hamish (our Sebastian) was whispering in her ear.

"I can only hope nothing happens to Jane, or this play may be the cause of a divorce," Quentin muttered before whirling back around to pay attention to his actors on stage.

Jane was our Olivia, and Amanda her understudy. While Jane was mature, professional, and madly in love with her wife, Amanda was a senior at Edinburgh University, smart but immature, single, a self-proclaimed flirt, and she loved being the center of attention. Olivia and Sebastian were love interests in *Twelfth Night*. Not a problem for Jane and Hamish.

If Amanda were to take over the role, however, I wasn't sure how that would work out for Hamish. He was fifteen years older than her, married with two kids, and apparently bored by that because the man clearly did not have the willpower to resist Amanda's charms.

I frowned at them, shaking my head in disgust. Amanda and I didn't exactly rub together very well. I'd watched her go through a shit ton of men since meeting her last September. A lot of them were already with someone else. It would seem that she got off on being able to capture men's attention from their girlfriends and wives, and as soon as she'd won, she dumped them, bored.

Poor Hamish.

What an idiot.

I looked down at my laptop, thinking it shouldn't have surprised me that joining a theater company would throw me into so much drama on stage and off.

However, it wasn't *my* offstage drama, and that's all I really cared about. My life was officially drama-free and it had been for a while now. It was exactly how I liked it.

I was content. Finally.

It hadn't been an easy road to get here, and by God, I would hold on to what I had with everything I had.

"Okay, where's my Valentine and Duke?" Quentin called out.

Duke Orsino was being played by Jack. He was a good-looking guy a few years older than me, medium height, athletically built with lovely dark eyes that constantly glittered with mischief. He was a flirt like Amanda, except he stayed away from attached women and he was actually more a serial monogamist than an outright player. He'd had two girlfriends since we'd met, dating each for a few months before breaking it off. While he was with a girl, he was *with* her, as far as I was aware, but that didn't stop him from flirting with every breathing female in Edinburgh.

Except Amanda.

He made it obvious she irritated the hell out of him.

Jack was a car salesman but he really wanted to be an actor. He'd been an extra in movies, had small, one-off parts in TV shows—he'd even done a couple of commercials. But nothing that would pay the bills on a regular basis.

Still, he persevered and got his acting fix as a player in this company.

He'd been sitting a few chairs down from me, his legs up over the seat in front of him, ankles crossed lazily. He and Jane, our Olivia, had been sitting watching the rehearsal in between playing with their phones. Other cast members with smaller parts were scattered around the small theater, waiting for Quentin to call them up.

I shifted to the side, holding my MacBook out of the way as Jack shuffled along the aisle to get out. He smirked down at me as our bodies brushed and tapped the top of my laptop. "This is why ye'er single. Too much work and not enough play makes Nora a dull girl."

I gestured for him to move along. "I'm single because I want to be single, Jack."

"Oh, that's obvious, gorgeous." He winked as he stepped into the aisle.

"Make haste, Orsino," Quentin snapped. "We haven't all bloody evening."

Will, who was playing Valentine, was already up on stage with Gwyn.

"Okay," Quentin said, once Jack was standing offstage ready to enter. "Act one, scene four." He pointed to Will.

Will strode out to the middle of the stage with Gwyn. "'If the Duke continues these favors towards you, Cesario, you are like to be much advanced; he hath known you but three days, and already you are no stranger.'"

Gwyn looked blankly at Will.

He whispered something to her and she flushed, turning to Quentin with an apologetic look. "Line?"

Our director rolled his eyes to the heavens.

Before he could feed her the line from the script book rolled in his hands, I called out, "'You either fear his humor or my negligence, that you call in question the continuance of his love. Is he inconstant, sir, in his favors?'"

"Thanks!" Gwyn called back. "I remember now."

Quentin shot me a thoughtful look and then swung his attention back to Gwyn. "No doubt you can guess how I feel about the fact that your understudy is feeding you your lines, Viola."

"She has a script," Gwyn argued.

"No," he shook his head, "that was from memory."

I flushed at the frown she sent my way, my eyes flickering to Pete who looked bored, and then Jack who was grinning at me like I was in trouble. Ignoring him, I concentrated on my paper.

Never feel ashamed about being smart, Nora. I should have encouraged it more. I'm sorry.

My mom's voice echoed in my head and I looked back up at the stage. It wasn't my fault I knew the part inside and out. I wouldn't let Gwyn make me feel bad about it. I was over self-recrimination. Every day I had to remind myself that I wanted to be a different person from the one I was eighteen months ago.

The change had begun that fateful morning I lost what felt like everything. As I'd been overcome with the kind of pain I'd never experienced before—the agony of losing someone because they wanted to be lost—Seonaid came to my rescue. She pulled me together and told me no man was worth it. She told me it was time to take control of my life.

And her fierceness mixed with my anger at *him* had lit a fire inside me.

I wanted to be the strong person she swore I could be, so I'd packed some clothes in a backpack, borrowed enough money from Seonaid to get a cheap flight home to Indiana, and I'd gone in search of my parents. It all started with them and I knew if I wanted to begin my life over again, I needed closure. I needed to know I was forgiven. Or not.

I had no way of knowing if I'd ever be able to afford to come back to Edinburgh but Seonaid said she'd make it happen, that she had to because Angie and Roddy were going to kill her for putting me on a flight to the States without saying goodbye.

But she could see in my eyes how I felt.

I needed to do it then, to have something to focus on, something to get me through having my heart broken by the man I loved.

DONOVAN, INDIANA
NOVEMBER 2015

CONFUSED, I FROWNED AT THE WOMAN WHO WAS STANDING IN MY PARENTS' *front doorway on West Washington. If it had been any other street in any other town, I might be forgiven for knocking on the wrong door due to jet lag and grief.*

But this was Donovan and my parents' house stood out for its smallness on the street. And there was the matter of the big-ass tree in the front yard.

The lady was perhaps in her early forties and vaguely familiar. She scowled at the sight of the bedraggled young woman on her doorstep. "Can I help you?"

"Um ... I'm looking for my parents. O'Brien?"

Surprise pulled her eyebrows up toward her hairline. "You their kid who ran off?"

The joys of living in a small town. "That would be me."

Her lip curled in a sneer. "Well, your momma doesn't live here anymore. She lives out on Willow, east of the Northwood Farm. She built it. Called Willow House."

Her words swirled around in my head but I didn't get a chance to ask anything further because she'd shut the door in my face. I stumbled off the small porch and almost tripped over my own feet as I walked down the garden path. How on earth could my mother afford to build a house on land not far from our very first home? And why did the woman make it seem like my mother had done it alone?

Where was my dad?

Pulse racing harder than it already had been, I walked.

At first, I was glad for my coat because it was a chilly forty-eight degrees and there was a blustery wind trying to blow me back the way I'd come. However, after fifty minutes of marching toward Willow on the outskirts of Donovan, I was sweating. The fact that I was nervous as hell might have had something to do with it.

I was worried about missing the house if it was built off the main road, but as I walked, I saw Willow House. It was larger than the home on West Washington but still modest. Two stories and clad in white shingles, it had a porch that wrapped around the whole house and a pretty garden out front that looked like someone actually tended it.

Feeling my palms slick with cold sweat, I stopped. It was like my feet had a mind of their own and they did not want to walk up there. Pretty curtains hung in the large dual picture windows at the front, a vase of lilies and roses in one.

A newer, cherry red Jeep Renegade in the driveway at the far side of the house caught my eye. Very cute.

Very not my mother.

Definitely not my father.

What the hell?

I was jolted out of my confusion by the sound of a deep bark. The front door opened and a big black dog burst out of it, throwing open the screen door and loping toward me. Fear unstuck my feet and I stumbled back as the black Labrador came at me.

"Trixie, stop!"

The lab skidded to a halt at my feet, her tail thumping the garden path as she peered up at me with excited brown eyes.

I raised my gaze from the dog to its obvious owner.

And I couldn't believe what I was seeing.

It was my mom, but it wasn't.

She wore skinny jeans that fit her still-slender figure and a big slouchy green sweater that was a great color on her. Her dark hair, rather than being scraped back from her face, hung in loose, attractive waves around her shoulders. And although she looked startled and wary to see me standing outside her house, the tired, pinched expression she used to wear, like they were a permanent part of her, were gone.

"Mom?"

My voice prodded her into action and slowly, as if in a daze, she made her way down the porch stairs toward me. I couldn't read her expression, so I tensed, bracing myself for vitriol. She passed the dog and kept coming. She walked right into me, our bodies colliding as she wrapped her arms around me so tight.

Shock stunned me for a second.

My mom was hugging me.

Hugging *me.*

"Nora," she whispered, sounding choked.

The fear I'd been holding onto for years shattered and I half laughed, half cried as I hugged her back.

We held each other until Trixie started to get impatient and jumped up on Mom. She laughed and let go of me. "Down, you silly girl." She pushed the dog's head away playfully and I studied her, thinking once again, Who is this person?

Seeing the questions written all over my face, Mom's laughter died. "Come on inside."

"Where's Dad?"

Avoiding my eyes, Mom turned on her heel and walked toward the house. "Inside, Nora."

It wasn't until we were standing facing each other in a stylishly decorated front room I never imagined would belong to my mother, all soft grays and buttercup yellows, that I got the news I'd been dreading for the last hour.

"Your dad is gone, Nora. He passed away about nine months ago. Heart attack."

It was too much.

It was all just too much.

"Malvolio!"

I gasped, coming out of the memory, and flushed, horrified at the thought of having been heard. But no one was watching me, and Terence, our Malvolio, was climbing over chairs to get to the stage.

"There is an aisle for a reason, you miscreant," Quentin scowled.

"I hardly think climbing over a few chairs warrants the insult. I, sir, am no villain. Well ... I am when you want me to be." He winked at him.

Suppressing a giggle, I watched as Quentin struggled not to smile. It should be mentioned that Terence was Quentin's lover and had been for three years. He was younger than Quentin by thirteen years and to the outside world, they seemed as different as apples and oranges. While Terence was playing the stoic, almost puritan Malvolio, in real life he was anything but. He was fun, sarcastic, a little wild, and gregarious, the opposite to Quentin who could be a wee bit uptight.

However, that was probably why they worked so well together. Terence was the light Quentin needed, and Quentin forced Terence to take life a little more seriously.

"Begin!" our director demanded.

Derek, who was playing Clown, strode onstage with Olivia and Malvolio.

"'Wit, and't be they will ...'"

I let them drift off in the background, trying to read my notes again when Quentin pulled me out of my concentration. "It's your debut line, Malvolio."

"I can't remember it," Terence said, giving him a boyish smile. His eyes flew past his boyfriend to me. "Perhaps Nora knows it."

"How can you not remember your first line?" Quentin asked.

He did remember it. He was just being annoying. "C'mon, Nora. Show off. I bet you know every line in this play."

"As impressive as that would be," Quentin said, "we do not have time for this. Line!"

But Terence smirked at me, taunting me. I huffed, sure I could see smoke billowing out of Quentin's ears. "'Yes; and shall do, till the pangs of death shake him.'"

"Ah there, see!" Terence clapped and then gestured at me to continue. "Go on."

I made a face. "Learn your own lines."

"You're all amateurs," Quentin growled.

Jane made a face. "Well ... yeah."

"It's kind of in the company name, darling." Terence continued to grin unapologetically.

Our director muttered something but he was too far away for me to hear.

"Is it just me," I lurched forward at the sound of Jack's voice right behind me, "or are they all particularly annoying tonight?"

"I would include you in that," I huffed, gesturing to his seat and then the stage. "When did you get there from up there?"

"While ye were staring at yer laptop pretending to work but secretly daydreaming about me."

I sighed and turned back around. "I'm not going out with you, Jack."

"I wasn't going to ask again. At least not tonight."

"You don't want to date me. You're… confused. No woman has ever said no before."

"True, but it's not just that. Ye'er a mystery, Nora O'Brien. I haven't met a lot of those lately."

"Too bad for you I don't want to be solved."

Quentin frowned over at us.

Jack leaned in closer so his mouth was near my ear. "What is it, then? Tragic past? Heartbroken one too many times?"

I pretended to look around. "What is that incessant buzzing noise?"

He chuckled. "Or maybe heartbroken the one time but it was enough to make ye gun shy."

"I certainly won't be handling your gun anytime soon."

"Or maybe it's daddy issues. I've dated women with those before. Is it? Is it daddy issues?"

I tensed, glaring sullenly at my screen. "My dad is dead."

DONOVAN, INDIANA
NOVEMBER 2015

"*I* GOT ALL YOUR LETTERS," MOM SAID THE NEXT MORNING. WE SAT AT *the breakfast counter in her beautiful New England-style kitchen. "I just didn't feel like I deserved to read them, to be a part of your life, after the way I'd treated you. Back then I thought you deserved to be free of me."*

That wasn't something I'd ever expected my mother to say.

But nothing about this trip home was going as expected.

After the news of my father's death, we didn't do much talking. At first, I cried and then I grew cold and words failed me as I processed the fact that my dad had been gone from this world for nearly a year and I'd had no idea.

Rather than continue the conversation about my letters, I let my anger lead me. "Is that why you didn't contact me to tell me he'd died?"

"No, I wrote you about your dad. Sent it to the last address you wrote from but the letter came back unopened."

Shit. "I moved."

She nodded. "I thought so. I tried social media but I couldn't find you."

Because I'd deleted my Facebook account after Jim died.

Shit.

"I'm sorry," I whispered, my anger dissipating.

"I figured I'd hear from you eventually." She studied my naked ring finger. "Divorced?"

I flinched. "He died. Early last year."

Horror filled my mother's expression. "Nora ... I am so sorry."

Exhaling shakily, I said, "It's been a crappy few years." Then I caught sight of the photo of us I'd liked best—the one of my mom cuddling into Dad's side and Dad holding me tight. I was about eight or nine in the picture. Mom had hung it near the kitchen door. "Did he hate me?"

"No," she said instantly. "He blustered about it but I knew your father better than he thought I did and he was mad at himself. He blamed himself for driving you away. Didn't make him any less mean. In fact, he only got worse." She sighed. "I'm afraid to say that hardship did not bring out the best in your father."

"I'm sorry for the way I left," I said, looking her directly in the eye. "That's what I came here to say. And to see if I'm forgiven for running away when you needed me."

Mom's brows pinched together. "There's nothing to forgive. We were the ones who needed to be forgiven, Nora. I understand why you left. You were a smart, great kid and I made you think that you didn't deserve to reach for something outside of this town. I was bitter. And I'd been bitter a long time and it wasn't until you left us that I woke the hell up. Too little, too late."

"You're so different," I mused, studying her, gratified to see her eyes were no longer dull and tired. "And this house ...?"

Smirking at my unfinished question, she replied, "This was all your dad's. The son of a bitch was sitting on **money**, Nora. Inheritance from his uncle who'd passed it to him 'cause he had no kids of his own. It was the money your dad used to set up his construction company. Money the sneaky bastard kept from his wife and invested well. Not to mention the fact that I found out from Kyle Trent at your dad's goddamn funeral that he paid decent money for your dad's company and the house but your dad asked him to keep it quiet from me."

Shocked, I couldn't quite comprehend what she was saying. "But why would he lie about it?"

And then realization hit me.

I could have gone to college.

"School," I whispered.

Guilt filled my mother's eyes. "I really thought we couldn't afford it. If I'd known that we could send you to school and then some, I swear ..." She shook her head. "I had a lot of anger toward your dad after he died and I came into all this money. He and I never had the greatest relationship and I knew the only way it would survive is if I worked all the damn time. I liked working. I liked being social. But I was bitter over losing our nice house and that my kid, who listened to her daddy fill her head with big dreams of an Ivy League education, was going to end up working jobs she hated. To realize he kept you from school, kept us all from comfort and security ... I wanted to resurrect him just so I could kill him."

I felt my own anger burning in my gut, along with incredible amounts of hurt. "I thought he loved me. Why would he lie?"

"He did love you. I think he was scared you'd go off to college and leave him alone with me. Irony was you ran off anyway."

We sat in silence for a minute and then I looked around at the pretty kitchen. "So, you spent the money?"

"Building this was therapy. It helped me get over what he'd done."

"It's beautiful."

"Thank you." She sat back on her high-backed stool and said, "And you are welcome to stay here as long as you want. But you should know that I put money in an account for you, in case you came back."

"Mom, you don't have to give me money. I didn't come here for that."

"Of course you didn't. But the money is yours." She cocked her head to the side. "Did you ever make it to college?"

I shook my head.

She grinned. "Well, if you still want to, there's enough money in that account to get you where you want to go and keep you there for four years."

The utter disbelief I felt must've shown on my face because she laughed and leaned over to pat my hand. "I knew it would feel good telling you that, but I never could've imagined it would feel this good."

chapter 23

"Nora? Nora," Jack whispered in my ear. "I said I'm sorry."

I dismissed the memories and threw him a look over my shoulder. "It's cool."

"Understudy Viola and Duke Orsino," Quentin said, turning to us, halting the rehearsal once again. I slumped in my seat with a groan. "Please desist with your nonsensical jibber-jabber."

"Apologies," Jack called out. "I'll stop the jibber and Miss O'Brien here promises to quit the jabber."

"You're all going to be the death of me." Quentin ran a hand through his thick, dark hair. "My father was right. I should have invested my money in Facebook shares. But no, I had to open a theater."

I coughed to cover my laughter and closed my laptop. There was no way I was getting this paper written at rehearsal. It was silly of me to have thought so.

"Hey."

I rolled my eyes and looked back at him. "What?"

Jack's countenance was surprisingly serious. "I really am sorry about yer dad."

Nodding my thanks, I turned back around and focused on the stage, trying to concentrate on the play. But my thoughts kept drifting back to Donovan. I'd stayed with my mom for a few months, reconnecting with her, and I actually got to know her. She only worked a few hours a day at May's Coffeehouse because she had Trixie to look after. It galled me somewhat that a dog was getting more consideration than her kid ever did, but I didn't want to hold any grudges. Not against her or my dad. I was too tired of it all. Plus, it was obvious my mother had changed.

We had a good few months together where I learned more about my dad in the years after I'd left. Being there allowed me to grieve more than anywhere else could have. I could do it freely because only mom understood how complicated my feelings were toward my father. He was the hero who let me down, but I'd forgiven him a long time ago for that. If I was honest, I didn't like the man he became, but I loved the man he had been with all my heart and soul. In a way, I'd already grieved losing my father a long time ago. What I needed my mom's help with was getting over the fear that he'd never forgiven me for leaving him.

Moreover, I told my mom the truth about my life in Edinburgh, about Jim, Seonaid, Roddy, and Angie. And about Sylvie and the man who'd made me flee home to Indiana.

There was no judgment from her; she was only sorry she hadn't been there to help me through.

What surprised me most about leaving for Edinburgh was how hard it was to get on that plane and leave my mom. We'd somehow, miraculously, bonded and I wasn't sure I was ready to let her go yet. But Donovan wasn't my home. Edinburgh was in my blood now and it called for me to return.

As did Seonaid, Roddy, and Angie, every Sunday on Skype. Seonaid had been inspired by what she considered a brave decision to head home and face my fears.

She faced her own.

She told Roddy she was in love with him.

His reply, "About fuckin' time, woman."

Oh, and he told her he loved her too.

Now they were either bickering or making out. They couldn't keep their hands off each other and as happy as I was for them, I also secretly envied them.

When I was in the States, though, I missed them and was desperate to get home and see what the world was like when Roddy and Seonaid were an item.

My last push to leave Donovan was my mom herself. She told me she didn't want to hold me back anymore and that she would come visit, and vice versa. So far that held true. Mom came to stay with me for a few weeks in the summer before I started my first semester at Edinburgh University. I got into their English Literature and Language program and had every intention of going on to get my master's in education so I could teach. Once upon a time, I might have been interested in the psychology of others, but after my time with the kids at the hospital, I realized that I loved being around them. Teaching seemed like the next best thing.

As for my kids at the hospital, I'd arranged with Jan so that I could Skype that first Wednesday I missed them. Although we were both sad to say goodbye, I told them I had to go home to the States to be with family, which wasn't actually a lie.

I missed them.

So yeah, teaching was the right path for me.

However, I didn't want to give up on my dream of being on stage again. Pushing past my fears, I auditioned for Quentin's company and to my surprise and delight, he let me in, even though he said that I was—and I quote, "From the blasted colonies."

Seonaid, honest as always, told me only a few weeks ago how proud of me she was for pulling my life together, and she'd never seen me so content, so at peace. It was like she was looking for reassurance too, though, that I was happy. And I told her I'd never been happier.

It wasn't true.

But how I felt was *real*. I had been determined to change my life. I'd forgiven myself. I'd stopped berating myself. And I never wanted to feel like I wasn't good enough for anyone ever again. Moreover, I was never going to put myself in the same situation I'd put myself in with Aidan Lennox.

There.

I said his name.

What was Aidan Lennox but a *fantasy* created by my longing and circumstance? Yet thinking of him still hurt, so I rarely allowed myself to, which meant I rarely allowed myself to think of Sylvie, either.

And I wouldn't think about them now.

I glanced over my shoulder at Jack who was playing around on his phone. "Rehearsal is running a little late tonight, right?" I whispered.

"His Majesty forgets some of us have lives outside the the-ah-ter."

I grinned and was about to joke that we should pull the fire alarm when the large double doors at the back of the auditorium opened. A tall man stepped inside but it was too dark to make out his features.

Jack followed my gaze. "Hey," he called, "private rehearsals going on tonight, mate."

The man didn't reply.

Instead we heard Quentin yell, "Is that who I think it is?"

The man strode down the aisle toward us and the light started to crawl up his body the closer he got. "Told you I'd be here," his reply was deep and rumbling.

It sent a shiver down my spine.

I knew that voice.

His face was suddenly alight and as he passed, his eyes flickered down to Jack and me.

There was so much fire in those green eyes, I thought I might go up in flames.

He certainly looked like he wished I would.

Aidan?

His expression blanked, like an eraser had come along and wiped it clean, and he jerked his face forward and strode to meet Quentin, holding his hand out. Our director grabbed Aidan's hand and shook it, smiling from ear to ear. He clamped his other hand on Aidan's big shoulder and shook his head in wonder. "Aidan Lennox, I can't believe it."

"Believe it." Aidan grinned at him.

I sat stunned, wondering if I'd been spun into an alternate reality. Or the past. Or some weird mix of the two.

"Everybody," Quentin gestured to us all, "this is my good friend Aidan Lennox. He's a very successful music producer and composer. And for some ludicrous reason I will not question, he has agreed to write original music for our production!"

Everyone clapped, excited about the idea.

Me?

I could wave goodbye to no offstage drama.

chapter 24

IT WAS HARD TO MAKE FRIENDS WITH THE PEOPLE IN MY CLASSES. THERE weren't a whole lot of mature students, and those who were had partners and kids to go home to right after class. This meant, other than taking Jack up on his offer, I had no one to go to after rehearsal who wouldn't see that I was distracted. Seonaid, Roddy, and Angie would all know something was up and I didn't want to talk about Aidan's sudden reappearance in my life.

Not once in the five minutes Quentin took to introduce Aidan had my past love acknowledged me or the fact that we knew each other.

He treated me like I was a stranger. One he looked through.

After what he did to me?

Laine was right—he could be an asshole to women.

It was hard for me to reconcile the man that was just introduced to our company—that cold, aloof man—with the one who'd looked at me like I was the answer to everything good in his world. Was that what losing Sylvie had done to him?

I cursed myself for the concern that overtook me. And for the way he was already consuming my thoughts. This wasn't what I wanted. I needed a distraction!

Quentin had called time on the rehearsal to hang out with Aidan and talk shop, and I didn't need to be told twice to get the hell out of there. However, as I was leaving, I swore I could feel that chilly gaze on my back. Not able to help myself, I glanced over my shoulder before following the others out into the night.

Aidan wasn't looking at me. He was smirking at Amanda who gave him a little flirtatious finger wave as she walked away.

To my horror, I felt a flare of possessive jealousy so intense, it was like the last eighteen months hadn't happened.

I went home. I avoided a call from Seonaid knowing as soon as she heard my voice, she'd know I was *not* okay. And I glared at my English paper, thinking how impossible it would be for me to work with Aidan on this play. My life was good. I was finally in a good place where I actually liked myself and the plans I had for my future. Why do anything to shake that up?

It was time to find another theater group.

———

THE MONEY MY MOM HAD GIVEN ME WAS ENOUGH TO AFFORD THE luxury of only working a few nights a week at a pub on the Grassmarket. I kept my flat in Sighthill to keep costs down, and bartending at The Tavern covered my food and electricity.

Rehearsals for the play were Monday and Wednesday evenings, and I worked Thursday and Friday evenings. We were always busy at the pub given our close proximity to student housing. During classes that day, I'd vacillated between the need to fall asleep (I had *not* slept well the night before) and wanting to tear my hair out in frustration because my thoughts would not abandon Aidan Lennox. Moreover, I was trying to work myself up to call Quentin and tell him I was out. Knowing that was going to be unpleasant, it was taking me a while to gather the courage.

I was on break at work that evening, considering using work as an excuse to leave the Tollcross Company, when my phone rang.

Spookily, it was Quentin.

Quentin never called.

Texted demands, yes, but never called.

"Are ye gonna answer that?" Kieran, my Irish colleague, scowled at me. He was a law student at Edinburgh and studied during his breaks in the tiny staff room at the back of the bar.

"Sorry." I stepped outside into the narrow hallway that led to a small courtyard at the back. "Hello?"

"Good, you're there." Quentin heaved a dramatic sigh. "Change of plans. You're now Viola."

"Uh ... what now?"

"Gwyn quit. Apparently, her dissertation is suffering and she needed to cut something out of her life. Considering she couldn't learn her lines, I'm not exactly in mourning. So. My little Rain Man, you are now Viola. Congratulations. Be at rehearsals, usual time."

And he hung up before I could say another word.

At once I wanted to fist pump the air because there was no way I expected to get a major part in any play so soon. We may have been an amateur theater company, but Quentin had worked hard for more than a decade to build up its reputation. His productions always sold out because he offered quality, affordable entertainment. The local media reviewed them. Jack had gotten work on an episode of a national TV drama because of his performance in *A Streetcar Named Desire* a few years ago.

How could I turn down the chance to play Viola?

Yes, I didn't want the drama of having to deal with Aidan or the way he clearly could invade my every waking thought. But wasn't running away from the situation something the old me would've done? This was *my* life. Mine. It was time to stop letting other people dictate how I lived it.

That didn't mean my hands weren't shaking when I wandered back into the bar.

———

"ARE YOU AVOIDING ME? I FEEL LIKE YOU'RE AVOIDING ME," SEONAID said as I hurried along Home Street, trying to block out the noisy traffic so I could hear my friend. She'd called as I was on my way to my first rehearsal as a major player.

"I told you I had a paper to finish this weekend. How is that avoiding you?"

"For fuck's sake, Cee Cee, stop interrogatin' the poor lassie. Ye ever think maybe she just wanted some peace and quiet fae ye?" I heard Roddy call from the background.

I snorted, listening as she retorted, "She's not you, Roddy. She actually likes having me around."

"I like havin' ye aroond tae. I just like it better when ye'er no' yappin'."

"You are lucky I know you're trying to wind me up, Roddy Livingston, or I'd advise you to get reacquainted with your right hand."

"Remember he's ambidextrous?" I said at the same time he said the same thing.

Seonaid huffed but I heard her amusement. "Stop avoiding the subject. Is everything really okay?"

I hesitated, wondering if I should tell her about Aidan. Seonaid was so good at bolstering me, inspiring me to be a better version of myself. But somehow, I couldn't get the words out. Telling her that he'd walked back into my life like a stranger would make it more real, and there was still a part of me hoping I could bury my head in the sand and pretend he'd been a surreal dream.

"Nora?"

I scrambled for a lie. "I ... um ... I've been feeling a little swamped with school lately and I didn't want to complain because I want this, and it seems so ungrateful to complain."

That sounded plausible.

Seonaid apparently thought so too. "You're still allowed to get stressed about it, though, babe. Let me know if there's anything I can do to help."

"Thank you. I'm fine, though. I'm heading to rehearsal, in fact. I ... uh ... the woman playing Viola dropped out so they gave the part to me."

"Oh, Nora, that's brilliant!" she cried. "I can't wait to come see you in it."

"Thanks." I smiled, still giddy that I'd actually be on stage playing this part.

"Shame you grew your hair out, though. Doesn't your character dress like a boy for most of the play?"

I snorted. "Yeah, she does."

Once my hair had hit my chin, it grew like wildfire and to my delight, it now reached my shoulder blades. I usually wore it in soft waves created with my hair straightener—Seonaid showed me how.

"Anyway, I'm almost there. Speak soon," I promised.

"Okay. Speak soon, babe."

We hung up and I attempted (and failed) not to feel guilty for lying to her. But I was already trying to deal with my own reaction to Aidan's return. I didn't need to deal with Seonaid's too.

By the time I walked into the building on Gilmore Place, it felt like there were small creatures surfing waves inside my belly.

Do not be sick, Nora. Whatever you do, do not throw up.

I'd like to pretend it was all about being nervous for my first day as Viola, but it was, of course, more than that. And the "more than that" was standing near the stage talking with Quentin and Terence.

Quentin looked up at the sound of my entrance and gestured to me. "Viola arrives!"

I flushed but attempted a smile. It may have come out a little grim.

My director didn't seem to notice, however. "Ready?"

"As I'll ever be," I said, coming to a stop near them.

To my disbelief my body hummed with absolute awareness of Aidan, like it used to. Would that damn feeling never go away? How was it possible to still feel that way when the bastard left me? Left *me*!

Because of the awareness, the way the hair on my arms stood on end, my eyes were drawn to him, despite my anger. He was concentrating on his phone, texting someone. His top lip was pressed into his full lower lip and the strong muscle in his jaw popped out, like he was gritting his teeth beneath his cool façade. As always, he was unshaven, scruffy in a way that worked for him. I flushed, remembering how the scratch of his stubble elicited tingles through my body when we kissed. Once upon a time, he'd promised me I'd feel it everywhere, but we never got the chance.

And now here he was.

Ignoring me.

Well, then.

In denial of the pain that scored across my chest, I said, "No one else here yet?"

Terence nodded to a door at the left side of the stage that led to dressing rooms and a small kitchen and public room. "Having a coffee. Still waiting on a few others."

I flicked one last look at Aidan but he was determinedly not looking anywhere in my vicinity.

Asshole.

Anger swirled in my belly and took out the earlier surfers, and I strode away like I couldn't care less. I found most of the cast in the kitchen.

"Here she is!" Jack boomed, standing up and holding his arms out wide. "Our lovely Viola!"

I rolled my eyes at him and then blushed when everyone cheered and whistled. "Stop it," I said, gesturing for them to hush.

"We're pleased for ye, Nora." Jack grinned.

"No, Jack is pleased for himself." Will smirked. "Now he can snog you and you have to snog him back."

While everyone chuckled and teased us, I took it in stride as I poured myself a quick coffee. "Yeah, pity Quentin isn't strictly sticking to the original play, huh?" There wasn't any kissing on the lips in the original.

Jack held a hand to his chest. "Oh, how ye wound me."

We stood around talking and joking for a few minutes until Terence popped his head in to tell us we were ready to start. As we wandered out to the theater, I heard Jane asking when the costume mistress would be taking fittings. We'd already had our measurements taken but I wondered if I'd need to have another session with her now that I was Viola.

Quentin's vision for the production was a dystopian twist. To him it was set way in the future after a cataclysmic climate disaster and Illyria was an island that had survived and thrived. Our clothing would be modern meets *Mad Max*, and although our dialogue was from the original play, Quentin had sexed it up a little. There were moments when I, dressed as Cesario, would appear as if I was going in for a real kiss after Orsino kisses my cheeks, for example. Those moments were supposed to be thick with sexual tension on my part. And Quentin also wanted me to kiss Orsino as Viola when he finally learns the truth that I'm a woman. He said it gave the audience the satisfaction they were looking for, rather than questioning whether Orsino really loved Viola or was simply glad someone loved him when he'd been rejected by Olivia so many times.

That last bit pricked me, reminding me of Jim. Although I was learning to forgive myself, I still wasn't completely there, and I still questioned how I'd really felt about him. Had I run off and married him because I was allured by how much he loved me?

Shaking the thoughts out of my head—I didn't need them hanging around when Aidan Lennox was near—I grabbed a seat with the others. Jack took the stage with Terence, who was playing Curio as well as Malvolio since the characters never share the stage. We were starting from the top secondary to Gwyn's departure.

I chanced a glance at Aidan who stood beside Quentin, and I frowned, watching him watch the actors. Why did he have to be here? Did he really need to be? Couldn't he just study Quentin's production notes and the costume and set designs? It wasn't like we were in dress rehearsal.

From the angle I was sitting, I could only see Aidan's profile. A rush of feeling flooded over me as I studied his familiar face. Memories flooded me. Smiles. Laughter. Kisses. Soft touches. Tears. Him falling to his knees. Not meeting my eyes and telling me to leave and get rest. The last thing he ever said to me.

I'd never felt such a confusing mix of fury and longing in my entire life. I at once wanted to go to him, make him look at me, hold me, and I also wanted to march up to him, grab his sweater in my fists, and shake him, even though he'd barely budge under my assault.

I remember you, Pixie.

I closed my eyes, in pain at the memory. If he called me by his nickname for me again, I didn't know whether I'd burst into tears or smack him across the face.

Probably both.

"Viola!" Quentin spun on his heel to look at me. "On stage."

Nerves hit me in a massive wave and I took a moment to exhale slowly before I stood and walked toward the stage. I hoped I appeared calm and ready to do this because inside, I was under attack.

I joined Eddie up on stage; he gave me a bolstering smile.

In my entrance on performance nights, I would be accompanied by Eddie as Captain and we'd have extras with us as our sailors. "'What country, friends, is this?'" I said in a faux upper-crust English accent, slowly walking across the stage, looking awed.

"'This is Illyria, lady,'" Eddie said, following me.

I swiftly turned to look at him. "'And what should I do in Illyria? My brother he is in Elysium …'"

We fell into the scene and I was feeling pretty good about it when it came to an end, until I looked over at Quentin and Aidan. Finally, I had Aidan's attention. But I'd take him ignoring me over the scowl he wore.

As my director opened his mouth to speak, Aidan called up to me, "You need to work on that accent."

I flushed, turning expectantly to Quentin. He looked a little taken aback by Aidan's input but he nodded at me. "If one person thinks it's not great, others might. Practice it. It's not a huge concern yet."

"The way she's wandering around the stage like a bewildered child is," Aidan said, like he hadn't insulted the hell out of me. "Viola is bold enough to dress as a man in order to find her brother. She wouldn't be wild-eyed and frightened."

Wild-eyed and frightened?

I hadn't been acting wild-eyed and frightened!

Quentin quirked a brow at his friend and then smirked up at me. "Play it a little less vulnerable in your next scene."

Seething, I could only nod. Completely unable to look at Aidan, I turned to Eddie. He gave me a sympathetic smile and we left the stage together. The actors playing Maria, Sir Toby, and Sir Andrew took the stage.

Ignoring Aidan, I strode farther down the aisle to get away from him, and Amanda gave me a smug smile from her seat next to Hamish. "You'll get better with practice," she said.

I returned her smile with a tight one of my own and flopped down on a seat near the back.

It wasn't much later, however, that Quentin was calling me up to stage again with Will and Jack. After Aidan's criticism—something he did not dole out to anyone else—I was on edge but fighting the feeling because I didn't want it to affect my performance.

We were halfway through the scene when Quentin called up for us to stop. Dread filled me as we looked down at him.

But it was Aidan who spoke. "You're doing it again. All doe-eyed while he's talking." He gestured to Jack.

Anger flared out of me. "I'm supposed to be in love with him," I argued.

"And you're masquerading as a man. You're good at deception," he bit out, and I couldn't miss the hiss of anger in his words. Were we still talking about the play? "At this point in the play, you can control your feelings for this man."

Reeling from his words, I couldn't argue this time. In fact, the whole atmosphere in the theater had changed, as if everyone else had heard the underlying fury in his words and were confused by them.

As confused as I was.

Why the hell was Aidan mad at me?

Attempting to shake him off, I stepped back into character and tried to rein in the vulnerability. Jack was incredibly charming as Orsino, playing him with the right amount of sensual masculinity and silly, lovelorn comedy.

When he'd finished his last line of the scene, I gave him a bow. "'I'll do my best to woo your lady.'" And then I strode off, as if exiting stage, but stopped and turned to the audience. I gave them a pained look, my hands in tight fists at my sides. "'Yet, a barful strife. Whoe'er I woo ... myself would be his wife.'"

"Again!" Aidan called up.

I gawped down in astonishment and even Quentin was gaping at him. Aidan caught his friend's look. "I can't get the feel of the play until all the actors are doing what they're supposed to be doing."

"What do you think was wrong here?" Quentin, to my utter surprise, entertained Aidan's overstep.

"Now she's not giving enough emotion. I need emotion to write music." He cut me a sneer. "This one needs more practice than the others."

This one? This one!

Quentin frowned. "It's the first rehearsal, Nora. You'll get there."

I nodded, grateful for his kindness, but my cheeks blazed with mortification at Aidan's hurtful critique. As I walked offstage, I heard Jack hurry to catch up with me. He threw his arm over my shoulders and squeezed me into his side. For once he wasn't smiling; he actually looked annoyed on my behalf. "Ye did great."

"Thanks. Apparently not."

"What the fuck does he know?" he whispered. "He's just some jumped-up music producer."

Whom I used to be in love with until he left me.

Which apparently wasn't enough damage.

Furious, my eyes went to Aidan as Jack walked with me, his arm still around me in comfort. Aidan was glowering at me with such vitriol, my muscles locked as if preparing for battle.

Dazed, I couldn't even remember getting into the seat next to Jack. I couldn't take my eyes off Aidan, not even when he whipped his fiery gaze from mine to turn back to the stage. But I knew him. His body was stiff with tension, with anger, and I was a mass of confusion.

How Aidan had treated me on that stage, deliberately humiliating me, was so out of character. It was like I was faced with an entirely different man. A stranger, like he'd made himself out to be. The only time in our past that Aidan had been truly angry with me was when I'd deserted him at lunch after he'd confided in me about his sister's death.

He'd treated me with cool aloofness then too.

With cold anger.

Looking at it rationally, the Aidan I had known would only be this angry with me if he thought *I* had done *him* wrong.

Cold sweat prickled under my arms.

"Yesterday after you left, he suddenly started making arrangements to leave the country. He took a job in LA so he can be close to Sylvie but it meant leaving early this morning."

I'd taken the word of a woman I didn't trust over a man I'd grown to trust more than anyone.

What if Aidan hadn't left? What if Laine had orchestrated the lie somehow?

No.

That was too ridiculous, right?

But then why was Aidan so furious with me? That kind of fury could be born of the fact that I had left him the day after his kid was taken from him. Right?

Yet … Aidan had texted me.

Aidan *had* texted me, right?

I tried to put the pieces together, the entire theater falling away as I thought back to that time eighteen months ago. I had left that night. My phone didn't work in the US so I'd left it, and I got a new number and cell when I returned months later. The old contract had ended and I threw out the old phone.

So if Aidan had tried to contact me, I wouldn't have known.

But he knew where I lived. He knew where Seonaid worked because I'd told him. Wouldn't he have gone to Seonaid when he couldn't get in touch with me?

And still, what about his phone? If he hadn't text me, if it had been Laine all along, then why didn't Aidan know about it?

Nothing made sense.

But something was wrong.

I looked at him, fear coalescing inside me, and I realized I was more afraid of discovering it had all been a huge misunderstanding, a deliberate manipulation on the part of his jealous friend, than I was of being faced with an indifferent, cold Aidan.

The Aidan I'd loved terrified me more.

Because I was finally in a good place, taking care of *me*, and I was nowhere near ready to face the kind of volatile emotions Aidan Lennox brought out in me.

chapter 25

THE SOUND OF GIRLS' LAUGHTER DREW ME OUT OF MY CONCENTRATION, and I glanced over at the group of eighteen-year-old freshman giggling under a tree. Like me, they'd decided to make the most of the beautiful spring day and were sitting out on The Meadows behind the main campus.

I was by myself. As usual.

It wasn't that people in my classes hadn't made overtures of friendliness toward me. They had. Because of my height, some had even mistaken me for their age, surprised when I told them I was twenty-four. Six years didn't seem like a huge spread, but the difference between eighteen and twenty-four was massive, especially for someone like me who'd been married, widowed, and lost a child and a man I'd loved.

As if conjuring her ghost, a little blond girl dashed by the students, turning to laugh behind her. A woman, presumably her mother, hurried after her. She was much younger than Sylvie had been when I last saw her.

God, Sylvie.

I didn't often let myself think about her because all that came with it was longing and worry. She'd be twelve now. Was she happy? Was Cal taking good care of her?

Looking beyond The Meadows to across the street, I felt a sudden urge to go to the hospital. I hadn't visited since returning to Edinburgh. It was too full of ghosts. But I found myself packing my books into my shoulder bag and getting to my feet. My steps took me out of the park and across the street and up.

Maybe it was Aidan's return in my life that finally pushed me toward the hospital. I wasn't sure what I was looking for as I walked toward the red brick building. All I knew was that before Aidan came back, I was feeling pretty sure of myself and of life, and now I felt like I was floating untethered again. Totally lost.

Aidan's cruel behavior at rehearsals wasn't helping.

I'd had two more rehearsals with him and each time, he'd found something to criticize in my performance. I wanted to believe that Quentin was getting as impatient with him as I was. Jack definitely was.

Tomorrow I had rehearsal again and I'd have to see him. I longed for Quentin to tell us it was Aidan's last day in the theater.

Pushing through the hospital's entrance door, the familiar smell brought with it a wave of memories.

Sylvie running to hug me. Grinning up at me with a mouthful of mac and cheese. The kids laughing as I prowled around the room like Count Olaf in *A Series of Unfortunate Events*. Aidan's face close to mine as we braced on the Twister sheet, his sexy smile making my heart flip in my chest.

I wrapped my arms around myself, as though to keep my insides from falling out. Why did I come here? It was stupid.

"Stupid, stupid, stupid," I muttered, turning away.

"Is that *you*, Peter Pan?"

I spun around, coming face to face with Jan.

She smiled at me tenderly.

And I rushed her.

Jan laughed, rocking back on her feet as I hugged her. She returned my hug and then pressed me gently away. Concern and fondness mingled in her expression. "What brings ye to my doorstep, Nora?"

"I don't know," I answered honestly.

Twenty minutes later, Jan had me seated in the quiet cafeteria with a cup of coffee, and I told her everything.

Absolutely everything.

It blurted out of me, uncontrolled, word after word.

"It doesn't sound right," Jan mused. "That definitely doesn't sound like Aidan. He'd never treat someone he cared about so poorly."

"Well, he is."

"I think ye'er right. I think his friend must have deliberately misled ye. As far as I'm aware, Aidan never went to California back then. He certainly still lives here."

"It doesn't matter." I said. "We're better off as we are."

"Then why do ye look so sad?"

I gave her a strained smile, my fingers gripping my coffee tightly. "I miss Sylvie."

"Sylvie's doing fine." Jan patted my hand.

Stunned, my heart rate sped up. "You've heard from her?"

She exhaled slowly. "Aidan drops by every now and then to let me know how she's doing. I ... uh ... knew something had happened between ye because when I mentioned ye, he clammed up. Everything makes sense now."

"And Sylvie?"

"She likes California. She's doing well. Her dad let her stay with Aidan for a month last summer, and he brought her back to Scotland at Christmas so she could see Aidan then too."

I wondered if she'd ever asked about me. If she missed me or worried where I'd gone. But above all, I was relieved to hear she was happy. "He's taking good care of her, then?"

"Do ye think Aidan would allow anything else?"

"Right."

"Ye need to talk to him," Jan said. "Explain and get this misunderstanding sorted out."

"I hate when he looks at me like he loathes me," I confessed on a whisper, "but I think I'm more afraid of him looking at me like he used to."

Confused, Jan shook her head. "I don't understand."

"I'm finally doing okay, Jan." I touched my book bag. "I'm at school and I'm in a play, and my life is not complicated. For the first time in a long time, I'm where *I* want to be. Aidan and I ... we were what each other needed back then. Not now. Now we're two completely different people on completely different paths."

She stared at me so long I began to shift uncomfortably in my chair. Finally, she said, "If that's true ... why are ye here?"

"I was missing Sylvie." It was a half-truth.

And we both knew it.

———

FOR NOT THE FIRST TIME IN THE PAST WEEK, I WAS FACED WITH AMANDA flirting with Aidan and him grinning down at her like he enjoyed it. When she touched his chest and giggled at something he said, using the motion to bring them closer together, I turned away.

Why was I doing this to myself? Jealousy burned in my gut.

Quentin had asked to take a five-minute break while he answered an "important phone call" and I'd used the time to pull out notes for the Classics course I was taking.

However, Amanda's laughter kept grabbing my attention and I could feel myself growing more and more agitated by the second.

The main doors to the auditorium squeaked open and I turned in my seat to see a tall brunette strolling down the aisle like she was on a runway.

My God, her legs went on forever.

I glanced across the aisle and saw Jack's tongue practically fall out of his mouth as she passed him. About to ask the model-like creature if I could help her, I noticed her exotic-shaped eyes were trained on Aidan.

I felt like someone had kicked me in the gut.

Amanda stepped back from Aidan, scowling as the woman

strolled right up to him, leaned into him, and pressed a kiss to the corner of his mouth. Aidan's hand rested familiarly on her hip, and I felt myself die inside.

Looking down at my notes, I couldn't breathe.

I was near tears.

Of course he was dating someone else. And of course she was five foot ten and looked like an older version of Gigi Hadid.

I shifted uncomfortably in my seat, pretending my notes were the most interesting thing in the world when really, I was wondering how on earth Aidan could have been interested in me when he could get women like that?

No!

I mentally slapped myself for the thought. That was *not* happening. I was not going back there to that insecure girl who constantly wondered why Aidan wanted to be with her.

No, I did not look like Gigi Hadid. I wasn't beautiful but I was pretty. I could finally look in the mirror and see that now. I was the pretty girl-next-door type, and I was okay with that.

Damn Aidan Lennox for re-entering my life and kicking up my self-esteem issues.

"Seriously?"

I jumped in my seat and looked up at Jack who was standing by me, his gaze hostile on Aidan who still had the model buried into his side. "Who does this arsehole think he is?"

"Have you Googled him?" I said.

He shook his head.

"Google him. He's kind of a big deal."

Jack looked down at me. "He treats ye like shit, Nora. He's kind of scum."

Grateful, I smiled up at him and something mischievous came over me. "Then why don't you show his girl how much more charming you can be? You know you want to."

A slow smile spread across his face. "She is pretty gorgeous."

"She is."

To my surprise, he leaned down and pressed a kiss to my cheek. "You're just as gorgeous, gorgeous."

I laughed and swatted him away playfully. "Liar."

He winked and turned away, and my eyes flew over to Aidan. I stiffened in my seat to find him glaring at me.

But I didn't look away this time.

Instead, I locked mental horns with him, willing him to back down first.

I wondered if either of us would have if it hadn't been for Quentin reappearing and clamping a hand on Aidan's shoulder, breaking our staring contest.

———

"'WHAT THRIFTLESS SIGHS SHALL POOR OLIVIA BREATHE. O TIME, THOU must untangle this, not I.'" For some reason, my attention fell on Aidan as I said that line. He sat in a seat in the front row and as our eyes connected, his expression darkened. The woman who'd crashed our rehearsal was still there, sitting beside him. I ignored her and finished my monologue. "'It is too hard a knot for me to untie.'"

"Terrible," Aidan announced immediately and loudly. "The accent, the lack of emotion. You're all alone up there. You need to command the attention of the audience. Even as Cesario, the men in the audience who know better, should wish they were Orsino. They should desire you. You're as appealing as a fart in a spacesuit up there."

"Now, wait a minute—" Jack started but I lifted a hand, halting him. He stood on the aisle near the edge of the stage and clamped his mouth shut in frustration. But I must've looked pretty pissed off because he remained silent.

And I turned my fury on the man who'd caused it. "Who the hell do you think you are?"

Aidan looked surprised. "I'm—"

"That was a rhetorical question," I snapped, my voice ringing out loud and clear in the auditorium. Tense silence followed but I didn't let it settle. "You have done nothing but insult me—not critique me, which I might add is not your place to do so—since the moment you entered this theater. You want to play the part of the egotistical asshat, go ahead, but I am playing Viola, and I am a member of this company, so you either show me some goddamn respect or you get the hell out."

It wasn't *my* place to say so.

But I said it nonetheless.

Aidan's eyes blazed up at me but this time, I couldn't read his expression.

"Nora."

My stomach sank as Quentin's voice rang out from behind Aidan. When my eyes connected with my director's, I was surprised he was smirking at me. I'd thought he'd be livid. "Thank God you finally reprimanded him for his ghastly behavior."

Relief moved through me as Quentin got to his feet and walked around to face Aidan. "We're friends, mate, and I am truly grateful you want to write music for this, but I have to support my actor."

Aidan stood up and patted his friend's shoulder, looking apologetic. "You're right. You're right. The girl is fresh and needs encouragement, not harsh words. It's not my place, either. It's the bossy arsehole in me, I'm afraid." He turned to me, a false smile on his lips. "Apologies, Miss O'Brien. It won't happen again."

We eyed each other, like two opponents in a boxing ring, until Quentin called time on rehearsals. I hurried offstage and Jack caught up with me as I gathered my stuff to leave. "Well done," he said under his breath. "Ye needed to do that."

"I know," I agreed. "Hopefully he'll back off now."

Jack looked over his shoulder. Aidan and his model were approaching.

"Nicolette, it was a pleasure," Jack said pointedly to the woman.

She gave him a flirtatious half smile back.

"Goodnight, Jack," Aidan nodded his head in acknowledgment.

He didn't look at me.

I didn't exist.

And off he walked, out of the theater with his arm around the beautiful Nicolette.

I attempted not to feel hurt but it was impossible.

"Ignorant arsehole," Jack huffed. "Why is he such a dick to ye?"

Because I think he thinks I broke his heart.

"I don't know."

"You know he and Nicolette aren't exclusive. Apparently, the jammy bugger has a woman on every fucking continent. And she's okay with it," he said incredulously.

The news was like a knife between my ribs. I gave my friend a bleak smile. "Good news for you."

"Aye." He grinned. "She gave me her number."

I wasn't surprised. Jack was no Aidan Lennox, but he could charm the pants off most women.

"As for you," he said, "don't listen to him. Ye'er brilliant up there."

I returned his kiss on the cheek from earlier. "Thanks, Jack," I said sadly, unable to hide my feelings now that Aidan was gone and I didn't have to.

However, I didn't want Jack's pity. I grabbed my stuff and high-tailed it out of the theater, dreading the next rehearsal.

And boy, did that piss me off even more. Why the hell was Aidan here? This was merely a favor to him, but the theater was my joy.

He was ruining my freaking joy!

chapter 26

TO SAY I WAS IN A FOUL MOOD AFTER REHEARSAL WAS THE WORLD'S biggest understatement, and that foul mood continued on into the week. My colleagues at the pub avoided me like the plague and I didn't contribute much to the tip jar at the end of the bar, so I offered to let Kieran and our other colleague Joe share that between them.

Thankfully, that made them hate me less.

I've never understood people who want to be around others when they're in a black mood. If you can spare people being infected by that crap, why wouldn't you? So I stayed home alone on Saturday, but there was no avoiding Seonaid on Sunday. She called and when I tried to bail on our monthly Sunday catch-up with Angie, she threatened to come personally haul my ass there.

Angie's delight to see me somewhat soothed my irritation, and it was nice to be fawned over by a mother figure as she ushered me into the kitchen where Seonaid and Roddy were. They were standing by the coffee machine, Seonaid backed up against the counter, Roddy's body pressed into hers, and he murmured something against her mouth that made her smile.

Envy unlike anything I'd ever experienced around them slithered through my veins like a poisonous serpent. It fueled my frustration with its toxin and it started to transform into suspicion and anger.

Angie cleared her throat. "Not in my kitchen," she warned, but she looked anything but annoyed.

She was happy her daughter and the boy she considered a son were happy.

I was happy for them too.

I was.

But right then, my theory about Aidan was making my gut churn with irate anticipation.

"You're here." Seonaid brushed by Roddy and came toward me, wearing a big grin on her lovely face, a grin that fell when she saw my expression. She stopped. "What's wrong?"

Something took over me. My need for answers. And it didn't care if Angie and Roddy were in the room. "Did Aidan come looking for me? When I left?"

She paled.

And the breath was knocked out of me. "Oh my God."

"Nora." she stepped toward me, appearing panicked. "He showed up at the salon a few days after you left."

My confusion and rage exploded out of me. "Why didn't you tell me?" I yelled.

Seonaid flinched and Roddy was at her back, glowering at me. "Want tae cool it?"

"This is none of your business," I snapped at him. "Seonaid?"

"He asked where you were and I told him you'd gone back home. He stormed out as soon as I told him. That was it. That was the extent of our conversation."

"That doesn't explain why you didn't tell me. I thought he was in California!"

"I couldn't assume that he hadn't come back. I didn't know why he was there, Nora."

"But you could have told me!"

Her expression turned pleading. "He wrecked you, Nora. I thought he was back to mess you up again and you needed to be at peace for once. Okay, I'm sorry if that was high-handed of me, but I didn't see any point in telling you. And when you came home, you were so content and so focused on *you*. Life was about *you* for once.

You didn't seem to care anymore about Aidan, and I assumed that he was a blip in your history." Tears shone in her eyes. "I'm sorry. I'm sorry. I don't know what else to say."

I slumped, the fight draining out of me at her words. Why the hell was I yelling at my best friend when I completely agreed with every word coming out of her mouth? Except one thing. "I wasn't over him," I whispered.

"Oh God, Nora—"

"But I am now," I cut her off. "I have to be. You're right. My life is finally where it should be and he made it messy."

There was a moment's quiet and then Angie spoke up. "I have absolutely nae idea who or what ye'er talking about … but sometimes the most beautiful things in life are the messiest."

My chest ached a little at her wisdom, but I remained strong. "And sometimes something comes along that's so beautiful, it's agony to lose it. I've had enough loss to last a lifetime." I looked at Seonaid. "I'm sorry for yelling. You did the right thing."

Seonaid didn't look so sure. "Did I?"

DESPITE SEONAID'S WARNING THAT I COULDN'T KEEP MY FEELINGS bottled up, I tried very hard to convince myself that I was okay with how things had played out with Aidan. That I needed to be okay so I could go on living my life in perfect contentment. While he gallivanted around the theater with his beautiful women and horse-assery.

Finding my Zen, however, was proving more difficult than I'd thought. I was a bundle of confused feelings. At war with myself.

So it wasn't any wonder I reacted the exact opposite of how I'd hoped when Aidan finally confronted me in private.

Having to meet up with another student to work on an assignment we had for a tutorial, I hadn't seen any point in heading home to Sighthill only to have to return to Tollcross for rehearsal. I'd grabbed a salad from a shop on Potterrow, and walked to the theater. I was ninety minutes early so no one was there. Thankfully, Quentin was usually at the theater during the day so the doors were open. When I got inside the auditorium, however, it was pitch black.

"Quentin?" I called out. "Are you here?"

My voice echoed.

Nothing.

"Anyone?"

But the silence told me I was alone. I wondered if Quentin had accidentally left the theater unlocked. I'd need to let him know.

Switching on the stage lights to make me not feel like I was about to become part of a horror movie, I found my way into an empty dressing room.

Eating my salad, I worked on a paper, waiting for the minutes to tick by.

A noise far off in the distance made me still like a rabbit caught in headlights. I cocked my head, listening, and sure enough, footsteps approached. Blood rushed in my ears as my pulse raced. I then cursed myself for being freaked out when it was obviously a cast member who was—I glanced at my watch—an hour early.

I waited, and the dressing room door I had left slightly ajar squeaked open.

My breath caught at the sight of Aidan filling the doorway.

He crossed his arms and his ankles and leaned against the jamb, staring at me dispassionately.

All I could do was stare back, my emotions whirling in a mess of feelings, like a tornado, with no thought to what it was sucking up into its wind funnel. "What are you doing here?" I finally said, my voice hoarse.

"I was sitting in the coffee shop across the way and I saw you come in."

"You followed me?"

"I argued with myself about it for a while. But aye."

Adrenaline coursed through me and made my hands shake. I

curled them into fists and hoped I looked back at him with as much boredom as he was bestowing upon me. "Why?"

"Curiosity." He shrugged.

"Curiosity?"

"Were you always such a heartless robot and I was just too fucking blind to see it?"

I flinched, knowing this was the moment I should tell him that Laine had lied to me. But I couldn't get the words out. I wanted to and I didn't want to.

So fear of him hating me and fear of him loving me left me in some kind of exasperated, frustrated no-man's land. I shot to my feet. "If you came here to use me as your emotional punching bag, you can leave," I hissed.

His eyes flashed and he pushed off the jamb, coming into the room. For the first time, I hated that I had to tip my head back to look up at him. "Not before I tell you what I really think of you, Nora, instead of hiding it behind the subterfuge of giving a fuck what happens with this play."

"Aidan—"

"You are the biggest coward I've ever met in my life. You're weak and emotionally defunct. What's worse is how fucking manipulative you are—"

"Aidan—"

"I've never met anyone who had me so fucking fooled!" His chest heaved as his cool fled in the wake of his rage. "You lied and strung me along, fled when the going got tough, not once but goddamn twice, and I'm the idiot who let you do that to me."

"Aidan—"

"But rest assured, Nora, you are the last woman who is ever going to make a fool out of me. I see you now. Who you really are. A fucked-up, selfish, self-involved, immature little—"

Whatever horrible thing he was going to call me next, I swallowed it in my kiss. Unable to bear his contempt any longer, but not knowing how to make it stop, I went with my gut.

And my gut told him to grab his T-shirt in my fists and use it to haul him down to my mouth.

What a mistake.

Because I remembered him now.

I remembered how beautiful he felt.

So when his hands gripped my forearms and tried to pry me off, I let him, only to slide my arms around his neck and cling on tighter, kissing him in desperation.

He grunted and grabbed my arms again and just as I feared he would shove me away, he broke. Aidan jerked me closer, his mouth opening under mine, his tongue searching for my tongue.

Quite abruptly, he was in charge.

I found myself lifted off the ground and then dropped on the dressing table counter. He forced my legs apart as we continued kissing hungrily. Our hands were everywhere, just as starved. Mine slipped under his T-shirt, roaming the hard muscles of his abdomen, while his roughly caressed my sides, squeezed my breasts, and finally delved under my dress.

I gasped into his mouth as his fingers slipped under the waistband of my underwear and fisted, ripping them down to my knees. His lips abruptly left mine, his angry glower burning into me and holding me totally captive as he hurriedly unzipped his jeans and pushed them down his hips to free his cock.

My eyes dropped to it, but I only had a second to take it in and question the fit of the huge, throbbing erection pointing right up at me, before Aidan gripped my hips, his fingers bruising. He drew my gaze back to his as he tilted my hips upward. Face fierce with need, he guided his dick between my legs and slammed inside me so deep, it was painful. I whimpered, clinging onto him as my inner muscles pulsed around him, trying to get used to the overwhelming hot fullness of him inside me.

His hold on me tightened, his movements rough, hard, and frenetic, but I didn't care. I wanted him to stay so deep inside of me, no one would be able to pull us apart. Already the tension had started to coil within me, and my sputtered breaths and cries for more mingled with his animalistic growls and grunts.

My skin was on fire, my thigh muscles burning, but every thrust of his dick brought less pain and more and more pleasure until my own fingernails were digging into his lower back and my hips undulated against his drives, reaching for more.

I wanted to rip off my clothes so my skin was against his, finally, both of us bared to one another, but that would mean stopping, breaking apart, and I couldn't. I couldn't stop. I wanted more. I wanted it forever. "Aidan," I begged.

One hand left my hip to grasp the back of my head and he crushed his mouth over mine in answer, a panting, gasping, slide of lips and tongue, no finesse ... just a wild need to mimic with our mouths what his dick was doing to my insides. He tilted my hips up further, dislodging my mouth from his as I held on. His green eyes were like a dark forest of possessiveness as he pounded into me.

Each thrust was like a hit to my internal thermostat, each slide into me stoking my flames, until I wasn't sure I could come without taking the whole building out in a fiery explosion.

The orgasm hit in wave after wave, and I yelled out his name, the sound garbled in pleasured shock when he came with a "Fuck!" and I felt the delicious sensation of my inner muscles contracting around his pulsing cock. His hips jerked against mine and my hold on him slipped, my muscles liquefied. Aidan collapsed against me, his hands caressing my thighs as if to soothe them from his harsh grip. I felt his breath as he panted against my neck, and his chest heaved inches from my face.

It felt longer. The entire explosive encounter. But when I looked back, I realized it had all lasted minutes.

However, he didn't even stay inside me a minute and as he pulled out, I froze with the cold, hard reality of the fact that we'd had sex without protection. I was on the pill, thankfully, and had been since Jim, and saw no point in coming off it because it regulated my period.

But if Aidan was out there screwing a ton of women, I was stupid for letting him inside me without a condom.

I was the stupidest woman on the planet.

Completely controlled by my freaking hormones.

Aidan cursed and grabbed tissues out of a box on the dresser beside us. He turned from me and presumably cleaned up before zipping his jeans up. Feeling more vulnerable than ever, I used the moment while his back was turned to slip off the counter, clean myself with the tissues, and pull my underwear back up and my dress down.

When I looked up again, Aidan was glaring at me like he *loathed* me.

I withered under that expression, fighting the need to burst into tears. Instead I tipped my chin up haughtily, like him hating me didn't matter.

"Are you on the pill?"

I nodded. "Are you clean?"

He nodded.

I scoffed. "And I'm to trust you?"

Aidan sneered. "Out of the two of us, I'm not the one who can't be trusted." He shook his head, dragging his eyes up and down my body like I was a slug he'd found in his salad. "I can't believe I used to care about you. What the fuck did I see?"

I'd never been shot or stabbed, but I had to wonder if anything in this life could've hurt as much as Aidan Lennox saying those words to me after we'd had sex.

After I'd had the roughest, most pleasurable sexual experience of my life.

After I'd had sex for the first time since my husband died.

I turned away so he couldn't see my tears and pretended to put my school papers away.

Tell him!

But I couldn't. I was bleeding internally from his words, and that was all the evidence I needed to know this had to end. Aidan Lennox had the power to hurt me more than anything else in this world and

I was done with that shit. Why I reached for him, I didn't know. But it was time to try harder to get over my confusion when it came to him. His words helped.

They helped a whole lot.

"Nora—"

"I got what I wanted, Aidan." I grabbed my bag. Without looking at him, I marched by him and said the words I knew would end this for good, "I scratched a two-year-old itch. Let's leave it at that."

chapter 27

To my utter relief, Aidan didn't hang around for rehearsal. It was bad enough I needed to shower him off me, I didn't need him watching me in revulsion while I was on stage. But I couldn't get through the night with his smell on me, with the feel of him between my legs.

So I faked sickness and I must've been pretty convincing because Quentin told me to get out of his rehearsal in case it was something the rest of his actors could catch.

Without looking at anyone, I left, so desperate to get home and shower that I grabbed a cab rather than take the bus.

I was shaking.

Trembling to my core.

Deep down I was filled with dread, that awful feeling you get in the pit of your stomach when you know something is gone or lost or over for good.

I refused to allow the feeling to float up to the surface, however, creating a metaphorical hard layer of concrete in my mind that bricked over those emotions so I could function.

Once in my flat, I hauled my dress up over my neck and threw it and my underwear in the wash. Then I got straight into the shower and I scrubbed. I scrubbed my body hard in hopes of cleaning away not just the smell of him but the feel of him. I didn't want to remember his hands on my body or how he felt inside me. Who wanted to remember something like that when they were never going to have it again?

It was emotional torture.

I was proud of myself I didn't cry. Finally, I had a lock on my emotions.

Afterward, I pulled on a robe, wrapped my wet hair in the towel, and I'd walked into the kitchen to make myself tea when there was a knock at my door.

Aidan? I instantly thought, feeling rapid flutters in my throat.

"Nora, are you home?"

It was Seonaid.

I snorted at my ridiculousness and wandered over to open the door. "Hey."

Her eyes narrowed on my dishabille as she pushed past. "I thought you would have just gotten home from rehearsals by now."

"I left early. You want tea?" I gave her my back as I moved into the kitchen.

"Aye, sure. Why did you leave early?"

Why lie?

"I was there early, first there, in fact. Then Aidan appeared. He's friends with the director and has been at a few rehearsals lately. He's angry at me because he thinks I left him after Sylvie was taken from him. So he called me some nasty shit. I kissed him to shut him up and we ended up fucking." I called it that because there was no other word for it. "Afterward, he told me he didn't know what he'd ever seen in me and I told him I was just scratching a two-year itch."

At first, she gave me nothing.

Then suddenly, her hand was on me, forcing me to turn to her. Her concerned eyes searched my face and whatever she saw there made her jaw muscles lock with tension. Confusing, because I was doing a wonderful impression of a blank piece of paper.

"You sound like you're reciting something that happened to someone else."

"It might as well have for all that it affected me."

"You're lying."

"I'm not."

"Nora, he's the first man you've had sex with since Jim and it sounds like ugly hate sex. How is that okay?"

"It's fine."

"Stop saying that," she huffed. "Stop acting like this."

"How would you have me act?" I said calmly, crossing my arms over my chest. "Wailing and crying and acting like a weak fool? I'm not *her* anymore, Seonaid. I'm in charge of my life."

Her face crumpled. "At least that Nora felt something. This Nora is scaring me."

"I'm fine."

"What happened between you? I've been thinking over it since you told me last Sunday that he never left for California. Did his friend lie? Why did she lie? Does he know she lied to you?"

"Yes, she lied. I don't know why but I think she was jealous. And no, he doesn't know."

"So you let him treat you like that when you could have told him that this was all a big misunderstanding? Why?"

"Because my life is calmer without him in it," I explained patiently. "Life has been good for me lately, Seonaid. I don't need the complication."

Anger clouded her expression. "And I would totally bloody agree if you weren't looking at me with dead eyes right now."

I looked away because I didn't know what else I could say to convince her I was okay.

With a noise of exasperation, my friend turned and marched toward the door.

"What about your tea?" I asked.

"Drink it yourself. Maybe it'll heat the bloody chill out of your heart." The door slammed shut behind her.

"Shit," I muttered, collapsing against my kitchen counter. I was pushing everyone away. "Nice job."

———

APRIL IN EDINBURGH, I'D COME TO FIND OVER THE YEARS, WAS WET. Very, very wet. I finally understood the term "April showers." It was only the first week in April, but already it had rained every day. It wasn't constant, which made it worse—I'd go outside wearing stupid little ballet flats because the weather was dry and then ten minutes later, I'd get stuck in a deluge. The downpour usually only lasted thirty minutes but by that point, I was soaked to my skin.

I didn't mind it too much. If the days had been filled with the delights of spring sunshine, I wouldn't have been able to enjoy it anyway. I was pretending I was numb, after all.

Pretending and actually being that way were, of course, two different things. As I made my way to rehearsals on Wednesday, I was filled with trepidation, wondering if Aidan would be there. I hoped, after our encounter on Monday, he'd see sense and stay away. We were terrible for one another.

Turning up for rehearsal later than usual, I discovered Jack outside the building talking on his cell. He glanced up from the side-walk, saw me, and said into the phone, "Hang on a sec, babe," he pulled the phone from his ear and warned me, "the arsehole is here."

"Aidan?" My belly flipped with nerves.

"Aye."

"Thanks for the warning," I murmured, wanting to turn around and go home. But I didn't. I threw back my shoulders and forced myself to enter the building.

Feeling anxious, I took a deep breath and pushed open the double doors to the auditorium. Chatter from the stage end reached my ears as I took in the sight of our cast hanging around on seats and talking. Quentin stood by the stage with Aidan at his side. They'd been speaking about something but both looked up at my entrance.

They both stared.

My pulse fluttered.

As I approached, my gaze unwillingly drew toward Aidan and my breath stuttered at the anguish in his eyes. Not loathing. Not hate.

Pain.

And if I wasn't mistaken: guilt.

What the hell?

"There you are. I thought for a second you weren't going to make it," Quentin said to me, yanking my eyes to him. "You're better, yes?"

"Excuse me?"

"You left rehearsal early on Monday because you were ill," he reminded me.

Discombobulated by Aidan's expression, I could only nod, not quite sure what I was nodding for.

"Fine, let's start. Where is our Orsino?" Quentin looked beyond my shoulder. "No doubt conversing on that dratted phone to an unsuspecting soon-to-be-infected-with-an-STD female."

We eventually made it on stage but I could feel Aidan's eyes on me the whole time. My lines eluded me, and I felt uncomfortable in my own skin, like I might burst out of it at any second. I couldn't have been further from Illyria if I'd tried. Selfishly, I was glad when it seemed some of the other cast members, including Jack, were equally distracted.

Quentin called time on rehearsals early, yelling, "And when you return next week, I expect to be greeted not by this talentless, tatterdemalion cast! Understood?"

"If I bloody well knew what tatterdemalion meant, then aye," Jack muttered as we walked offstage.

I gave him a weary smile of agreement and wished him goodnight. He left while I found my way over to the seat I'd been using and started to put my schoolwork back in my bag.

"Nora."

My breath caught at the sound of Aidan's voice at my back. Slowly, I turned, lifting my bag onto my shoulder and reluctantly looked up at him. Was it just me or did he look nervous?

What the hell was going on?

"Can we talk?" Aidan asked.

Suddenly, I was seeing him glaring down at me with fierce need as he pounded into me, feeling him stroke in deep, rough thrusts.

I flushed, breaking eye contact.

Nope. I should not be allowed to be alone with this man. We were magnets, he and I, and I couldn't deny that. Staying away from him was my only course of action. "I have to go," I said, turning to leave.

But he followed. "We need to talk."

"There's nothing left to say."

"Apparently, there is a fuckload to say."

What the hell did that mean?

I didn't ask, even though my curiosity was tickling my tongue. "Aidan, I don't know what you're after now, but I want to be left alone."

Marching out into the damp, dank, spring evening, I hurried along the road onto one of the main streets in Tollcross, Leven Street, and as soon as I spotted a cab, I lifted my arm in the air. The driver saw me and began pulling toward me.

"Nora, I'm not going anywhere."

I sucked in a breath at finding Aidan right beside me.

Everything around me was dulled with the rain. The buildings, the road, and the people hurrying along in their dark-colored raincoats and umbrellas. The only startle of color was in the brightly painted doors of the shops and flats here, and in the banner across the entrance of the King's Theatre opposite us, advertising a musical.

And Aidan.

To me he was a bright, vivid beacon in the dreary world around me, and I knew that more than anything, I needed to shut whatever this was down.

Glowering up at him, I said, "Well, I am. I'm going home. You should go home too." The cab came to a stop and I reached for the door only for Aidan to beat me to it. I found myself ushered into the car. And then he got in beside me!

"Fountainbridge Square," he told the driver.

"What are you doing?" I looked at the driver frowning at us in his rearview mirror. "Not Fountainbridge Square, it's—"

"Fountainbridge Square," Aidan insisted.

"Are you kidding, mate?" the driver gaped. "That's just around the bloody corner."

"*I'm* going to Sighthill."

Aidan scowled down at me. "I know everything, Nora. Seonaid tracked me down at the music studio yesterday."

I had no words.

Inside my head, I was screaming at my best friend, but for Aidan, I had no words.

He looked at the driver. "Fountainbridge Square and then possibly Sighthill." He stared at me with a mixture of remorse and frustration. "Why the fuck did you not tell me?"

"Tell you what?" I murmured, feeling all the emotions I'd kept under that concrete layer starting to poke through little cracks.

"Tell me what?" he asked in disbelief. "That Laine lied to you."

"I wasn't sure she had," I lied.

Aidan's expression darkened. "She and I had words last night. She fucking lied, Nora."

"You texted," I said, dazed, stupidly trying to hold onto the misunderstanding. "You told me you were leaving. That it was over."

That made the muscle in his jaw pop as he grit his teeth together. His hands curled into fists and then flexed as he exhaled, like he was trying to control his temper. "I lost my phone the day after I last saw you. When you left, I let fucking Laine talk me into getting a new number so you couldn't contact me. I was so angry at you for leaving that I thought it was a good idea. I didn't realize she was trying to make sure I never saw the last text sent from it to you."

God, she was despicable. Truly despicable.

"Oh, it gets worse. Cal made it clear he wanted space for him and Sylvie to bond so even if I'd decided to leave, I couldn't go to California. And I certainly wouldn't have gone without you." His expression turned so pained I glanced down, unable to bear seeing him look at me that way again. Like he cared.

Like he *more* than cared.

Oh God, Seonaid, why did you do this?

"When you weren't answering your phone and there was no answer when I came to your flat, I remembered the salon Seonaid worked at. I found her and asked her where you were. She told me you'd left. That you'd gone home to the States.

"No word of warning, no goodbye, just gone. During the worst time imaginable, I thought you'd left me."

"I know," I whispered, and then cleared my throat of emotion. "I didn't. I went to see you the morning after Cal took Sylvie. Laine let me up. All of your instruments were gone and she told me so were you. That you had packed up and gotten a job in California to be close to Sylvie but the job meant leaving right away. I didn't want to believe it, but all your stuff was gone … and then when I tried calling you, I got no answer. I texted you and you confirmed what Laine told me. I couldn't … I … I needed to leave, get away, so I did."

His warm, large hand with its calloused fingers slid over mine and I wanted to pull away from his touch but at the same time, I wanted to hold on tight. Tears burned my eyes as I let him hold my hand.

"I was at Cal's, seeing Sylvie. I know a woman who runs a home removals company and I called her and paid her an obscene amount of money to get out there with a team and pack up Sylvie's stuff. I was drunk. Miserable. And I didn't want to have to deal with it. So they took it all to Cal's that night, and I moved all my instruments into Sylvie's old room. The next morning, I felt like shit. I didn't want Sylvie to think I was throwing her away, so I went there. It was just Cal, no Sally, and he felt bad for doing what he'd done, so he let Sylvie and me have the day together. I was out all day and I didn't have my phone on me because I'd left in such a rush that morning."

"Oh my God." I felt sick that someone could lie like that. "Laine should've been an actress."

"She admitted to deliberately misleading you." His grip on my hand tightened. "She stole my phone. She was the one who texted you."

"She's not well, Aidan," I stated the obvious.

"She has feelings for me that I don't return. I knew that. I thought we'd gotten through it over the years. Obviously, I was a fool. She decided you were too young for me, too immature to handle every-thing I was going through. I told her—" His voice began to rise in anger and he stopped himself. "I told her she was vindictive and jealous and she tried to ruin the best thing that had ever happened to me."

I gaped at him in disbelief, his words so beautiful but so painful. "She succeeded, Aidan."

His eyes darkened at my comment. "My relationship with Laine might be well and truly fucked. But *our* relationship needn't be destroyed, Pixie."

My eyes closed against the nickname. I couldn't see him stare at me with affection and hear his name for me at the same time. It was too much. Way too much!

Like he sensed my thoughts, he slid his hand around the nape of my neck, gently forcing me to look at him. His smell, his warmth surrounded me, and I found my eyes dropping to his lips, longing for them even though part of me wanted to jump out of the moving vehicle.

Voice hoarse, he told me, "I have missed you so damn much, Pixie."

"We're a mess," I whispered, thinking of the last few weeks.

"I'm sorry I treated you so badly. I was a bitter arsehole. But you have haunted me for eighteen months, and I resented the hell out of you for it. I thought you'd betrayed me, Nora, at a moment I needed you the most. That's my only, and terrible, excuse for what I've done the last few weeks."

"Did you know I was a member of Quentin's cast?"

"Aye," he admitted. "He asked me to help him out and I saw your name on the list of players. I had to see if it was you."

"So you could torture me." I pulled away from him, remembering his callous treatment and my equally horrible treatment of him after we'd had sex.

"I wanted closure. I couldn't find it." Aidan brushed my hair off my face, refusing to let me create a physical distance between us. "I still wanted you, even when I'd thought you betrayed me."

"Yeah, I got that."

He was silent and then he leaned in and I felt his warm breath on my ear as he whispered, "If coming inside you is the last thing I ever do, I'll die a happy man, Pixie."

Tingles fizzed to life between my legs and despite my fight against him, my whole body swelled toward in him in arousal. "Aidan," I breathed.

His lips whispered across my jaw and I felt his fingers press gently to my chin, forcing me to look at him again. He spoke his next words against my mouth. "Let's start over."

Images of us together, laughing, making love, talking, and being at peace with each other flitted through my head. However, those images were quickly crushed by the agony I had experienced when I'd lost him once before. The pain was too fresh, too sharp to have forgotten what it felt like to lose Aidan Lennox. More than that, however, I was afraid of losing myself. It had been a messy, twisted, unpleasant road to liking myself, forgiving myself. I feared that somehow being around Aidan would take me back to the person with insecurities and little self-worth.

I shook my head, dislodging his hold. "I can't."

Disbelief quickly turned to frustration. "If it's because of how I treated you, or about Nicolette, I promise you she and I aren't together. And I won't see her again. As for how I treated you, it fucking guts me to remember. I promise that will never happen again. Never. Please say you understand."

"I do understand. It's not about that or Nicolette." I brushed my fingers along his cheek, feeling the familiar bristle. "This isn't punishment, Aidan. I would never want to punish you. I just can't be with you. I'm not her anymore. I'm not the girl you cared about. I have a good life now and things are the way they're supposed to be."

Before Aidan could speak, the driver announced impatiently, "Look, I can't sit here all bloody night."

It was then I realized we were at Fountainbridge and probably had been a while.

Aidan shot him a glower and then turned it on me. "You need time to think."

"No, I don't."

"Then I need you to take time to think."

"I don't need time," I insisted and said to the driver, "Sighthill."

The driver nodded and looked at Aidan expectantly.

My disgruntled Scot whipped out his wallet and handed the driver enough money to cover the entire car journey. "Aidan—"

"This isn't over, Pixie," he said, exasperated, as he threw open the cab door and got out.

I tried and failed not to look back at him as the taxi pulled away into traffic. My whole body hummed with nervous energy and I knew I wouldn't sleep tonight.

Because Aidan Lennox had said those words to me before and the determined, beautiful man meant them *then*—and I knew he meant them *now*.

chapter 28

"WELL, I'M NO' SURE I SHOULD LET YE IN WI' A FACE LIKE THUNDER." Roddy braced his arm across the doorway of Seonaid's flat.

"A face like thunder?" I pointed to my face. "This is not thunder. This is … irritated confusion."

"Either way, yer claws are oot and I like ma woman's face the way it is, thank ye very much."

"Roddy, get out of my way."

"Who is it?" Seonaid's voice sounded distant, suggesting she was in the sitting room.

Roddy frowned at me. "Whit has she done now?"

"Meddled."

Sighing heavily, he stood aside and rolled his eyes to the ceiling. "I couldnae settle doon wi' a quiet wee lass wi' nae pals."

Ignoring his teasing, I brushed past him and wandered down the hallway to the sitting room. I found Seonaid sitting at the dining table using her laptop. She twisted in her seat and smiled at my appearance. "Hey, babe, this is a nice surprise."

Ugh, she made it so hard to be pissed at her.

I dumped my bag on the floor and flopped down in an armchair. "You meddled."

Her eyes grew round. "Did he come see you?"

"Did who come see whit?" Roddy asked, coming into the room.

Seonaid waved her hand dismissively. "Too long to explain. Why don't you make us all a cuppa?"

"I'm watching the fitbaw." He pointed to the TV where he had a soccer game on pause.

"It'll be here when you're done."

He looked between us and rather than leaving, he sat down on the couch and waited expectantly for me to speak.

Seonaid, uncaring that Roddy was being nosy, hurried over to me, settling down on the couch at the end nearest to me. "Well?"

I raised an eyebrow. "You don't think I should be a little angry that you went behind my back and told Aidan the truth?"

My friend shook her head. "Absolutely not. You no longer have dead eyes so I'm going to be able to live with my decision."

"Meddler."

"Well?"

"Well what? Thanks to you, I've got a sexy-ass Scotsman determined to pick things up where we left them."

"Yay!" She clapped her hands in delight, and then sobered so quickly it was comical. "He was pretty shell-shocked after I told him and he didn't want to believe it. But I guess he confronted that bampot and she fessed up?"

"Laine fessed up. And like I said, now he's all about 'starting over.' Thanks, Seonaid. This is just what I need."

"This *is* just what you need," she argued. "I got to spend half an hour with that man and bloody hell, Nora he's lethal! Why would you want to resist that?"

I glared at her. "I told you why!"

"You're happy with your life the way it is and blah, blah, blah."

"Nice."

"Look, your life is good. I couldn't be happier that you finally got over yourself and started giving yourself the life you deserve."

"Again ... nice."

She rolled her eyes. "Anyway, in my eyes, deliberately not making an attempt to start over with Mr. I'm So Fucking Hot Eyes

Burn Just Looking at Me is doing the opposite of giving yourself the life you deserve."

"It's not. I'm protecting the life I've built. Aidan makes me messy and confused and emotional and wrecked. Absolutely wrecked. I'm not going back there."

"So you told him no and he's gone?"

I thought of the determined expression on his face before he got out of the taxi. "No. He said, 'This isn't over.'"

A huge smile spread across her pretty face but I glared at it sullenly. She didn't get it.

"Mr. I'm So Fucking Hot Eyes Burn Just Looking at Me?" Roddy queried.

His girlfriend took in his look of disgruntlement. "Oh, don't worry, gorgeous, he's her man."

"He's not my man. He's not my anything."

"Totally her bloke."

"Seonaid—"

"But ye found him hot?" Roddy persisted.

"I have eyes."

Used to them winding each other up but too tired to play referee, I stood and grabbed my bag. "Okay, I'm out. Bye, guys."

Roddy gave me a chin nod, but Seonaid followed me into the hall. She pulled the front door open and stopped me. "You're not really mad at me, are you?"

"You make it really hard to be mad at you."

She hugged me tight. "I want you to have everything good in the world."

"Which is why I'm not mad at you."

When she finally let me go, she said, "I still think letting Aidan back into your life isn't going to be the catastrophe to your well-being that you think. Things are different now."

"I hear you and so noted. But I've made my decision and I really need you to support me."

"I'll always support you. Only… don't be a daft bampot, Nora. When that man found out it was all a misunderstanding, that you were an injured party in all of this too, I saw the pain it caused him. Whatever you do … try not to cause him anymore pain."

———

"RIGHT, PEOPLE, FROM THE TOP!" QUENTIN CALLED.

I sat in the audience, no schoolwork with me, and watched as Jack and Terence took to the stage to rehearse act one, scene one.

"'If music be the food of love, play on,'" Aidan's scrumptious, deep voice rumbled in my ear, making me jolt. I shivered at his hot breath on my skin as he continued, "Is it, Pixie?"

"Is it what?" I whispered.

He leaned further forward in the seat behind me and I felt his fingers in my hair. "Is music the food of love?"

"No," I decided.

"Damn. That would've made things easier for me."

I turned to look at him and whispered, "I thought you were leaving me alone?"

For the past week, it had certainly seemed that way. After he'd gotten out of the cab, I hadn't heard a word from him. Seonaid tentatively asked about him when we were out at lunch, but I honestly had nothing to report. It was a relief to not have to deal with him, to not have to explain to a man I cared about that I was planning on being selfish; that when I said I didn't want to start anything new with him, it was because I was protecting my future happiness.

Still, the fact that he had retreated altogether and had done nothing to pursue me was a little irritating. It had only emphasized to me that I was doing the right thing by keeping this man at bay.

"I said I was giving you time," he whispered back. "I've done that."

"Less than a week?"

"We both know I'm not a patient man when I want something, Pixie."

"Don't call me that."

"Your face gets soft every time I say it." He reached out to run the back of his finger along my cheek. I jerked away from his touch. "Pixie …" He sounded sad.

My chest ached with guilt. "Aidan, please, don't."

"Not until you tell me you don't love me."

Suddenly, it wasn't so easy to breathe. We had never used the L Word before. "What?"

"I said, not until you tell me—"

"Jesus Christ, Aidan, why are you disrupting my rehearsals now?" Quentin called over to us.

The entire theater went quiet and I glanced sheepishly at Quentin and then up on stage where Jack and Terence looked put out. No wonder. It was intolerably rude of us to whisper during their performance.

I opened my mouth to apologize but Aidan beat me to it.

"Apologies, Quentin, but Miss O'Brien and I have some unfinished business."

"Like what?" My director crossed his arms over his chest and waited expectantly.

"Aidan—"

"Nothing I'd like to share with the room," Aidan cut off my protest.

"Well, if that's so, then perhaps you would be so kind as to shut the fuck up?"

I heard Aidan's quiet chuckle. "Of course."

He did shut up but I could feel him at my back, his eyes boring into me, and I was never so relieved as to get on that stage and away from him. My whole body thrummed with awareness of him, and I had excited, wild butterflies in my belly that I wished I could say were due to my upcoming performance. But they weren't.

Those butterflies didn't belong to the theater.

They all belonged to Aidan.

I forced him out and let Viola/Cesario in.

"'How does he love me?'" Jane asked, playful, suspicious as Olivia.

"'With adoration, fertile tears, with groans that thunder love, with sighs of fire,'" I replied.

"That was perfect, Pixie," Aidan called from offstage.

"Pixie?" Quentin huffed. "Who the hell is Pixie?"

I glowered at Aidan. "I am. And that's enough chatter from the peanut gallery."

He laughed. "Merely giving you a compliment. You know how I love to give you compliments."

"Oh, really? Flattery? Because lately there have only been insults."

"You know why, Pixie. I've apologized. And it's not flattery. It's compliments. There's a difference."

I tried not to smile at his charm. "Well, I'm still stinging from the insults."

"I can kiss those away." He grinned unrepentantly up at me.

My lips twitched but I refused to give in. "Your lips are no good here."

"Oh, Pixie ..." His smile turned wicked. "We both know that's a lie."

Heat licked through me and my breath stuttered. "Asshole."

Looking much too happy and smug for someone who had just been called an asshole, he replied, "Angel."

"Prick."

"Gorgeous."

"Demented."

"Addictive."

"Aidan," I snapped.

"Well, as entertaining as this is, I'm also completely flummoxed," Quentin said. "Anyone else?"

There were murmurs around the room and I flushed, realizing I'd been carrying on a private encounter in front of absolutely everyone. Damn it! How did he make me forget myself?

"You know this is important to me. Stop interrupting."

He studied me thoughtfully. "If I leave, Pixie, it's not for good. You'll see me again."

"Make sure to bring your boom box blaring out Police's 'Every Breath You Take' and I'll know you're coming."

Aidan laughed. "Fuck, I've missed you."

My insides got all squishy but I refused to let him see those feelings on my face.

He nodded. "I'll go. But I'll see you soon."

I watched him stride down the aisle and out of the auditorium doors, and I hated how I wanted to jump off the stage and run after him.

Once I'd dragged my gaze from the doors, I faced the curious and very confused stares of my fellow company members. Then they volleyed their questions. How did Aidan and I go from him insulting and critiquing me constantly to us acting like we were flirty friends who knew each other?

I shrugged. "We're old friends, okay?"

"Old friends?" Quentin asked.

"Yeah."

"And why didn't you say something before?"

"Because we were mad at each other about something and I didn't want it to affect the play, but now we're not mad. Well, not in the angry sense. I think *he* might be a little crazy."

"Crazy in love with you," Jane said quietly at my side.

I looked at her startled. "What?"

"Nora—" She laughed, looking at me incredulous, like she thought I might be a little insane myself. "I have never seen a man look at a woman the way he was looking at you. Now all that fiery anger with you before makes sense. Only love can make someone act that way. Trust me, I know. One minute, my wife adores me and the next, she wants to kill me while still wanting to make love to me."

My heart raced. "Aidan doesn't love me," I denied.

"If that's true, he's certainly good at acting like a lovelorn idiot."

———

I LOOKED AT HIM ACROSS THE BAR. "WHAT ARE YOU DOING HERE?"

He leaned across it, seemingly to hear me over the noise of the pub.

Not even twenty-four hours later and here he was, back again. To torment me. His look said it all.

"Aidan, this is my job." I gestured around the pub. "I'm busy."

"Then serve me." He gave me a boyish, mischievous smile that melted my insides.

"Aidan—"

"I'm with some friends." He glanced over at a table near one of the stained-glass windows. Three guys were sitting at the table, grinning at me. It was strange but in all the time I'd known Aidan, I'd never met any of his friends—except Laine.

We really had existed in a little bubble together.

I was more curious about his friends than I cared to admit. "What are you guys drinking?"

He ordered four pints of Guinness and I felt his eyes on me the entire time I pulled them. "Do you like it here?" he asked as he handed over money for the drinks.

"Yeah. Why?"

Aidan's countenance grew so serious that I saw behind the cocky smiles and teasing to a sadness I detested seeing in him. "I want to make sure you're happy."

My hand closed around the twenty note he'd given me, clasping his fingers. "Are you happy, Aidan?"

"Do you still care, Pixie?"

"I want you to be happy," I evaded.

"Oi, what's the hold-up?" One of the guys from Aidan's table appeared, clapping Aidan on the shoulder. I let go of Aidan's hand and turned to the till to finish the sale.

"Nora, this is Colin. We're old pals from school. Colin, this is Nora."

After I handed Aidan his change (which he immediately put in the tip jar), I smiled politely at Colin. "Nice to meet you."

"We're *all* old school pals of Aidan." Colin gestured behind him at the table. He was almost as tall as Aidan with broad shoulders and massive arms. He had a bit of a gut but there was no mistaking this guy was strong. I looked past him at the others and noted they were all pretty big.

"Huh. You weren't on a rugby team together, were you?"

"Under 19s," Colin said, grinning through his scraggly beard. He was dark like Aidan and he had flecks of gray in his hair. "How did you guess?"

I smirked at Aidan who was looking back at me, his feelings shining out of his eyes. I lost my smile as Jane's words from yesterday came back to haunt me. Was Aidan in love with me?

He was looking at me like he was in love with me.

To my annoyance, I found myself getting turned on at the thought, tingles prickling in places they weren't invited, while my bra began to feel too tight.

I turned to Colin to break the intense eye contact. "You're all pretty big guys."

"Do you like rugby?"

"Honestly, I can take it or leave it."

Colin smiled. "We can work with that. I'm telling you, darlin', by the time we're through with you, you'll be a rugby fan."

"By the time you're through with me?"

"Well, once Aidan's convinced you to forgive him for being a pure bastard, we expect to see you around more." He clapped Aidan supportively on the shoulders, deftly handled three of the pints, and walked them over to their friends.

I glowered at Aidan. "You told them?"

"They wanted to know why my friendship with Laine is over."

Understanding that her betrayal was so much harder for him than it ever could be for me, I offered, "I'm sorry, Aidan. I know you were friends a long time."

"Aye, well, no one can believe it." He shook his head. "I don't want to dwell on it. I want to move on."

"So do I."

"Nora!"

I squeezed my eyes closed for a moment and turned in the direction of the yell. Kieran glared at me from the other end of the bar.

"Want to stop flirting and help us out?"

Flushing, I pushed away from the counter. "Duty calls."

"I'll be over there." Aidan grabbed his pint and pointed to the table.

Knowing there was little I could say to make him change his mind, I nodded and moved to serve a customer.

For the rest of the night, however, I felt him, even when he was engaged with his friends and not even looking over. I felt him. And I couldn't get the look of sadness in his eyes out of my head.

Aidan had lost so much in such a short time, and back then we'd connected because I understood that like no one else had.

I was afraid of losing who I'd become—someone I liked, someone I respected—if I started a relationship with a man who had, unwittingly, made me question my self-worth with regard to his affection. But I was also afraid for Aidan. And I wondered if he needed someone to talk to.

I still cared too much.

chapter 29

FORGETTING IT WAS APRIL, I MADE THE STUPID DECISION TO TRUST THAT the sun was out and it was an unseasonably warm spring evening. Having stayed at the university library to work, I made my way to the theater the following week dressed only in ballet flats, a summer dress, and a cardigan. As I left the library and walked onto The Meadows, I saw the dark clouds roll overhead in warning.

"Please don't rain," I murmured under my breath.

But my pleading fell on deaf ears.

The rain lashed down in diagonal sheets that battered and plastered my hair and clothes to my skin. Shrieks erupted as park-goers got caught in the downpour, and I lifted my bag to cover my head and started to run toward Gilmore Place.

My shoes slipped on the slick sidewalk, and I cursed as I narrowly avoided face-planting in the middle of the road. Stalled by traffic lights on the corner of Leven and Home Street, I ignored the sympathetic smile of a driver as she passed and catcalls of the guys in the car behind her as they drove by.

I glanced down at myself, flushing at the way my clothes molded to my body.

Brilliant.

There was no use hoping that Aidan wouldn't be at rehearsal to see me like this. Although he hadn't turned up at the pub on my next shift, he had promised to see me at rehearsal, and on Monday, he was there. To flirt with me. Charm me. And generally piss off Quentin and Amanda (who was not too thrilled about Aidan's focused attention). Though it was annoying, the other half of me, as we all knew, was a weakling who loved his attention.

I eventually got across the street and ran down Gilmore, splashing dirty puddle water up my bare legs.

I pushed at the doors to the building, expecting them to swing open, and grunted when they resisted. Grabbing the oversized door-knobs, I shoved again.

Nothing.

I rattled them.

Nothing.

What the ever loving ...

Shivering, I ducked under the tiny overhang of the building and looked up and down the street for signs of my fellow company members.

No one.

Sighing in exasperation, I rummaged through my bag, digging past papers and books, to find my phone. I flicked through my messages for any explanation of why the theater doors were locked when it was time to start the damn rehearsals. Nothing.

Cursing, I hit call on Quentin's name.

"What?" he answered on the third ring.

"Where is everyone?" I said without preamble. "The doors to the building are locked."

"You're at rehearsals?" he asked, sounding as irritated as I felt. "Terence, you were supposed to text everyone!"

"I did text everyone!" I heard Terence's distant yell.

"Well, you didn't text Nora, you wretch!"

"I did text Nora!"

"He didn't text me." My teeth started to chatter. "What's going on?"

"I broke my bloody foot last night."

Concern distracted me from the cold. "How?"

"Terence left a shoe on the stairs. Suffice it to say he's now my personal go-fetch boy. Anyway, I'm in a little of bit of pain, so I moved rehearsals to Saturday midday, much to everyone's disgruntlement. Very kind. Our cast and crew, I mean. Very concerned. That was sarcasm. They were mewling villains, the whole lot of them."

"I hope you're okay."

"Of course, you do, Nora, you're a sweetheart. Sorry, Terence is such a complete and utter wanker sometimes. I hope you didn't get caught in the downpour."

"No, I'm fine," I lied. "Feel better. See you Saturday."

We hung up, and I wrapped my arms around myself, praying a taxi would appear so I wouldn't have to run out into the deluge again. I shivered and shook like a wet dog, feeling miserable and sorry for myself, when a dark green Range Rover turned down the street and stopped outside the building.

The window rolled down on the passenger side and Aidan's face appeared. "Get in!" he yelled through the rain.

My heart pounded so hard in my chest, I couldn't move much less react to his sudden appearance.

"Nora, get in!" This time he sounded annoyed and it broke me out of my stupor. Whether I'd decided I'd rather be in his company than catch the flu, or if it was merely an excuse to be near him without feeling like I was betraying myself, I didn't know.

I gripped my bag and flew down the steps toward his SUV.

Warmth suffused me as I bundled into the passenger seat and closed the door. He had the heating turned all the way up.

"Your seats," I said, avoiding looking him in the eye.

"Like I give a fuck about my seats right now. You're soaked."

"Just a little." My teeth chattered. "Or a lot."

Cursing under his breath, he took off back into traffic. "You didn't get the text that rehearsal was moved?"

"Apparently, I was the only one."

"Well, thank God I was on my way home from the studio and decided to swing by in case someone didn't get the memo."

"Yeah, good thinking." I still couldn't look at him. "New car?"

"Aye."

I sat quietly, shivering, as he drove to Fountainbridge. "I don't suppose you could drop me off at my place?"

"By the time we get there, you could fall ill," he said impatiently.

Worry gnawed at me as he parked in the garage beneath his building and hopped out of the car to come around to my side. "Aidan, I'm fine," I said as he opened the door and held his hand out to me.

When he refused to move out of the way, I had no choice but to take his hand.

The sound of him drawing in a sharp breath brought my head up.

And his eyes were on my body and the way the dress stuck to me, leaving little to the imagination.

I flushed and tried to draw my cardigan closed.

Aidan grabbed my hand and looked away, but I saw the flush of red high on his cheeks.

My nipples were already hard from the cold and the wet, and now my breasts felt swollen, high, and tight.

Run, Nora, run!

I didn't run. I let Aidan lead me silently into the elevator. Once inside I let go of his hand as gently as possible, not wanting to hurt his feelings.

"You can take a hot shower while I find some dry clothes of mine that'll do while I put your dress in the dryer." He stared stonily ahead.

"That's kind of you," I said.

We sounded like strangers.

But the electricity between us in that elevator crackled and sparked so much, I was shocked my hair didn't frizz.

When the elevator door opened, we both moved to leave first, and I ended up walking into his side, my breasts pressed up against him. Aidan winced as if in pain and gripped my biceps a little too tightly as he removed me from his person before I could remove myself.

"I was going to open the door," he explained.

For a moment, I looked up at him, the blood rushing so hot inside of me, I could feel my rationale and common sense flying out the window. Whatever he saw in my expression opened the lock he'd had on his desire, and it blazed at me from his eyes.

"Door," I whispered, reminding him.

He nodded, his features strained with tension, as he marched out of the elevator and across the hall.

As soon as I walked into his apartment I felt winded, like someone had kicked me in the gut. It was almost as if by crossing the threshold, I'd been hurtled back in time eighteen months ago. A dining table and chairs were now set up where the small music studio had been, but otherwise, it was the same.

My eyes flew to Aidan who had stopped and turned when I'd halted to take in the space. His longing matched my own when our gazes connected. He was remembering too.

I remembered how much I loved him.

Needed him.

Wanted to crawl so deep inside him, we wouldn't be able to tell each other apart.

And right then, with lust pumping through my veins and tears of the past in my eyes, those feelings weren't ducking for cover.

They were consuming.

Aidan cleared his throat. "The shower in the master suite is more powerful. You can use that. There are clean towels in there. Leave your …" he looked away, "clothes outside the bathroom door and I'll stick them in the dryer while you shower. I'll put a dry T-shirt or something outside for you."

Somehow, I nodded. Somehow, I slipped off my ballet flats so as not to traipse my muddy footprints across his floors. Somehow, I walked past him and down the hall. But the farther my cold, bare feet took me, the more wrong it felt to be parted from him.

My body felt tight, wanton, and dissatisfied with the distance.

More than dissatisfied.

Uncooperative with the distance.

Looking back on it, I don't know what came over me.

I think I was exhausted with fighting something that I longed for.

Entering his bedroom, that tight, coiling sensation of need in the pit of my stomach worsened. The room smelled of him, and he hadn't made his bed that morning. The vision of him sprawled there, naked, caused a flip low and hungry in my belly.

I walked over to the bathroom and pushed open the door. The shower cubicle was much bigger than the one in the family bathroom out in the hall, and I shivered, looking forward to feeling the hot water sluice over me. But I wanted more than that. I didn't have the words or the power to use the words, still afraid of saying them out loud.

I stripped out of my clothes in the threshold of the bathroom and left them on the floor.

I kept the door open.

Wide open.

I reached into the shower and switched it on, waited for the hot water to come on, and stepped inside, closing the glass cubicle door behind me. When I turned around, I could see right out into the bedroom.

My heart pounded. Thud. Thud. Thud. Thud Thud. Thud Thud Thud. Thud Thud Thud Thud Thud. Faster and harder.

Then my breath caught as Aidan came into my line of sight. He gave me his profile at first, and I could see the little frown between his brows. Then he tensed, and I knew he'd caught sight of me in his peripheral. When he turned, first his eyes went to my pile of clothing on the floor and then slowly, they rose. They dragged up my body.

I washed my breasts and shivered as Aidan watched me.

Finally, our eyes met.

His so fierce with need, I felt my legs wobble.

Still, I continued, using his shampoo and conditioner to wash my hair, and I luxuriated in the way he was hypnotized by my breasts as they bounced with the movement.

His erection pushed against the zipper on his jeans and I grew slick between my legs.

Once I was clean, my skin hot from the water and arousal, I turned off the shower, squeezed the water out of my hair, and stepped out. The cold air prickled over my skin, making me shiver, making my nipples bead into tight buds.

And Aidan drank in every inch of me.

Goosebumps broke out all over my skin at his perusal.

I didn't feel insecure or too young anymore.

I felt bold and needy and desired.

"Aidan," I whispered.

Everything he wanted to hear was in that one word, and suddenly, he was unbuttoning his shirt. Relief moved through me. I wouldn't be forced to say the words I couldn't, but I was going to get what I wanted anyway.

I watched as he undressed, his eyes never leaving me, and a little whimper escaped me when his hard cock was revealed, straining toward his belly, hot, throbbing, and desperate for me.

I did that.

Me.

"Get on the bed, Pixie. And spread your legs."

His hoarse demand might as well have been his tongue on my clit for the way my body responded. Limbs shaking with desire, I walked by him, torturously close, and climbed onto his bed, giving him an eyeful of my ass before I turned around and lay on my back.

A spike of vulnerability, of nerves, halted me from opening my legs.

"Legs. Now."

I bit my lips on a smile. "No please?"

"I'm grappling to take this slow, Pixie," he admitted.

I opened my legs.

He appeared, approaching the bed, and I felt a rush of wet as he looked at me there, hunger on his face. Unexpectedly, he didn't take what I was offering. He crawled over my body and hands braced on the mattress on either side of my head, he looked down at me.

"Aidan?"

"Are you really here, Pixie?"

Not sure if that question was loaded with more than those simple words, I reached up to cup his cheek in my hand, rubbing my thumb over the bristle there like I used to. "Let's forget everything else and just have this. I feel like I might shake apart if you don't come inside me."

"Fuck," he groaned and bent his head to take my mouth. The kiss was impatiently hard. I moved my lips beneath his, our tongues stroking one another in deep tangles that mimicked what our bodies wanted to do. My hips tilted toward his in want.

I gripped Aidan's waist as the kiss grew rough and breathless; I whimpered again as his hips moved against mine and his erection skated, teased across my belly. He released my mouth only for his lips to whisper across my chin, down my jaw, like he couldn't rest easy until they had touched everywhere. He kissed his way down my body, his mouth hot, hungry, and I held on, caressing his muscled back, sliding my hands up toward his shoulder blades and into his hair as he moved downward.

When the Saharan heat of his mouth closed around my right nipple, my hips slammed against his in reaction. My thighs gripped him as I urged him closer, my back arching for more as he first licked me and then sucked hard, all the while pinching my other nipple between his forefinger and thumb.

I felt a wet rush between my legs.

He lifted his head, his eyes forest green as he undulated against me, his cock between my legs now, kissing my throbbing heat. "More, wee Pixie, or straight to the finale?"

As much as I longed for it, I wanted him to have what he wanted. "You know you want to torture me, you bastard," I groaned, needy. "So why ask?"

His laughter rumbled against me, and I squeezed my eyes closed because the sound elicited so much more than sexual desire.

"Open your eyes."

I did.

Satisfied, he dipped his head again, licking, teasing, and torturing my other nipple now. I felt the coil of tension tighten in my lower belly.

"Aidan," I panted hard, clutching his head in my hands as he circled his tongue around my areola. "I need you."

He moved, sliding down my body, his lips trailing open-mouthed kisses down my stomach as his hands cupped and shaped my breasts on his descent. I shivered at the touch of his tongue across my navel and sighed happily as he pressed my thighs open.

Aidan settled between my legs, and his calloused, beautiful hand glided along the inside of my thigh until I felt his fingers slide inside me.

"Oh God ..." I threw my head back at the sensation, never having reacted to this act quite so explosively before. It felt like I was already seconds from coming.

How could that be?

My reaction brought Aidan's eyes up to my face. They were intense, the mischief gone and replaced by ferocious sexual intent. His fingers slipped out of me and then back in. My hips pushed against them, trying to catch rhythm.

"You're soaked, Pixie," he said, his voice thick, guttural. "Drenched. Are you always like this? Or is this just for me?"

"Just for you," I bit out, truthfully. "Only you do this to me."

He bared his teeth, satisfaction slicing harshly across his face, and I swear the potent masculinity of him made my belly squeeze deep and low, giving him more of my wet.

Aidan dipped his head again. His fingers slipped out of me but before I could bemoan the loss, he parted my labia and my hips nearly came off the bed at the feel of his tongue on me.

Finally.

He circled my clit, teasing it, pressing it ... and then he sucked it.

I cried out, unable to control how loud my response was, reeling as my orgasm started building in me. My thighs automatically closed on him, wanting to draw his mouth deeper into me, and at the scratch of his stubble against my skin, lust took over entirely. My hips surged against him, trying to ride his mouth as he thrust his tongue into my channel before licking it back up to my clit. Then he sucked.

The tension inside of me burst apart so hard, my head slammed back on the mattress and my eyes rolled. I also screamed.

I'd never screamed during climax.

But there was no holding it back as my inner muscles pulsed in hard wave after hard wave. And still he continued to lick me through it until I was writhing against his mouth, my fingers curled into the bedding beneath me.

It faded into aftershocks and my limbs grew so heavy, my legs collapsed against his side as he drew himself up to stare down at me.

I didn't know why he was looking at me in wonder.

I was the one in awe.

When he pulled back and got off the bed, I whined—actually whined!—"Where are you going?"

Aidan didn't say anything. I heard some rustling, and then he was back, crawling

up my body. He straddled me, his impressive erection standing to attention, and he watched me watch him as he ripped the condom wrapper with his teeth and rolled it onto his dick.

His big hand coasted up my torso and despite the fact that I'd been drained of energy seconds ago, I arched my back into his touch. Heat shot through me from the inside out as he squeezed my right breast with one hand while his other hand slid between my legs. I jolted, my clit overly sensitive.

Aidan groaned. "I need you."

"Then take me."

Features strained with the barely there hold he had on his control, he nudged my legs apart further and braced himself over me. And then he pushed inside of me. His eyes closed as if he was in pain as he pressed through the tight resistance of my body, my muscles squeezing around him. I stifled a whimper. It burned. A pleasure pain like last time. He was so goddamn big and I was so goddamn tiny. Aidan panted, and his arms shook a little.

"Aidan?" I lifted my hips, trying to get him to sink in deeper.

"You're tight and swollen." His eyes flew open, and the fire in them made my inner muscles squeeze around his dick. "Ah, fuck," he breathed in reaction.

I caressed his back, pressing my nails so they scratched lightly over his skin. "Stop being gentle," I taunted.

He glared at me. "I wasn't gentle last time."

"And it was wonderful." My hips lifted, asking him to thrust and Aidan practically snarled, pulling back out of me. And then he drove back in. My head flew back and I grinned.

"Animal," he teased, grunting out a laugh.

"Look who's talking."

He smirked at me, his eyes drifting down over my face, my lips, down my breasts, and then to where he was inside me. He began to move. Aidan watched himself sliding back and forth out of me, and his chest moved up and down in shallow breaths as his excitement increased.

His gaze flew to mine and I nodded at the silent question in his eyes.

And just like that, Aidan began to power in and out of me with hard, deep thrusts that dragged across my clit and stirred me again.

"Come all over me, Pixie," he demanded, fucking me harder, his teeth gritted together as he held off his orgasm. "Let me feel it around my cock this time." His words triggered his climax and seeing him fall apart for me was the last thrust against the growing tension inside of me.

I blew apart, gripping him in voluptuous tugs that made Aidan's eyes widen ever so slightly. "Fuck," he bit out and then grew still for a second before his hips shuddered against me. His cock pulsed and throbbed inside me as he came gratifyingly long and hard.

Collapsing in an astounded grunt, Aidan crushed me into the mattress with his weight, his lips pressed against my neck.

I laughed breathlessly and nudged him. He rolled off me, muttering a drowsy apology. Grinning at the absolute slack, relaxed expression on his face as he lay on his back, his leg still tangled with mine, I couldn't remember the last time I'd felt like this.

So happy, I could float up off the bed and dance across the ceiling.

Then Aidan opened those beautiful eyes and said, "I'm not letting you go now, Pixie."

And I came crashing back down to the bed with a bump called reality.

chapter 30

<small>I HAD TO UNDERSTAND WHY AIDAN WAS SO DETERMINED TO HAVE ME.</small>

I considered it, listing the reasons in my head as we stood in his apartment staring at one another. After his declaration, I'd shot out of his bed, grabbing the shirt he'd been wearing, throwing it on, and hauling ass into the front of the apartment, hoping I'd be safer from my lust there.

Aidan, of course, followed.

Annoyed.

And now here I was. Thinking of the reasons he wanted me to be with him. The relationship we'd shared during our time with Sylvie was molded by circumstance. We were brought together by a shared feeling of being haunted by the ghosts of our pasts. We *got* each other. We made each other feel less alone. And the three of us were like a little family unit for a while. That created a feeling of extreme closeness between Aidan and me.

Then there was the fact that we'd never had much of a physical relationship during that time. Lots of heat and sexual chemistry—a ton of pent-up sexual frustration—so that tension had kept us drawn together like the proverbial moth to a flame.

Which led me to the sex in the dressing room at the theater, and then the sex we'd just had.

The sex in the dressing room ... I felt hot all over thinking about it again. That was a sexual fantasy come to life. It was passionate and rough and epic. All that anger and bitterness and desire collided in an orgasmic explosion that I was never going to forget.

And the sex just now had been born of that same frustration and longing.

However, that did not mean that sex would be like that between us all the time! Those moments were a huge, almost two-year build-up. Of course sex was going to be off the charts AMAZING between us at first.

Which meant it was part of a fantasy.

It wasn't real.

Just like who we were back then with Sylvie was no longer real. Those people were gone. I knew I'd changed.

Yet these were all the reasons Aidan wanted us to try again. He was clinging to something that no longer existed.

Then show him. Show him what it would really be like.

I scoffed at the thought.

That was my desire talking. I wasn't going to continue this with Aidan so I could have sex with him and prove to us both that it was all going to be average in the end.

No. But we could have sex. Friends with benefits. Until he grows bored and realizes we are not meant to be.

That was the most fucked-up thing I'd ever thought.

My eyes locked with his as he waited for me to answer his question when he chased after me. "What is going on in your head?"

Maybe there was something in the whole friends-with-benefits option.

Maybe we would tire of each other.

"I can't be in a relationship with you, Aidan. But if you want, we could have this," I gestured between us, "for however long we both want it. But only sex."

Funny, but I didn't know what I was more scared of, that he'd agree or disagree.

He glared at me incredulously. "Are you suggesting I be your fuck buddy?"

I flushed. "Well, I wouldn't put it so bluntly, but yes."

"Are you insane?"

"There's nothing insane about it. It's my offer. Take it or leave it. But it is all I'm willing to give you."

"Sex?" He crossed his arms over his chest. "Just sex."

"I thought that would be easy for you considering you have a Nicolette on every continent."

His eyes flashed with smugness. "Jealous? Because last I checked, jealousy usually means you care for more than just sex."

"Don't taunt me."

"Aye, I had Nicolette and a few others that meant nothing to me. I can't take that back. But I can say I used to hope to hear from nearly every woman I've ever been with that all they wanted was just sex. But it was always me saying those words and them agreeing, hoping somehow, I'd change my mind and give them more. How ironic that the first woman to propose it to me is the only woman I've ever wanted to try permanency with."

Feeling guilty, I couldn't hold his gaze. "I don't know what to say," I whispered.

"Aye, I can see you don't." The bitterness in his words hurt my chest. Aidan sighed. Heavily. "Fine. If it's the only way I can have you, then I agree. I don't understand it. But I agree."

I looked him in the eye now, hope blooming. "Really?"

He nodded.

And I allowed myself to smile. "This is a better idea than what you had in mind."

Aidan didn't respond. Instead, he marched across the room and bent, lifting me up onto his shoulder, causing the breath to escape my body. "Aidan!" I wheezed, in shock as I found myself being carried to the back of the apartment.

"If this is all I get, then hear this," he said, dumping me on the bed and pulling me toward him by my ankles. His green eyes gleamed with intent. "Tonight, you're mine and I intend to make the most of it."

———

"You're a total and utter bastard," I muttered, swatting at the air above me as he pressed a kiss to my bare shoulder.

The sun streamed in through the blinds on his bedroom window, a natural alarm clock that raised the lazy curtains on my eyes.

I felt him shake with laughter against me, heard the delicious rumble in my ear. "You say such sweet things to me."

I smiled sleepily, my vision adjusting from blur to focus, and took in the clock on Aidan's bedside table. Ten thirty blinked up at me. Ten thirty. Ten thirty! I shot up straight, hearing him make a disgruntled sound at my back. "Is that the right time?"

"Aye, what of it?"

I whipped around to glare at him, wishing I could shield my eyes against the gorgeous sight of him sprawled on the bed, one arm above his head on the pillow, the other on his stomach. The bed sheets stopped below his navel, and I could see the man was already half ready to go another round. As earth-shattering as last night had been, I was afraid I wouldn't be able to walk if he touched me again. Plus, I was late.

"I have classes. You know, commitments. Don't you? Have commitments, I mean?"

"I can work later."

"I can't do my classes later."

Aidan sat up, sliding an arm around my waist and pulling me against him, bare skin against bare skin. His eyes moved over my face with such intensity, I wanted to dive back under the sheets. "Surely, you can miss a class or two."

I could miss a class or two without the world coming to an end, but that wasn't the point. "I don't like to."

"So, what you're telling me is that you would rather have gotten up early for class today than have the multiple orgasms you had last night?"

I huffed. "No."

His hand delved beneath the sheets.

"Uh-uh." I reached for it, dragging it back into the light. At his raised eyebrow, I flushed a little. "I'm sore."

The boyish grin that spread across his face was almost irresistible. "Cocky bastard."

"That's the second time you've called me a bastard." He tickled my ribs, and I squealed, trying to get away. He was persistent, though. Giggling and begging for release, I found myself flat on my back on the bed with a brawny, amused Scotsman braced over me.

Not exactly a bad way to greet a new day.

"Okay, okay!" I laughed. "I'm sorry! Stop!"

His tickling ceased. His kissing commenced. I wasn't surprised when my skin grew hot, and my thighs automatically gripped his hips. Despite my complaints of feeling tender, I was lost to the addiction of his touch. Last night we'd kissed and touched each other everywhere, passionate sex mixed with tender lovemaking. Afterward, I'd drifted to sleep only to be awoken sometime later by Aidan's searching mouth and hands on my body. To my complete befuddlement, rather than growing tired of one another as I'd hoped, each touch increased our addiction.

And I couldn't stop myself from tasting him again.

Aidan paused briefly to put on a condom and the whole time I lay there panting for him, not even thinking about putting a halt to it. Then he was inside me, and I was sore and tender, crying out in discomfort.

"Pixie," he murmured, kissing me to soothe me, as he stilled to allow me to adjust to him again. "I can stop."

"Don't," I whispered.

So he didn't. He moved and I clutched his sexy, sculpted ass in my hands as he glided in and out of me.

"Aidan!"

At first I thought maybe I'd called out his name.

But then …

"Aidan!"

He stopped moving, looking down at me, puzzled. "Was that—"

"Aidan, are you home?" The voice was closer now, heading toward us.

Aidan pulled out of me, yanking the bed sheets to cover us both as the door burst open.

To my complete horror and confusion, Laine stood in the threshold.

"Oh my God," she said, looking more horrified than I felt. "Oh my God."

"Laine, get the fuck out!" Aidan snapped, trying to shield as much of me as possible.

"Oh my God." She spun around, almost walking into the door before she hurried out of sight.

We waited a moment.

But the sound of the apartment door opening and shutting didn't come.

I immediately glared up at Aidan. "She's still comfortable enough to walk into your bedroom. That really must've been some falling out between you two."

He glowered back at me. "I haven't spoken to her since."

"Well, I guess you better get out there, then." My tone was ugly. I knew it. However, the cold, hard bite of jealousy had returned as if the last almost twenty months had never happened.

"I will. And you're coming with me." He got off the bed, striding across the room in his glorious nakedness to the adjoining dressing room. When he returned, he was wearing sweat pants.

I sat up. "Uh ... where's your T-shirt?"

"Really?"

"Yeah. Really."

He grinned at me. "Feeling possessive again there, Pixie."

I jutted my chin in the air. "It would be inappropriate, that's all."

"Aye, sure." He disappeared back into the dressing room and returned wearing a T-shirt, holding another in his hand. He tossed it to me. "Put that on."

"You don't seriously want me to go out there with you?"

"I seriously do. Now."

"Why?"

"Because I have to go out there and make perfectly clear what I already thought I'd made perfectly clear, and that is that I don't forgive Laine for what she did. I don't want her in my life."

I studied him thoughtfully. I too would never forgive Laine. However, I also hadn't known Laine that long. She and Aidan had been friends since they were schoolchildren. My worry was that his decision to withhold forgiveness was based on what he thought I wanted.

"Don't throw her out of your life for me, Aidan. Especially when I can't offer anything ..." I said. He knew what I was trying to say.

Taking a step closer to me, I saw the slash of pain across his features and heard it in his words. "Laine took away the one thing holding my world together when Cal took Sylvie. She did it selfishly and without thought, excusing her actions under the guise of caring for me too much." He shook his head, and I saw the anger alongside the pain. "The only person Laine cared about in that moment of deception was herself. And now I finally have you, and I don't actually have you, do I, Nora? As far as you're concerned, you're already a ghost in my bed. I'm so fucked in the head over you, I'm willing to be haunted."

He gestured behind him to the door. "But I can't even be haunted in peace without her interrupting us. She has a fucking key to my apartment. I want it back."

"You need to change your locks." I winced as soon as I said it. Aidan bared his soul, and I couldn't even take the time to explain myself better to him?

His lips pinched together for a moment. "Are you coming out there with me or not?"

"Why do you really want me out there? To humiliate her? Because I think walking in on the man she loves having sex with another woman might have already done that."

Aidan appeared to process that and his face softened. "How many women in your position would give a damn? Fuck, you drive me crazy, and I don't understand you half the time, but I've never met anyone who cares like you care. Where did you come from, Pixie?"

"Up there. In the sky," I whispered sadly, pointing upward. "Second star to the right and straight on till morning."

Recognizing the quote, he braced a hand on the bed and reached out to cup my face. His thumb whispered over my lips. "You're still that lass who dressed up as a storybook character to make sick children's days brighter. Stronger, more together, but still her."

"No, I'm not." I was afraid of her.

"No one changes that much." He brushed a kiss across my lips. "And why would you want to? That woman was just as bloody magnificent as the woman you've become."

"Magnificent?" I gave him a teary-eyed smile, remembering.

He remembered too. "Magnificent."

But I *wasn't* her—I forced myself to remember that too. I jerked back from his touch and shook my head. "I'm not her, Aidan. You'll see that soon enough."

He blew out a breath of frustration but got up off the bed. "I'll speak to Laine. You can stay here if you want."

I did.

Kind of.

I got out of bed and put on Aidan's T-shirt and tried not to shiver at how good it felt to wear it, to feel like I really was *his* in it. Standing in the doorway of his bedroom, I eavesdropped.

Not cool.

I know that.

But I wanted to be able to go to Aidan if he needed me.

"I didn't mean to barge in like that," I heard Laine say. "I stopped by the studio and Guy told me you weren't coming in this morning so I thought I'd ..."

"Use a key you're not welcome to have anymore."

"Aidan, you won't return my calls. I had to see you."

"Which part of I don't want to see you don't you get?"

"But I need you to forgive me. For us to be friends again. Please, Aidan, I miss you."

He was silent a moment. And then he replied, his tone gentle but his words not so much, "All I heard in your words was 'me' and 'I,' just as that was all I heard in your explanation for lying to Nora and for letting me think she'd abandoned me. Doesn't it compute, Laine, that you chased off the person I needed the most after my niece was taken from me? Don't you understand how fucking awful and selfish you had to have been to have done that to me? And even now, all you care about is what *you* want and what *you* need. You don't care about me."

"I do, Aidan, I love you," she sobbed.

I closed my eyes, hearing so much pain in the confession. It wasn't easy to hear that kind of pain, no matter her misdeeds.

"Then you love selfishly."

She cried harder.

"Maybe over time, I'll learn to forgive you but I'll never forget. And I'll never trust you. But even if I could forgive you, that time is not now. *I* want you to leave. *I* need you to stay out of my life."

"Aidan—"

"And I'll be changing the locks to the flat *and* to the building."

Another sob. "Aidan, I'm so sorry."

"Aye, I know. I can see that. But I still believe you're only sorry you got caught. You're not sorry you did what you did, Laine, and until you are, our friendship ceases to exist."

There was silence, followed by the soft sounds of footsteps, then the door to the flat opened and closed.

Feeling sick for Aidan that he'd had to have such a confrontation, I hurried out to find him sitting on the couch, staring out the window. I took the couch opposite him. "Are you okay? Can I get you anything?"

He looked at me, his handsome face bathed in the glow of the morning sun, his green eyes so bright with the sunlight dancing in them. My breath caught. Not at how attracted to him I was because I knew I might never get used to that.

No, I gasped at his expression. It was open, bare, like he wore his soul upon his face for me to see. And all I saw was love and anguish.

"Tell me. Explain to me exactly why we can't have a proper relationship. Explain it again. Make me understand."

My chest felt heavy, like something was pressing down on it, and I could hear my shallow breaths. I knew that something was happening here. Something that was going to decide our fate together in that very moment. Moreover, after hearing Laine and Aidan's brief encounter, I knew this man was owed honesty.

"I don't know how to explain without seeming as selfish as Laine."

"I want the truth, no matter how it sounds."

"It's like I told you before. The truth is that I like my life now, Aidan. I'm in school, and I have the play, and it's everything I dreamed of having. You and I are messy and complicated, and we hurt. It's all too much with us, and I don't want to go back to the girl who was afraid of losing you. She wasn't strong. She was in pain. And that was mostly because I didn't like her very much. But I like myself now. I'm not the girl who used to think she wasn't good enough for you. I don't need you to bolster my self-esteem. I like myself," I repeated.

He frowned. "I'm glad, Pixie. I really am. But did you ever think that maybe I'm the one who doesn't like themselves very much?"

No. I hadn't. "Why wouldn't you like yourself?"

"Because I resented my sister for dying. And just when I thought maybe I wasn't such a bad guy, the kid I loved was ripped out of my arms and I couldn't do a fucking thing to stop it." His voice broke. "She doesn't look at me the same way, Pixie. Ever since … I'm not her hero anymore."

Tears filled my eyes, remembering the way Sylvie loved him. I hadn't asked him about her enough. I hadn't wanted to cause him pain, but maybe *he* needed to talk about it. "I don't believe that for a second."

He looked away, but not before I saw the wet in his eyes. "Aye, well, you weren't there to see Sylvie when she saw me for the first time after their move over there."

I knew if he felt that way that there wasn't anything I could say or do to make it better. Only time would handle those feelings. However, I needed him to understand something too. "Us being in a real relationship won't bring her back, if that's where this conversation is going."

He jerked like I'd hit him. "I don't fucking think that."

"Well, do you think being with me will miraculously make you like yourself better, because I can tell you from experience, Aidan, it won't. Only time can give you that."

"Aye, no doubt you're right," he said, eyes blazing. "But in the meantime, I don't want to lose the one thing in my life that makes every other thing in it worthwhile. You're everything to me, Nora. Every bloody thing. I never knew happiness like it until I met you. And maybe that scares the shit out of you, but news fucking flash: it scares the shit out of me too. I don't know if it's fear holding you back or if what you really need right now is to be alone. All I know is that I won't love you selfishly. I was going to keep you in this fucked-up arrangement you suggested, hoping that somehow loving you, even if only through sex, would bring you back to me."

He stood abruptly, looking down at me with that love and anguish that made me shiver in my seat. "But I can't do it, Nora. I can't take what you don't really want to give me. If you're to be mine, I need all of you to be mine, because all of me is yours."

Tears spilled down my cheeks, and I couldn't speak for the lump thick in my throat.

Crushing disappointment strained his expression and he looked at the floor. His voice was hard as he said, "I've been offered a job producing a studio album in New York. I'm going to take it. I'll most likely get a flight out on Monday. Concerning you and me? Once I'm gone, I'm gone for good. I won't stay on this roller coaster."

Leaving me?

Aidan gone?

I couldn't process that properly.

NO!

I'd already lost him and now I was going to lose him again.

This time … my fault.

"I'm going for a walk, and when I come back, I'm sure you'll be gone." He strode toward the door, bending down to put on shoes that didn't match his sweat pants. He didn't even seem to see them. As he stood, the scream inside of me threatened to burst out, and I felt the sound coming as he opened the door.

But before it could, before he left, he turned back to me. "If you figure out that everyone changes, bit by bit, day by day, Nora, while somehow staying the same, then come find me. If you figure out that we've got nothing to fear from the people we were yesterday, and that you certainly don't, that I know who you are and I love you, then come find me. Just because it takes more than falling in love to find yourself doesn't mean that losing yourself in another person can't be fucking beautiful. I promise you, Pixie, being lost in each other for the rest of our lives will be the best thing to have ever happened to either of us.

"And if you figure that out in time, come find me before I leave."

chapter 31

TO SAY I WAS LOST IN A FOG OF CONFUSION OVER THE NEXT FEW DAYS was an understatement. I felt an itch inside me, a constant reminder that Aidan was walking out of my life. It didn't seem real to me that Thursday morning in his apartment could be the last time I'd ever see him.

It didn't have to be.

Aidan loved me.

Loved me.

Loved *me*.

Just me. Not the ghosts between us or all those reasons we were drawn together in the first place.

Just me.

Like I loved him.

So why couldn't I shed my fear that by being with him, I'd become someone broken and lost?

"Because that's who you were when you first met him?" Seonaid said when I finally got up the courage to ask her.

It was Saturday night, I'd blown through a terrible rehearsal with the rest of my cast members, and Seonaid had come over after I'd called to explain the countdown to Monday.

She brought beer.

"Thanks."

"Well, you were. That's nothing to be ashamed of, Nora. You lost a lot as a child, and then you left your family to be with a man who didn't really get you, loved you, but by God, he didn't understand you, and," she sucked in a teary breath, "he died. Too much to lose and all it did was fill your head with guilt that didn't belong to you. You were broken and lost. Finding Aidan made you feel less alone when you needed it most. He mended you, babe, whether you want to admit it or not. Finding him gave you faith that this world is filled with good. And then you lost him. You thought he walked away. And it broke what was left of you.

"But this time, you knew you had to put yourself together. And you did. You became a survivor and a fighter, and you went after all the things you wanted in life. That's who you are now. So why on earth would you run from this thing you want in life? Because we both know you want Aidan Lennox more than you want anything. He's consumed you from the moment you met him."

That word, though: *consume*. That didn't sound very healthy. Not at all.

"Does Roddy consume you, Seonaid?"

She smiled, lowering her eyes to the glass of beer in her hand. "I know to everyone else it looks like the bugger bewitches and bothers and bewilders me. But when we're alone, he's someone else. He gives me a piece of him that belongs to only me. And aye, he consumes me with it." She looked at me. "If that's madness, Nora, then I gladly give myself over to it."

I envied her, her clarity of mind. "I don't know what to do."

"Talk to Jim," Seonaid said.

"What?"

"Visit Jim. I like to believe he's not really gone." Tears wet her eyes. "And I talk to him, liking the idea that he understands us all now better than he ever did when he was alive. So talk to him. Maybe everything that has happened will start to make sense, and all the pieces will make a path that'll lead you to the right decision."

I took a swallow of my beer to avoid bursting into tears. And when I thought I could speak without crying, I said, "You're the wisest, dearest friend I've ever known, Seonaid McAlister."

The pressure of her smile caused her tears to spill over.

———

Sun dapple from the leaves on the tree above Jim's grave caused patterns to dance across the dark gray of his headstone. I hadn't been to visit since before I left for Indiana, afraid of seeing it in the same way I was afraid of returning to Aidan.

"I'm sorry, Jim." I placed a hand on the top of the stone. "It's about time I stopped evading the things that scare me."

I studied the gold lettering on his stone.

> *James Stuart McAlister*
> *June 12, 1990 to July 15, 2014*
> *His life a beautiful memory, his absence a silent grief.*

I didn't remember discussing Jim's epitaph. I know Angie wouldn't have gone ahead with something without my approval, but for the life of me, I couldn't remember discussing it. She'd chosen beautifully.

I hadn't been in love with Jim.

But he'd been my closest friend for a number of years, and I loved and missed my friend.

The memories of our life together flooded me as if Jim were pumping them up into the hand I'd placed on his headstone. The nervous excitement of running away together, his patient gentleness the night we made love for the first time. How scared I'd been. How it took weeks for me to feel comfortable enough around him to start enjoying sex with him. How when we were together like that, I used to stare into his eyes, wishing that the connection I sought would somehow magically appear between us. I'd get lost in his lovemaking because Jim was good at it, and he was not a selfish lover, but afterward when we were finished, I'd feel more alone than ever.

As alone as I'd felt in that small, cramped room back in that unhappy house in Indiana.

Jim wasn't the reason I'd lost myself.

I lost myself the moment my dad stopped loving me and started hating the world. Or maybe that wasn't right, either. Maybe I was too young then to have even have found myself. Maybe Dad had thrown me off course. And Jim's waves had buffeted me to the wrong shore.

And losing Aidan had forced me to get up and keep moving until I found what I was looking for. I found me.

I knew I'd never have found myself with Jim by my side. That I would've walked away from him. Hadn't I already made up my mind to do so before he died? I could've done it too, because he never made me feel like Aidan does. I cared about Jim, but it wasn't unselfish affection. I would have hurt him to walk away. And the sad truth is that as badly as I'd have felt doing it, it wouldn't have broken me.

But walking away from Aidan, hurting Aidan, was going to break me.

There was no denying I was unequivocally in love with Aidan Lennox.

And by choosing my fears over him, I was loving him selfishly.

Wasn't it time to trust him? To believe him when he said that he would love me for who I was now?

"Thank you, Jim, for bringing me here," I bent down to whisper against the stone. "I did love you. In my own way."

I straightened and walked swiftly away, making a vow that I would visit Jim more often. It was unwise to sweep the pieces of my past behind me simply because some of those pieces were jagged and painful. Each was a piece of a jigsaw, and I was the puzzle. I wasn't complete without them. Jim deserved to be remembered, and I needed to embrace the memories of the old me too.

Because Aidan was right.

I was still that Nora. I was also eight-year-old Nora and twelve-year-old Nora, and I was Nora today. I couldn't be who I was now without them all.

And if I liked myself as much as I proclaimed to, then why was I desperate to forget them, as if ashamed they'd ever been me? There were going to be days, hopefully few and far between, when I didn't love myself very much for whatever reason, because I was human and no one liked themselves every day. Trying to protect myself from that was futile, and pushing away Aidan to protect myself from that was sightless and thoughtless. Totally unwise. That was a diplomatic way of saying I'd been a blind fool!

I sighed, feeling the pressure that had been on my chest since Thursday morning lift. I breathed deep but not easy. There was a man out there, after all, who I needed to convince to stay.

To forgive me.

To love me, even on the days I didn't love myself.

chapter 32

A NEIGHBOR WAS COMING OUT OF AIDAN'S BUILDING AS I APPROACHED, and I hurried toward him. "Hold the door."

The man, perhaps in his fifties, startled and stopped, the poodle on the lead in his hand tugging forward. The door started to shut, and I launched into it, accidentally knocking the man out of the way.

"I'm so sorry." I rushed past him.

"I hope you know someone—" His words were abruptly cut off by the building door slamming shut.

Palms slick, my underarms in much the same condition, I hit the elevator door button and bounced on my feet as it opened.

The ascent to Aidan's floor seemed to take five million times longer than usual. I blew out an agitated breath between my lips, praying he was home.

The elevator binged, and I swear my heart stopped as those doors rolled up. Aidan's door stood beyond, aloof and solid.

There was a giant possibility my future was on the other side.

"Don't be sick, Nora," I whispered to myself as I stepped off the elevator. "Not sexy."

It took me a moment, staring at the brass number on his door, to gather the courage to lift my arm. Another moment to curl my hand into a fist.

And a few after that to knock.

The quiet behind it only increased my pulse until there was so much blood rushing in my ears, I wondered if I was imagining the footsteps on the other side of the door.

Suddenly, I was flooded with light as the door opened.

Aidan looked down at me.

Waiting.

Expectant.

"I love you too," I said.

chapter 33

I GASPED FOR BREATH, FALLING BACK ON THE BED, NAKED AND COVERED in sweat.

Aidan collapsed next to me, his breathing also shallow as he tried to catch it.

"I take it that means I'm forgiven for being a drama queen and that you love me too?" I asked the ceiling.

The mattress shook beside me with his laughter. "I love you too, Pixie."

Joy suffused me, and I turned my head, my hair rustling on the pillow, to meet his gaze.

His reaction to my confession had been gratifyingly fast and demonstrative. One second I was on the other side of the door, and the next I was in his bed and we were tearing each other's clothes off.

I didn't see much as he dragged me like a caveman to his room, but what I did see was no evidence of his departure tomorrow for the States. "When is your flight supposed to leave?"

"What flight?" He frowned.

"Your flight. To New York."

"Ready to be shot of me already?"

I smacked him playfully. "Of course not."

"I didn't really take the job."

Confused, and feeling outrage building, I sat up. "What?"

He sat up too, his expression placating. "Look, I would lose my good name if I agreed to a job and then backed out at the last minute, which we both know I would've done when you came back to me. I was only going to accept the job if you didn't come to me."

Yes, definitely outraged. "So you lied to me? You manipulative ass!" I attempted to lunge off the bed but his strong arms wrapped around my waist, hauling me back down onto it. Then he pinned me to the mattress with his hands wrapped tight around my wrists.

"What? No. Off. Now, Aidan."

"I love it when you're bossy," he growled playfully against my lips.

"Aidan!"

He rolled his eyes and pulled back, but I could see that amusement still dancing in his eyes. "I told a wee white lie. A little story ... for my storyteller."

"Oh, don't get cute. You lied."

"I played with the truth a wee bit. But just a bit." Aidan let go of my arms, but he didn't get off me. His expression changed. "I didn't know what else to do. When you left the first time, you know it had a massive impact on me. I hoped that the idea of me leaving you would provide you with perspective—a real chance to work out whether you loved me without it dragging on for ages. You know I'm not a patient man, Nora."

"It wasn't about whether or not I loved you, Aidan. That was never in question. I've loved you since that day on Portobello Beach. I was afraid of myself and the past." I sat up, curling a hand around the nape of his neck and drawing him close to me. "But I love you more than anything else. I'm done *telling* everyone that I've moved on; now I'm actually going to *live* like I've moved on. With you by my side."

He closed his eyes and leaned his forehead against mine. "And I'll never leave your side, Pixie. I'm yours."

"And I'm yours."

He lifted his head but only to draw me tighter against his chest.

His hands caressed my naked back, his eyes filled with desire and tenderness.

I leaned in to brush my lips over his. "Love me in the knowledge that you're the only man I'll ever want like this." I kissed him with all the fierce love and need I had inside me. My tongue danced with his in a deep, drugging kiss as we crushed tight against each other.

Aidan broke the kiss to follow a path down my throat with his mouth. I gasped for breath, my hips surging against his erection as he kissed his way down to my breasts. When he wrapped his lips around my nipple, I lost all control.

I pushed up on my knees, wrapped my hand around him and guided him to my entrance. I lowered down, and we panted as he slid inside me. The thickness of him took my breath away for a moment, and we both held still as my body eased into accepting him.

I sighed when I moved up on him slightly and back down, shivers exploding down my spine.

Aidan pulled my mouth back to his, kissing me with a hunger that seeped into me—I couldn't get enough of him. I began to ride him. Slowly, savoring each deep tug of desire in the pit of my belly as I slid down on him and dragged up.

Our hot breaths mingled as sweat slickened our skin and our moans filled the bedroom. Our eyes locked on each other, never breaking the connection, as we undulated together, our movements growing steadily faster as we sought completion together.

What we both realized as our fingers bit into each other's skin was that we already had it.

A connection no one could break.

"I love you," I whimpered against his lips.

"I love you too."

His words were a trigger, and my shout of release was swallowed in his kiss, followed quickly by his groan reverberating in mine as the pulsing clench of my climax around his cock wrenched his orgasm from him.

I collapsed in his arms, my face buried against his neck, and I felt his soft lips kiss my shoulder. He gently threaded his fingers through my hair to clasp my nape and brought my head back. I looked into the face I loved more than any other and wondered when I'd stop kicking myself for prolonging this moment.

"I was too long without you," he said, sounding pained.

I brushed my fingers tenderly along his cheeks, still scratchy with bristle. "Never again," I promised. "I've never been this happy." It scared the hell out of me, but I wouldn't run from it.

And I knew he was thinking the same thing.

Aidan Lennox and I never seemed to make sense on paper. He was older, worldlier, and more experienced.

Good thing I finally found the sense to rip that paper into little pieces that I then set alight.

Until it was nothing but dust floating in the wind.

epilogue

BEING ONLY A CHILD THE LAST TIME I'D STOOD ON STAGE, I'D FORGOTTEN how difficult it was to see the faces in the dark audience through the blaze of stage lights. It was impossible on a stage like the one at the Tollcross Theatre, and the realization startled me a little when I first stepped out during dress rehearsal.

I was prepared for it on opening night.

However, I wasn't prepared for the colossal waves of nervousness in my gut or the way I'd needed Aidan more than I'd anticipated. Unfortunately, he was working on a studio album after he'd finalized the score for our show. We didn't have an orchestra, just a sound guy who cued the digital music on a computer and sound system.

Since there was a piece of his creativity in the show, and the fact that it was my first performance, Aidan had promised to be there, but he couldn't get away from the studio long enough to escort me to the play. He'd said he'd be in the audience.

I was disappointed but I understood. For the first few weeks of our reconciliation, he'd put so much of his work on hold to be with me. It wasn't fair to pout now that he was getting back to the work he loved.

In the end, I pulled it together and forced myself onto that stage, with Jack murmuring jokes in my ear to calm me.

Before I knew it, the play was almost over, our words having disappeared into the dark of the audience even though it had been two and a half hours including a ten-minute intermission. The layers of cotton and leather I wore, resembling a mash-up of *Mad Max* meets steampunk, meant I was sweating under the stage lights. And I longed for Aidan to be there after my first real performance. But all these thoughts were tucked in the recesses of my mind so that Viola's thoughts and feelings and actions could move me across the stage.

I was Viola kissing Duke Orsino, not Nora kissing Jack.

I was Viola taking Orsino's hand as he asked to see me in my own clothes and not Cesario's. I was Viola as I clung to his side and told him that my friend the Captain had my clothing but that he was in prison because of Malvolio.

And that was it.

That was my last line.

I almost couldn't believe it.

Still, I continued to act, reacting to the words of my fellow players until finally Orsino said his last line and we, except for Clown, left the stage. Clown's monologue drifted offstage as we quietly waited for him to bring the play to a close.

"'But that's all one, our play is done, and we'll strive to please you every day.'"

Silence.

Then the uproarious applause that brought a huge grin to my face. I turned to find Quentin standing with us now, grinning back at me. He looked to us all. "Bravo, my miscreants. Bravo."

I laughed, remembering the sound of the audience's laughter throughout the performance. Of the little noises of surprise they made, their claps and cheers as the comedy progressed.

They liked us.

Jack grabbed my hand and led me back on stage where the flood of applause hit me like a wave crashing over my head. I was stunned until Jack bowed, and still holding my hand took me with him.

We'd rehearsed this part too.

Jane and Hamish stepped forward and bowed.

Then Jack and I to a thunder of clapping.

And so on as the other actors took their applause.

Quentin's turn came. After he'd bowed, he stepped back, and we all bowed once more together as the curtain came down on us.

Excitement and chatter buzzed around me as my cast members congregated momentarily on stage. I wanted to cheer with them. I did.

However, more than anything, I wanted to celebrate this moment with my friends and family. Hugging my fellow players as briefly as possible, I managed to get off the stage without being rude and made my way to my dressing room where I'd told my loved ones to meet me afterward.

I was in the room but a moment, having wiped off as much stage makeup as possible much to the relief of my skin, when there was a knock. The door opened to reveal Seonaid's head. "Can we come in?"

"Of course!"

"Ahhh!" she screamed, barging in and throwing herself into my arms. She danced and jiggled me around, laughing. Then she shoved me away playfully. "You didn't tell me you were bloody awesome!"

I thought my face might break from grinning so hard. "Did you think so?" My eyes flew to Roddy and Angie ... and my mother.

"Mom," I whispered, tears in my eyes.

It still made me emotional that she flew all the way over to see me perform in an amateur production.

She strode forward and hugged me. "I'm so proud of you. You were amazing." She pulled back and cupped my face in her hands. Concern pinched her features. "How on earth did you handle all this with your school exams too?"

It was such a motherly thing to say, I wanted to burst into tears. Who was this woman? Seriously! I laughed, hugging her again. "I can handle it," I promised.

And I had.

It wasn't only Aidan who'd been busy lately, what with my first-year exams only a few weeks ago. It hadn't been easy to juggle studying, the play, and getting closer to the man I loved, but it all made me so endlessly happy …

Angie drew me into her arms as soon as my mom stepped back. "Ye were wonderful. I'm so proud of ye."

My arms tightened around her. "Thank you, Angie."

When she let me go, Roddy approached wearing that little smirk of his. "Aye, ye werenae bad."

"Werenae bad?" I raised an eyebrow. "Faint praise indeed."

"Well," he hooked an arm around my neck and drew me into him with a grin, "wouldnae want ye gettin' a big heid an flyin' off tae Hollywood, no' wid we?"

Giggling at his ridiculousness, I shook my head. "You thought I was good."

"You were brilliant." Seonaid shook her head in amazement, looking teary all of a sudden. "You really were."

Feeling overwhelmed and emotional, I waved her off. "Stop, or I'll cry."

She shared a laugh with Angie, while my mom smiled and Roddy rolled his eyes.

And I realized we were all alone. I stiffened, feeling disappointment grow in my belly. "Where's Aidan?"

A rap on the door sounded, and that horrible feeling fled as his head appeared around it. "He's here, Pixie." He smiled fondly, but he didn't come into the room. "But, eh …," his eyes flew to Seonaid, "would you mind giving us privacy?"

Something about the way he said it made Seonaid's eyes widen, like he'd communicated something silently to her. Bemused, I watched as Aidan ducked back into the hallway and Seonaid ushered my mother, her own, and her boyfriend out of the room.

As she was leaving, she threw me a mischievous grin I did not understand at all.

Then the door opened again, and Aidan appeared. "You were magnificent, Pixie," he said.

"You really think so?" I started walking toward him, needing to hold him.

But he stopped, and I realized he had something or someone tucked behind him. "And I'm not the only one who thought so."

The someone stepped out from behind Aidan, and I felt my breath fly away.

She looked at me with cautious, hopeful eyes, her light blond hair longer than it used to be, braided in a fishtail down her left shoulder.

"Sylvie?" I whispered, disbelieving she was here.

Four weeks into our new relationship, Aidan had asked me to sit in his weekly Skype call with Sylvie. It had been strange and awkward at first because of the time that had passed, but over the weeks it felt like all three of us had never left each other.

As far as I'd been made aware, however, she wouldn't be visiting Aidan until late June.

"I wanted to see you in the play," Sylvie said.

And then like she'd done so easily before, she rushed forward and threw her arms around me. I immediately wrapped my arms around her, feeling a piece of me that I'd been missing slot back into place. With tears of gratitude, I looked up at Aidan, and he took us in with such love in his expression, I thought I would burst.

Finally, with the realization that Sylvie's affection for me had never waned, I felt the last of the guilt I'd carried over the years of my young life detach from my soul and float far away. Without even meaning to, I'd blamed myself for not being able to stop Cal from taking her that day.

Now I knew better.

It was easy, when you loved people, to find ways to blame yourself when you couldn't protect them from the hurts of the world. That was an impossible task, and we only ended up hurting ourselves by believing that it wasn't.

The only thing that was in our power was to love through the hard times, to hold onto that love, and not allow blame and guilt to blister it.

I had all the love I needed in that theater building, and I swore to myself as Aidan approached us and wrapped his big arms around Sylvie and me that I would protect our love with my body and soul.

More importantly, I'd forgive myself on the days when the rain came out of nowhere and soaked us to our skin. We'd have those days.

Everyone had those days.

But with Aidan, I could find the laughter in those days, as well hidden as it may be, and I could strip off my dress and seduce the sadness out of him. Our passion wouldn't ever be a solution, but it would be a constant reminder that the hard days were worth getting through to keep safe what we shared.

It was a well-known fact that the Scottish used humor and light-ness to get through difficult times. To play on, to laugh on, and to dream on, even on the days they felt abandoned by hope. I under-stood that now. I got it. I respected it.

This place ... well, it fit me.

Indiana and my mother would always have a piece of me.

But this place ... these people ... this man ...

They fit beautifully.

acknowlegments

It has been a long, very busy year in writing for me, and I would not have had so much time in my writing cave if it wasn't for the support of the people around me. First I'd like to thank my parents for dogsitting on more than a few occasions so I could disappear fully into the writing cave to write Aidan and Nora's story. And a ginormous thank you to my dad for doing more than a few odd jobs around my house because I was too busy to. Everyone should have a dad like mine.

Moreover, I'd like to thank the rest of my friends and family for being so patient with my absence these last few months while I wrote and wrote... and wrote some more.

A massive thank you to my personal assistant Ashleen Walker for taking care of so many other things so I could concentrate on the writing part, and for organizing promos and tours and generally being a freaking rock star. I'm lucky to have my best friend work with me, and even luckier that you're so great at everything you put your mind to.

I must thank my incredibly smart and hilarious editor Jenn Young for editing PLAY ON on a tight schedule and for being so insightful, witty and encouraging. It can be a nerve-wracking business this writing malarkey and you helped soothe some of those nerves, my friend.

Also a thank you to Amy Donnelly at Alchemy and Words for jumping on board last minute to proofread and catch all the little things missed in the first few rounds of editing. I'm so grateful! Oh and any errors in the acknowledgments are entirely my fault.

And thank you to Jeff at Indie Formatting Services for always doing such a spectacular job making my books look stylish and professional in ebook and print.

The cover for PLAY ON was designed by the tremendously talented Hang Le. Hang, you blew me away with your cover concepts. This cover is stunning and more than I imagined it could be. Thank you, thank you, a million times thank you!

The cover, blurb and the story found their way into readers' hands with the help of fantastic book bloggers. I want to thank everyone who has supported the release of PLAY ON and given their time so generously to the book world. There aren't enough thank yous for what you do, but just know that I appreciate every single one of you.

These acknowledgments are never complete without thanking my agent extraordinaire Lauren Abramo. Thank you, Lauren, for working so passionately to make sure the stories I write get to travel the world. I have the best agent. EVER.

And finally the biggest thank you of all is to you: my reader.

Thank you forever and always for reading.

I hope you enjoyed Aidan and Nora's love story.

SAMANTHA
YOUNG

NEW YORK TIMES BESTSELLING AUTHOR OF
ON DUBLIN STREET

A Joss & Braden Novella
STARS OVER
CASTLE HILL

Joss and Braden Carmichael are blissfully married living in their townhouse on Dublin Street with their three beautiful children. It's a life Joss never expected to have, and one she's grateful for every day.

But... what if she never met Braden and Ellie Carmichael on that fateful day when she was only twenty-two years old?

When Joss is asked to write a story about how her life might have turned out if a pivotal moment in it never happened, she thinks of the day she met both Braden and Ellie Carmichael. If she had never met them where might she have ended up? Joss believes no matter where life may have taken her it would have inevitably led her to Braden. But what if she was thirty instead of twenty-two when they met? How would she have felt about risking her heart then?

And even if she was older and wiser and ready to fall madly in love, what if too much had happened to Braden to make him the man that would risk his heart to save hers?

Will time be their enemy... or is it possible that two souls are meant for one another in any reality?

Stars Over Castle Hill **is an alternative reality novella of the #1 international bestselling romance** *On Dublin Street,* **a story that captured the hearts of readers all over the world. Joss and Braden are back with a tale that is just as emotional, passionate and sexy as their first!**

Continue on to read the first two chapters…

THE WORLD WE MADE

Usually when I finished a book I felt a level of apprehension before sending it to my agent and editor. That was natural, I guessed. But as I watched my printer whipping out the novella I'd spent the last month writing, I had to admit that what I was feeling was a different kind of apprehension.

This was the first time I wanted Braden to read one of my stories before anyone else. Even before beta readers.

It was mostly due to the personal nature of the story.

"Mum!"

I squeezed my eyes shut, knowing my twelve-year-old daughter was about to bust into my office, even though my "Crabbit Writer at Work" sign was on the door. Everyone in our family knew I only put the sign up when I was in the zone and really didn't need interruptions creating havoc with the flow of words.

Braden bought me the sign. After eighteen years in Scotland, I knew that crabbit meant "grumpy as hell."

As much as I appreciated the sentiment, I argued that I was not grumpy.

I was temperamental. There was a difference.

Braden just laughed but I was being completely serious.

I told him that, too.

He laughed harder.

Impossible man.

"Mum!" Beth threw open my office door but I was braced for it. I was already facing the door, waiting to hear her latest catastrophe or thrilling story. Every day in a preteen's life was wonderful and horrifying and life or death.

At least in *my* preteen's life.

"Mum, we need to go shopping on Thursday night. Please! It's Cassie Hogan's birthday party and I can't go in a dress that everyone in my class has already seen."

"You own a thousand dresses."

Beth made a face. "Mum, let's not exaggerate."

"No, because we wouldn't want to do that."

She ignored my sarcasm, very much used to it and adept at it herself. "Please, Mum. Amanda and Sarah said they're getting new clothes for it."

"And if Amanda and Sarah ju—"

"Don't say 'jumped off a bridge.' Everyone says that. And you're a writer, Mum. Doesn't that mean you have to be original or something?"

I stared at her, trying very hard not to burst out laughing. It would only encourage her and the girl teased me enough. I didn't think a day had gone by when she didn't tease me about my accent. Living with Braden for so long, I'd picked up Scottish inflections in a way I hadn't when my mom was alive. Now I had this weird American-Scots accent that Beth loved mimicking. "I'm sorry, were you asking me for something?" I asked.

Beth smiled sweetly. "Please, Mum."

Shopping. Hmm. I knew only one way we'd get through it.

Ellie.

Ellie was much better at the shopping thing than I was. It was hilarious how my kid could be so much like me, and yet such a girly girl like her Aunt Ellie. Beth had more clothes and shoes and nail polish and pink and posters of an irritating, globally successful boy band on her bedroom walls than twenty preteen girls put together. "Fine. But we'll ask Aunt Ellie if she's free to come with us."

Beth patted my shoulder, giving me an unintentionally (or at least I hoped) patronizing smile of sympathy. "Already did. We both know you hate shopping. I only asked you to join us out of politeness."

"And I have the credit card to pay for the dress," I reminded her.

"That too!" Beth grinned cheekily and sauntered out of my office. "Mum's busy," I heard her say snottily.

"You went in!" my nine-year old son replied.

"I'm older."

"That's your answer for everything," Luke whined as he barged into the room. "Mum," he raced toward me with all the exuberance and energy of his age. Fuck, I envied him. "Where's my football socks?"

I brushed his dark blond hair off his face and he ducked to the side to avoid any more grooming. "Which ones?"

"My lucky ones," he said, like it was obvious. Only nine, and already giving me the "duh" voice. I wanted him to be four again and always running to his mommy for cuddles.

"Damn time and its envy," I muttered.

Luke made a face. "What?"

"Remember talking rule number two."

"Mum," he whined, lolling his head from side to side, "I'm too old for that."

"Rule number two," I insisted.

"It's not 'what,' it's 'pardon.'" He rolled his eyes.

Seriously. I was so sure the rolling eyes thing happened later with boys. Of course, Beth had been rolling her eyes at me since she was three.

"I haven't washed your lucky socks yet. You don't have a game until next Saturday."

"But I'm going to play Five-a-Side on The Green with Allan."

"And you need your lucky socks for that?"

"Yeah. I want to win."

"Baby, I'm guessing by how thin those lucky socks of yours are getting, they only have so many more games in them. Do you really want to waste their luck on a non-game game?"

As he opened his mouth to speak, I said, "And you're not playing Five-a-Side football that far away from the house."

I had to stop myself from smiling. When my son frowned, he *frowned*. Somehow he managed to put all of his face, not just his brows and eyes, into the expression. It was impressive. And adorable. Which I'm sure is not at all what he was going for. "It's only five minutes away."

"In a city, five minutes away is far enough for some miscreant to steal you from us."

"What's a miscreant?"

In answer, I handed him my dictionary. Accustomed to my method of teaching them to reach for knowledge themselves as much as possible, Luke flipped through it for the answer. "Did you ask your dad if you could go?" I said.

"Yes, but he said no." Braden strode into the room with our youngest, Ellie (so named after her aunt), in his arms. Ellie was eighteen months old and already a total daddy's girl. I couldn't blame her really.

Right now, however, Braden was scowling at Luke. "What have I said about going behind our backs to ask the other once one of us has said no? When one says no, the answer is no, Luke."

Luke scrunched up his face, and I could sense a tantrum on the horizon. "I'm bored!"

Yup.

"And I said that I'd come with you if you wanted to play football on The Green."

"No one else is bringing their dad! I'll look like a wee kid!"

"News flash," Braden leaned down, shifting Ellie in his arms, "you *are* a wee kid. And if you raise your voice at me again, I will ground you for a week."

"Ground me, then, because I cannae go out anyway!"

"It's can't," I threw in.

"Cannae, cannae, cannae!" he yelled, jumping up and down.

I winced. My kid was loud when he wanted to be. Too loud! "Ah, *can it*."

"Right, you're grounded," Braden declared.

"Oops!" Ellie cried out and then giggled.

Braden and I looked at each other and struggled not to laugh.

Luke was not in the mood for laughter. "Mum!" he hurried over to me, shifting from side to side like he needed to pee. "Tell him!"

"Kid, bring the noise level down. And you heard your dad. You're grounded. Believe me, it pains me more than you."

"Ha ha!" Beth shouted from outside the door.

"You'd better be laughing at your own brilliant thoughts, Beth Carmichael, and not at your brother's incarceration!" I called.

"Definitely the first one." She peeked her head around the door-jamb. "And not the funniness of Luke talking himself into a grounding."

"Shut up!" Luke lunged toward her and Braden caught him by the back of the shirt as Beth took off squealing.

"Oops!" Ellie cried again.

"We need to teach her a new word."

"I don't know," Braden said, letting go of Luke, "it does seem to fit the situation when she uses it."

"Oops!"

"Or not," I said.

He snorted as Ellie reached out her little arm toward Luke. "Uke! Uke! Want Uke!"

Luke obliged and held out his arms for her. Once she was settled in his strong little-boy arms, my chest filled with more emotion than I could cope with. "I wish Beth was like you, Ellie," he said.

Braden smirked. "Don't worry. One day she'll be old enough to be just as annoying. Enjoy this while you can."

Luke sighed, as if he had the weight of the world on his shoulders. "Fine. We'll watch cartoons. Since I'm grounded." He grumbled to his little sister all the way out the door.

And there was blissful quiet in my office.

Braden turned to stare at me.

I stared back.

And then I huffed, "You're the one that wanted kids."

"Yeah, well, I'm not the one who was so damn sexy I couldn't keep my hands off you or my powerful, baby-making semen out of you." He grinned.

I wrinkled my nose. "Charming."

"Always, babe."

"Okay, I thought you knew this already but clearly not, so heads-up: Semen? Not a sexy word."

He wandered over to me, sliding his hand around my waist to pull me into him. "Noted."

I melted into his strong heat, unable, even after all these years, to be in a room with my husband and not eventually end up attached to him in some way.

He kissed the side of my neck, and then my printed manuscript caught his eye. "What are you working on?"

"On that subject … my 'Crabbit Writer at Work' sign apparently no longer works."

"Do you want me to get something with a more aggressive tone?"

"Like, 'Fuck off'?"

"I think that might offend our kids."

"I don't think anything offends our kids. We grew those babies with abnormal amounts of emotional thick skin and way too much energy."

He laughed and reached for the paper. "Enough of the subject change. What is this?"

I turned to face him, absentmindedly tracing patterns on the fabric of his shirt at his chest. "Actually something I wanted you to read before I consider submitting it."

Curiosity flared in his pale blue eyes. "Oh?"

"I was approached by this author. She asked me if I'd like to participate in a digital anthology. We are to write a novella that's kind of personal but fictional."

"How so?"

"The concept is that I write a novella based on what might have happened to me if a pivotal moment in my life hadn't occurred."

He shifted, craning to get a look at the pages. "It sounds interesting."

"That's what I thought. So I wrote it. I chose to write an alternate reality based on what might have happened if I'd never answered Ellie's ad for a flatmate."

"And you want me to read it?"

I picked up the manuscript and held it out to him. "If you're not busy."

"Of course not." Braden accepted the papers. "I'll read it now."

That little flurry of apprehension sprung to life in my belly again. "You're sure?"

He gave me a quizzical look. "Is there anything in here you're worried about?"

"No. It's ... you might think it's cheesy."

He threw his head back in laughter and then laughed harder at my scowl. He kissed the pout off my lips. "You're Jocelyn Carmichael. You couldn't be cheesy if you tried."

I pushed him away playfully. "Once upon a time I would have agreed with you, but then you came along, made me all mushy, gave me three adorable kids who have completely messed up my hormones so I cry at yogurt commercials."

Chuckling, he settled into my chair and shooed me away. "Go play with the kids. Leave me to read in peace."

I huffed at the order but moved to exit the room.

At the door, I glanced back to watch as he settled in, kicking his long legs up onto my desk.

I imagined the first words he'd read and wondered what he'd think about where those words were about to take him ...

STARS OVER CASTLE HILL

By J. B. Carmichael

AUTHOR NOTE

WHAT IF, WHAT IF, WHAT IF? I'M SURE THAT'S A QUESTION WE ALL ASK ourselves at least once in our lives. For many of us, I'm guessing we ask ourselves it more than we'd like. Before the year I turned twenty-two, that question haunted me. So much so, I'd confused existing with actually living. But then I met a certain man and a certain young woman on the same day: a day that would change my life forever.

Since meeting them, I've asked myself that question a lot less. And in recent years, I haven't asked myself that question at all.

Until someone asked me to.

What if?

And the words you're about to read are my answer. I choose to believe this answer because I know with certainty I can't explain that no matter what time, what day, or what age, I was fated to meet that man and that young woman.

But still … what if?

Time changes us minute by minute. Circumstance, experience, it all changes us.

So … just because you're fated to meet someone doesn't mean that your interactions with that person will play out exactly the same; the ending you share with them will be the same in an alternate world where you met before or after your meeting in this one.

The possibilities are endless.

And exciting.

And terrifying.

THIS IS MY WHAT IF ...

THE FEAR

IF SOMEONE HAD TOLD ME EVEN TWO YEARS AGO THAT I WOULD FREAK out about turning thirty, I would've laughed at the absurdity. Age didn't freak me out. There were worse things in life than growing old.

Like never getting the chance to.

But shit fuckity shit fuck, as it turned out, I was turning thirty and freaking out.

I wasn't where I wanted to be in life at thirty.

Glancing down at my watch as I poured a customer a draft beer, I sighed. In two hours, it would be midnight and my golden carriage of the twenty-something life was about to turn into a giant, decaying pumpkin.

My early twenties had been fine. I perfected the art of avoiding making real emotional connections with anyone and I was certain that was the way I wanted it. No, *needed* it. The thought of actually letting someone close enough to me for them to be worth grieving over when I lost them made me suffer full-blown panic attacks.

It was easier to be the friend and not the best friend.

Even my once best friend Rhian thought so. We used to be close in that we didn't want to let the other too close. It worked for us. It was comforting having her there but not really there. But she married her college boyfriend, James. That changed her and we didn't really have a lot in common anymore.

The same thing happened with my friend Jo. She worked the bar here with me at *Club 39*, until Mr. Good-Looking-Arty-Tattoo Guy showed up and she became Mrs. Jo MacCabe. I hadn't spoken to Jo in … God … I couldn't even remember how many years it had been.

The guy I was serving lifted his gaze from my breasts and gave me a big, flirtatious smile as I handed him his change. I turned away to deal with my next customer because me and men … yeah … that hadn't happened in a while.

Like, a depressingly long time.

Like, born-again-virgin long time.

Oh, all right, it had been three years since I'd had sex. There was this incident when I was eighteen … I was sleeping around a lot and I woke up one morning with a guy on either side of me and couldn't remember how the hell I'd gotten there.

Scary, I know.

So I quit the whole sex thing.

And then when I was in my early twenties, I had a fling with my coworker Craig after a seriously delicious kiss at the bar one night. From then on, I had a one-night stand every few months or so, to curb the need.

Until three years ago when I had a one-night stand with a guy who got extremely clingy afterwards. He started turning up at the bar and watching me. When I asked him to stop, he didn't, and then I slammed him against the wall, grabbed his balls, and threatened to castrate him if he ever came near me again. Thankfully, he didn't get off on stalking a woman who wasn't intimidated by him, and I never saw him again.

So that put me off the whole one-night-stand thing.

I'd been through many a vibrator in the last three years.

God, I missed sex.

Maybe three years was enough time to trust that not every guy was a weirdo stalker.

"You're quiet tonight, Joss?" my colleague Jeb said to me. "You thinking about writing?"

Jeb was nineteen years old and he thought it was cool that I had a book published. In fact, I'd had several published. Fantasy and paranormal fiction. They did okay. I was nowhere near as successful a writer as I wanted to be. I was currently flirting with dipping my toes into contemporary fiction. When I told Jeb that, he thought that meant I wanted my characters to be disapproving and disdainful.

I really hoped it was a case of mishearing me. I hadn't the heart to correct him.

Plus, it was funny.

For not the first time that night, I asked myself why the hell I was still working in a club with nineteen-year-olds when I didn't have to. My writing didn't pay very much, but I had a huge inheritance. I hadn't been that comfortable using that inheritance, but I started easing up on that a couple years ago. After five years of living in a student flat, I finally had enough. I was twenty-eight at the time. I needed a respectable home. So, I used a small percentage of my significant inheritance to buy a nice two-bedroom flat in Morningside. I turned the other bedroom into an office.

"So why the heck am I still working here?" I grumbled under my breath.

Oh yeah.

Because without this job, I'd be a hermit and if I wanted to write contemporary fiction, I needed to, you know … experience life. If only through others.

However, over the last year I'd started to fear getting older and ending up alone. I never thought I'd fear that. I was supposed to be happy alone.

Fuckity fuck.

My biological clock was ticking and I had to wonder if ending up alone and childless was scarier than the thought of possibly losing again to that sneaky bastard Death.

Some days I would ache deep in my chest, this horrifying longing for a child gripping me. And then other days the thought of having a child, only to lose it, scared the shit out of me.

I was a tangled mess of yucky emotions and at midnight that mess was going to look a lot messier.

"Jeb, we're out of lime. Can you get some from the back?"

He nodded and disappeared to do so.

"A fellow American. And a beautiful one to boot," a deep Southern voice said from my right.

I turned and found myself staring at a tall, blond, very handsome guy. He had green eyes and right now they were focused solely on me. "A fellow American. And a Southern gentleman to boot."

He held out his hand. "Travis."

I shook it, getting a little sexual thrill from the strength in his big hand. "Joss."

"How long have you been in Edinburgh, Joss?"

I glanced down the bar to make sure Jeb was back and dealing with the customer who was waiting. I looked back at Travis. "Twelve years."

He raised an eyebrow. "Twelve years and you've still got your accent?"

It was true I hadn't picked up any Scottish brogue living here. I think it was because I didn't spend nearly enough time around Scots unless I was working. And even then, we got an eclectic group of accents coming through *Club 39*.

"I guess not."

"I'm here with the U.S. soccer team. I leave tomorrow." His eyes drifted over me, blatantly sexual. "I can't believe I've been here all week and I've only just met you."

A snort escaped me before I could stop myself. "Really? Does that work for you normally?"

Travis grinned, unabashed. "Usually."

"Maybe it's the accent. That drawl probably has them panting for you over here."

"I'm not going to lie—it definitely does." He crossed his arms on the bar and leaned toward me so we were almost touching. "Is it working for you at all?"

I considered the handsome American. If I were a soccer fan, I'd probably be wetting my pants about now. And he was heading home tomorrow. Famous soccer player and heading home to America.

Those things made me feel pretty certain he wasn't going to turn into a scary stalker.

At midnight I was turning thirty years old.

Did I want to do that alone?

Surely that would epitomize my fears and everything I had to look forward to in the coming years.

Maybe I should fight that idea. Push my crippling issues aside for one night and have sex with this handsome soccer player to prove that I could change my life!

Before I could really think about it, I blurted out, "Do you want some company your last night in the windy city?"

Travis's green eyes burned with anticipation. "I would love that." He reached for a napkin on the bar and leaned over to take the little pencil I had tucked behind my ear. After he'd written on the napkin, he handed both back to me. "My hotel and room number. Stop by when you get off work."

What the hell was I doing?

"Great." I gave him a saucy smirk. He laughed.

"Looking forward to it, Joss."

"See you in a little while, Travis."

He walked away, joining a group of men who I guessed were teammates. As they were leaving, Travis threw me a smoldering look that should've burst my underwear into flames.

Don't get me wrong, I tingled a little.

I think if my head weren't so messed up, however, there would've been a lot more tingling.

I hated how the mind could mess with the body.

For the rest of the shift I worked in a daze, wondering what the hell I'd been thinking arranging to meet a man at his hotel room after talking to him for ... oh, three seconds.

I glanced down at the napkin in my hand. He *was* staying in a fancy-ass hotel.

So!

Serial killers could stay in fancy-ass hotels.

He's not a serial killer.

What was my problem? I'd gone back to strange men's apartments.

That doesn't make it any better.

Shouldn't turning thirty bring with it some maturity and common sense?

"You sure you're okay?" Jeb appeared at my side. He put his hand on my lower back and I tensed. "Su let it slip you're turning thirty at midnight. That must be rubbish ... working and turning thirty. Not having a boyfriend."

I tried to make him spontaneously combust by mind power alone.

Unfortunately, Jeb wasn't good at reading a situation. Instead he leaned in closer. "I usually don't dip my wick into anything older than twenty-five but you're fit, Joss, and you've got great tits. If you want, I'll sleep with you tonight?"

Did he ...

Was I ...

Did he just offer me a pity fuck?

Did a nineteen-year-old *boy* just offer me a pity fuck?

I shuddered and shoved him away. "Ugh, Jeb, you're a baby. Fuck. *Fuck!*" I made a face of revulsion and strode away from him before I decided to knee him in the balls.

I was *so* going to meet yummy soccer man for some sex, if only to cleanse myself of what had just happened.

———

"WHAT THE HELL WERE YOU THINKING?" I HISSED AT MYSELF AS I STOOD outside Room 343 at 1:30 a.m.

After what Jeb had said to me, I left him to clean up the bar after closing.

Idiot child.

Although now, I was seriously regretting my impulsive decision to come to the hotel to have sex with Travis.

Yes, I was afraid of turning thirty and being alone, something I never thought I'd feel. But wasn't another one-night stand the exact opposite of what my heart was telling me I wanted?

You don't know what *you want.*

Shit.

Feeling suddenly cold—and yes, I admit it, scared—I wrapped my arms around my waist and backed away from the door. I couldn't go in there. Maybe I was finally growing up because the idea of having sex with a stranger didn't appeal to me. My body wouldn't react. At least not in a sexy way.

Decision made, I hurried down the hotel corridor on light feet, breathing a sigh of relief when I stepped into the elevator.

I was exhausted, and ready to sleep away my worries.

To my irritation, the elevator stopped on a ballroom floor. *Oh God, please don't let there be a function going on that involves the soccer team.*

That would be just my luck.

Holding my breath, I waited as the elevator dinged as the doors opened. Only one man stood on the other side. A very tall, rugged-as-hell man staring wearily at the floor.

As he stepped inside the elevator, a strange current of electricity zipped down my spine, and all of a sudden I wasn't exhausted anymore. He was so big, his powerful shoulders stretched the beautiful fabric of his expensive tuxedo as he moved. I felt overwhelmed by him as he filled the space.

I peeked over at him where he leaned against the side of the elevator and ran a hand through his hair. He had a sharp jawline, a cleft chin, wide cheekbones, and a roman nose. Dark stubble shadowed his cheeks and his hair was kind of messy, even before he put his fingers through it. Altogether, his rugged unkemptness seemed at odds with the stylish tuxedo.

And then he lifted his gaze to me; as I froze, he seemed to also.

He had startling pale blue eyes framed by long dark lashes.

He wasn't classically handsome, but those eyes … gorgeous.

Eyes that instantly sharpened with interest as they moved down my body, lingered over my breasts and legs, before traveling back up to my face.

I felt like all the air had been sucked out of me, and the only way to get the oxygen back was via this man.

Oh boy.

Buy Now

CPSIA information can be obtained
at www.ICGtesting.com
Printed in the USA
LVOW07s1824130917
548611LV00004B/759/P